THE TIME JUST BEFORE

Peter Deacon

Dedicated to my late father who flew and
returned.
Also to the 55,573 who did not come back.

Published by NTS Books
booksnts@gmail.com

All rights reserved 2019

Copyright: Peter Deacon 2019

First published 2019

Foreword

Although the characters and the story itself are fictional, the details of flying and combat are not. The raids happened on the dates stated and in much the manner described. Similarly, other events are true to the times given.

The outline of this novel reflects the experiences of my late father. Along with many others, he assisted in rescue efforts during the Blitz, volunteered for aircrew, trained in Canada and flew operationally - although the rest is in no way his story.

I have drawn on my own experience of the military to ensure that the narrative is as accurate and factual as I can make it. I would also like to thank Dr Elizabeth Carrington and Col Bruce Burnett for their invaluable advice on medicine and aviation. Also, to Paul H for his guidance.

Those eagle-eyed will spot some deliberate errors. For example, RAF Oakley housed OTU and not HCU squadrons and there was no RAF Blackbrook. However, I have kept these departures to a minimum and only then to ensure that real people are not mistaken for the ones I have invented.

If you do read on then I thank you and hope that you enjoy the story.

Chapter 1

London - 25th October 1940

London was on fire. Blazing refineries and storehouses near the Thames billowed columns of thick black smoke high into the dawn sky. Far below, three RAF Albion trucks ground slowly through Greenwich, snaking between piles of rubble and along roads strewn with debris. The lead driver craned his neck through the cab window as he navigated the obstacles. Inside the vehicles, exhausted aircraftmen jolted against each other as they tried to sleep. Eventually, a policeman waved at them and pointed to where a few figures clambered over the wreckage of demolished buildings.

Parking well away from the rescue work so that their engines would not mask sounds from inside the debris, Sergeant Mackenzie swung to the road and walked along the line of vehicles, banging his fist on their sides. 'Out, out, out,' he yelled hoarsely. They had been on duty for days, snatching only minutes of sleep while being shunted from one bomb-damaged building to the next. Disembarking clumsily the aircraftmen blinked at the now bright sunlight, battling against numbing weariness. Quick glances showed them an avenue of neat houses, but now four were rubble and the windows and roofs of the others were either missing or damaged. Curtains fluttered like distress signals through broken glass, while a few dazed householders piled rubble beside their homes as though imposing order on the destruction somehow reduced its potency.

George Watford stumbled as he dropped to the road, almost falling to his knees. His last solid night's sleep had been so long ago that he could barely remember it. Just nineteen, years of farm work before the war had made him strong, but over the past few weeks the Luftwaffe's air raids had been relentless and he had been in the thick of it. Like the others, he was exhausted. An ARP warden broke away from the rescue effort and hurried across and Sergeant Mackenzie gathered them to listen.

'An unexploded bomb went off just over an hour ago, demolishing four houses,' the warden spoke quickly, eager to get back. 'A neighbour reckons those two have basements and so we're digging there first.' He pointed at the closest pair of wrecked buildings. 'She also thinks there were people in most houses at the time, but doesn't know how many.'

'Right,' Mackenzie replied, glancing up the road. 'Any leaking gas or other UXB's?'

The warden shook his head. His dark blue uniform was tinged grey with dust and sweat ran down from under his tin hat leaving vertical lines in the grime on his face. 'The gas main's turned off. There's nothing else dangerous that we know of.'

Mackenzie nodded thankfully. 'Any sounds from inside?'

The warden shrugged. 'Thought we heard something from the second house about fifteen minutes ago, but nothing since.'

Mackenzie quickly allocated his men across the four buildings. By now, they knew their jobs without detailed instructions and moved off carrying a selection of picks, wrecking bars and shovels.

George walked to the furthest bomb-damaged house and eyed it warily. He hated finding bodies, but even when they found survivors there was often little joy in it. Many of the youngsters evacuated at the start of the war had returned to London and in every raid, children lost mothers and mothers lost children. Last night they recovered the body of a young woman, her face purple and bloated. Nearby small children wailed pitifully as neighbours clung to them. He found the grief of the living hardest of all to bear.

Arriving first, he quickly tied a broken lace and examined the ruins. The interior partition wall dividing the houses was still standing, but the exterior walls had collapsed. What remained of the roof following the explosion had simply broken and dropped either side of the partition.

'If there's a bed in there, I'm crawling into it,' Roy Clark said behind him. George glanced at Clark and saw him stagger slightly.

'There might be someone in it already,' George said clambering up the rubble.

'Well if this lot landed on them then I don't think they'll be too bothered by me.'

'Even a dead woman wouldn't stay in bed with you, Knobby,' George told him.

'I wouldn't care if it was Gracie Fields herself. She'd have nothing to worry about but my snoring.'

Debris slipped treacherously as George climbed higher and dislodged slates sped down the rubble like toboggans on a snow slope. He could see that the wooden floor joists had snapped, but most still leaned against the partition wall forming a right-angled triangle and giving the possibility of a void underneath. Behind him, Clark and the others formed a line, ready to pass back rubble as he freed it. Dulled by lack of sleep he worked mechanically, pulling away tiles, bricks and pieces of wood, pausing every so often to call into the wreckage below. Suddenly the air raid sirens started again, their familiar sound winding into a howl.

'Jesus,' Clark cursed. 'Don't the flaming Luftwaffe ever take a day off?'

3

George smiled grimly and tugged at the last few bricks covering two of the joists. 'I heard that Hitler pays overtime,' he replied and went back to work. Minutes later, he removed a brick and saw a space below, a good-sized space. The trouble was that the more rubble they removed the weaker the structure grew. If they took away too much it might collapse altogether. He lay on his stomach and slithered over the hole, manoeuvring a flashlight to the side of his ear. Through the dust, he examined what was left of the room, a fireplace, a rug, a settee and a woman's body partly buried under rubble.

'I can see someone down there,' he called over his shoulder.

'Alive?'

'Don't think so. She's not moving anyway.' The beam cut through the murky air, lighting up her face and he saw her eyes flick open.

'Hang on, she is alive. I just saw her stir. Can you hear me down there?' he called through the hole. Her right arm lifted slightly in acknowledgement, but she said nothing.

'Can she get out?'

'No chance, she's trapped from the waist down under piles of the stuff. I'll have to go in,' he added and pulled away more wreckage. The gap was narrow and he doubted that the joists would hold if he swung from them. He grimaced at the thought of dropping into the wreckage with so much rubble above his head. His grandfather had died working in the coal mines near his Somerset village, trapped deep underground in a pitfall that killed ten men. Crushed or suffocated no one knew because the bodies were abandoned, impossible to recover. He hated enclosed spaces.

'Send back for the medic and pass me a bar once I'm down.' George called urgently. There was no reply so he turned and saw the others transfixed, staring at the sky. He followed their gaze and caught his breath. In the far distance, a silver cloud was coming towards them, a huge silver cloud that glinted in the sunlight. The Luftwaffe was back and more than ever.

Puffs of white flak peppered the sky around the horde while a few tiny dots of RAF planes darted at them. Higher still, twisting white con-trails showed where RAF and German fighters battled. However, the Luftwaffe swarm slogged on, far too many for the defenders to stop. The usual anger at the bombers coursed through him and deep frustration because he could do nothing to stop them. Every day hundreds of rescue workers sifted through the destruction like ants scurrying over a split anthill, only for the maniac with the spade to return the next day.

'Bloody hell,' Clark said quietly, watching the approaching maelstrom. 'The buggers are coming right at us.'

George gave a final glance and turned away, determined to carry on. Slipping between the joists, he dropped onto the settee with a jarring thud that rolled him onto the floor. For a second he tensed, winded, half expecting the ruins to collapse. Then pulling out his flashlight he clambered across to the woman. The air was thick with dust and he shivered. It was too much like being in a pit shaft, dark and claustrophobic. A part of him wanted to scramble back out, but instead he knelt by her side.

'Are you hurt?' he asked, prizing masonry from her legs. At first, the covering of grime on her face and hair made her look grey and elderly, but as he wiped away dust and rubble from her eyes and mouth, he could see that she was young.

She closed her eyes and seemed half-asleep. Eventually, she said weakly, 'Ich glaube, mein Bein ist gebrochen.'

'What?' he asked taken aback. 'I don't understand. Can you speak English?'

'Was?' she looked at him strangely, her pupils unfocused. Then she recovered. '...I think my leg is broken.' Her accent was now English but with a hint of somewhere foreign.

'Is there anyone else in here?'

'No, just me.'

'George!' Clark shouted down the hole. 'The sergeant says we're to take cover under the railway arches, can you get out?'

A rolling crump of explosions sounded in the distance and he felt a shiver of fear, but glancing at the girl he saw her watching him and he knew he could not leave.

'No, I'll chance it in here. Pass me a couple of bars and a canteen too if you've got one. Then go. I'll be fine.'

Through the hole came two wrecking bars and a canteen of water, and he set to work in the void, his actions quick and urgent. Balancing the flashlight on the floor, he smashed two small holes high in the chimney breast with the bars. Next, he rammed a bar into each hole as far as it would go, wedging them in place. Finally, he placed a few lengths of wood across the bars to block the wooden beams if they slid down the wall. There was a chance anyway; it was all he could think of doing.

'I'm going to have to move you to the fireplace,' he said and without waiting for a reply, lifted her as gently as he could. She was lighter than he expected but tiredness made him stumble and she screamed as he knocked her leg against one of the broken beams.

'Gott, es tut weh!'

'What?'

'...That hurt. My leg hurts,' she said. He saw there was a bulge in her shin and it bent at a slight angle.

'Sorry, but it has to be done, you'll be safe by the chimney,' George tried to sound confident, stifling his anxiety, but feeling certain they would die if the rubble collapsed. He kicked cushions from the broken settee to the fireplace and laid her on them as gently as he could. She grimaced as he set her down. 'Sorry. It must be painful.'

The spasm passed and she looked up. Her pupils were wider and she seemed more alert. 'Please... stay with me,' she whispered through gritted teeth. 'I don't want to be alone again.'

'As long as nothing lands too close we'll be fine.'

'You're a poor liar,' she said with a pained expression.

'I'd almost convinced myself.'

'That just means you're a fool, a double fool for not going with the others.'

He settled on the floor next to her and with both their backs to the fireplace, it felt oddly companionable. Closer now, sharp explosions rumbled like thunder.

'Is it just your leg that hurts?' he asked shakily, wondering if he really had been foolish to stay.

'Yes. My shin feels like it's on fire... It must be broken,' she winced and touched it gently.

'Can I do anything?'

'Just stay with me.'

George glanced up at the hole he had made in the rubble, wondering if he should have tried to get her out, but he knew it was too small. 'Where are you from? You're not from here are you?'

'No, I'm not English,' she answered and said no more.

'You sound Scandinavian.'

'Scandinavian?' she repeated, confused. 'No, I'm not Scandinavian.'

'So where do you come from?' he pressed her, wanting to think of anything but the approaching bombs.

'Is it important?' she snapped and her evasiveness made him even more curious.

'It sounds like you don't want to tell me.'

She thought for a moment before replying. 'I... I don't want you to leave.'

Now he was really curious. 'Why would I leave because of where you're from?'

Again, she hesitated and he thought she was ignoring him. Eventually, she answered. 'Because I'm German. Those are my countrymen dropping bombs.'

'German!' George exclaimed, so surprised that he almost stood up. 'How can you be German?'

'Because I was born there. How else?' Her tone was weary, defeated.

'But... but why are you here?' He did not know what else to say. 'We're at war.'

She turned her head away as if she was tired of explaining her nationality. 'I'm here because I'm Jewish. We aren't liked by the Nazis so my parents sent me here to be safe.'

The bombs were getting nearer. Tremors bounced through the floorboards and brought down a haze of dust from the rubble, stinging his throat and making breathing difficult. He unscrewed the canteen and offered it to her. She drank deeply and then splashed water onto her face. With much of the dust washed away, she looked to be about the same age as him. The beams groaned ominously and he stared at them fearfully. *Cheap wood,* he said to himself. *Unseasoned. They'll snap rather than bend.*

'And what about you?' she asked. 'You're in the RAF, why aren't you flying?'

George shook his head. 'I'm what's called an 'Erk', an aircraftman. I don't fly.'

'That's like a sailor never going to sea. Why be in the RAF if you don't fly?'

He managed a wry grin; it was something he had asked himself many times. 'I've always loved aircraft, so it seemed the service to join.' He took the canteen and swirled some water in his mouth before spitting it out. 'I've applied to become aircrew, so you never know.' However, he doubted that would happen now and that thought bothered him almost as much as the approaching bombers. Flying had fascinated him since childhood and at times, he wanted it so badly he ached.

Suddenly the ground shuddered, followed immediately by a loud explosion and she shrieked. 'My God, they're getting very close!' She reached for his arm and pressed her face into his dusty uniform. George curled into her, feeling her body shake with fear. *Oh you bastards*, he said to himself. *You bloody bastards!*

More jagged explosions followed and the rubble jumped sharply. Bits of plaster and stone dropped onto them and the wooden joists slid down the wall until stopped by his makeshift barrier. He looked up at it silently, praying it would be strong enough.

'I think your support has worked,' she said at last, shaking plaster from her hair.

'For now,' he replied quietly. They had shifted a lot of the rubble heaped above them, so they might survive if it collapsed. It just depended which way it fell. The flashlight toppled over so he grabbed it and sat back down, the urge to scramble up through the hole and run for shelter was almost overpowering. 'Where will you go now?' he asked, feeling the need to talk, to say something above the creaking rubble and approaching bombs, like whistling against the darkness.

'This place is rented. I can get lodging with my job.' The next blast was much closer and the ground shook sharply, dropping and bouncing back up. A shower of soot fell down the chimney and swirled around them like mist. She coughed and grabbed at his jacket again, clinging to it like a lifeline. 'I'm scared, bloody terrified. Please keep talking, say something, anything. What's your name?'

He pulled her into his chest, trying to hide her from another shower of debris, but his arms shook so badly he could hardly hold her. 'I'm... George,' he told her, forcing out the words. 'George Watford.'

'I'm Millie,' she almost screamed. 'Millie Horowitz.' For an instant, the void lit brighter than daylight and he could see every detail within the space. Then the explosion struck, the beams collapsed and there was only darkness.

His first thought was that he was waking from a deep sleep; it was the same soft, warm mugginess. Then his back began to throb and he rolled over but that was a mistake. Pain lanced through his shoulder so sharply that he cried out. Still half-asleep, he struggled to sit up, but his back was tearing itself apart. He tried to open his eyes but could see nothing. Firm hands grabbed him and pushed him back down.

'Lay still, damn you,' a man's voice said harshly. 'You'll break the bloody stitches.'

'What's happening?' George mumbled. 'Where am I?' No one answered.

'Get the bandage out of his eyes,' the man snapped. 'He must have pulled it down. And fetch the morphine, he needs another half grain.'

Gentle hands touched his face and something slid over his nose and onto his brow. The light was sudden and dazzling and he clamped his eyes closed. When he opened them again, stark bare walls and metal framed beds surrounded him, and standing beside him was a white-coated doctor and a nurse.

'Where am I?' he repeated in confusion. Then the memory of the bomb blast flicked into his muddled mind. Snapshot images of an explosion, brilliant light and falling rubble. 'Am I hurt?'

'Hush,' the nurse said gently. 'Just be still.'

'Where's the bloody morphine?' the doctor called and pushed George onto his side and held him firmly. 'He's bleeding, the wound has opened. Get a needle and thread and some fresh dressings while I hold him.'

The throbbing was intense, sharp and searing. He remembered an enclosed space, an injured girl and approaching bombers. Flickering images like a worn Pathé Newsreel in the cinema. He clamped his teeth together and tried not to cry out.

'Is it serious, doctor? What's happened to me?' Pain swept away the last vestiges of sleep. He was now alert and fighting the discomfort.

'Nothing serious,' the doctor answered at last. 'You've got a deep laceration on the right shoulder, the trapezius muscle and a smaller one on the back of the head. Something sharp and heavy fell on you but you're young and strong so you'll be as good as new in a few weeks, as long as it doesn't become infected.'

'What about the girl?' George asked, remembering. 'There was a girl with me, she had a broken leg. I was trying to get her out.'

'I don't keep track of everyone admitted to the hospital,' the doctor said briskly. However, after some seconds he added, 'Is she young with black hair?'

'Sounds like her.'

'I was on duty when a girl came in with a fractured tibia. A broken shin bone,' he explained. 'I can see she was lucky.'

'Lucky?' George repeated through gritted teeth. 'How was she lucky?'

'Because the building collapsed on an ox like you rather than her. Now don't move or I'll have to redo all of the stitches.' George chuckled and immediately regretted it as the pain returned. 'At last,' the doctor said at the sound of approaching footsteps. 'Hold him while I thread the needle. Stay absolutely still, I can't wait for the morphine and this is going to hurt.'

Sergeant Mackenzie visited the next day, just after they returned from the basement following another air raid. The familiar face looked tired and bits of dust showed in the joints of his uniform. He carried a kit bag on his shoulder that George recognised as his own.

'You're an idiot, Watford,' Mackenzie said in a gentle Scottish burr. 'You should have sheltered with the rest of us.'

George looked up and smiled. Mackenzie's voice was loud and harsh when he was truly angry. 'Sorry sergeant, I couldn't just leave her there.'

Mackenzie dumped the kit bag on the floor and sat on the edge of the bed. 'Aye an' I'm sure you'd have done the same if she'd been some old granny,' he said sarcastically.

George shrugged. 'I think I would,' he replied, suddenly wondering.

Mackenzie laughed. 'Yes, I dare say you would have.' He pulled some papers from inside his jacket and handed them to George. 'Anyway, you're a lucky idiot. The Flight Lieutenant asked me to bring you these. They've accepted your application for aircrew. You're off on education courses from December and then you report to an Initial Training

Unit at Torquay in March. In the meantime you're no use to man nor beast with that injury, so you're on convalescence leave until you start.'

'A month?' George said incredulously. Up to now, a forty-eight-hour pass was generous.

'Six weeks to be exact.' Mackenzie shook his head at the craziness of his superiors. 'Apparently, they're keen to get their hands on anyone daft enough to volunteer for aircrew and they don't want your chances spoilt by injury.'

George was speechless, selected for aircrew training and two months convalescence seemed too good to be true. He needed time to absorb the news and all it meant. 'How are the lads?' he asked, changing the subject.

'Pleased you're going,' Mackenzie replied. 'You make them look bad with all these heroics.' He laughed and went to slap George on the shoulder, but then appeared horrified as George recoiled. 'Och, sorry lad, I completely forgot.'

He forced a quick grin for Mackenzie's benefit. 'I bet the Flight Lieutenant put you up to that, just to make sure I really needed the leave.'

Mackenzie smiled sheepishly. 'I've got to be off, George. You take care of yourself and good luck with ITU.' They shook hands and Mackenzie was about to go when he turned back and stared hard for a moment. 'You're a good man and I was glad to have you in my flight. Just remember that most heroes get their medals posthumously.'

George watched Mackenzie walk away down the ward with a tinge of sadness. He would miss him. The Scot possessed the rare ability to combine humanity with discipline. Sergeant Mackenzie cared about his men and they would never dare take advantage of that fact. As the doors swung shut on one part of his RAF career, he closed his eyes and relaxed into thoughts of the future. Education courses and two months at an Initial Training Unit followed by ten weeks of Elementary Flying Training to see if he had what it took to become a pilot. Success there would mean a further year at an Advanced Flying Training School abroad. Finally, there would be more courses to learn the skills needed for combat. In all, he would have almost two years dedicated to a thing he had dreamt of since childhood. That was if he was good enough. So many things could go wrong, so many tests to untried aspects of his character. He sighed and forced the thoughts away, he was determined to succeed. After rereading the orders for the third time and savouring each line, he decided he needed to share his news with someone. So clad in hospital pyjamas and a robe he went in search of Millie.

The woman's wards were on the floor below and he walked quickly past rows of beds, trying hard not to stare. At the end of one ward, he saw a girl lying in bed. Her plaster cast leg hoisted by a metal gantry.

'Hello Millie,' he said. With the dirt washed from her face and her hair brushed, she looked so different. She had collar length black hair, high cheekbones and a thin face. However, the most striking feature was her eyes. Brown and penetratingly bright, they gave the impression that she was both amused and critical at the same time. She was, George decided, beautiful and for a moment, he found it hard to breathe.

For a second she stared back before recognising him. 'Hello George Watford,' she said, smiling. 'How strange, I was just thinking about you. I wondered what had happened to you.' Her pronunciation was now precise, almost accent-less.

'Just a few cuts,' he said. 'It's nothing serious. The doctor told me your shin bone is broken.'

'It itches so much,' she replied and frowned, rubbing the skin above the plaster cast. 'I thought it would only do that when it was healing, but it's already driving me insane.' She looked at him quizzically. 'You look very happy, considering what happened to you.' She followed his eyes down the bed and ruffled the nightdress further over her legs.

Flushing with embarrassment he looked up. He had been wondering whether he should offer to sign the plaster cast. 'I've just found out I'm going to flying assessment. I'll become a pilot if I pass.'

'Congratulations,' she said. 'Come and sit by me. Is this something you want?'

'For as long as I can remember,' he said and slowly relaxed into the bedside chair. As they talked, her brown eyes watched him keenly, encouragingly, as if his news was as important to her as it was to him. He felt lightheaded with pleasure and secretly examined every curve of her face and curl of her hair, drinking it into his memory.

'Where will you go now?' he asked, suddenly conscious that he was talking about himself too much. He wanted to ask about her and her family, but other patients were close and he guessed that she might not want it known that she was German.

She paused briefly as if considering an answer. 'As I said yesterday, my employers have lodgings I can use.'

'That's lucky,' he replied, feeling disappointed. 'Still, if it doesn't work out, you could always come home with me,' her expression hardened and he instantly regretted making such a clumsy offer.

'Go home with you?' she repeated, looking worried.

'To my parents,' he scrambled. 'But only if you can't manage by yourself. Mum always wanted a daughter; she'd love to look after you.'

She stared for a second before breathing a small sigh of relief. 'Oh, I see. Thank you, I'll think about it.' She looked away as if deciding something. 'And you, George, will you look after me too?' she asked quickly turning back.

'Of course. Well, I've tried to so far anyway.' He smiled in what he hoped was a guileless way.

She nodded. 'Yes, you have. You could have left me.'

Then he suddenly realised she was concerned about more than her injury, something else worried her. 'You sound bothered by something?'

She bit her lip. 'I... I think there will be... difficulties for me soon,' she said slowly. 'I may need a friend to turn to.' She tensed and her expression became apprehensive as if picturing some future event.

'I'll always help you, Millie,' he assured her, puzzled by the change. Seconds before she had seemed bright and happy, now a cloud had formed and her eyes looked afraid.

'Do you promise to help?' she asked suddenly and took his hand, staring directly at him. 'Will you promise me, George.' She squeezed tightly in emphasis.

'I promise. But what sort of problem is it?'

'You shouldn't be in here, young man,' a harsh voice said. 'Visiting hours are over.'

George turned quickly, the movement tugging painfully at his stitches. Matron was a large woman who filled her voluminous uniform so tightly that it seemed inflated. Her hard, clever eyes had seen every trickster and malingerer and found them all wanting.

'Sorry matron,' he began. 'We were injured together. I just wanted to see how she is.'

The eyes flicked from George to Millie and back again. 'So you're the one who stayed with Miss Horowitz through the bombing?'

'We kept each other company,' George replied, pleased that Millie must have spoken about him.

'Well, that was brave of you,' the matron said and for a moment he wondered if she might let him stay. 'I'm sure Miss Horowitz will look forward to seeing you tomorrow, during visiting hours. Come along now, it's almost time for ward rounds.'

'I'd better go,' George said, wondering what she had been about to say. 'We'll talk tomorrow.' Millie shrugged sympathetically and nodded, holding eye contact until he turned away.

Walking back up the stairs, he felt a surge of happiness, almost euphoria. The fact she was worried about something bothered him but tomorrow he would go back early and make sure they had plenty of time together, certain that he could help with whatever it was. For now, all he could think of was those eyes, her face, her voice and the cleverness in the way she said things. Millie had affected him in a way that he did not fully understand and at that moment, he wanted nothing more than to be with her. He would write to his parents and tell them of his injury, that he would be home in a few days. Although he would not say so in the letter, maybe, just maybe, he would bring Millie with him. Give her a place to recover and escape any worries. She could see the farm and the countryside and perhaps love it the way he did. Although how his parents would react to a German girl would be interesting. Less of a mystery would be their attitude when he told them he had volunteered for flight training. That would be a conversation needing perfect timing.

Early the next day he went back to the women's ward. Curtains surrounded Millie's bed and he approached warily in case she was changing. There was no sound or movement so he edged to the curtain and called her name. When there was no reply, he peaked through a gap and was startled to see an empty bed. At the end of the ward, the matron was in animated conversation with a nurse. She looked irritated as he approached.

'Excuse me, Matron,' George asked warily. 'Has Miss Horowitz been moved?'

'Moved.' she replied impatiently. 'No, of course she hasn't been moved.'

'She's not there,' George said simply.

'Don't be ridiculous,' she snapped. 'Where else would she be?' The matron stormed along the ward and threw back the curtain. 'Nurse!' she yelled when she saw inside.

Chapter 2

London - 27th October 1940

'But she can't have just vanished?' George's voice leaked frustration. He had allowed himself such high hopes and now they were gone. 'People don't just vanish.' After waiting all day and assuming she was in another ward or even transferred to another hospital, the matron's explanation was bewildering. Millie had simply disappeared.

'I've checked with the night nurse and the porters,' she said briskly, clearly not used to having her word questioned. 'No one saw anyone entering or leaving the ward. Even the other patients saw nothing. The nurse said that Miss Horowitz seemed agitated last evening and asked for curtains to be put around her bed. She heard nothing else from her and because of the disruption from casualties arriving in the night, decided not to disturb her in the morning.'

'It doesn't make sense,' George shook his head. 'There was no reason for her to leave, especially with a broken leg. Someone must have made her go.'

'That's impossible,' matron shook her head. 'The night nurse would have seen an intruder and in any case, Miss Horowitz would have struggled and the other patients would have heard.'

George scrambled for an explanation. 'Not if she was chloroformed.'

'Chloroformed?' Matron tilted her head at him. 'You've read too many penny-dreadfuls. It takes at least five minutes to put someone under with chloroform and believe me, she would have struggled. In any case, she changed into her old clothes, so she must have been conscious.'

That made him think and he searched for another explanation. 'What about the police? She's German. Could they have taken her?'

The matron pursed her lips. 'The authorities have to speak to us first to make sure the patient is well enough to travel. I can only assume that she wanted to leave.'

'But why?' George asked her uncertainly. 'That's what I don't understand.'

'I don't understand it either,' Matron replied blankly and then looked at him appraisingly, her expression softening. 'I don't think it was anything you did if that's what you're wondering.' George shrugged, that was exactly what he had been thinking. Had he scared her into leaving? Had the clumsy offer of staying at his home frightened her? Matron put a hand on his shoulder. 'I think she was quite taken with you. After you'd gone she spoke very highly of you, so I really wouldn't fret on that score.'

Which left one other option, that something else scared her? Maybe because she was German she feared internment. The Nazis were arresting Jews, so maybe she thought the same would happen to her here. Although how she could compare Britain to Nazi Germany beat him. Matron turned away and walked back to the million other problems awaiting her and George began packing his belongings, he was leaving. The more he thought about it, the more convinced he became that Millie was running from the authorities. Why else would she have voluntarily dressed and left the hospital with a broken leg? The image of her alone and frightened, hiding away somewhere tortured him. He had no idea where she might be, but she had called him her friend and he had promised to help, and that was enough for now.

The Victory Services Club in Seymour Street was the only place that he could think of staying. Twice damaged by bombing, it stubbornly remained open to all ranks and was somewhere to avoid difficult questions about why he was not in the hospital or at home recuperating. Dumping his kit bag in a room that he scarcely noticed, he stretched his arms to relieve the throbbing. The dressing on his back would need changing soon, but he had no idea how to do it without help.

It was the first time that he had been on his own for months and it felt oddly lonely. He had written to his parents and they would be expecting him, but he could not face them yet. Especially when he would have to tell them about flight training, something they would hate. A dull headache was growing and he pressed his forehead against the dusty window glass, enjoying its soothing coolness. Then air-raid sirens wailed and the steady bark of anti-aircraft guns marked another raid's progress. Below the street emptied as people hurried for shelter, but the prospect of sitting for hours in a cramped basement seemed worse than risking the bombs, so he lay on the bed and darned the jagged tear in his uniform jacket.

The council official's shoulders slumped and he looked tired. In the middle of his desk sat a stack of ledgers and to the side of these, an ashtray threatened to overflow. 'I'm afraid that this is an office for people who go missing because of the bombing, not who wander off,' he said wearily, pointedly glancing over George's shoulder to the long queue behind.

'What's the difference?' George asked. 'She's still missing.' he had queued for over an hour and his shoulder burned.

The official rubbed his red eyes and reached for another cigarette. 'Look, the missing people we record haven't simply wandered off; they're either dead or injured. This office is just for the next of kin to find out whether they should go to a hospital or a mortuary. We don't record what happens to people after they leave the hospital.'

'Just check the name,' George snapped, not wanting to argue the point and he leaned on the desk, making it clear that he was not going away without some effort, no matter how pointless. Sighing, the official again glanced at the queue and reached for a pencil and paper.

'Name of the missing person?' he asked irritably.

'Millie Horowitz,' George replied and waited while the official selected a ledger and flicked through its pages.

Finally, with a small smile of triumph, the official shook his head. 'Nothing,' he said.

George stumbled back into the street and pushed his way through the crowd, wondering why there was no record of Millie even going to a hospital. It was beginning to feel like she did not exist, that he had imagined her. He had spent days asking at police stations, ARP offices, hospitals and left his name and address in a dozen places. No one had any information about Millie. Was it just stubbornness that made him keep searching, the need to solve a mystery? Maybe in part, but it was more than that, much more. She had made him promise to help, and also, for the first time he had met someone he cared for deeply, someone who perhaps cared for him too. There was no way he could just walk away and forget her, especially since she might be in trouble.

The flight office had stamped his pay book with an infantry base in Bath, the nearest city to his home and it was impossible to draw wages elsewhere without a good reason. Moreover, some bright spark might decide that if he was capable of searching London for a missing woman, he was well enough to return to duty and he definitely was not fit for that. He calculated that he had enough money to last another day but after that, it would be over, he would have to go home. There was just one more day to find her and he had no idea where to go next. He trudged on and on, searching faces and wondering what to do. Of course, there was no chance that with a broken leg, Millie would be out walking the streets, but still, he looked, searching every face. Eventually, he arrived at the Embankment, just down from Parliament and leaned against the stone balustrade, taking the weight from his shoulder. Palls of smoke drifted upwards from fires downriver and dozens of barrage balloons floated high in the air, tethered to the ground by long metal cables. Looking across at the south bank, he strained to catch sight of Greenwich where Millie had lived. Suddenly the thought struck him that her belongings were still in the ruins. That there could be letters from an employer or from people who might know where she was. He cursed himself for not thinking of it before and set off; deciding to walk the six miles to save what little money remained.

The ARP post in Greenwich marked each bomb-damaged street on a wall map and George quickly found the avenue where Millie had lived. By now, his shoulder felt on fire and was so tender that he walked lopsided in an effort to reduce the pressure from his uniform. Stopping at the end of the road, he noticed a car parked beside the wreckage of her house and three figures clambering over the rubble. He walked faster, trying to ignore the pain. Closer, he saw that two were female and the third was male. They were stacking recovered items in piles beside cardboard suitcases.

'What are you doing?' George asked them as he drew close. At first, he thought they were looters but their clothes looked unsuitable for sifting debris. More like they had taken time away from an office to be there. The two women glanced at him and then at the man, before continuing with their work. However, they now worked faster, quickly filling the cases from the piles.

The man stepped carefully over the rubble towards George. He was stocky and had a hard face, someone used to trouble and unafraid of it. He paused just in front and inched forward, forcing George backwards. George could barely move his right arm without searing pain. He had no choice but to give way.

'I'm looking for Millie Horowitz,' he said to the man. 'Do you know her?' There was no reply, just a menacing silence.

'Do you know Millie? he then called to the two women. They exchanged looks and seemed to redouble their efforts. 'Just tell me if you know where she is. Has she been arrested? Is she well?' The women closed the suitcases and lugged them towards the vehicle. 'For Christ's sake, I just want to know if she's OK!' he called after them.

They scrambled into the car and the man again stepped closer. Frustration boiled over and George pushed him backwards with a hard shove from his left arm, tripping him onto the pavement. Quickly he strode towards the car, but one of the women ducked back out and aimed a revolver straight at him, stopping him dead. The cold look on her face told him that she was prepared to kill. 'Look I only want to know if Millie's safe,' he said, shocked by the gun and by her expression.

The blow to his back was so sharp and painful that he toppled forwards, collapsing onto the road and crying out in agony. By the time the pain subsided and he could look up, the motor was at the other end of the street and disappearing around a corner. George slowly staggered to his feet, his heart beating so fast that he felt faint. Damp stickiness from what he knew was blood spread across his back. Completely bewildered, he had no idea what was happening or what sort of trouble Millie was in. He hung his head and tried to think what to do next, but he had run out of strength, money and ideas. Air raid sirens began wailing and with a deep sigh of frustration, he shuffled towards the train station. It was time to collect his things go home. For now, it was over but he would not give up.

Chapter 3

Somerset - 8th December 1940

'Pleased?' George's father shouted his face livid with rage. 'You think we should be pleased?' Jack Watford was tall like his son and there was a similarity in the shape of their faces, but their temperaments had always been poles apart. The morning milking had just finished and his father brought the smell of cattle dung into the room. The harsh odour seemed to increase the hostility of his presence.

'This is something that I've always wanted.' George explained again, forcing his voice to sound reasonable. His father was volatile and in a strange way, he envied him these bursts of raw passion. It was probably healthier than the calm and rational emotions he usually felt. However, maybe that was no longer the case. London had changed him. Seeing the dead and injured and then meeting Millie exposed deeper feelings, a fervour and determination he did not realise he possessed.

Of course, it was always going to come to this scene, just as it always had whenever he suggested something new or different for the farm. But there was the faint possibility that the time spent away in the RAF would have persuaded them that he was no longer a child. Not someone to forge into their image of a son. There had been a slight chance, but inside he always knew how they would react, especially his father. His mother sat on a chair in the parlour and just stared at him. Normally she was sensible and calm, a peacemaker, but for some reason, she now chose silence, as if too shocked to speak.

'If you think I'm pleased that you might become a pilot, think again,' his father bellowed. 'If you think that then you're a bigger fool than I take you for,' and he slammed his hand onto the table in exasperation. 'You had a safe job on the ground and you throw it away to go flying.'

George felt a flash of anger, there was never any compromise with his father. It was always his way, his view that must prevail and nothing could make him understand, nothing could change him. Standing up he shook his head. 'I'm sorry that's how you feel, but like it or not it's going to happen,' and he started towards the door.

'What about us, this farm? Did you think at all before volunteering?' His father spat the words bitterly as if George had deliberately spited his plans. 'There's three hundred acres of good pasture here that are just beginning to make us money. You could have carried on with it.'

'I still can, dad,' George replied quietly, 'once the war is over.' Although farming held few attractions for him currently. Fewer when he thought how claustrophobic it would be working under his father's gaze.

'Not if you're dead or maimed you can't,' his father snapped. 'You only tell us on the day you leave because you knew how we'd feel.' The older man spat the words accusingly and leaned both hands on the table as if preparing to pounce.

George paused; that was true of course. For weeks he had put off telling them. But like a gambler playing one bad hand after another, he hoped the next day might bring a change. Now there were no days left.

'I can't hide away from fighting,' he said quietly. 'I saw too many dead bodies in London, came close to being one myself. I can't leave the fighting to others. I have to take my share.' He wanted to describe what he had seen, tell them about the young mother whose children wailed at her lifeless corpse. Instead, he said, 'I want to fight and this is the best way I know.'

'But it's so dangerous,' his mother spoke at last. 'Why did you have to do it?' The news was full of the air war and even though the BBC talked in terms of aircraft losses rather than aircrew deaths, the high number of casualties was obvious.

George looked at her and tried to smile reassuringly. 'Even if I'm successful it will be almost two years before I go into combat. The war could be over by then.'

His mother looked optimistically at her husband, but his father waved a dismissive hand. 'In the last war, everyone said it would be over by Christmas. Uncle Fred's sons, Dick and Lorrie wanted to join up before they missed it. That was in fifteen and both of them were dead two years before it ended. It's how we got this farm, boy. Have you forgotten that?' They inherited the farm when the Great War claimed the two boys, but because Jack Watford was new to farming and inexperienced, there followed years of mistakes and backbreaking toil to pay off death duties. Now there was another war and he knew his father feared they might end up like his aunt and uncle, without a child to inherit the farm, working the land until they were too old and it passed to another relative or was sold.

'Not everyone died in the war. Most came back.'

'And you're certain to be one of those?' his father asked contemptuously. 'I suppose you're smarter than the dead ones? You're too clever to die.'

'No. But, I can't hide away either,' George answered defiantly.

'I won't let you do this,' his father ordered. 'I want you to stop this bloody foolishness and get your old job back.' In the past, this tone had worked and George invariably backed down. But then he had nowhere else to go, no options. Now it was different.

He stared at his father for a moment. 'Sorry. I understand how you feel, but I won't do it. I want this chance. Not just to fight, but to see if I can be a pilot.'

The older man shook his head, turned and walked away. George watched for a moment and wondered if he should go after him, but suddenly he remembered the day in the hospital when Sergeant Mackenzie gave him the letter and he talked to Millie. A door cracked open onto a world of possibilities. One where you shaped your future, not just accepted it passively and he wanted that world again. Returning home ill and defeated he was grateful for his parents care. However, he knew now that the direction of his life had turned away from them, at least for a while. The failure to find Millie stung him each day, but he was not going to give up on this dream too. Meeting Millie and the things he had seen in the blitz brought out a determination so deeply hidden that it surprised him. With a last look at his mother, he went to change; there was a train to catch.

Chapter 4

Perth - 16th May 1941

'Good morning, gentlemen. Welcome to Perth and Elementary Flying Training. Please sit.' The squadron leader perched casually on the edge of a table and waited for the trainees to settle. 'I am Squadron Leader Wilson and these gentlemen are some of my instructors. The people who will begin turning you into pilots.' He paused, allowing the students' time to examine the men behind him. The instructors stood in a row, hands clasped behind their backs and staring at some fixed point above the student's heads. They looked businesslike and their worn Sidcots reeked of experience.

'Now, contrary to popular belief, we are not here to teach you to fly. Our job is to assess your potential to become pilots and to make sure that only those with genuine ability pass on to the next stage. Those of you failing to meet the standards will muster into other aircrew trades. The new heavy bombers have a crew of seven and so you will not be wasted.' Wilson looked at the assembled faces as if searching for likely candidates to chop and George settled lower into his seat, hoping the gaze would pass him by.

'You will be with us for ten weeks,' Wilson continued. 'In the first few weeks, you will either fly solo or fail. However, I warn you now; there are many ways of not making the grade. Do something stupid and you will be scrubbed, show the wrong attitude and you will be scrubbed, fail to learn and you will be scrubbed.' He smiled grimly at the young men below him. 'In fact, there are so many ways to fail that I haven't found them all yet. However, there is only one way to pass. Listen to your instructors, do what they tell you and learn quickly. Gentleman, good luck.' With that, he stepped from the platform and marched off. The students digested his words silently and George glanced at the people nearby, watching their reactions. All of them wanted to wear the pilot's double-winged insignia on their breast and their faces showed that they too dreaded the prospect of failure.

'And happy Christmas to you too,' James Dickinson, the trainee pilot sitting next to George said quietly. 'Cheerful blighter isn't he?'

'Yes, very encouraging.' George replied. 'It's like being back at school.'

'Not my school. There they expected you to succeed and beat you if you didn't. Here they just seem to beat you.'

He shared a room in Torquay with James during the previous two months of Initial Training and they developed if not a close friendship, then a sort of mutual curiosity about each other. Mainly, this was because of their completely different backgrounds. James joined the RAF a few months before, almost straight from public school. Lean and tall with a mop of black hair that flopped forward over his brow; he had a relaxed, lazy manner as if little was important. However, his eyes told a different story; they were restless, constantly searching and recording, missing little.

An aircraftman stepped forward and read a list of names, allocating each student to an instructor. George found himself paired with Prendergast, a slight man with thinning hair and dark rings around his eyes.

Dickinson nudged him. 'Your bloke looks a complete bastard,' he said with a smile. 'I wouldn't bother unpacking if I were you, old son. Doubt you'll be here long.'

Then a bull of an instructor called Kellick stepped forward and the aircraftman said Dickinson's name. 'Oh Christ,' he swore. 'Don't suppose you'd consider swapping?'

'No, but I'll wave to you when you leave,' George whispered from the corner of his mouth.

'Ok, but no tears. I hate emotional farewells.'

Chivvied by a sergeant, they queued at the stores building and received Sidcots, suede overalls, fleeced flying boots, helmets, gloves and goggles, along with threats about what would happen if these were lost or damaged. While most carried their bundles to classrooms, George and a few others walked to the crew room and changed. With fifteen minutes to go before the lesson, the tension became unbearable and so brittle it threatened to unnerve him. The memory of scaling his father's barn and looking down at the valley beyond clicked into his mind, of crinkling his eyes and imagining soaring above the fields. Now, at last, it would happen. He was going to fly. The blackboard showed his name written beside an aeroplane number so he went to find it.

The Tiger Moth pulled him like a magnet and he traced its lines with his eyes, admiring the rakish back sweep of the biplane's wings, the two open cockpits and the slender fuselage ending in a delicate stub nose. It looked refined and purposeful. On the other hand, this machine looked worn and surprisingly frail and that gave him doubts. It looked as though one good tug would pull the wings off. The exhausts were blackened and greasy smears stretched down the cowling below them. Much use had stripped the propeller's varnish and numerous repair patches on the wings and fuselage stood out like sticking plasters on skin.

As his eyes travelled the aircraft, he began to wonder just how strong it was and felt anxiety gnawing the pit of his stomach. Fascination with aircraft was one thing but the skill and confidence to pilot one was an order of magnitude again. He suddenly had doubts about himself and the aircraft.

A movement to one side caught his attention and he turned to see Prendergast striding across the grass pulling on thick leather flying gauntlets. 'You must be Watford?'

'Sir.' George saluted in textbook fashion, longest way up and shortest down. Just in case the instructor was old school.

'At ease. No need for formalities when we're flying.' Prendergast replied and then quite unexpectedly smiled. 'What do you think of her?'

George looked back at the aircraft. 'Beautiful. I've only seen them in the distance before.'

'I take it you've never flown?'

'Never, I always wanted to but it was too expensive.'

'Well, now you're being paid to fly,' Prendergast said cheerily. 'Do you think you'll make a pilot?'

George thought for a second. 'I think so,' he decided, not wanting to show either too much confidence or the lack of it. 'I'm going to give it my best shot anyway.'

'Good,' Prendergast said and tapped a wing with his knuckles. It gave a muted, insubstantial sound. 'There are four things to remember. The first is that an aircraft must be light to get off the ground, so you can't build them from girders. The second is that hollow metal tubes can be stronger than solid bars and the third is that if the wings didn't flex, they'd snap.'

George nodded; he could accept all of that. 'You said there were four things?'

'Ah yes, well spotted. Well, the fourth thing is that if it wasn't safe, wild horses wouldn't get me up in one.' Prendergast chuckled but then became serious. 'Everything will snap or break if you apply enough force. The key to flying is precision. Know the limits of your aircraft, stay within them and you'll be safe. OK? Good. Now, it's time to fly.'

Once George was strapped in, with double straps, as it was an open cockpit, Prendergast showed him the controls and seemed pleased that he already had some knowledge. 'Once we're airborne, I want you to hold the stick lightly and rest your feet on the rudder bars so you can feel me controlling the aircraft. Under no circumstances are you to apply positive pressure until I tell you to, understand?' George nodded, just sitting in the cockpit seemed right and he suddenly felt a surge of determination. *Just keep your nerve and it'll be OK,* he told himself. *This machine is designed to fly, it's at home in the air.* Come what may he would give the next hour everything he had.

'Finally, if you're sick, make sure you do it in your gauntlet and not the aircraft. The ground crew doesn't clear up puke, you do.' Prendergast said with a smile and checked the aircraft before swinging into the front seat. His voice became tinny and distant through the Gosport Tube intercom. 'I'm going to talk you through the procedures as we go. Try to remember as much as you can. Firstly, before starting the engine, check the throttle is closed, the switches are off and the stick is hard back.' He then gave a circular wave to the fitter, indicating for him to swing the propeller. 'Now, crack open the throttle an inch and switch on magnetos.' The engine fired immediately with a throaty roar that filled the air with noise and exhaust fumes.

Prendergast gunned the engine until the blades were a blur and the rev-counter showed nine hundred. 'We wait a few minutes for the engine to warm and monitor the oil pressure,' he stated calmly. 'You also need to check the windsock to make sure you're taking off into the wind.' The aircraft trembled like an excited dog eager to be loose. 'Lastly, always remember to pull the stick back when taxing onto the runway to avoid the propeller tipping forward into the ground.' He swung the Tiger Moth onto the grass runway. The aircraft's raised nose blocked much of the forward view so George craned his head sideways out of the aircraft. The cool May wind driven by the prop whipped across the cockpit and pummelled his face, sliding the goggles up his nose and threatening to rip off his leather flying helmet.

'You can't see much forward on the ground, so always look for reference points on either side. That's also important once we're airborne.' Prendergast's voice was slow and easy. It was just another day at the office. 'Check the sky for other aircraft. Good, all clear. Now we gently open the throttle for a full power takeoff.'

The engine roared louder and they bounded forward, bouncing across the grass. 'Once we get going, push the stick forward a little to lift the tail. Feel it? That's the back coming up. We control any swing with the rudder now.'

As they accelerated, George checked the instruments, determined to miss nothing. The grass blurred on both sides and the jolting increased until quite suddenly he felt a change in motion. The bouncing stopped the front of the aircraft rose and gravity pressed him gently down into his seat. They were airborne. He wanted to shout with excitement. It was a feeling of pure elation. For so long he had dreamt of this, although Prendergast's warning came back and he hoped he would not be airsick.

'What was the takeoff speed?' Prendergast asked, snapping him back to reality.

He thought for a second, 'Sixty miles per hour, sir?'

'Are you asking me or telling me?'

'It was sixty, sir,' George said, biting back the euphoria.

'Closer on fifty-five, but good enough. Where's the aerodrome?'

They were banking to the right and so the aerodrome must be behind and left. 'Behind and to the left, sir.'

'No, I'm circling, so it's right below us. See what I mean about visual references? You must be aware of where you are at all times. Now gently take hold of the stick.'

At three thousand feet, the buildings below looked like toy houses and the fields a patchwork of shapes and colours. The wind, the noise, the smell and most of all the pure sensation of flying was so much better than he imagined. With his hands resting lightly on the stick, Prendergast manoeuvred the aircraft so that he could feel the effect of the controls.

'Now it's your turn,' the instructor said. 'Hold the stick firmly and press your feet on the rudder bars. Got it?'

'Got it,' George confirmed. After they had flown straight and level for a time, Prendergast said, 'You now have control. I want you to climb up to five thousand feet and then down to four.'

George hesitated; this was the beginning, the start of his testing. Would he be good enough?

'When you're quite ready, Watford.' The instructor chided, but good-humouredly as if sensing George's awe. 'Remember that pulling the stick back makes the houses smaller and pushing it forward makes them bigger.'

The session lasted an hour and by the end, he was exhausted and convinced he would never become a pilot. Although he loved it, every second of it, he was certain that his co-ordination and reactions were nowhere near good enough. Prendergast took back control for landing and George eyed the countryside wistfully, wondering if this would be his one and only flight. He fully expected Prendergast to scrub him the moment they landed. As they walked from the aircraft, the instructor patted him on the back and he flinched, waiting for the words of condolence.

'Well done Watford, a good start. Keep this up and we might just make a pilot of you.' George stood stock-still and watched Prendergast stroll to the instructors' hut. Slowly a smile formed on his face and he laughed aloud.

They billeted several of the trainees at a large private house in Perth, requisitioned for the duration. An unseasonably late snowfall and near-freezing temperatures turned the residence into an icebox, so the second night they built a roaring fire in their room. Dickinson lolled on his bed reading while George hauled a bucket of coal up the stairs.

'I don't suppose you'd like to help, would you?' he asked Dickinson.

'Can't I'm afraid old boy,' came the languid reply. 'Psychologically incapable.'

'What does that mean?' Dickinson's laziness and excuses had become the stuff of legend. Initially, it was amusing but now it irritated.

Dickinson lowered his book and ran his fingers through his hair, sweeping it off his brow. 'It means my brain prevents me from fetching coal, much as I'd like to. Sad really, but there you have it.'

'That's utter cock.'

'No it's all true, I'm a tragic case,' he lay back on the bed and stared at the ceiling. 'You see before you a casualty of the public school system.'

'You're saying that you can't fetch coal because of where you went to school?'

'More or less.'

'Well, you'd better explain because I'm not getting another bucketful while you laze in bed.'

'Then you force me to reveal dark memories,' Dickinson said shaking his head regretfully. He leaned on one arm and stared at George. 'They made me fag for Brown when I was just a child. Every morning I fetched his coal and lit his fire. It destroyed my innocence and left me incapable of going near another fireplace.'

'What? Just fetching a bit of coal?'

'Not fetching! The swine tried to bugger me every time I bent over the mantle. Simply can't go near another fireplace.' He picked up his book and began reading again.

George shook his head, not believing a word. 'Well if I was that way inclined I'd want someone prettier than you,' he said and placed the bucket on Dickinson's chest. 'It's time to conquer your fears,' he told him. Although he liked Dickinson, he was damned if was going to be treated like his family retainer.

As he lay on his bed and watched Dickinson go reluctantly for more coal, he thought again of Millie and her disappearance. The suddenness of the woman aiming a gun at him shocked as much as it had on the day. The coldness in her eyes and the certainty that she would have killed him. Despite hours of wrestling with the question, he was no closer to understanding who they were or their connection with Millie. As usual, he sifted a range of possibilities, from them being the police to fellow Jewish escapees or even part of a criminal gang. Nothing seemed to fit the circumstances. The police would surely have said who they were. There were probably plenty of escapee Jews in London, but why would they carry guns? Criminal gangs carried weapons but he doubted they employed many women. Each solution seemed as unlikely as the last and gave him no clues about where to search when he next had leave. Maybe she was no longer even in London. It was so frustrating but above all, he felt a deep and rending sense of loss. Millie felt like a missing jigsaw piece. A piece that when added had shown him a different and unexpected picture of himself. On top of that was the fact that he had failed her after promising to help. Although there was nothing he could do now, it did not stop him from wondering and fretting.

Just before nine, they both went down to the dining room to listen to the BBC. As ever, there was little good news and only the daily courage of RAF fighter pilots brought any comfort from the constant threat of invasion. Fierce fighting followed a landing by German paratroops in Crete, while elsewhere in the Mediterranean the Italians had bombed and sunk the destroyer, HMS Juno. The report ended and George turned the dial to Radio Hamburg. Static noise changed to beer-hall music and then to the hated voice of Lord Haw Haw, his upper-class accent lazy and sneering.

'*Germany calling, Germany calling. The great offensive against France has been brought to a glorious conclusion and people throughout the world now wonder when the final act, the offensive against British soil, will come. In Germany and many other countries, particularly in England, people are now with the firm conviction that it would come soon and that conviction remains. The day and the hour are the Fuehrer's secret...*'

The men of his village said every woman must jump in the river and drown themselves if the Germans invaded and he wondered whether his mother would do that. Knowing her, she would be more likely to grab a shotgun and go after the invaders.

'*The great exodus from Britain is well underway. The rich and affluent are removing themselves and their valuables as fast as they can. Great stretches of the coastline have been evacuated to a depth of twenty miles. Hastily improvised defences are being erected, which are things of Papier-*

Mache and cardboard in comparison with the Maginot Line and the forts of Liege'.

Which might be true, but France and Belgium did not have sea surrounding them and the Royal Navy guarding the approaches.

'The political prisoners that have been arrested and thrown into jail without trial are, it is said, to be transported to Canada. This is a fresh crime to be perpetrated by the corrupt dictator of England against men and women who have dared to say that peace offers the only hope for their country....'

That made him think and he hardly listened to the rest of the broadcast. Could this have happened to Millie? Was she some sort of political agitator? Had they arrested her rather than sending her to an internment camp?

On day five, Prendergast gave a lesson on spinning. Following the pre-flight check, George took control. Once they were rolling he pushed the stick forward and the tail came up nicely. Not too far in case the propeller tipped into the runway, but enough to raise the tail, minimise drag and allow speed to increase. Then, with a small back pull on the stick, they were airborne. George held the aircraft level to build more speed before banking into a right turn and climbing to five thousand feet. It was a bitterly cold but beautiful day for flying. Hoarfrost glistened in the shade below, the sun shone on golden bracken and stubble, while the river Tay twisted its way through woods and fields as snow-peaked mountains loomed in the distance.

After demonstrating a spin, Prendergast handed over control. 'Your turn now,' he said. 'Take us up to six thousand feet, climb steeply and reduce power. She'll stall at about thirty miles-per-hour. Just as she does, put on a bit of bank to drop one wing. Then kick in plenty of rudder to swing the nose down and we'll have a nice steep spin.'

George was anxious about this manoeuvre, in fact, it near terrified him. It was common knowledge that spins killed as many pilots as the enemy in the last war. At the given height, he took a deep breath and pulled the nose up sharply, simultaneously reducing power. Airspeed dropped quickly and just as it fell below thirty the aircraft shook, the propeller clattered and she began to stall. Steeling himself, he immediately banked and kicked the right rudder. The nose fell sideways and they spiralled downwards.

'Idle the engine and hold the stick in the central position, ' Prendergast shouted.

The Moth toppled earthwards, gyrating as it fell. Ahead a checkerboard of fields span dizzyingly around the propeller, while in his periphery he could see the wings flutter and vibrate alarmingly. It was like a crazy roundabout ride, dropping as it span and very disorientating.

'Kick in opposite rudder to oppose the spin,' Prendergast ordered, 'and push the stick forward to gain some airspeed.' George instinctively wanted to pull the stick back, but he knew that would be fatal. Doing so would tighten the turn and make the spin worse until they either ran out of sky or snapped off the wings. After a few more turns, the spin slowed and stopped and they were in controlled flight again.

'Well done, Watford. Not bad for a first attempt.' Praise indeed. His arms and legs trembled and his heart raced, although he was not quite sure whether this was from fear or excitement. He hoped it was fear; it would be completely insane to enjoy spinning. 'Now take us back up to six thousand and do it again, but this time without any help from me.'

After more days, he felt comfortable in the air and constant repetition of the manoeuvres quickly built his confidence. As they walked back from a lesson Prendergast chatted happily, demonstrating the correct stall and recovery angles with his hands. Suddenly he stopped mid-sentence and looked up at the sky. 'Bloody hell!'

High above the edge of the aerodrome, a Tiger Moth was in trouble. Instead of spiralling earthwards with its nose down, the aircraft was flat and level, spinning horizontally. It was like watching a sycamore seed drop through the air. Without forward motion, there was no airflow across the wings and so no chance of regaining controlled flight. George ran with Prendergast to his car and they raced towards the plane, certain of finding wreckage and two bodies. Amazingly, behind a stand of trees, they discovered the aircraft sitting on its wheels and looking almost undamaged. The instructor and trainee climbed out as they pulled alongside. Simmons, a student who George knew vaguely stood with his head bowed while 'Killer' Kellick roared at him.

'You complete flaming idiot,' Kellick bellowed furiously. 'You great clodhopping fool. Can't you follow the simplest instructions? If you want to kill yourself that's fine, it's no loss, but have the decency to do so when I'm not in the bloody aircraft.'

A fire tender drew up with its bell clattering. 'What happened?' Prendergast asked Kellick, amazed they were both alive and there was so little damage to the aircraft.

'We were at seven thousand feet and just as we stalled this bloody idiot decided to level off. Then he kicked in some rudder for good measure and got us into a flat spin.' Kellick shook his head in astonishment. 'The aircraft had no forward speed, nothing at all. We came down like an autumn leaf.'

The undercarriage and a wingtip absorbed most of the impact. Otherwise, there was surprisingly little damage. A white-faced Simmons waited by the aircraft while George and both instructors drove off. George gave Simmons the 'thumbs up' but Simmons could only manage a small nod in return. They both knew it was the end of his flight training.

Flying and lectures filled the trainees' days and in their free time, they talked about flying and swapped stories of their instructor's anger and frustration. Usually, this was at the Salutation Hotel in South Street, an impressive white-fronted building with a large and comfortable lounge. A dozen students were already at the bar when George and Dickinson arrived. Most were in high spirits except for one who sat alone at a table with head in hands, staring morosely at an untouched beer.

'Evening chaps,' Dickinson called out as they walked to the bar. 'How're tricks?'

'In the pink, old darling,' a trainee called Marshall replied. He and Dickinson knew each other through family connections. Marshall was stocky, with an honest face and a nose that had been broken while captaining his school's rugby team. 'Although sadly, the same can't be said for young Brooks over there.' Marshall indicated to the solitary drinker.

'Yes, he does look a bit down. What's the story?' Dickinson asked while George nodded to Brooks who looked up at the mention of his name.

Marshal, beckoned them forward and spoke confidentially. 'Bit of a disaster, really. We popped in here for a few stiffeners last night. Nothing too serious you understand.'

'Of course,' Dickinson acknowledged and raised his eyes at George in disbelief.

'Well, this morning old Brooks wakes up feeling a tad under the weather but absolutely insists on pressing on like the trooper he is. Goes up with your man 'Killer Kellick', who decided to sit in the back and chuck the kite all over the sky in a most irresponsible manner. End result is that while inverted, poor old Brooks loses his breakfast and the Killer gains it.'

'He threw up over an instructor while they were upside-down?' George repeated doubtfully. 'That's impossible.' If true then it had not been a good day for the Killer. First Brooks and then Simmons. Little wonder some instructors hated students.

'As you rightly say Watford old man, it defies belief.' Marshall acknowledged. 'However, to my mind, that sort of precision shows Brooks that is just the sort of chap Bomber Command needs. Instead, he's up for a progress check with the Squadron Leader tomorrow.' They shook their heads sympathetically and raised their glasses to Brooks. A progress check was the last chance before the chop.

'Did you hear about Simmons?' George asked.

'Saw him walking out the gate with his bag,' Marshall replied. 'To be honest I think he was happy to leave. Better suited to the Navy than our lot if you ask me. There's a bit more time to think when you're stunting a frigate.'

'I can't help but notice how the class is thinning somewhat,' Dickinson mused. 'I'd say we've lost half a dozen already.'

'Yes, it's getting a bit like an Agatha Christie novel.'

'And no prizes for guessing who's next,' George added and they again raised their glasses to Brooks, who groaned and buried his head back in his hands.

Chapter 5

Perth - 24th May 1941

They ordered everyone into the main hall the following morning and the trainees waited apprehensively, wondering what was brewing. Squadron Leader Wilson marched to the front with a sheet of paper clenched in his hand that he thrust forward as if it had a bad smell. He looked deeply shocked and his normal air of assuredness was completely missing.

Someone behind tapped George on the shoulder and whispered. 'Have you been pinning 'kick my arse' notes on his back again?'

George smiled. 'No, it's his mess bill. Marshall has been buying drinks on his mess number,' he murmured back.

'Please sit,' Wilson said and George noticed the instructors gathering at the back. This looked serious. 'At zero six hundred today in the North Atlantic, the battleship *Prince of Wales* and the battlecruiser *Hood* engaged the German battleship *Bismarck* and the heavy cruiser *Prinz Eugen*.' He paused and scanned the paper, reading it again before addressing the crowd. 'I very much regret to tell you that *HMS Hood* was hit by a salvo from the *Bismarck* and exploded. She sank immediately with the loss of all but three of her crew of fourteen-hundred.'

The *Hood* was the pride of the Royal Navy, a darling of the public and a symbol of the steel ring protecting Britain. The shock of the disaster stunned them. George shook his head in disbelief, staggered that the Navy sent an ageing cruiser and a new untested battleship against the *Bismarck*. In fact, the *Bismarck* outclassed the *Prince of Wales* even if she had been ready for battle.

The squadron leader waited for the noise to lessen. 'Gentlemen, gentleman,' he said and once it was quiet he continued. 'The signal states that the fleet is even now steaming to the area. They are confident of destroying *Bismarck* in the next few days. The *Hood* will be avenged,' he shouted. 'But now please join with me for a minute's silence as we pray for those brave sailors who perished this morning.'

Everyone felt the loss of the *Hood* keenly and an air of melancholy settled over the aerodrome. So far, little in the war had gone well for Britain or her allies. A few weeks before, British and Australian troops retreated from Greece and now Crete seemed about to fall. In North Africa, Rommel drove the Eighth Army back into Egypt. Each setback seemed quickly followed by the next and most good news was only the staving off of a disaster. Only the RAF's bombing raids took the fight to Germany itself in any significant way.

The first trainee soloed after just six hours tuition. However, even though Prendergast was consistently marking him above average and things seemed to be on track, George felt he still had much to prove before flying solo himself.

'Hold her steady!' Prendergast snapped. The wind was fluky, buffeting the aircraft as they rolled down the airfield. It seemed to blow from one direction and then immediately from another. George was in a sweat, trying too hard and overcorrecting, swinging the plane too much.

Once they were airborne, Prendergast said in a more even tone. 'It's a common problem, Watford. When the wind is eddying, all you can do is to take an average course and stick to it. Don't try to chase the wind or you'll flip over, especially once you're operating from a fixed strip.' George tried to calm himself and concentrate on the rest of the lesson. Nevertheless, he knew it was a bad start.

At seven thousand feet Prendergast made him perform a series of loops and stall turns, which went surprisingly well given the jittery state he was now in. For the final thirty minutes, they went back to the aerodrome and practised 'Circuits and Bumps', which meant touching the wheels to the runway and taking straight off again. Clearly, Prendergast wanted to ensure that George had learned from his earlier mistake. By the end of the lesson, he was again exhausted.

Neither George nor Dickinson felt like studying that night and so they went back to the Salutation. A crowd of trainees were already there, some raucously celebrating the classes' first solo flight, while others were more subdued, digesting the news of *HMS Hood*, the lost battlecruiser. They sought out Marshall and found him drinking at the bar on his own and looking sombre.

'Evening, Marshall,' George called but received the barest smile in return. 'You look glum. Did you know someone onboard the *Hood*?'

'What? Oh no, nothing like that. No, I was just mourning the other recently departed.'

Dickinson nodded at the barman and leaned his back against the bar while he worked out what Marshall meant. 'Ah, I see young Brooks is missing. I presume his progress check went badly.'

'Badly isn't the word. In fact, I don't think there is a word that properly covers it.'

'What happened?' George asked, sorting through his pockets for coins. His wage was the princely sum of half a crown each day and after deductions, it did not go far.

Marshall took a deep pull of his beer just as the barman placed three more glasses on the bar. 'Bloody Bismarck, that's what happened. The CO was in a thunderous mood after the news. He took Brooks up and proceeded to stunt the kite all over the sky as if he was chasing Admiral Raeder himself. Once he had thoroughly put the wind up Brooks, he told him to repeat the manoeuvres. Scrub one Brooks.'

George shrugged, 'Well maybe it's for the best.' The truth was he did not know Brooks well, but the little he did had not impressed him. He seemed standoffish with anyone other than his own set, which did not include George. Secretly, he was far from unhappy to see Brooks fail.

'I don't give a fig about Brooks,' Marshall sighed. 'It's his sister that's the issue.'

'His sister?' Dickinson asked with renewed interest. 'Should I know her?'

'Bunty Brooks,' Marshall told him. 'You must remember Bunty. Come hither eyes and a chest you could practise Circuits and Bumps on.'

'Yes... Yes of course. Well, well, so Bunty's his sister.'

Marshall drained his glass and reached for another. 'Cheers. Anyway, the thing is that Bunty asked me to look after her brother because I'd been his rugger captain at school. She wanted me to make sure the little blighter didn't get himself killed and so on. We had a sort of understanding that if I looked after her little chap, then she'd look after mine.'

'Oh, what rotten luck,' Dickinson commiserated. 'I guess all bets are off now?'

'Bound to be. Damn shame really, damnable shame.'

Dickinson looked puzzled. 'But if memory serves, Bunty is a bit on the large size,' he reflected. 'I mean to say; when she launders her drawers the washing line must look like HMS Victory under full sail.'

Marshall held up his hands in exasperation, 'I dare say you're right Dicky, but can I help what appeals to the little fellow? He likes big popsies and I try to accommodate. I play fair with him and he plays fair with me.' They both nodded sympathetically.

'Give it a rest you two. It's like being in a second-rate music hall.' George said.

'Look here, Watford,' Dickinson rounded on him. 'In a few months time we could be laying down our lives for womankind and it's only fair that they lay down for us beforehand. I for one do not intend to go back to my maker in the same mint condition that he dispatched me. It's like the parable of the talents and He would be quite offended. In any case, Marshall here has yet to kiss a girl,' he said patting Marshall on the shoulder. 'Mind you, they can't be criticised too harshly for that, especially given his proclivity for larger ladies.'

'Even big girls need love,' Marshall stated wisely.

George decided to change the subject. He really did not want to hear about Marshall's preferences. 'I wonder which SFTS they'll send us to?' he mused. The next step after Perth was a Service Flying Training School and these were located in Canada, South Africa and Rhodesia. It was the icing on the cake as far as he was concerned. Perth was the furthest from home that he had ever been and the prospect of learning advanced flying in an exotic location was a double dream come true.

'Somewhere in Africa for me,' Marshall stated. 'Went to Canada once and the wretched place was covered in snow.'

'It was probably winter,' Dickinson told him. 'Less snow in summer I'm sure.'

'Yes, but SFTS lasts for a year. Bound to get plenty of the white stuff at some point, Dicky,' Marshall shivered. 'This place is bad enough, but can you imagine trying to navigate when everything below you is white?' They debated the advantages of each country before moving on to the other big unknown, their selection for multi or single engine aircraft, bombers or fighters at the end of the course.

'Naturally, Marshall and I shall go to fighters,' Dickinson assured George. 'No disrespect intended, but a good public school makes one a natural knight of the air. Setting out each day to slay the Hun dragon, followed by a good supper in the Mess and then relieving some popsy of her virtue at night.' Marshall nodded sagely in agreement.

'Whereas your own bucolic upbringing makes you more suited to driving the corporation omnibus.' Dickinson continued and winked at George. 'You my friend are a natural for flying transports.'

'What rubbish,' George laughed. 'The only thing public school equips you for is holding hands in the shower.' Although he enjoyed their company, he knew they would never see him as one of them; he would always be an outsider in their world. 'Anyway, they stream you according to temperament, not background and I want to fly bombers. A Lancaster or Halifax does more damage in one night than a Spitfire or Hurricane can all year.'

Marshall wagged a finger as if he had found an obvious flaw in George's reasoning. 'Yes, but answer me this. How do you find floozies if you're flying at night? That's how the bomber boys fight and that's the problem.' He puffed up like a barrister delivering the crushing argument. 'You don't find attractive females at afternoon tea dances.'

'Or even the sort that Marshall prefers,' Dickinson added.

'Exactly,' Marshall agreed. 'It is the God-given right of every warrior to sip from the cup of carnal knowledge after battle and if you work nights you just can't do it.'

'Speaking of which,' Dickinson stated as he surveyed the room. 'There is a bevy of lovelies over yonder desperate for company.'

George and Marshall turned and saw some girls seated by the window, watching the trainees with interest. 'I suppose you will shun the ladies?' Dickinson asked and George nodded.

'I'm flying first thing,' he replied. However, the truth was that no one else ever compared to Millie. No other girl had her quick eyes, so full of life and understanding. Some nights he yearned to see her again, just to make sure that she really was as he remembered.

'Well Marshall, it's up to me and you to uphold the classes' honour,' Dickinson sighed.

'And to rob them of theirs,' Marshall replied. 'You may have the skinny ones, I shall go for voluptuousness.'

George watched them go, his thoughts straying back to Millie. The moment he saw her in the hospital ward something happened that he could not understand. Just like the Luftwaffe swarm above London, her image burnt into his memory. He might grow used to the loss of her, even learn to live with it, but he could never forget her and that seemed so unfair. Millie exposed emotions that he had been blind to before and that he longed to find again. It was like having a limb amputated but the nerves still registering its presence. At times, he felt crippled.

He took his beer and went to talk to Bill Lane and Geoff Walker. Dickinson and Marshall were wrong about the type of aircraft they would fly. He could tell now who were natural fighter pilots or multi-engine flyers. Fighter pilots tended to be self-contained, judgemental and preferred snap decisions, whereas bomber boys were team players, leaders and far more calculating. Of course, that may not be universally the case, but from what he had heard and seen so far, it certainly applied to the good ones.

Prendergast outlined a route along the Tay to Dundee, before cutting across country to Forfar and back to Perth. This was flying at its best with clear skies above and the land and river inching past far below. The view of houses, roads and moorland made him ache for the chance to fly alone and indulge his curiosity and sense of freedom. He no longer felt uncertain about the aircraft, instead, he enjoyed controlling it, feeling its responses and gaining every inch of performance that he could.

With the map case open on his knee, he compared features on the ground with those on the paper. The Tay was easy enough to follow to Dundee, but once they turned inland, he was anxious about picking out Forfar from all the other small towns nearby. In the end, he simply followed the road, but it emphasised just how fraught night flying would be without a good navigator. Before arriving back at Perth aerodrome, Prendergast made him perform a spin and then a loop before landing. Everything seemed to have gone well and they taxied to the apron.

'Don't switch off the engine,' Prendergast instructed, climbing out of the front seat. 'I want you to take her back up, do a circuit of the aerodrome and land again. Good luck.'

And that was it, he was going solo. The familiar green of the aerodrome stretched away towards the distant hills, but it all looked quite different without Prendergast in the front seat. After cockpit checks, he eased the throttle wide open and went bumping away across the grass. Soon there were no more jolts and he climbed smoothly with only the familiar sound of the Gypsy engine and the slipstream buffeting his helmet for company. He gave a shout of joy and then forced himself to concentrate; one mistake now would ruin everything. Orbiting the field in precise turns, he flew onto the downwind approach and began losing height. Making sure the fuel mixture was fully rich, the wing slots were unlocked and the airspeed was around sixty miles-per-hour, he dipped the nose and with a touch of rudder to line up, the Moth descended nicely. A small bounce and all three wheels struck the grass at the same time.

He was down.

He had done it!

For the rest of the day, George floated on air. The next few weeks would mean many solo flights in the Tiger Moth along with training on the twin-engine Airspeed Oxfords and time in link trainers learning instrument flying. Then there would be twenty-hour and forty-hour progress checks to pass, but he had crossed the biggest hurdle, he had soloed. That night there was a celebration in the Salutation's bar for George and three others who had gone solo that day. However, Dickinson was worried. His lesson had not gone well.

'Doesn't help that you were out until four this morning,' George said, shaking his head theatrically in reproof.

'My dear Watford, sometimes statements of the blindly obvious aren't helpful.'

'Well if you need a few pointers, just let me know.' George offered brightly. He could barely contain his amusement. The farming lad from the sticks had beaten the public school boys to the prize.

'Your words of kindness are touching and duly noted. Tomorrow will be a better day I'm sure.' They carried their beers to a table and joined a knot of others. Marshall was holding forth about a manoeuvre he had performed, describing it energetically with his hands.

'So the 'Killer' tells me to demonstrate a few aerobatics, anything I wanted. So I barrel-rolled at five thousand and dived straight down to four, then up into a stall and a lazy-eight down to three thousand, where I came out in a loop.'

'And was he impressed? Geoff Walker asked.

'Very. Starts shouting that I'd nearly had the flaming wings off and that if I pulled a stunt like that again I'd be out the gate,' he grinned. 'Bound to get fighters now.'

'Sounds more likely that you'll get the chop,' Geoff told him.

'Nonsense. Two sides to every story,' Marshall replied enigmatically. 'I believe it shows a certain *Joie de vivre.*'

'Joy Davis?' Geoff asked, winking at George. 'Is that the fat floozy you took home last night? I bet she wasn't any more impressed with your performance than the instructor.'

'You ignoramus. I mean it shows that I have that *je ne sais quoi*.'

'Sounds bloody painful,' Geoff continued innocently. 'Probably caught it from Joy Davis. No wonder you flew badly.'

'God give me strength,' Marshall shook his head. 'Flying used to be for gentlemen, I shouldn't have to mix with the lower orders.'

George felt the mellowness of contentment drift over him as he listened to their banter. For once in his life, he had achieved something significant. He crossed a barrier between his origins and his potential. He was going to be a pilot.

Less than half of the class soloed by the end of the third week, around the fifteen-hour mark. However, this included

Dickinson and Marshall who both just scraped an 'acceptable' on their logbooks. As they walked back from their aircraft after a navigation exercise, Dickinson suddenly halted them.

'Hello, hello,' he said. 'Looks like someone's going to solo.' Across the field, a Tiger Moth landed and the instructor climbed out, leaving the pupil alone at the controls.

'Who is it?' Marshall asked.

'Looks like Geoff Walker,' George said. 'I think he was flying this morning.' The night before in the Salutation, Geoff fretted because he had still not soloed and so they had spent an hour reassuring him. Geoff was one of nature's gentlemen, mild-mannered and deferential, but he lacked confidence and so it was a relief to see he was going up alone at last.

'Good for Geoff, it's about time too,' Dickinson said and they watched as across the strip the engine gunned and the aircraft rolled forward.

'A bit bouncy I'd say,' Marshall observed. Having now soloed he felt himself the seasoned aviator.

'Strong breeze, the windsock's almost straight out.' George reminded them. The wind had increased in the last hour. It now ruffled his hair and flapped the arms and legs of his sidcot. Above them, small fluffy clouds chivvied along as if they were running from something. Safe to fly, but you had to be careful.

The aircraft gave a final bounce and it was airborne. However, Marshall was right, it was a shaky takeoff and Geoff climbed too steeply and too soon. As the aircraft's angle increased, the wind that had surged across the wings providing helpful lift suddenly found its way blocked and began pushing from underneath. This slowed the aircraft and forced the nose even higher. *Never be low and slow*, the instructor's mantra came to mind.

'Get the nose down,' George shouted in alarm and started walking towards the instructor. The moth's gipsy engine stuttered and then shrieked as the pilot applied full power, but it was too little and too late.

'My God, he's going to stall her.' Marshall cried out. This was no longer just poor flying it had become dangerous.

At about two hundred feet, the Tiger Moth stopped in mid-air, toppled sideways and plunged nose first into the ground. The wings snapped forward and the front of the aircraft crumpled. Without thinking they ran towards the wreckage, racing to get there. Hoping that because Geoff was in the rear seat the engine might not have crushed him. The instructor reached the aircraft first but instead of climbing into the debris, he stopped, turned and ran away. Immediately a whoosh of flames erupted into an inferno as leaking petrol ignited. An explosive wave of heat swept over them, tossing the instructor to the ground. They got to within feet of the pyre but the flames forced them back. George tried not to look at the brief movement he saw within the burning aircraft, praying that it was smoke.

Chapter 6

Perth - 1st August 1941

By the end of the course, only about half of the original candidates passed for further training, the rest left to become navigators, bomb aimers or flight engineers. That morning a paper appeared outside the adjutant's office listing which Service Flying Training Schools or SFTSs the successful candidates would attend next and importantly on which aircraft type they would train. George fought his way to the front and scanned the list until he found his name. Canada and Multi-Engine. Bombers! He stepped back in a daze as the others pressed forward. Around him, trainees gabbled excitedly, but he could only think of spending a year on the British Commonwealth Air Training Plan in Canada.

Back at the building's entrance, he found Dickinson and Marshall smoking cigarettes and looking miserable. 'Bloody bombers!' Marshall spat disgustedly when he saw him. 'Dicky and I are to fly bombers.'

'I don't understand your problem. The new heavies are great kites,' George replied, trying to edge past them and be away. Nothing was going to dampen his spirits today, not even these two. 'The Lancaster and Halifax are superb.'

'George, old darling, we've explained this *ad nauseam*.' Marshall began and George feigned an interest he did not feel. He wanted to go to the admin office, find out when the next posting would start and ask whether he could take leave. He was going back to London and search for Millie. 'You cannot find totty flying bombers. Bombers fly at night for God's sake!'

'Yes but not every night,' he said. Over Marshall's shoulder, he could see others heading to the admin office. He would be at the back of the queue if he did not hurry.

'What?'

'They fly two or three times a week at most,' he told them patiently. 'That leaves plenty of time for hobbies.'

'Weekends as well, or just during the week?' Marshall's interest rose and his eyebrows crushed together like a pair of caterpillars wrestling.

'I'm sure if you asked the CO of your squadron nicely, he'd let you off fighting on weekends.' George said innocently.

'Really?' Marshall's face took on a hopeful look.

'Don't be an ass Marshall,' Dickinson told him. 'Watford's sporting with you. But now I think of it, one of the instructors did tell me something similar. Bombers don't fly every night. More to the point, floozies can come for a joy ride in a big crate. The fighter boys can't take totty up in a single seater, can they? D'you know, I think we may be better off.'

'Let's go to the mess and get drunk,' Marshall suggested brightly.

'Coming, George?' Dickinson asked. 'We've finished the course and there's nothing better to do.' Then Dickinson stood back, turned to one side and saluted smartly. Marshall did the same. From the corner of his eye, George saw a figure approach and assuming it was an officer, copied them. The young WAAF Section Officer returned their salutes and walked straight up to him. Her face tilted downwards and the rim of her hat almost covering her eyes.

'Would you come with me, please,' she ordered and turned smartly away without waiting. He glanced at the others before following, feeling panic rising. They had seen this happen before when the bombing killed a family member or a relative was lost on active service. Then admin staff took the person away and sent him on compassionate leave. Dickinson and Marshall stared back sympathetically.

Behind the Adjutants Office, the pathway narrowed as it wove between two stores buildings. Here it was shaded and unobserved. The Section Officer stopped suddenly, glanced sideways and turned back. 'Hello George,' she said and kissed him lightly on the lips, pulling away so quickly that it might never have happened. 'I never thanked you properly for saving me.'

'Millie?' he muttered in confusion not believing his eyes. The uniform had completely fooled him, but now he recognised her and struggled to believe it. 'It can't be you... I thought you were from admin... that something had happened to my parents,' he said knowing he was blathering like an idiot.

Her smile froze. 'Sorry, I never thought about that. I just didn't want to surprise you in public.' She then added coyly, 'Is it a surprise?'

Euphoria quickly replaced his shock. 'Surprise? Yes. Officers hardly ever kiss me.'

'I mean to see me, you idiot.'

'You disappeared.' The words tumbled out before he could stop them. 'I spent a week looking for you, asked everyone. Where did you go?' He had so many questions.

'Let's leave that until later,' she said. 'Come on, I've got a car here. We'll go for lunch somewhere and talk.'

'I'm not supposed to leave base without permission,' he said apologetically.

'Why not?'

'Because... '

'Stop being so bloody stiff and British. I'm ordering you to come to lunch with me,' she said with her hands on her hips.

He thought for half a second. 'Well I suppose I can't refuse an order,' he said and then held her by the shoulders and looked at her. 'I can't believe it's you. I thought I'd never see you again. What happened to you?'

She stared at him curiously. 'I'm truly sorry. They searched for me when I didn't turn up for work and I was transferred to a private hospital. They came in the night, there wasn't time to say goodbye or leave a note. Sorry.'

'But why did they have to move you?' he asked, confused. 'It was a broken leg, not a major injury.'

Her eyes flicked away. 'Who knows?' she replied slowly. 'I guess its standard procedure.'

George could tell this was not the whole story, but she was here now and as they had known each other for just a few hours, the briefest of times, he had no right to expect more. Pressing her suddenly seemed unreasonable and might spoil things. It was mad enough that he felt this way, but the shock of meeting her again so unexpectedly made him light-headed.

A military green Austin Tourer was parked on the gravel space adjacent to the CO's office and they sped past the guard post and out onto the Perth road. The wind whipped over the windshield and he took off his forage cap and grabbed her barathea hat before the slipstream snatched them both away. He could not stop looking at her. After thinking about her for so long, of looking for her in every stranger's face and of coming to terms with the possibility of never meeting her again, here she was. It was only as they neared Perth and he glanced at her hat that he wondered how she could possibly be in the RAF.

'Where shall we go?' she asked, smiling in a way that made his emotions do a double loop.

'The Salutation Hotel,' he replied. 'I'll direct you.' And he hoped none of the others would go there.

'Did you come all this way to see me?' he asked hopefully.

'Mostly,' she replied, concentrating on the road. 'I'm going to our base at Arisaig on the other coast and tied the two together.' Immediately she frowned as if saying her destination was a mistake.

Arisaig meant nothing to him other than a vague name on the map, but he did wonder why a base would be in such a remote location on the west coast of Scotland. 'It's lucky you came today otherwise I might not have been free,' he said, suddenly wondering at the coincidence.

'It wasn't luck. I asked an RAF Officer I work with to make inquiries. He tracked you down and found out when your course finished.' She spoke casually as if this took no more effort than browsing a telephone directory. 'Anyway, you've got your wish; you're going to be a pilot. I remember how excited you were at the prospect back in the hospital.'

George sat back. Today was the first time he really believed it would happen. 'Yes, it hasn't sunk in yet. I'm going to Canada for a year to qualify. I've never been abroad before, I can't wait,' he said happily, but then saw the irony of leaving now that he had just met her again.

'A year's a long time,' she replied quietly, almost as if she could read his thoughts.

Not yet midday, the dining room was almost empty. Below a vaulted ceiling, paintings of Scottish landscapes hung from panelled walls, interspersed with mounted antlers. Settings of silver cutlery and condiments sat on starched white tablecloths, rigid with formality. The only other diners were four businessmen talking quietly at a table by the door. The maître d' showed them to a table nearby, but Millie asked for

61

one by the end window and he smiled knowingly as he led them the length of the room.

It was dim and cool after the rush of the journey and George felt awkward in such formality, especially where every noise seemed to echo from the walls. It was so frustrating to sit and talk when all he wanted was to take her in his arms and hold her. They ordered the set lunch of soup, game pie and treacle tart, and to his relief, Millie asked for a beer. He had not acquired a taste for wine yet.

'Are you over your injuries?' George asked. He had so many questions, but he felt it best to start slowly.

'Just about,' she replied, sipping her drink. 'I still get a few aches, but nothing serious. And you?'

'I've got a scar down the back of my shoulder. It was sore for weeks, but its fine now.'

'You'll be quite the warrior, covered in battle scars.'

George smiled. 'Hardly. With a scarred back, it looks like I was running away.'

'There's no shame in running, George,' she said, quietly.

He cursed himself. 'Sorry, I didn't mean to imply...'

'I know.' Millie interrupted. 'But believe me; I fully intend to run away whenever I can.'

It seemed a strange remark for her to make but he let it pass. 'How do you come to be in uniform? I mean British uniform.'

'Well, I decided that RAF blue goes better with my complexion than Wehrmacht grey. Do you like it?' She held up her hands as if modelling a costume.

'Were you in the RAF when I met you?' he asked, completely confused. Especially when he reminded himself that she was German.

'Oh, I'm not really,' she answered carelessly as if commenting on the weather.

'What?' George almost choked. 'But the uniform. The car?'

She laughed, the same tinkling, musical sound that he remembered from the hospital. The waiter brought their soup and a basket of bread. 'I work for a government department where there are military and civilians. Many are foreigners like me and although we are not strictly military, the staffs wear uniforms so we don't stand out. It makes life so much easier these days when everyone is in uniform. For women, the choice is either to become a WAAF or join the Women's Transport Service. I chose the RAF because the army uniform looks so frumpy.' She said this as if it answered the entire question and crumpled some bread into her soup before spooning it into her mouth.

'So what do you do?' he asked, but then realised the reason for her evasiveness. 'I guess it's all hush-hush?' Secrecy had become second nature to everyone. Posters adorned walls warning that *loose talk costs lives* and even films had that theme.

Millie shrugged. 'Sorry, but I can't talk about my work, I'm sure you understand. Anyway, I thought you would be more interested in other things.' She watched him over the soupspoon. 'Like me.'

George would not be deflected. 'I went to your house and there were two women and a man collecting your things. One of the women pulled a gun on me,' he told her, suddenly embarrassed that his tone sounded so indignant.

Millie smiled at his expression. 'I am sorry, George, especially that Jorgen hit you. I had strong words with him when they told me.'

'He hit me from behind,' George protested, and then smiled as well.

'That's tricky foreigners for you. We're very protective of each other.'

However, this did not explain why the woman carried a gun in London. Millie's answers were just raising more questions, but he forced himself not to press her too far. There was more at stake than his curiosity but frustratingly, he felt no closer to understanding who she really was. He tried a different tack. 'In the hospital, you talked about problems and made me promise to help. I thought you were in trouble.'

'I know,' she said. Her smile faded and became serious. 'I realised that you were looking for me and I can't explain just how much that means.' Her eyes widened as she spoke into a sincere expression. 'You kept your promise.'

'But what were the problems?' he asked again, hoping the mystery that had puzzled him for so long would be explained.

For a second she looked about to say something, but then choked back the words and instead said. 'Before you came to the building, when I was trapped and dazed, I kept thinking about the terror of being alone and in danger. It shocked me. Well, I'd volunteered for something at work that I wasn't sure I could do. I thought I might just run away instead. I know it's infuriating for both of us that I can't say more, but please don't ask because I feel such a prig not being able to tell you.'

George looked at her for a second and nodded. 'Ok, but are you happy now? Is it sorted?'

Millie shrugged. 'I'm more... comfortable about things,' she said quietly and then her eyes flicked onto his. 'But I still want to know that you will be there if I need you. I need to know that I can always rely on you.'

'Always. I will always be there for you,' he told her firmly. She nodded and gave a small smile of appreciation. Although he desperately wanted to ask more, he knew she would not tell him and decided to let the subject drop. The last thing he wanted was to mess things up between them by pestering.

However, he could make an educated guess. It was obvious that being both intelligent and German she would be useful to the war effort in many ways, from translation to advice on bombing targets. He suspected something of the latter because she mentioned working with an RAF Officer, although why they had a base in remote Arisaig was another mystery. Maybe it was the prospect of working against her homeland that gave her problems. Perhaps conflicting loyalty was the difficulty she mentioned before.

'Blue suits you,' he said at last.

'I think so too,' she replied, her tone making it clear that she was eager to talk about something else. 'But not the Black-Outs.'

'Black-Outs?'

'RAF issue knickers, very itchy and unattractive.'

George looked away, embarrassed. 'I'll take your word for it. Although I'm sure my friend Marshall would disagree.'

'He likes them?' She asked incredulously.

'He likes... unusual things.' George replied evasively and wished he had not mentioned Marshall.

'And you George? What do you like?'

'Me?' he said and hesitated before looking in her eyes. 'I like you. If you hadn't vanished, I was hoping... I'd hoped that...' But he was too embarrassed to continue and felt in danger of making a fool of himself.

She watched him carefully, working something out. 'I like you too, George and not just because of what you did,' she said at last.

It felt as if he were teetering on a springboard, wanting to jump but not having the nerve. He jumped. 'If you hadn't disappeared I was hoping that we might have become close, maybe become more than friends.'

Her response was easy and instantaneous as if this was expected. 'That sounds nice. Perhaps once we get to know each other I would like to be your girlfriend.' She smiled and reached for his hand. 'But I'm afraid it can't happen yet,' she continued. 'You are going away and my job will not allow it at the moment. We'll keep in touch and when you return, who knows?' She seemed sincere or at least instinctively, he felt she was. There was a year to get through and many things could change, but he truly loved her, he knew that beyond doubt now. At that moment, he wanted to laugh aloud with the pleasure of being with her again. So many good things had happened today that it was almost too much. The unknowns surrounding her and the year away suddenly seemed just frustrations.

'I understand. We'll meet when I get back.'

'I really hope we can,' she said genuinely. 'I would like that a lot.' However, something in her voice and the way she spoke suddenly made him doubt she would be there. Maybe it was just her German intonation, but he sensed uncertainty about her future.

'You'll wait for me?' he asked, hoping that it did not sound like a line from a second rate movie.

'I'll wait for you,' Millie replied quietly and then she grinned mockingly. 'Well, if we hope to become more than just friends, I should know about you. Tell me about yourself?' she said and waited for him to speak.

'There's not much to tell really. I come from a small village in Somerset. We're farmers, or at least we have been since my great-aunt and uncle died. They owned the farm originally. Unfortunately, both their sons died in the last war. When they lost them I think they both gave up on life.' He did not tell her that his great-aunt wasted away and shortly afterwards his great-uncle took a one-way stroll to the fields with his shotgun.

'Now tell me about you,' he asked. 'What happened to your family?'

Millie raised the spoon to her lips. 'Family?' she repeated slowly, savouring the word. 'I haven't heard from my family in a long time. We were close and very happy and I think of them constantly.' She stirred her soup, watching the lumps of bread swirl in circles. 'Sometimes I feel that bad news would be better than not knowing.'

'What happened before you came to England?' he asked gently.

Suddenly the energy surrounding her seemed to fall away leaving her vulnerable, exposed. She shrugged. 'We lived in München, Munich, in a nice part of the city near Rosenheimer Platz. Our lives were good. My Father is a Civil Engineer with his own business and my mother is a concert musician, mainly the flute but she is qualified to teach piano. I have a younger brother and sister who were at school, and I myself studied at the Ludwig Maximilian University.' She emphasised the name with obvious pride and as she spoke of her past, her English accent slipped and became more German. It made her seem different, more exotic.

'When the Nazis came things changed. Some people became scared and others more confident. We are not devout, but we are Jewish. The laughable thing is that my father is a proud German. He loves his country. We were all good citizens.' She pushed her bowl away, drank some beer and grimaced. 'After the war, you must come to Bavaria and taste our beer. I will take you to a good München Biergarten. We'll sit in the sun, drink Weizenbier and eat wurst with pretzel and sweet mustard.'

George had no idea what those things were, but he nodded politely as if it might happen. It felt decidedly odd for a Somerset lad to be sitting in a Scottish hotel talking to a German girl. 'I think I'll be going to Germany before long,' he said thoughtfully. 'Not sure I'll try the food though unless I get shot down of course. Anyway, this is wartime beer. It's watered and poor stuff. So, what happened to your family?'

Her eyes became distant as if picturing past events. 'My Father was not permitted to work and we survived for a while from my mother's music lessons. Then, one day he was badly beaten and decided we must leave Germany. They could not get travel papers but I came here on a student programme. My parents packed me off with all the jewellery they could buy. I had their life's wealth hidden in the linings of my trunk. The plan was that I would sell them and rent a house for our family. Then my brother and sister would come on the Kindertransport, and finally, my parents would join us, somehow.'

'But it didn't happen.'

'No. It started well enough. A Jewish organisation in London sold the valuables for me. Not for as much as we'd hoped, but I think it was fair. They also tried to discover what happened to my family. Apparently, my little brother and sister managed to leave, but they went to France rather than Britain and they were still there when the French surrendered. I received a letter from the Red Cross stating that my parents were arrested after Kristallnacht, but I know no more.' George noticed tears forming in the corners of her eyes and he reached for her hand.

'So you rented the house in London and that's where I found you.' He wondered how she came to be living alone in Greenwich.

68

'Yes. You were the first honourable thing to happen to me in a long time,' she said quietly, like an uneasy confession.

'Did you have a boyfriend in Munich?' George made it sound like friendly interest, but a morbid curiosity made him want to know.

Millie flinched as if stabbed by a sharp pain. 'I had a friend at the University. Rather, I thought he was a friend, but it turned out that he was a Schweine an Arschloch.'

George guessed at the words meanings and knew he should change the subject, talk about something happier, but he had to ask. 'What did he do?'

She breathed raggedly and stared at nothing in particular. Eventually, she spoke without looking at him. 'Don't ask me that, George. Maybe one day I will tell you, but not now. He betrayed me and until you risked the bombs to stay with me, I thought I would never trust anyone again.'

'Then one day we'll talk.' George squeezed her hand and let go, feeling a stab of guilt at the word 'trust', knowing he was not behaving particularly honourably by asking so many questions. She probably wanted little more than friendship while he wanted so much besides. 'But remember that you have a friend in me. I'll write to you from Canada.' The businessmen at the other end of the room laughed and clinked wine glasses, their deal done. The sudden noise snapped her reverie, the cloudy expression vanished and a sparkle returned to her eyes.

'Good, because I would like that, I would like you to write to me very much and I shall write to you whenever possible.' She paused and crinkled her brow in thought. 'Then here is to us and the future,' she raised her glass and toasted. 'May the next year bring us safety and success and find us together again at its end.' They touched glasses and he again wondered at her choice of words, but then the waiter arrived with a trolley, took away their soup bowls and laid out the next course. Millie watched him until he was by the door.

'How do you feel about helping the British?' George asked her circumspectly. It might be a tactless question, but he guessed other Germans would consider her a traitor and he wondered whether this was another thing causing her problems.

Millie flicked her eyes at him as if she had been stung. 'I suppose you think that I betray my country?' she asked slowly and tilted her head to one side as she considered the question.

'Not betray,' he explained quickly, trying to reassure her. 'But it must be difficult working against your homeland, despite what they've done.'

Her response was immediate and passionate. 'Well, I feel fine about it. In fact, better than fine, I feel very good. The Nazis are the real traitors, the ones who betrayed Germany. They seduced the people and led them to war. Worse, they made us Jews the scapegoat for our nation's ills and destroyed the lives of many good people. The Nazis are a rot to be cut from the tree before it can be healthy again.'

'But the German people elected them. You can't kill everyone.'

'The majority were deluded, they voted for a dream,' she said, pointing with her fork. 'During the depression we had nothing and Hitler returned our self-respect. He gave us pride and purpose again, but it was all a deception. He is a skilful politician and a great leader in many ways, but no one knew he was evil.' She grinned. 'Sadly that wasn't mentioned in their party's manifesto. If he had turned his skills to commerce instead of conquest, to unity rather than division then Germany could have thrived and become a world leader.

Instead, he brought out the worst in our people and now we spread our canker across the globe.'

'So you're against Nazism, not Germany?' he asked slowly.

'Obviously, at certain levels, they are the same thing, but yes, that's right. I love my country and I wear this uniform to fight the Nazis for what they have done to it.'

'And for what they have done to your family?' he asked shrewdly.

'Especially for that, but wouldn't you? If the British government took away your family for no reason, I'm sure you would fight to save them,' she said and he nodded. 'I will do everything I can to make them safe, absolutely everything and anything.' Millie looked at him, and her expression confirmed that he had discovered her secret. She glanced at her watch and frowned. 'I am sorry, but I need to be going. Do you mind if we skip dessert and just leave?'

George shrugged. 'I've never liked treacle tart much,' he smiled and waved at the maître d'.

She parked out of sight of the gatepost and stepped from the car. It was the moment he had thought about and dreaded since leaving the hotel. Should he tell her that he loved her and risk sounding like a moonstruck adolescent, or just enjoy a few uncomplicated moments? In the end, Millie made the decision for him when she turned her lips towards his in a lingering kiss.

'I want you to have this,' she said afterwards and took off her necklace. It was a silver star of David on a chain. 'This was given to me on my Brita, my naming day.'

'I can't take it,' he said, horrified. 'It's far too precious.'

Millie took his hand and dropped the chain onto his palm. 'Please, I want you to have it and think of me whenever you look at it. In any case, I have my mother's.'

After a moment's thought, he pulled off his identity tags and slipped them over her head. 'Then you have these to remember me by as well. I'm sorry they're not valuable.'

They kissed again and she turned abruptly and got back into the car. Then, with a wave and a smile, she was gone. The day had started so well and now the thought of not seeing her again for a year was more than he could bear.

Chapter 7

Alberta - 17th February 1942

Yesterday it snowed in a miserable haze of powdery flakes that chilled hands and faces and slithered under collars. In complete contrast, the skies today were crisp and crystal blue. Just a few fluffy blobs of cumulus floated like candyfloss at three thousand feet. Much higher still at around eighteen thousand feet, 'Mares Tails' of cirrus streaked white ribbons through the air.

After checking the sky, George zipped up his fleece-lined Irvin Jacket and strode from RCAF Claresholm's mess hall towards the admin block. It may have been sunny, but the temperature in Alberta hovered around minus six degrees centigrade and had done since sunrise. In a few months, he would leave Claresholm and transfer to RCAF Pennfield Ridge on the east of the country to begin Operational Training. It surprised him just how quickly time passed and how soon he had become used to Canada. The vastness of the country with its prairies, mountains and unending forests were such a complete contrast to his Somerset village that at first, he marvelled he was still on the same planet. Instead of the gentle valleys of home, the land around Claresholm was completely flat and stretched as far as the eye could see, except to the east where just visible on the horizon was the grey line of snow-clad Rocky Mountains.

Two letters from Millie had arrived overnight. The first, dated months before, was little more than a hastily scribbled note. The second, dated just two weeks ago was long and full of gossip. Correspondence across the Atlantic was slow and tenuous at the best of times, and occasionally nonexistent when it ended up on the seabed along with the ship transporting it. Maybe that had happened to her other correspondence. Maybe she had written more often and her letters were lost in transit, but if that was the case, how could these two have arrived at the same time? To be fair, she apologised for not writing more frequently and put the blame firmly on pressures from work. Although it was hard to imagine any job being too demanding to write a letter. George frowned. The obvious explanation was that she did not want to write, but Millie was a straightforward person and he believed that she would tell him if she had met someone else. His relationship with her had become one mystery after another.

Having flown until late the previous evening, George was due the day off. Instead, he reported to the Squadron Engineering Officer. He knocked on the SEO's office door, entered and saluted. The SEO was the Squadron Leader responsible for all one hundred and twenty aircraft on the base. Good-natured and professional, the SEO fussed over his aircraft like a mother hen with her chicks.

'Ah, Watford. Good of you to come,' he called brightly as if George had a choice. 'I know it's a rest day, but I've got a quick hop for you.' George was happy to hear that. Although he had accumulated over one hundred flying hours on his logbook, he needed more before he could earn his pilot's wings.

'Not a problem, sir. What's the trip?' He sat in the chair indicated and watched the SEO shuffle some papers before handing one across.

'We've just finished refitting an Anson and she needs a shakedown flight. In addition, the stores' Johnnies want this list fetched from Red Deer. So putting the two together, I'd like you to fly over and get them.'

George knew RCAF Red Deer well, it was another aerodrome about one hundred and fifty miles due north and he was pleased that the SEO had chosen him for such an easy hop. A shakedown flight and the chance to see the sights, nothing too onerous, maybe two hours duration there and back, not including lunch at Red Deer if he could scrounge one. Three hours total. The list comprised clothing and stationary so weight was not a concern.

'The 'Ops' people have a crew for you, some new boys fresh from home who need a familiarisation flight,' the SEO continued. 'They've done the basic courses so they know enough to be useful.'

George was less happy to hear that. It was always reassuring to have experienced hands onboard. Still, it was only a quick flight and in good weather. He mentally added an extra hour for training and to show Calgary to the new boys.

The Met Office was on the way to the crew room, so he called in to check the forecast. This close to mountains, conditions altered quickly and weather information was sometimes little more than an educated guess. Each day the meteorological staff chalked forecasts and wind speeds across a number of blackboards. George wandered from board to board, making notes on his flight pad.

The three trainees waited in the crew room, looking cold and ill at ease. George smiled to himself, remembering how awkward he felt when he arrived just a few months before. They stood up, shook hands and introduced themselves. The newcomers were Beck, Gordon and Sherman, trainee navigator, bomb aimer and wireless operator.

'Welcome to RCAF Claresholm,' he said. No one had lit a fire yet and it was so cold that his breath steamed as he spoke. 'I suppose you've come straight from the ship?'

'We've been travelling by train for three days and got here late yesterday.' Gordon said and yawned deeply.

George was sympathetic, but their training would be intense and constant tiredness was something they would have to deal with. 'Everything will be a bit bewildering at first, but believe me, you'll soon be enjoying yourselves. How were things back home?' Uncensored news was hard to get this far away and anyone from Britain endured a barrage of questions.

Sherman creased his eyebrows. 'I don't know how long you've been away. The people are bearing up and there's more optimism now the yanks have joined in. Plus the bombing's got less recently. It's just that there's never much good news from the war and everyone's tired of rationing and shortages.'

'Well, there I can give you some good news,' George said brightly. 'They haven't heard of rationing over here and the food is first rate, also there are no blackouts to bother with either. When we set off, I'll make a low pass over Calgary. It's the nearest city and you can usually scrounge a lift there on days off.' He asked a few more questions about home, before guiding them to a series of maps pasted across one of the walls. The first was a large scale of Canada and he pointed to the bottom left-hand corner.

'You're in Alberta now, the other side of the country from where you came ashore. This aerodrome is part of the British Commonwealth Air Training Plan, set up to give us a safe place to learn away from enemy fighters. There are dozens of other aerodromes across the country, marked with the red crosses.' He waved a hand at the symbols speckling the map. Most were near the border with the United States, with about half on the east of the country and slightly more on the West. 'Every base has its own purpose. Some teach single engine flying for the fighter boys, then there's navigation and bombing schools and so on. Here at Claresholm, bomber pilots learn multi-engine flying.'

'So why are we here?' Beck the navigator asked abruptly.

George looked at him. Beck was a tall youth with an unfriendly air about him. Arrogance? Boredom? He couldn't decide which. 'Well, they sail us across when there's space on a ship. It doesn't always tie in with the start of a course. I guess they sent you to Claresholm to gain some experience while you're waiting for your courses to start.'

'More inefficiency,' Beck sneered. 'No wonder the war's going so badly.'

George frowned but did not argue. Someone with Beck's attitude would never agree, no matter what he said. It was easier to ignore him. 'Once your course starts you'll be pretty busy. If I were you I'd take every opportunity to learn as much as you can beforehand.' Beck looked away and shook his head.

The next map was of Alberta and George pointed to a red cross on the bottom left. 'This is us at RCAF Claresholm, we're about eighty miles south of Calgary and eighty miles east of the Rocky Mountains. Today's flight is straightforward. We're going to get some supplies from another aerodrome at a place called Red Deer.' and he pointed to a mark higher up the map. 'We'll be flying an Avro Anson just out of refit, so we'll stooge about a bit at first to try her out. I've checked with the Met people and they say there's a chance of thunderstorms further up country. They usually get it wrong, but all the same, I want you to stay on top of your jobs. This close to the mountains the weather changes quickly. Are you happy with that Nav?' George asked Beck pointedly.

Beck looked up. 'My happiness isn't your concern. You do the flying and leave the navigation to me.'

Because they were the same rank, on the ground George had no real authority over the trainees, but most aircrews treated pilots with deference. In the air, of course, it was a different matter. There the pilot was in charge and insubordination was a hazard not tolerated. But that did not mean he had to accept rudeness passively. He slowly drew himself to his full height and stepped inches from Beck so their eyes locked. 'Just make sure you do Nav, or your flying days will be over. Right, let's get going,' he ordered. Beck glared for a moment and his jaw twitched as if he were about to say something else. Then he turned and stalked towards the door. As George watched him go, Sherman hung back and grabbed George's arm, holding it until the others were outside.

'What is it, WOp?' George asked the Wireless Operator.

'Look, don't worry about Beck. He's still upset because he was scrubbed from the pilot's course. He gets a bit moody about it.'

'Well, he's not going to make any friends like that,' George told him, removing Sherman's hand from his arm. 'Aircrews are a team, not rivals.'

'He'll get over it,' Sherman assured him, but George did not think he would.

As the four of them crunched across the snow to the aircraft, he tried to concentrate on the flight. The twin-engine Avro Anson was not fast enough to use in combat, but she had found her place as a training aircraft. Slow and steady, safe and with few vices, she gave good visibility from the cockpit and with long glass panels down both sides, from the fuselage too. The crew sat in a line behind the pilot, starting with Beck at the navigator's desk, then Sherman with his wireless and finally Gordon took the spare seat at the back next to Sherman. He would stay there until it was time to come forward for a practice bomb run. Although it was always nice to have someone helping in the cockpit, being alone was not a problem in the Anson. Steering was through a solid column with a 'u' shaped yoke, and the dials and levers were all easy to see and reach, she was a good kite to fly.

Maybe Gordon was right, perhaps Beck did just need time to adjust to his disappointment. He would give him the benefit of the doubt for now and see how he shaped up in the air. Despite having flown the previous evening, George looked forward to flying again. It was part of him and seemed as natural as combing his hair. Because of the cold, the ground crew had already spun up the aircraft's engines. George simply went through the checks and flew away. This was definitely the life and as they climbed away from Claresholm, his good spirits returned and he hummed a song from the Mess.

'You can keep your Moth and Battle,
Your Harvard and your Crane,
Give me the good old Anson
In which our pilots train.'

None of the trainees knew Calgary, so he did a low circuit over the city and pointed out the Eighth Avenue shops, the Hudson's Bay Company department store and the Palliser Hotel, the tallest building in Calgary.

'Look down to the right,' George told them and banked the aircraft around the hotel. Below them was a huge twelve-floor building with three wings like teeth in a comb. 'If you fancy spending some of your flying pay, people joke that the Palliser's steaks are so large they ask whether you want the horns trimmed and the hooves polished before they serve your order.'

'Have you eaten there?' Sherman asked.

'I have and the steaks are gigantic,' he replied. 'but they didn't polish the hooves.'

Further north he flew over a couple of isolated ranches so that Gordon could see what low-level bomb runs would be like. Climbing back to ten thousand feet, the cumulus had developed thick cauliflower tops, a sure sign of bad weather. More worrying was that far away to the east, dark clouds were spilling over the mountains like dirty foam and spreading quickly. Not good, he would have to hurry.

Thirty miles out from RCAF Red Deer, the aerodrome advised that it had just closed down due to an electrical storm. Through the windscreen, he could see a long line of black clouds hanging over the Red Deer area, illuminated by forks of lightning. For a moment, he debated whether to press on anyway, but there was little point in taking unnecessary risks. Wind shear and turbulence from storms could be deadly when the aircraft was at low speed for landing. The stores were not vital and the Anson had been air tested, so he had done the most important part of the job. He could always come back tomorrow and get a few extra hours flying time as well. Swinging the aircraft around he hauled back south to home. Lunch and the stores could wait.

'Pilot to crew. Red Deer has closed because of a storm, so I'm heading back to Claresholm. Hopefully, we can stay ahead of the weather, but it could get bumpy. Make sure you haven't got anything loose lying around.'

Ten minutes into the return journey, the cumulus turned into a blanket of stratocumulus, completely obscuring the ground. Way above them, the mares' tails of cirrus expanded to hide the sun, but this was still no great problem. They could fly on instruments, work out their position from compass and clock, even get heading and bearing information over the wireless, and Claresholm was still clear.

Suddenly, towering black storm clouds formed in front and around them, heavy and threatening. The Anson immediately pitched in the volatile air, bucking up and down like a wild steer. Gusts of hail slashed across the windscreen so heavily that for seconds at a time there was little forward visibility. Unpleasant, but not necessarily dangerous. George told the crew to strap themselves in and he tightened his own harness. This was going to get interesting.

Lightning crashed out of the clouds, close enough to bathe the Anson in electricity. Sherman, the wireless operator, shouted that his set was smoking, so he shut it down. Beck, the navigator, added that the compass was spinning like a top and useless. Now they were in trouble.

George pressed the intercom switch. 'Nav, I need our position.' With a fix on their location, he could estimate a course and use the clock to time an approach to Claresholm. There was no reply.

'Nav. Get your finger out and give me a position.' He asked for a second time, his frustration with Beck was growing. Again, no reply and for a moment George wondered whether the intercom was damaged.

Then a voice said, 'Nav to Pilot. Not possible to give a position at this time.' The plane bucked and dropped, and George fought to bring it back to ten thousand feet.

'For God's sake, Nav. It's not that difficult.' He snarled at the effort of wrestling with the control column. 'Add side-wind and speed to the time from our last plotted position. Assume a constant heading.'

No reply. 'Nav?'

'Nav to Pilot. You do your job and I'll do my mine. I repeat it's not possible to calculate our position.'

George swore with anger at Beck's stupidity. The navigator should have plotted their position at every stage of the journey, but he would bet a month's wages that the idiot had slept instead and now they were lost near the Rocky Mountains. Clouds heavy with moisture and dark with thunder rose in pillars, stretching way up to twenty thousand feet, far higher than the Avro Anson could climb. Navigating around them was like flying into a maze, where each turn might bring a dead end. Then they would have to enter the storm clouds and risk ice forming on the wings, making the aircraft heavy and unstable. As minutes ticked by, the clouds became closer and more frequent, massive lumps of black and grey that lit like lamps when lightning exploded within.

Avoiding one pillar the Anson suddenly bucked and dropped like a stone. He became weightless and floated up from his seat into the harness. It felt like driving off a cliff. Even without the intercom, he could hear the panicked cries of the crew behind. For seconds he battled with his senses, trying to understand what was happening. The Anson's nose was down, the engines shrieked and they were in free fall.

Then he realised they had flown into a downdraft, a block of warm air that cold air cascaded down. For seconds he froze, uncertain what to do. Then pulling back on the column, he jammed the two engine throttles to the stops. With only thin air for the blades to bite into, the propellers span faster. Much too fast. Their whining filled the aircraft with a painful noise, but he could not reduce power. He needed to claw every available molecule of air. The temperature gauges leapt up, but not as fast as the altimeter unwound. This could not continue. Either the engines would explode or they would run out of sky. One way or another it would end soon. He felt helpless and that scared him as much as anything. In those seconds, his thoughts tumbled like a flickering film. *Dear God, I don't want to die, please give me some solid air*, he prayed. Their only chance was to reach the other side, but there was no knowing how wide the vortex was. Although they still had forward momentum, the aircraft dropped a dozen feet for every one forwards.

The altimeter wound down through seven thousand feet. They had fallen three thousand feet in seconds. George desperately pushed the throttle levers again, even though he knew they were already at the stops. With his other hand, he heaved the column further into his stomach. As they fell through five thousand feet, the engine temperature gauges redlined. He was little more than a passenger; nothing he did was having any effect. Glancing sideways out of the window, he saw the lower clouds rushing up to meet them. It felt like falling into a canyon.

George held the yoke so tightly that his hands cramped. How much longer could they stay airborne? Twenty seconds, thirty? *At least it will be quick.* Then they hit a solid lump of cold air and the Anson juddered, jerked and finally bounced with such force he was surprised the wings stayed on. From the rear of the aircraft, cries and thuds overlaid a bitter stench of vomit, but they were through and into colder, denser air. He pulled the throttles back an inch or two so the overheated engines could cool. But they were now in the middle of the storm and needed power to get above it. Electrical storms created the worst forms of turbulence. For miles around the air was shattered, creating invisible quagmires of swirling ether, but he could not risk increasing power and climbing until the engines cooled.

With another almighty thud, the aircraft hit a pocket of severe turbulence, tossing it onto its starboard side. The control column shook like a wet dog and he wrenched the yoke to port, knowing that if he lost control now they would flip over and topple from the sky. The aircraft's sharp angle threw him sideways against the harness and the strap dug painfully into his neck, forcing his head onto his left shoulder. He fought the controls as the Anson hurtled in tight circles, losing more altitude with each orbit. Within seconds, they fell into a cloud and became enveloped in muggy whiteness. The temperature was coming down and speed and oil pressure were OK, but he could not get the aircraft to level out. Altitude was just three thousand feet and they were still spiralling. His brain screamed that this was a death spin. Fighting every instinct, he reduced power and pushed the column forward, the opposite of what fear was telling him. The nose dropped and he kicked in some port rudder. Miraculously the wings levelled off at two thousand feet, but this was much too low to be in cloud near mountains.

In his fear, he saw grey rocks materialise in the gloom. He had to get higher. Slamming the throttles forward and pulling back the column, he circled the Anson upwards. The altimeter rose through three to four thousand feet. The cloud thinned to a wispy vapour and disappeared. Five, six, seven thousand feet and still he climbed, not daring to stop until they reached eight thousand feet and the Anson threatened to stall. Only then did he ascend more slowly.

The storm clouds were three miles behind and the air was smoother here, but his arms shook so badly that the control column rattled. His heart pounded and his mouth tasted of blood. He must have bitten his tongue, but could not remember when. For moments, he clenched the controls and stared blindly ahead. Never before had he been so scared. Breathing more slowly he patted the windscreen edge. *Thank you God and thank you old girl. Now get us home.* Altitude ten thousand feet, airspeed a hundred and fifty miles-per-hour, engine temperature and pressure normal. They were alive, but still in trouble. He must think clearly, plan the best thing to do. Glancing outside he tried to spot a gap in the clouds, but as far as he could see, the earth was covered in a bath foam of clouds.

'Navigator,' he called down the intercom, hoping that his voice sounded firmer than he felt. 'I could use some help.' There was no reply.

'Nav. Speak to me.'

Sherman, the wireless operator, spoke quickly, squeaky with fear. 'Beck's out cold. I think he might be dead. He wasn't strapped in.'

George glanced over his shoulder and in the edge of his vision saw a figure lying prone on the deck. *At last, some good news*, he said to himself bitterly. 'OK. Leave him. Nothing we can do now.' He thought for a moment. 'I need you and Gordon to keep lookout. One left and the other right. Watch for gaps in the cloud. Let me know if you spot anything. We need to get down and soon. Understand?'

'Do you think we'll be OK?' Shearman asked shakily.

He wanted to say something comforting, as much for himself as the others. 'We'll be OK if we can find a break in the clouds, even if I have to put her down on the prairie.'

'And if we don't?'

'Then we go down anyway and hope for the best,' and the best was that they did not fly into the mountains.

Their fuel was low, very low. Less than an hour's flying time left in the tanks, probably closer to forty-five minutes. *Think. Think. The bad things are; we are lost, solid cloud above and below, and mountains nearby. No radio, no compass, no navigator and low on fuel.* What were the good things? He must concentrate on those. *Well, the controls respond, height good, engines good and the thunderclouds are behind us*. It was not a lot but it would have to do.

George set the timer on the cockpit clock. Thirty minutes and he would circle down through the clouds and hope for the best, mountains or no mountains. Then the clock face reminded him of something, some snippet of information? *What was it...? Of course! Point a watch's hour hand at the sun and due south is halfway between the hour hand and the 12. But where was the sun?*

'Look for the brightest patch of cloud,' George shouted. 'Try to work out roughly where the sun is.'

After a few seconds, Sherman said, 'We think it's on the right, the cloud seems brightest there.'

This meant east was behind them. *Damn*. They were flying west towards the mountains, maybe already over them. He swung the plane around and checked the timer. Five minutes had gone. So, five minutes to get back to their previous position and twenty minutes of flight towards the prairie beyond. Then he would spiral down and with luck have fifteen more minutes of fuel to choose a landing spot. That was the best case. The worst case was that atmospheric refraction caused the sky's brightness and they were now flying towards the Rockies rather than away from them. If so, at some point in the clouds they would meet a large lump of mountain. There seemed no end to the clouds, every time he thought he saw a gap it turned into just another valley. There were only minutes to go before he must make the decision to descend.

'George! George!' Sherman's voice exploded from his headset, making him jump.

'What?'

'Over at three o'clock. An aircraft!'

For seconds George saw nothing except pillars and valleys of cloud. Then a mile to the right and three thousand feet below he spotted a silverfish darting through clouds on a parallel heading.

'Signal them with the Aldis lamp,' George shouted. 'Try to attract their attention. Quickly!' He banked the aircraft over, dropped the nose and increased speed, sacrificing fuel in a desperate attempt to catch the other aircraft. Several times he thought he had lost it, but each time the plane reappeared from a cloud further on. It was a Cessna Crane, another training aircraft. Eventually, it spotted them and flashed back in Morse.

'Problems?...' Sherman read out the message.

'Tell them we're lost, low on fuel and damaged. Ask them to guide us to the nearest aerodrome.' He reduced power just as the timer hit zero. Fifteen, perhaps twenty-five minutes of fuel remained, then nothing but fumes.

'Stay...close...' Sherman read.

Slipping sideways the Crane straightened onto a new heading and George closed until he was just twenty feet away. The other aircraft reduced power and slid into the clouds with the Anson so near they trembled from her wake. The cockpit darkened and visibility became just a few yards. Moisture condensed on the screen, running sideways in dozens of thin streams. Without knowing how near the clouds went to the ground, he had to stick to the other aircraft like glue. Despite the cold, he was sweating and rivulets ran from under his leather helmet and stung his eyes. He tried to blink them away but only succeeded in blurring his vision. Exhaustion from fear and constant physical effort sapped at his strength. Like the Anson, he was nearing the limit of endurance. He must keep the Crane in sight.

'Put on your parachutes,' he said into the intercom. 'You'll be safer jumping if we lose the engines.' Although there could be no escape for him, the aircraft would only remain stable with someone at the controls.

The Anson bucked in the cloud's turbulence, getting dangerously close to the Crane. He drew back slightly, but began to lose sight of the other aircraft and added power until her wing lights were clear. He was flying stick and throttle now, using all his skills to stay on the Crane's bouncing tail. Suddenly he had the distinct impression that he was banking to the right and corrected by turning left. Immediately he lost the other aircraft and in a panic, swung back the other way. The crane materialised, and a glance at the dials showed the Attitude Indicator was level. His senses were misleading him, he had vertigo. *This just gets better and better.*

At eight hundred feet, the cloud thinned and evaporated. Below a flat, snow-covered expanse of landscape appeared. Desolate, cold and unwelcoming in the fading light, but it was the best sight he had seen in a long time. They were safely through the clouds.

Both fuel gauges were flat against the stops. They were now flying on vapour and the dial's inaccuracy. The Crane banked to the right, extended flaps and lowered its undercarriage. George did the same, just as the starboard engine coughed, spluttered and stopped. The starboard tank was dry. He increased power to the port engine and applied port rudder to keep the aircraft straight. *Just another minute. Please.* They were down to five hundred feet and he recognised where they were. Fort Macleod, an aerodrome thirty miles south of Claresholm. His actions were slow and instinctive now, his thoughts sluggish from exhaustion.

Ahead, two rows of lights blinked on. Landing lights. The Crane dipped its wings in farewell and banked away to the left, leaving him with a clear shot at the runway. Seconds later the Anson sped over the boundary and he reduced power further, flared the wings and landed with hardly a bump. Scarcely conscious of the shouts of relief behind him, he taxied to dispersal and shut down the port engine. *Any landing you can walk away from is a good one*, he told himself, but this felt like one of his best. An ambulance pulled up and medics came onboard. He left them to deal with Beck, who he could see was breathing. Unconscious and not dead. Maybe tomorrow he would find out how he was, but not tonight.

A crowd gathered to watch the Anson's arrival. One of the figures detached itself and trotted over. 'Watford! My dear fellow,' Marshall cried out in surprise and grasped George in a bear hug. 'Delighted to see you again. You look bloody awful.'

'It's good to see you too, Marshal,' he replied genuinely. 'Do you have a bar here?' Marshall nodded knowingly and led him away.

Chapter 8

Liverpool - 6th August 1942

S.S. Mauretania, the pride of Cunard's White Star line had just run the gauntlet of U-boats in the Atlantic, part of a convoy of forty merchant ships and escorts sailing from Halifax to Liverpool. A heavy crossing with high waves and dank, squally weather forced all but the most seasick inside. Hundreds of servicemen crowded the lower decks where claustrophobic compartments, stacked with hammocks, reeked with the stench of vomit and stale tobacco smoke. The constant fear of U-boats compounded their misery and each day brought fresh alerts and drills. The *Mauretania* now approached Liverpool and the end of her journey.

George stood near the bow and waited for dawn to rise. A few nights before a submarine slipped into the convoy and torpedoed two merchant ships. Their blazing hulks drifted slowly astern until they were just bright specks on the horizon. That scared him and since then he spent every waking hour outside. Today was cold and a sea mist settled on the water, dulling the constant thrum of *Mauretania's* engines. England was so near now that he peered landward, desperate to glimpse it after so long away. He was almost home. Nearby a seagull rode the chill air currents, cawing noisily and he watched it curiously, wondering what sort of omen it might be.

As the light improved, a faint outline solidified into a shoreline and buildings. Other pilots gathered nearby and together they stared at the ruins. With a start, he saw that most of the structures lining the Mersey were bomb damaged and fire-blackened. The Luftwaffe had flattened this part of the city and hollow shells and piles of rubble were all that remained of building after building. Feelings of anger and guilt at the destruction welled through him. He had been far away and safe while his country suffered. Seeing the damage reinforced his determination. He wanted to repay the enemy. He wanted it very badly.

As soon as the liner docked, the pilots grabbed their kitbags and disembarked. They huddled on the dockside, longing for a mug of tea and wondering about breakfast, but grateful to be on dry land and away from the fetid lower decks. There was no band or welcome home speeches; instead, an official directed them to a large wooden hut that smelt strongly of creosote. Inside, four RAF administrators, headed by an elderly Flight Lieutenant, rummaged unhurriedly through piles of boxes, searching for their orders.

'Come on you blokes,' called one of the pilots. 'The war will be over by the time you've finished.'

'You should be so lucky,' the Flight Lieutenant replied tartly and that quietened them.

Eventually, the banter began again and someone called to Bill Lane, 'What's the first thing you'll do when you get home, Bill?' Bill was married and they all knew he was looking forward to spending the customary two weeks Foreign Service Leave with his wife.

'Never you mind, that's private between me and the missus,' he said to a chorus of hoots.

'OK. So what's the second thing you'll do?' someone else asked.

'Put my bags down,' he replied happily. George chuckled. He looked forward to telling Millie he was home and kindling a relationship. However, he had been away for such a long time and things change. Strangely, it was easier when he was in Canada because of the impossible distance between them. Now he was home he would know for sure whether she wanted him. Although her letters were warm enough, he still worried that their irregularity showed at best indifference. The time away had not dimmed his feelings and many nights he had fallen asleep planning a life after the war with her.

The administrators found their orders eventually and delivered the bad news that there was to be no leave. The pilots grumbled but the Flight Lieutenant just told them to take it up with the CO of their base. George received a rail warrant and instructions to make his way to RAF Oakley, a Heavy Conversion Unit. It was one of the dozens of new aerodromes built since the war started. Although he had no idea where RAF Oakley was, the rail warrant's destination was Bicester and he knew where that was, roughly.

Lorries ferried them to Liverpool railway station where they found a NAAFI van dispensing current buns and mugs of warm sweet tea. Thankfully, it was free of charge as no one had any British money. They stood in a group, talking quietly; watching dour-faced civilians hurry past. The people looked tired and weary, and the station was dirty and smoke stained. Things seemed to have changed during their year in Canada, the country seemed grimmer, smaller and darker. An hour later, a southern bound train pulled in, its carriages untidy and worn, and many of its windows cracked. Half of the group struggled onboard while the rest, heading to bases either north or directly east, waved them farewell. The train was already crowded and with no chance of a seat, they stretched out where they could on floors, toilets and even along luggage racks, all hoping to snatch a little more sleep.

At each major station, pilots left to journey to different destinations. They went without a fuss, just hitching kitbags on their shoulders and muttering farewells to friends. George changed trains in Birmingham and found a space on a corridor floor. He was alone now and it felt strange to be without the people he had trained with. This was yet another beginning and he began to feel that change had become the only constant. It made him think wistfully about his old life on the farm and the certainty of the passing seasons. He stretched out with his head on his kitbag and reread Millie's last letter.

The train's slow rhythmic rocking made him sleepy. Carefully he refolded the letter and closed his eyes, his mind drifting back to Canada. From this distance, it seemed like a different world and a different age. Someone once told him that a man could go into the wild north and with four pegs mark out as much land as he wanted and it would be his. That thought entranced him. He could stake out a few hundred acres, buy a small aircraft and make money from farming and flying people around. It was a fantasy, but he might try it if his father remained hostile or if Millie rejected him. It was a haven to run to if all else failed. One thing was certain; he could never go back to how things were at home. He was no longer the same person, not even close. Kipling's words came to him.

Where there's neither a road nor a tree -
But only my Maker an' me,
An I think it will kill me or cure,
So I think I will go there an' see.

It was a good fantasy, to be self-reliant and far from the responsibilities of family. However, deep inside he knew his old life would be like a rubber band that stretched but never broke; it would always tug at him. Maybe the war would change him, but now that he was back, he felt a love for the old country that went deeper than homesickness. Thinking of

Canada then made him wonder how Dickinson and Marshall were fairing. Both had gone across several weeks after him and as Marshall had predicted, he was finding navigation over the white featureless countryside a problem.

A voice called out as the train jerked away from Birmingham. 'Any danger of some space in here you blokes?' He cracked open an eye and saw a figure in the darker blue RAAF uniform stagger between the legs of dozing servicemen. Weighed down by a bulging kitbag, the Australian struggled to stay upright. No one moved and so George swung his legs sideways to free up some space.

'Down here,' he called.

The Australian stumbled over and dropped to the floor, and they sat facing each other across the width of the corridor. 'Thanks, mate,' he said and reached out his hand. 'Dingo Johnston. Good to meet you.'

George shook his hand, 'George Watford. Good to meet you too.'

'Bloody riot these trains,' the Australian complained. 'Couldn't get on the last one and the station bludgers won't tell you squat.' Dingo had a tight mop of curly brown hair, bright blue eyes and strong features lightly pockmarked from some distant illness. His eyes were narrow slits except when he smiled. Overall, his was a handsome face, if you liked the rugged outdoors type.

'I guess it's the war, the place has changed,' George said. He felt much the same as the Australian.

'Christ I hope that's the case. I've been looking forward to seeing the land of my father's.'

'Been here long?'

'Couple of days,' Dingo replied. 'The ship that brought us over had engine problems, so they crawled into Southampton yesterday and the drongos kicked us off. I've been travelling since then. I'm done in and that's the truth.'

George nodded sympathetically. He was about to ask where Dingo had trained, but curiosity about his name got the better of him. 'Is Dingo your real name?'

Dingo pulled a pack of Players from his greatcoat and offered one to George, who shook his head. Putting one in the corner of his mouth, he lit it with an easy flick of an American Zippo lighter. 'Me mates called me Dingo because I was a bit wild as a youngster. The old man farms five thousand acres in the Northern Territories and I guess I enjoyed the freedom too much.'

George was impressed; his father's farm was only three hundred acres. 'That's a lot of land. He must be rich.'

'Nah, it's all scrub, snakes and spiders. It's not fertile like here. Only worth something to those stupid enough to farm it, but it's a beauty of a place all the same.'

Dingo reached across, pulled open George's greatcoat and looked at the double winged insignia freshly stitched on the breast of his jacket. 'Pilot. You any good?'

'Same number of landings as take-offs.' George believed he was good, but he was not going to tempt fate by boasting.

Dingo looked thoughtful and took a deep pull on his cigarette. 'I'm a navigator, myself.' He opened his greatcoat to show the single wing emblem with the letter 'N' inside it.

'Any good?' George repeated Dingo's question.

'Any good!' Dingo laughed. 'Mate, give me a compass, a couple of stars and I'll find you the Popes private bordello. Half the jokers calling themselves Nav's couldn't get themselves home from the pub.' Dingo continued more seriously. 'You going to Oakley, too?' George nodded and Dingo said, 'You know what will happen when we get there?'

'Lunch in the sergeants' mess and then two week's leave?' George guessed, hoping it would be true. He was desperate to see Millie and his home again.

'Good luck with that, mate.' the Australian laughed. He leaned closer and spoke more quietly. 'I got the gen from a pal who went through this last year. First thing tomorrow morning they'll put everyone in an empty hangar and tell us to form crews.' Dingo stared at George seriously. 'Well, my mate told me to make sure I got in with a good bunch because the ones that don't click don't stick if you get my meaning?'

George leaned forward, interested. 'Did he say how to get in with a good group?' He had assumed they would allocate crews like rooms in the Mess.

'Nah. He didn't and I couldn't write back because the poor blighter bought it on the way back from Germany a week later.'

'Sorry to hear it.' George could think of nothing better to say.

'Yeah, me as well. He was a good cobber, one of the best. Good bush pilot too. He could land on an ant hill and drink like a sheep shearer on payday.'

'What happened to him?'

'Who knows? You fly in the dark and die in the dark in this game. I do know that he had a good crew though. Poor bastard almost made it; they were on the last trip of the tour. It was a bloody shame.' Dingo took another pull of his cigarette and stared at the glowing tip as he exhaled. 'He told me that you can't beat the odds, just stretch them far enough to get through your thirty operations.'

George straightened himself; his legs were beginning to cramp. 'I almost died in Canada once,' he said slowly, remembering. 'Bad weather, low fuel and a nav who didn't know where home was.' A figure shuffled between them, stepping slowly between the dozing servicemen. The Australian looked competent and if he was as good as his word, he certainly knew his job and understood the dangers. George wanted to fly with capable people. He made his decision. 'How about we stick together?'

Dingo smiled lazily as he considered this. 'Well, I reckon I could chance you for the skipper if you'll have me.'

'If you're as good as you say, I'd be mad to turn you down.' George reached out his hand again and Dingo took it, striking the deal.

'Well that's the pilot and nav sorted, we just need the rest. So how do we do it?' Dingo asked, staring at George across the glowing tip of his cigarette.

George considered the problem for a while and suddenly smiled. 'We don't wait for tomorrow, we pick our crew tonight in the Mess bar.'

Dingo looked sceptical. 'You plan to recruit a crew of booze hounds?'

'Got a better idea?' George replied. 'Course we could always wait for tomorrow and hold interviews. Ask them about their hobbies and why they're right for us. That's bound to get the pick of the crop.'

Dingo raised his hands briefly in surrender. 'OK, OK, point taken.'

'You never know, maybe the ones going to the bar will be more sociable, fit into a team better. At the very least it gives us more time to choose.'

Dingo still looked doubtful, but then nodded. 'It's a theory I suppose. But, when I'm guiding us to hunland and back, I need a fair go that I'll get home. It's hard to make calculations when you're looking over your shoulder for the parachute all the time.'

George shrugged. 'Then you do the choosing,' he offered. 'I'll sit at a table while you hang around the bar and pick the ones you like. Send them across and I'll make sure they're OK.' This seemed sensible because the navigator relied on the crew more than he did. The bomb aimer and two gunners spotted ground features, while the wireless operator passed on weather transmissions and could get a fix on their position from ground stations. Navigating at night was a team effort.

Dingo thought for a moment. 'Yeah, it could work. Better than just leaving it to chance, I suppose. So what do I look for?'

George gathered his thoughts. He often thought about crew qualities following his flight through the thunderstorm and decided there were a few essentials. 'Well, we can assume they're all at a good basic standard, so...' He began counting off his fingers, 'The two gunners must be the types who'll stay alert. They don't have to be good shots, just be able to spot trouble. Get someone short for the rear turret. It's as cramped as hell and I want the Tail-End-Charlie to be able to shift about while he's searching.' George paused to make sure Dingo agreed and received a nod. 'The Wireless Operator must have a high Morse speed and our Engineer must be a natural fixer because if the kite's shot up he'll be the difference between us getting home and going down. Lastly, the bomb aimer will be working closely with you to get us over the target, so as well as doing his job; he must be someone you can trust.'

'Quite a shopping list,' Dingo responded. 'I can see you've been thinking about this.'

RAF Oakley was a wartime construction and depressingly devoid of the comforts found in pre-war stations. Erected quickly and cheaply, its buildings had tin roofs, thin walls and inadequate heating. Similarly, the furniture was sparse and utilitarian. However, the organisation was good and as soon as they arrived, the admin staff allocated temporary accommodation and dinner was waiting in the Sergeants Mess. George and Dingo bolted down an indifferent meal of sausages, baked beans and potatoes, before heading next door to the bar. Some non-flying sergeants were already there, sitting in little knots and pointedly ignoring the newcomers. These men were regular RAF, people who had taken a dozen or more years to earn their three stripes and resented the aircrew sergeants who gained theirs in just a year. By signing up for the war's duration, George and the others became part of the RAF Volunteer Reserve, and regulars regarded VR sergeants as little more than civilians in uniform, people lacking tradition, discipline and respect.

'G'day mates,' Dingo made a point of calling out and laughed when they took no notice. 'Bunch of dunny rats, the lot of them,' he told George.

George glanced at the regulars and chose a table well away. 'I'll stay here and look welcoming; you set up shop by the bar.'

Dingo licked his lips, 'My oath, I'm as dry as a dead rat in the desert. Give me your mess number, mate and I'll bring you a glass of amber.'

The mess started to fill with aircrew and he watched Dingo circulating, holding snatches of conversation before moving on. He reminded George of a farmer inspecting livestock at the market. Behind the friendly smile, Dingo's eyes were icy cold, calculating and appraising. Once he had wandered up and down the room, he homed in for longer conversations. The first person he sent over was a sergeant with the letters AG inside his single wing insignia, an air-gunner.

'Watcher chum, the name's Max. Dingo sent me over,' he said looking at George shrewdly. 'He says you're crewing up?' Max had a strong London accent. He was short and had a ready smile that hinted at an equally ready wit. There was something else as well, a confidence and assuredness. George immediately took to Max and mentally ticked off the rear gunner's position as filled.

'Nice to meet you, Max, pull up a seat.' It had begun.

Minutes later an Air Engineer, with an 'E' in his insignia, introduced himself as Norman 'Chalky' White. Chalky was older than George by a few years and had a serious expression, but he also seemed steady and a bit of maturity in a crew was not a bad thing.

'What's your background, Chalky?' George asked him.

'I trained on the Tyne as a mechanical fitter with Swan Hunter and then worked in their Wallsend shipyard ever since.' George warmed to Chalky's lyrical Geordie accent. He definitely had the right background and seemed confident and friendly.

'Why not join the navy?'

Chalky smiled. 'I've had enough of ships. I fancied something a bit more glamorous.'

'And are you getting that?' George nodded at the sparsely decorated room.

'I'll let you know when I find it. But at least you come home every night in this mob.'

'That's as long as the skipper can find the aerodrome.' Max chipped in. 'I guess you can do that boss?'

'You need to ask Dingo. I only have to fly the crate, not navigate it.' They looked at Dingo who was laughing loudly with someone at the bar while trying to balance a pint of beer on his head.

'Why doesn't that fill me with confidence?' Max chuckled and then added. 'Hello, here comes the next recruit.' A slight, bookish-looking youth detached himself from Dingo and walked across. The letter B in his insignia told them he was a bomb aimer. He shook hands with George and the others with unusual formality.

'My name's Richard Scrivener, but please call me Dick.' He pulled up a chair and sat looking at them expectantly. 'I'm a bomb aimer.' He offered when no one spoke.

'Roll on. An' there was me thinking the 'B' stood for 'Bashful'.' Max replied.

Scrivener dusted his insignia. 'No, Bashful was one of the seven dwarfs. Possibly a relative of yours?'

'Cheeky bugger,' Max laughed. 'All the best things come in little packages you know, chum.'

'Yes, like my wages.' Chalky joined in.

'What did you do in Civvy Street, Dick?' George asked.

'Not too much. I'd just finished a degree in mathematics and was trying to decide on a career.'

George envied the casual way that university people talked about employment, as if it was a choice of entertainment rather than a route out of poverty. Max chipped in. 'You studied sums? Any good at working out the horses? Picking the winners? We could make some money together.'

Dick shook his head. 'I'm afraid there are too many random variables in horse racing to allow a reliable statistical probability.'

Max frowned and turned to Chalky. 'What did he just say?'

'Basically, that you'll have to stick to flogging knocked-off goods down the Mile End Road.'

Max's eyes widened. 'What? That's a bloody slander. I never worked the Mile End.'

Next came James Ambiolo, another air gunner and from Suffolk. Jim was blond, good looking and laconic. A silent type who watched cat like while the others talked, but smiled readily at their jokes. The final person recruited by Dingo was Edward 'Ned' Anderson, a Canadian who seemed much too young to be in uniform. His body was thin and gangly and his skin so smooth that it seemed unlikely to have ever felt the scrape of a razor. George would have put him closer to fourteen than the minimum age of eighteen. However, for better or worse he now had his crew.

'Right Skipper,' Dingo said pulling up a chair and sitting opposite him. 'Over to you.' He gave George a meaningful nod.

George had never made a speech before but sensed this moment was important if he was to give them the confidence to trust him. He took a sip of beer and slowly put the glass down.

'Tomorrow, we'll be asked to form into crews and that's a pretty big step for all of us.' He began, surprised by the firmness of his voice. 'We'll be fixed with the people we will depend on when we fly. I won't give you a load of bull about king and country, you all know why you volunteered for aircrew. Nothing guarantees we'll get through our tour, but we give ourselves the best chance by being a tight crew. Now, I'm not a bad pilot, but I'm going to get better. Likewise, if you join me, I'll expect everyone to get on top of his job and I'll tell you if you're not doing it.' He looked at them again and each nodded as he met their gaze. 'As I said, there are no guarantees. If a flak shell's got our name on it, then there's not a lot we can do. However, the odds get better if we're a good team and fly like professionals. If you buy into that and want to be part of this crew, then form up around me in the morning. Last thing, on the ground we're all the same, but in the air, I'm the boss, there can't be any question about who's in charge when we fly.' George finished, picked up his beer and waited for someone to speak, leaving an awkward silence. The others glanced at each other, unsure who would say something first.

'Well I reckon I'm in,' Chalky White said eventually in his strong Geordie accent. 'I know my job pretty well and I don't want to fly with a bunch of clowns. I've seen too many ships come up the Tyne that have been knocked all over the place. The German's aren't playing games.'

Dick Scrivener spoke next in his quiet considered way. 'As the Skipper says, statistically the better we are the better our chances. I'd like to join.'

One by one, they all nodded and spoke briefly to say they wanted in. George felt as though he had passed an interview. They got another round of drinks and began the business of getting to know each other. If Dingo was right, in the morning, they would become official and so without making it obvious, he took this last opportunity to watch them. In the weeks and months ahead they would become like brothers. They would share dangers and either survive or die together. He also knew that just how good they became would depend greatly on him, his abilities as a leader as well as a pilot. After a few more rounds, he felt the weariness of the day catch up and suggested they should call it a night. Tomorrow they could well be flying.

However, George was curious why Dingo had chosen these people. As they walked back from the Mess, he pulled Dingo to one side and asked him. Dingo took a pull of his cigarette and glanced at his feet before speaking, something was making him uneasy.

'Back home a few years ago, I was out late one night when my horse spooked. I don't know what at, a snake maybe.

Anyway, she jumped sideways, threw me and bolted. I landed badly and twisted my leg. So there I was, lying on the ground in the dark and can't move. Believe me mate, the Northern Territory is not a place you want to be when you're alone and helpless. I lay there getting more and more scared, but knowing that eventually my folks would come for me. Well, after my cobber bought it, I started thinking about things and decided to make sure I was in a crew I could trust like my family. People who would get me back home. Does that make sense?'

'I guess so,' George decided. 'So why pick these lads?'

Dingo took a final drag and flicked the burning embers away. 'Instinct mainly. The two gunners? Well, Max and Jim have good eyes and they listened carefully when I spoke. Plus they're friendly and not too full of themselves. Dick Scrivener, the bomb aimer, is intelligent and he'll do his job well enough. Also, he's sensible. If we're in a tight spot I think he'll drop the bombs and not want to go around again and get us the chop. Then Chalky is a steady hand and seems a thoroughgoing engineer. I think he's the type that if it can be fixed he'll mend it.'

'And Ned?' George asked. 'He's too young.'

'Yeah, Ned was difficult. My guess is that he lied about his age. I reckon he's only about fifteen.'

'So why take him?'

'Well, he came third in his Wireless course, so young or not he knows his stuff.' Dingo hesitated, waiting for someone to walk past. 'But truth be told, I guess I felt sorry for him. He reminded me of myself a few years back. I couldn't see the little blighter go off to a crook crew, it just wouldn't be right.'

Picking Ned was a mistake and they both knew it. Dingo meant well, but one weak link could kill them all. It defeated the purpose of selecting a crew beforehand. However, he had asked Dingo to do the choosing, so he had to accept his decision. 'Just remember, the first time he screws up will be the last time he flies with us.'

'Fair enough Skipper, but I think he'll do just fine.'

Dingo started to walk away but George held him back. 'So why did you agree to join me?'

'Eh?' Dingo feigned surprise.

'You heard.' Even in the dim light, he could see Dingo shift uncomfortably and guessed this was the real reason for his edginess. 'You're pretty choosy and the pilot's got the key job. So why go with me?

Dingo forced a laugh, 'Hey mate, maybe I just liked the look of you,' he said and patted George on the shoulder.

'Be serious Dingo,' George told him. 'You didn't ask me anything about my training or experience, yet you're happy to fly with me.'

Dingo frowned, suddenly serious. 'Skipper, I'm not going to lie to you, but I'm not going to tell you either. As it happens it's nothing bad, but it's my own reason, understand?'

'I want to know Dingo; I don't want to be wondering about it.'

Dingo stuck another cigarette in his mouth and took his time lighting it. Eventually, he spoke. 'Sorry Skipper, best I can say is that it's nothing bad. I'll tell you after the tour if you're still curious. Call it an incentive to get us all through if you like.'

George thought for a second and decided it was not important enough to fall out over. 'After the tour then, I'll hold you to it.' He shook his head and said jokingly, 'Christ, but you're irritating.'

Dingo laughed, a quick sound that George could tell came from relief. 'That's what the old fella said the day after I was born. '*Dingo*' he says to me, '*Dingo, you really are a pain in the arse. Why don't you go piss-off the Pommes instead?*' So twenty-one years later, here I am.'

They assembled in an empty hangar after breakfast. The pilots were told to space themselves in the centre of the building and the rest instructed to find a pilot and form a crew. Dingo was the first to join him, quickly followed by the other five. That was it; they were the first team to complete and he had his crew.

There were enough of them to form exactly a dozen crews and people circulated the hangar, looking for groups lacking their specialisations or willing to have them, or simply that they found appealing. One pilot backed away from the centre, avoiding attention. He seemed to want to form his crew from the six left over. Was it some form of superstition, or had the pilot reasoned that the last few would have something different about them, something no one else recognised, something special? However, George had his crew and now he could begin to make it a good one. Many thoughts swam through his head as he waited. There would be morale and confidence to build, and flying skills to hone, but first, they would fly together.

Once a dozen crews had formed, they stood in their small groups eyeing each other speculatively, each wondering whether they had made good choices. George knew that every crew would be particularly anxious about the skill of its pilot and the sort of leader he would be. His crew undoubtedly had asked themselves the same question last night and probably still did, but they joined anyway. The CO of the conversion unit clambered onto a packing case, coughed loudly and waited for silence. He was a spare man whose uniform hung so loosely it gave no indication of his physique other than the fact he was thin. Although stern looking, there seemed to be the potential for humour in the set of his eyes and mouth. George briefly wondered what it would take to make him smile and hoped that it was not awarding punishments and extra duties.

'Good morning gentlemen. Welcome to 3 Group and RAF Oakley. Firstly, congratulations on sorting yourselves into crews so quickly, at least one group has set a new record,' he said and glanced towards George. 'As you will be aware, this station is a Heavy Conversion Unit. Its job is to teach you to transition from twin-engine to four-engine aircraft. If you like, we are your finishing school. Thus far, you have learned your skills individually in Advanced Flight Training and later, alongside your peers in an Operational Training Unit. Now you will learn to operate as a heavy bomber crew. On completion of this course, you will be posted directly to one of 3 Group's Lancaster squadrons.'

'What about our Foreign Service Leave, sir?' a voice called out.

The CO was clearly expecting more enthusiasm and it showed in his expression. 'I'm afraid leave will have to wait until after the course, and for a very good reason.' The crews groaned and he glared at them. 'There's a bloody war on you know!'

After drawing flying gear and parachutes, they crowded around notice boards in the crew buildings and copied down flight information. They scribbled call signs, wireless frequencies, weather information and that day's Angel Number. This arbitrary figure was to hide their true height from the enemy. The crew added or subtracted the angel number to any height instruction broadcast over the wireless. Today it was ten thousand feet, which meant that a broadcast of angels plus ten meant a height of twenty thousand feet.

Similarly, a broadcast of angels minus five would mean five thousand feet. Nervous excitement built as they flowed around the boards. A few, like Max, talked endlessly, while others hardly spoke. Outside, buses waited to take them to the aircraft. It was time to fly.

As his transport cleared the last hangar, George saw the Lancasters waiting at dispersal. Black and powerful, huge in comparison to the twin-engine aircraft he had flown before. He felt a thrill of anticipation and involuntarily clenched his hands as if he were already holding the controls. In his mind, he went through the cockpit layout and drills learned in Canada.

When the bus reached the first aircraft, an aircraftman called a pilot's name and the crew departed. After two more stops, it was George and his group's turn. The bus trundled off leaving them alone to look closely at a Lancaster for the first time. M-Mother towered above and even her wheels came up to chest height. All George could think about was her size. She was a beast, a monster. Part of him felt apprehensive at flying such an aircraft, but that was just a small part. Mostly he wanted to so badly he ached.

'First time close to a Lanc'?' A voice behind asked and he turned to see a figure in flying gear wheel a bicycle across the concrete pan to the aircraft. Without waiting for an answer, the stranger lowered the cycle and walked to George, holding out a hand. 'Flying Officer Steve Smith.' He announced. 'I'm your instructor.'

George saluted and shook his hand. 'Sergeant George Watford. Good to meet you, sir.' Smith's battered peaked cap looked as though it had been thrust into his trouser pocket and sat on a hundred times. It was a dishevelled and faded thing, and the clearest badge of experience there was. George also noted the DFC ribbon on Smith's breast pocket and guessed that he had completed at least one thirty operation tour.

Smith smiled benevolently. 'The first thing to remember is the correct form. On operational squadrons, its normal practice to salute just once when you first meet and there's never any need to address an aircrew officer you know as 'sir'. It's strictly first names only unless you're being chewed out for something of course. So from now on, I'm Steve and you're George or Skipper. OK with that?'

'Sounds fine to me,' George replied, immediately warming to Smith.

'Good. Got your logbook?' George fished inside his pocket and passed across the record of his flying history. 'Thanks. I have a dekko at this while you start the ground checks.'

The rest of the crew stood in a huddle and watched. This was the first test of George's credentials and so he worked slowly and methodically. Smith watched too, his eyes following above the pages of the logbook. Although he had ground checked single and twin-engine aircraft a hundred times in Canada, the Lanc was a different beast altogether. George reached out and touched the riveted metal skin, feeling a thrill as his hand pressed on the surface of the aircraft. Starting at the entrance door, he went clockwise, checking tailplanes and mainplanes, fins, rudders and elevators for movement. Then a look at wheels and undercarriage, engines and propellers for leaks and damage. Lastly, cover plates and panels to make sure they were secure.

'All OK?' Smith asked and handed back the logbook.

'She's fine. One or two repair patches could do with some attention, but nothing to stop us flying.'

'So you're happy to board?'

George suddenly realised his mistake and cursed himself. 'No. Not yet.' Standing well apart from them was a knot ground tradesmen, headed by a sergeant. These people 'owned' the aircraft, George and his crew simply 'borrowed' it for the flight. The ground crew best knew the Lancaster's condition and he should have spoken to them first. He felt like an idiot, but Smith had the decency not to mention it. George waved to the sergeant and waited for him to come across.

'Sorry sergeant, I should have spoken to you first.' George extended his hand.

The sergeant glanced at Smith before taking it. 'That's OK. It's a busy day for you, we understand.'

'Any issues I should know of?' he asked, cringing inwardly. Having told Smith the aircraft was fit to board, he hoped he was right.

'Nothing to speak of, a couple of the patches need replacing, but they're not urgent.' George breathed again. 'Mother had a few knocks before she came to us and we haven't had time to spruce her up yet.'

The sergeant presented George with the Authorisation Book, which listed any current issues with the Lancaster and a form 700, which was George's agreement that the aircraft was fit to fly. George read both, signed and handed them back.

'I'll take good care of your lady,' George told him.

'See that you do, she's a plucky old bird.' With that, the sergeant nodded at Smith and went back to his men.

On their own again, Smith said. 'You'll find that the Lanc is a different beast to the kites you've flown before. She has a lot more power with four engines, but the principles are just the same. I'll fly a few circuits and bumps to show you the ropes, then maybe after lunch you can captain us.'

George hesitated before speaking. 'I've memorised the Pilot Notes. I'd like to take her up straight away.'

Smith's eyes narrowed. 'It's usual for the instructor to fly at least the first flight. I need to check you out on emergency procedures and so on.'

'Without wanting to sound over-confident, I know the drills backwards.'

Smith pushed his hat back and frowned. 'OK, I'll trust you, but just make sure you do exactly as I say if there's a problem. I suggest you take us up to fifteen thousand and head west over to Wales. Stooge about at first so that you can get a feel for her. Remember we are in an operational area. It doesn't happen often but the Luftwaffe has been known to send fighters over to catch bombers doing air tests. The guns are loaded so make sure your boys keep their eyes peeled.'

George nodded, from now on whenever he took off, someone might try to shoot them down. *The shape of things to come*, he told himself. It certainly added spice to the flight.

'OK to go?' Smith asked.

'OK to go.' George confirmed and nodded at the crew.

Max climbed in first and made his way to the rear turret, right in the tail of the aircraft. Dick went forward to the nose and the bomb aimer's position. Then Chalky, who sat beside George in the cockpit on the pull-down 'dicky' seat. Dingo went just to the rear of the cockpit in the curtained off navigation cubby. Young Ned followed to the Wireless Operator's spot, immediately behind Dingo. Back further, just under halfway along the aircraft, Jim Ambiolo climbed up into his buttock numbing canvas seat in the mid-upper turret. Finally, George, followed by Smith, clambered through the fuselage towards the cockpit. Inside, the familiar aircraft smells wafted over him. Metal combined with the scents of aviation fuel, oil and a whiff of chemicals from the

Elsan toilet. Halfway along, headspace reduced greatly as they stepped onto the top of the bomb bay. Shortly after that was the main spar, the beam connecting the two wings. Dressed in bulky flying gear and parachute, this waist-high obstruction presented a major obstacle. George struggled clumsily across it, deciding that the Lancaster was not an aircraft for the claustrophobic. However, the cockpit was the opposite. High up above the bomb bay and with plenty of glass surrounding him, the visibility was excellent and he was immediately happy with his place. For once, he felt this was an aircraft designed with the pilot in mind, and not as an afterthought. It would be a good place to work; he had the best seat in the house.

George adjusted the seat height, tightened the straps and gave himself a moment to survey the rows of dials and switches in front. He felt a jolt of nervousness at the extra complexity of a four-engine aircraft. With twin engines, the dials, gauges and levers came mostly in pairs and scanning them really meant just checking that both needles pointed in the same direction. Now he had four of everything and the extra seconds needed for checks would be time when he was not giving full attention to flying. Many things could go wrong quickly if you were not looking in the right place.

Flicking on the intercom George led the crew through the internal checks before he and Chalky prepped the cockpit. There were lists of checks to make at every stage. Before entering the aircraft, before starting the engines, before taxiing and the most important one the VAs, or Vital Actions, was just before takeoff. Although there were check-off cards, George remembered the VAs though the complicated mnemonic TMPFFGGH, standing for trim, medium-supercharger, pitch, fuel, flaps, gills, gyro and hydraulics. It could take as long as an hour to pre-flight a heavy bomber, and eager as George was to go; he was equally keen for this first flight to be incident free.

Smith stood behind the pilot's seat, watching him unobtrusively and thankfully saying nothing. Although George could sense him fidgeting and he chuckled silently. All pilots hated being passengers, especially to rookies, and especially to rookies on their first flight. 'Sure you wouldn't like me to take her up this first time?' Smith asked again.

'No thanks,' he replied. 'But please say if I do anything dangerous.'

'I will, never worry about that,' Smith said firmly. 'You'll be the first to know.'

'Start the engines, Chalky.' George said and watched carefully as the engineer indicated to the ground crew which engine he would start first. Chalky opened the fuel cocks, flicked up the engine starter covers and pressed the starboard inner button. This engine powered the aircraft's alternators and was the sensible choice to start first. The near propeller on the right wing rotated and after three spins the Merlin coughed, banged and roared into life. Tongues of flame belched from the exhausts and M-Mother trembled. George adjusted the setting to give one thousand two hundred rpm and gave the thumbs up to continue. Chalky next started the starboard outer engine, then the port inner and finally the port outer. With all four engines running, the aircraft shook and swamped the crew with noise. Either side of George, the airscrews were a grey blur of pure and brutal strength. The Merlin's power was intense; their force tangible and M-Mother shuddered like a thoroughbred at the starting gate. Ensuring his microphone was off, George laughed with happiness and pure exhilaration. He felt he was riding the storm or holding onto a tiger's tail, depending which way you looked at it.

Checks complete, the ground controller gave permission for M-Mother to leave dispersal and George signalled for the ground crew to remove the wheel chocks. He released the brakes and gave all four engines a burst of power. From stationary, the Lancaster turned by gunning the outer engine on the side opposite to the direction needed and then doing the reverse to straighten up. However, once the aircraft was moving, there was just enough airflow from the propeller wash to use the rudders, although this meant stamping on the rudder pedals to make even the smallest turn. The taxiway was to the left and so George increased power to the right outer engine. He was heavy-handed and M-Mother slewed too far, so he corrected with a burst of power to the left outer engine and the Lancaster snaked from side to side along the concrete dispersal and onto the taxiway.

Gradually the oscillations died as he became familiar with the controls. This was important to him as pilots built their reputation on small things, as well as flying skills. Although the newspapers now called him 'Bomber' Harris, the head of Bomber Command earned his RAF nickname of 'Butch' or 'Butcher' Harris by destroying several aircraft in heavy landings and not by an aggressive spirit. One Lancaster waited in front and as it departed, George nudged Mother forward to the runway marker. Chalky read out the final checks, the Vital Actions. *Propellers set for max rpm. Superchargers set medium gear. Flaps set twenty degrees down.*

'Take off positions everyone,' George said and spoke to the ground controller. 'M-Mother, ready for takeoff.'

'Wait one, M-Mother,' came the reply. George watched the glass dome in the roof of the runway controller's caravan to the right, waiting for the green flash of an Aldis lamp. He could feel his heart pumping faster, but why did his voice sound so calm? Suddenly the light flashed, bright and emerald.

'Here we go!' George called. This was it.

He smiled with anticipation at the runaway stretching away in front, readying himself for the acceleration and wondering how this massive aircraft would react. His hands moved quickly and firmly, releasing the brakes and pushing the four throttle levels gently forward until they reached the gate that marked a full takeoff power. He gave slightly more power to the port outer to counteract the swing to the left created by the rotation of the propellers and Chalky placed a hand behind his as a safety measure. The change was astounding, M-Mother leapt forward, bounding down the runway's white centreline. With her rudders in the slipstream, it was easy to keep the aircraft straight and within seconds, the Lancaster's speed was enough for George to push the stick forward and bring up her tail. M-Mother was rolling straight and level and her speed was rocketing.

'Fifty... Sixty... Seventy...' Chalky called out, each number tumbling after the other. The runway stretched out in front, while in his periphery, markers and lights zipped past. George kept his gaze outside for this first takeoff; he wanted to get a feel for the Lancaster. 'Eighty... Ninety... One hundred...'

Then the controls felt lighter, softening their contact with the runway. M-Mother strained to be free of the ground and with a gentle pull of the column the great aircraft's nose came up. They were airborne and he was a Lancaster pilot. There was so much power, far more than the Anson's, Cranes and Wellingtons back in Canada. At five hundred feet he raised the undercarriage and flaps. The speed increased rapidly to one-seventy and seconds later to two hundred miles-per-hour. George turned the yoke to the left and as the horizon tilted, he looked down the port wing at tiny uniformed figures, bicycles and trucks moving around the aerodrome roadways like so many ants around a nest. He climbed to ten thousand feet in minutes. It was wonderful, the Lancaster had so much lift and power, and the controls felt light and responsive.

'Oxygen on everyone,' George told the crew and hitched the mask across his face.

'Impressed?' Smith's voice chuckled over the intercom.

'She's superb,' George replied. He could think of no better word to describe his feelings. He felt Smith's hand pat his shoulder, sharing in his excitement.

'Of course, she won't be so responsive fully loaded with bombs and fuel, but she's good, damn good.'

George adjusted the trim so the aircraft flew straight and level. 'Pilot to crew, we're heading west at fifteen thousand feet, making two hundred miles-per-hour. Remember, enemy aircraft could be operating in the area so gunners keep your eyes peeled and let me know if you spot another aircraft. Nav, give me a course for Milford Haven and WOp, tell control that we're heading west at angels plus five.' Dick Scrivener stood up from his prone bomb aimer's position and climbed into the front turret. George felt the trim of the aircraft change as both he and Max in the rear, rotated their turrets and scanned the skies around them. All good so far.

Looping around Milford Haven, they began the return journey. This time George simulated bomb runs on Monmouth and Cirencester so that Dick Scrivener and Dingo could work together. He made Ned Anderson call up aerodromes for wireless tests, and then he jinked the aircraft while Max and Jim tried to track pieces of cloud with their guns. Later he would talk to Smith alone, but he believed he had the makings of a good crew and that in the weeks ahead they would become a tight one. George contacted Oakley's controller as they approached the aerodrome. 'Oakley, this is M-Mother approaching from the west. Request permission to rejoin, over.'

'M-Mother, you're clear to rejoin. Runway two-zero. QFE one-zero-one-one, wind twenty degrees from starboard, seven knots. Two aircraft in circuit. Call downwind, out.'

The QFE figure is the barometric pressure above sea level at the station. It had changed slightly since take-off and he set this figure on the altitude indicator. In front and below, he saw two Lancasters orbiting the airfield. He and Chalky hurried through the landing checks. 'Oakley, M-Mother downwind, over.'

'Mother, you're clear to finals. One ahead, out.' The first aircraft had landed and George could see that the second was in finals. He swung Mother onto the approach. As long as the other aircraft landed safely, they would come straight in behind.

Moments later, George called, 'Mother, finals, over.'

'Mother, you are clear to land, out.'

Chapter 9

RAF Oakley - 7th August 1942

They crossed the aerodrome boundary at one hundred and fifty feet and landed with just a small bump. Outside the crew room, Smith took George to one side and waited until the others had entered.

'So how do you think it went?' Smith asked.

George loosened his Irvin jacket and allowed the fresh air to wash over him. 'OK, for a first flight. What do you think?'

Smith glanced at the sky before replying, another Lancaster was coming into land, drowning them in noise. 'Your crew did their jobs competently and you handled the kite well, you clearly have confidence. During my last tour, we lost aircraft because pilots were nervous about chucking the crate around, but with a fighter on your tail, the only way to survive is to make yourself a difficult target.'

'And the bad things?'

'Not many of those, but some things to think about. First, your crew must cooperate more. When they're not busy, they should be trying to help each other and you need to encourage that attitude. Next, you must delegate more to the engineer; get him to do the donkey work in the cockpit. You adjusted revs yourself and that's his job. Also, check in on the crew every ten minutes or so, it's too easy for them to lose concentration and drift off, especially on long flights. The final thing is to bank the aircraft left and right from time to time, so both gunners get a clear view below. Bad things can creep up on a bomber from underneath and the first you'll know is when cannon shells shred your wings.' Smith paused and looked George in the eye. 'Overall, you did well. You flew competently and you have a good crew.'

George nodded, feeling disappointed not to have done better and it showed. Smith slapped him on the back. 'Now don't get down about it, George. You're a good pilot, but flying a heavy bomber is another matter altogether and that's what I'm going to teach you. There isn't a pilot or crew that hasn't been sharpened by a spell at HCU. More to the point, a lot would be dead if they hadn't been here.' With that, Smith turned and walked away, but stopped after a few paces and came back. 'By the way, that includes me. I thought the RAF was a flying club when I joined. It took an instructor by the name of Tom Sawyer to kick me into shape. Believe me, you are a lot better than I was at that stage.'

They moved out of the transit block and into a Nissen hut, a prefabricated structure built from half-cylinders of corrugated steel. Functional and drab, it contained seven beds, lockers and wardrobes, and a solitary pot-bellied stove. George chose a bed at the back of the room, as far away from the draughty door as possible.

'Home sweet bleeding home,' Max said, throwing himself onto a bed. 'What a dump.'

'Could be a lot worse,' Chalky told him.

'Maybe compared to up the north, old cock, but some of us are used to the finer things in life.' Max folded his arms behind his head and eyed Chalky speculatively, readying himself for some sport.

'Don't tell me the East End was better?' Chalky laughed.

'Better? My son, it was a paradise, at least compared to Newcastle.'

'A paradise? Sure you don't mean a piss-hole?' Chalky dumped his bag on the bed and began unpacking. 'From what I hear, the Luftwaffe did London a favour.'

'You cheeky bugger. The reason the German's don't bomb up north as much is that the locals would pinch their bleeding aeroplanes.' Max jumped up on the bed, did a Hitler salute with one hand and put a finger under his nose with the other. 'Mein Gott. You vill keepen mein Luftwaffe avay from der bleeding Geordies and Scousers, Goering mein old mucker. Dey vill half-inch der bloody lot.' Chalky tossed a shoe at Max and chased him up and down the room, the pair leaping over beds like steeplechasers.

'So, what did our boy Smith, have to say for himself?' Dingo asked above the noise.

George folded the letter he had been trying to read and slipped it back into the breast pocket of his battledress. He wanted to let Millie know that he had arrived back in England, but he felt too weary. The Merlin's throaty roar still thundered in ears and his arms ached from the constant pressure of the column.

'We did well, but he reckons there's room for improvement.'

Chalky made a grab for Max, stumbled and fell across Dingo's bed. 'Jeez, will you two drongos pack it in. It's like a bloody chimp's tea party in here!' Max pulled Chalky up and they wandered away.

'Don't worry about it, skipper.' Dingo lay back on his bed and lit a cigarette. 'Bound to be a few rough edges to sharpen.' He nodded towards Chalky and Max, who were now settling down to play cards with Dick and Jim, while young Ned watched. 'Especially considering what you've got to work with.'

'Well, you chose them.' George said and fished out Millie's letter again.

'Yeah,' Dingo replied blowing smoke rings towards the curved ceiling. 'An' that just goes to show you can't trust anyone in this game.'

Smith prepared a route for them the following morning. Northwest over Birmingham and Liverpool to the Isle of Man, then down the Irish Sea, passing Holyhead, Cardigan and Portmeirion. Finally, east to Worcester and then home. A total distance of six hundred miles. This time George banked the aircraft sixty degrees left and right every five minutes and checked in with each crew position at the same time. At the end of the flight, Smith was a happy instructor and George began to understand the physical as well as mental demands of combat flying. It was no longer enough to be a competent pilot, combat flying was far more proactive. From now on, he was the leader of a fighting team and that was a completely new job, and an extra one.

There was no respite that evening. After a few hours of rest, they took off again for their first night flight together. Fortunately, Smith had them follow the morning's route, so planning was minimal. George flew many times at night in Canada, but his inexperience in Lancasters made this a completely new challenge. The sun had set by the time they were ready to take off and a quarter-moon shone weakly. Silver blobs of altocumulus that he could cover with his thumb gusted at fifteen thousand feet. It would be windy up there. He kept M-Mother on the runway until she reached over one hundred miles-per-hour and pulled back on the column. She leapt up into the dark and climbed steadily until they were at twenty thousand feet and approaching Liverpool. In the moonlight, the propellers were silvery blurs either side of the cockpit and dim blue flames streamed from the exhausts. Dick Scrivener sat in the nose with a map spread across his knees, telling Dingo each time he spotted features in the dark landscape below.

'Bomb Aimer to Nav. Large 'U' shaped river coming up directly ahead.'

'Roger. That'll be the Mersey. Let me know when we cross the shoreline beyond.'

'Searchlights coming on in front, skipper,' Dick then told George.

George looked over M-Mother's nose and saw half a dozen beams slicing into the air. 'Roger. Pilot to WOp. Better throw out some flares. We don't want the pongoes in Liverpool shooting at us. Do you know today's colours?'

'Yep, it's red-yellow-red, skipper,' Ned replied.

'Roger. Well done Ned, I'd completely forgotten,' he lied.

As they turned south at the Isle of Man and set course down the Irish Sea, Chalky gave Smith his seat next to George. 'What's combat flying like?' George asked him.

There was a pause before Smith replied. 'I've heard it described as ninety percent boredom and ten percent terror. I'd say that's pretty accurate.'

'I don't mind boredom.'

'No, you can live with boredom, but the terror can kill.'

'Any tips?'

Smith thought for a few seconds before replying. 'The main thing to remember is that night-fighters are the biggest threat. Flak's bloody scary and it takes aircraft on every trip, but the real damage is done by fighters. Everything depends on you seeing them before they get into a firing position. Once you've spotted a fighter, you've got a good chance of getting away. It's damn difficult following a kite when it's jinking about in the dark, even a big one like a Lancaster. I've been on raids and never seen another aircraft.'

'Tell me about evasion techniques.' This was what he was most keen to learn.

Smith stretched his legs out and made himself more comfortable. 'Well, assuming you don't want to shoot it out with a night-fighter, which you don't because their cannons have twice the range of your popguns, then officially you have a couple of choices. You can either slow down quickly, causing the fighter to overshoot, or you can dive and corkscrew away from him.'

'Which one is best?' George knew the crew was listening and that was good. They all needed this information.

'Well, personally I've never met anyone who could slow a bomber faster than a fighter, although I suspect that France and Germany are littered with those who tried. The moment you spot a fighter, dive and then climb back up steeply, turning one way then the other. You fly the same shape as a corkscrew, hence the name.'

George pictured the movements and controls needed. 'OK, that makes sense. What are our chances against a night-fighter, I guess you've had experience of this?'

Smith gave a wry chuckle. 'I flew old Whitworth Whitley's at first and then Wellingtons, but I've never flown a Lancaster operationally. I'll be honest with you, when I did my tour the opposition wasn't as good as it is now and my crew always spotted their fighters, although plenty of others weren't so lucky. If there's a novice on your tail and you see him first, you should get away. If your boy is experienced, then you have problems. Worse still, they sometimes hunt in pairs, so while one has a go at you, the other keeps watch. Then it gets dicey.' He was silent for seconds as if the next part was difficult to tell. 'The best friend you have is the cloud; always try to hide in it if you have the chance. If there's no cloud, try to shake them off, frustrate them until they either run low on fuel or look for easier pickings. But that may take some time.'

Smith's reply was not as confident as George had hoped and he asked the obvious question. 'I guess if you don't see the fighter, you've very little chance?'

'The Lanc's a good crate, but you're a big target filled with fuel and high explosives. Even the airframe is a magnesium alloy, which will burn. Just hope you spot the fighter first. Whatever happens, always move never sit still. Even the best pilots can freeze when tracer comes at them and that really is fatal.'

Suddenly the Lancaster did not seem so powerful or so invulnerable. He remembered seeing caribou herds in Canada chased down by wolves as they ran. That image seemed to fit German fighters among a mass of bombers. However, maybe they could improve the odds. George breathed deeply. 'At what angle do you dive?'

Smith turned towards him. An oxygen mask and goggles covered most of his face, leaving only his eyes visible. He said, 'I'm convinced that more pilots could escape if they had the confidence to dive steeply. The makers say the wings will come off at four hundred miles-per-hour, but I've never heard of that happening. So if the choice is between sure death from a fighter and possible death from a steep dive, take your pick.' Even in the moonlight's dim glow and the gloom of the cockpit dials, he could tell Smith was smiling, a challenging smile.

'I guess we should practice,' George said. Smith was telling him that his chances of surviving a German night-fighter were slim unless he could chuck a heavy bomber about the sky and for an extended period. Well, there was only one way to practice.

'No time like the present,' Smith agreed. 'Another thing to remember, the steeper the dive, the harder it is to pull out. The Lanc has big control surfaces and air rushing over them at high speed makes them hard to move. But you must always claw back height after each dive, otherwise, the fighter will eventually drive you into the ground.'

'OK, let's do it.' George spoke to the others. He did not feel at all happy about throwing thirty-two tons of aircraft around the sky and he suspected he never would, but as with growing old, the alternative was far worse. 'You all heard Steve; evasion is something we need to practice. Get ready for evasive manoeuvres, I don't want any injuries.'

Smith leaned forward and checked the dials. 'We're at twenty thousand feet, bring the airspeed back to around two hundred miles-per-hour, that'll be your best speed when fully loaded.' He waited as George eased off the throttles. 'Right, when I say, I want you to throttle right back and drop down a thousand feet. Then bank to the right, climb five hundred feet and bank to the left until you're back at twenty thousand. Got it?'

'Got it,' George gripped the yoke more firmly with his left hand, ready to move his right hand to the throttles.

'Go!'

Immediately, George pushed the column forward and pulled back the throttles. As he watched the height unwind, he felt the familiar weightlessness lifting him up from his seat. He had dived many times in daylight and always found it exhilarating, but darkness was so different. There was nothing visible outside the cockpit and without visual references; the dive angle seemed much steeper. George concentrated on the instruments. Airspeed increased to over two hundred and fifty miles-per-hour and at nineteen thousand feet, he pulled back on the column and climbed to the right. The controls were heavy, slow to respond and the Lancaster dropped another five hundred feet before her nose came up. Once they were climbing right, he waited until the altimeter read nineteen and a half thousand feet and then banked left.

'OK. I think you found out a few things there, didn't you,' Smith said once they were level.

George was breathing hard, gulping down oxygen. 'Yes. I need to start pulling out of the dive earlier.'

'Right. Now this time when you bottom, put on twenty-five degrees of flap and trim up, that'll help. Also, don't power climb out of the dive. Take it slowly but steeply. Around one hundred and forty miles-per-hour at sixty degrees nose up is best. Fighters are not happy at low speeds, you want them to overshoot and lose you. Right, let's try that again.'

George winced, so many things to remember. 'Anything else?' he asked.

'Yes. I want you to dive steeper, much steeper. Ready...'

They landed back at Oakley early the following morning. Smith congratulated them on a good flight, climbed onto his bicycle and peddled off. As they watched him fade into the gloom, the seven stood in the darkness and waited for the crew bus. The only sound was the popping and hissing of the four cooling Merlin engines. No one spoke for a while, partly through weariness, but also, George suspected, because of gnawing uncertainty. Like him, the others believed that the risks would reduce if they trained hard and flew well. But now? Now, he was not so sure. It seemed to him that you might escape if you spotted a German night-fighter before it attacked. However, that was a big 'if'. Fighters are small, especially when viewed head-on in the dark. In seconds, a speck of dirt on the glass could grow wings and turn into an aircraft spitting cannon fire. Then there was the physical strength required. They practised evasion for just thirty minutes and George was exhausted. However, a raid deep into Germany could last over eight hours. At some point, he might not be able to force his arms and legs to haul the huge aircraft through those violent manoeuvres.

George knew that he should say something. He had hoped Smith would offer a few words of encouragement, just as a parent comforted a fretful child. However, the stark reality was that the bogeyman was out there in the dark and nothing could keep him away. A cold wind gusted across the aerodrome, bringing with it a fine drizzle. They huddled further under the wing and cursed the bus driver, who was probably asleep by a fire, warm and safe.

'Well, that was fun,' Max said, breaking the silence. 'Give us a ciggie Dingo. I'm knackered.'

Dingo reached deep into his battle dress and offered the packet around. Only George and young Ned declined.

'Let me get this straight,' Dingo began, once the five cigarettes were alight. 'We have to fly thirty operations to complete a tour?'

'If you don't think that's enough, you can always sign on for more,' George replied, trying to make a joke.

'Personally, and speaking just for myself, I was thinking that thirty might be more than enough. I mean you can have too much of a good thing.' Dingo blew a plume of smoke that the wind immediately snatched away.

'Does anyone get through thirty ops, d'you think?' Chalky asked quietly.

George shrugged, 'Smith did, so it must be possible.'

'Yeah, but that was early on before the Krauts had sorted themselves out,' Max chipped in. 'It was so bloody dark tonight; I couldn't see a thing, not a sausage. There could have been a whole squadron of Zeppelins queuing up to piss on us and I wouldn't have spotted them.'

George felt a stab of irritation. 'Look, no one promised this was going to be a piece of cake. Its war and bad things happen. But back in Canada I once had to follow another aircraft through clouds and I still don't know how I did it, and he was doing all he could to keep me on his tail. That's how difficult it is for the Luftwaffe at night. When there's better visibility for them, there will be for us too. Remember that.'

'But don't they have radar?' Ned Anderson asked softly. In his bulky flying gear, he looked like a child playing at dressing up in adult clothes.

'Their ground radar will only get them close; it can't put them on our tail. You and every other WOp will be jamming their frequencies and so if the fighters can't hear their controllers the radar's no use to them.' In the distance, he could see a faint movement on the perimeter track and hoped it was the crew bus. He turned to the others. 'The odds aren't going to get any better by whinging. We've as much chance as anyone else, better if we're a tight crew. Our best option is still to be as good as we can and train as hard as we can. I intend to get through our tour in one piece. OK?'

The six glanced at each other and nodded. 'Right skipper,' Max said, 'But if you get us killed, I'll kick your arse all the way to hell and back.'

'No chance,' George retorted. 'I've already got my wings; I'm going to the other place.' The crew bus pulled up alongside and they clambered on.

Chapter 10

RAF Oakley - 9th September 1942

Over the following weeks, they practised bombing, navigation, night flying and daylight evasion against Spitfires and Beaufighters. On the ground, they learned instrument flying in the link-trainer, a flying simulator, and attended lectures on operational flying. All the while, the crew came together as a team. Then a storm front moved in bringing a mass of dense cloud and with it the danger of collision. The CO cancelled flying and laid on buses to Oxford. George and his crew hurriedly changed into their best blues and, braving the rain, scrabbled onto the last bus. It was half-full and a dim blue interior light turned every face a deathly pale. George fell into a seat next to Dingo and the others sat near them, their breath steaming in the dank atmosphere. Ten minutes later the bus stopped again and a group of rain-soaked WAAFs struggled onboard. One sat next to the handsome Jim Ambiolo, who had taken a seat to himself and they immediately began talking and laughing.

Max looked back over his shoulder at George and Dingo. 'How does he do it?' he asked in amazement. 'I swear he's never met her before. It's like bees round a bleeding honey pot.'

'I guess he's got that certain something girls adore,' Dingo replied wistfully.

'No, he hasn't,' Max retorted. 'I looked when we were in the showers the other day. It's tiny like yours, Dingo.'

Dingo gave Max a playful whack on the head. 'Mate, I go for quality, not quantity. You Londoners think the height of sexual sophistication is to warm your hands and shout 'brace yourself'.'

Max looked thoughtful. 'You could be right, Dingo. I must try sophistication. You find that goes down well with the sheep back home, do you?'

The bus meandered through Headington and dropped them at the high street in Oxford, where the passengers headed off in different directions towards their favourite watering holes. Pulling up their greatcoat collars and clamping their caps firmly against the steady drizzle, George and his crew walked briskly to the King's Arms on the corner of Holywell Street, their footsteps echoing along the old narrow roads. Jim's WAAF joined them, along with three of her friends and Max was already trying his luck with one of them, his chirpy voice loud and constant. George watched him enviously; the Londoner was never shy or lost for words in the way that he so often felt.

The King's Arms had large rooms with low oak beamed ceilings and a guarantee of blazing fires in cold weather. It was a favourite with aircrews from Oakley and even the instructors used it, although George had yet to see Steve Smith there. After the rain, the inside was warm and welcoming, smelling of wood smoke, hops and tobacco. They hung their sodden greatcoats and caps on a rack near the fireplace and looked for somewhere to sit. It was busy but Dick spotted an empty table large enough for them all.

'Kitty time,' Max called above the pub's noise and they piled what coins they had onto the table. The WAAFs insisted on contributing, although they only drank halves, and Max deftly scooped up the coins and counted them into piles, one for each round. At five pennies a pint, there looked enough to last the evening and maybe provide a tuppeny bag of chips each before catching the bus back. As George waited for his beer, he eyed the rest of the clientele. Five other crews caught earlier buses and three had managed to secure the company of WAAFs. The crews sat apart, acknowledging but not mingling with each other. By now, each had firmly cemented their flying fellowships and individual crewmembers never socialised outside their group. To do so would be bad form, if not downright insulting. Crews were a tight, if at times claustrophobic, family.

Because Chalky was married and Ned too shy, neither competed for the WAAFs. This suited George and so he sat between them. Out of loyalty to Millie, he had stayed well away from girls in Canada, but a year was a long time and he could not imagine someone as intelligent and attractive as her being without admirers. The thought of her with someone else chilled him.

'Here you go, ladies,' Dingo said as he placed a tray of half-pints on the table. 'Knock the froth of these while I get the next lot.'

'I love his accent,' Brenda, one of the WAAFs sighed. 'It's sort of American but with a hint of cockney.' She looked dreamily toward the bar, where Dingo was placing pint glasses on the tray. 'When he speaks you can hear sunshine and warm seas.'

Max spluttered. 'Cor, you got a good imagination, girl,' he said. 'All I hear is a load of old kangaroo crap.'

'I bet the girls like him, a good-looking boy like that?' Dotty, another WAAF added, clearly fishing for information.

Max leant forward conspiratorially. 'I shouldn't be saying this, but that's the reason he's over here isn't it.'

'Really?' Brenda asked. 'Just because the girls like him? She was buxom and wore a little too much makeup for George's taste, but he could see that Max was keen. He had not heard this story before and wondered what Max knew.

'He only got caught in a barn having relations with a girl, and by her mother. That's all,' Max said, shaking his head reproachfully. 'He had to leave the country after that.'

'Goodness me,' Brenda glanced towards Dingo before turning back to Max. 'What did her mother say to him?' she asked quietly and George felt sure he knew the answer.

They watched Max expectantly. 'Her exact words were 'Baaa, Baaa'.'

Brenda looked confused for a moment and then burst out laughing. 'Oh, you are a one, Max. I fell for that didn't I?' She sipped her beer as Dingo put a tray of pint mugs on the table. 'I do like a boy that can make me laugh,' she added and gave Max a smile.

'Here we are, mates,' Dingo said and then noticed everyone was grinning at him. 'What is it?'

'Max has been telling us about you,' Dotty told him.

'Yeah, an' I bet it involved sheep too.' Dingo flashed a threatening look in Max's direction.

'I was just telling them about your winning ways.' Max replied innocently. 'Honest, on my mother's life.'

Dingo considered this for a second. 'Well, if you're swearing on your mother then I'll believe you. I couldn't say the same about your old man though.'

'What's wrong with his dad, Dingo?' Dotty asked, glancing suspiciously at Max.

Dingo took a pull of beer and licked his lips. 'Ripper,' he said and looked at the WAAFs with a serious expression. 'Because no one knows who his dad is, do they. Max's birth certificate just gives his father as the officers and crew of *HMS Ark Royal*.'

'Dingo, that's not very nice,' one of the WAAFs chided.

'God's truth, Vicky. It was lucky the fleet was only in port for one night or it might have been the *Vanguard* and *Repulse* as well.'

Even Max chuckled, but Brenda did not laugh. She put her arm around Max's neck and gave him a peck on the cheek, leaving a smear of red lipstick. 'Poor Max, it's not funny when you don't know who your father is. My old fella ran off when I was born, I didn't know my dad either.'

Max looked about to protest, but changed his mind and snuggled closer to Brenda. He shrugged tragically. 'You're absolutely right, Brenda. That sort of thing scars you for life. Some people will never understand, though.' Behind Brenda's back, he waved two fingers at Dingo.

George grinned and turned to Ned. 'So how are you settling in?' The youngster had hardly touched his beer and George sensed his awkwardness in female company. It could so easily have been him a couple of years before.

'Yeah, fine thanks, skipper.' Ned's Canadian drawl became stronger as he spoke louder against the room's noise. 'The grubs pretty bad, but flying is good and the boys are swell.'

'You're right about the food,' George agreed. 'If I eat many more baked beans I'll explode.'

'Especially at twenty thousand feet,' Chalky added. 'The change in pressure plays havoc with my bowels.'

'You're lucky being further back, Ned,' George said. 'There's a permanent fug in the cockpit once we get above ten thousand feet.'

'It's Dingo,' Ned explained happily. 'He lifts his backside every two minutes. Never stops working though, just rolls up and down like a sailor in a gale.'

'Whereabouts in Canada are you from?' Chalky asked. 'I did my training near Halifax.'

'I'm a 'Caper', I come from Louisbourg on Cape Breton Island. It's only about three hundred miles from Halifax, so you probably flew over it.' Ned's face lit up with the mention of his home and he took a sip of beer. George did not know the east coast of Canada as well; most of his flying was in the west.

'I was on the other side of the country, near Calgary, just west of the Rockies.' George said and then looked at the young Canadian. 'Although I did OTU in New Brunswick. You must miss your home.'

'Yeah, I guess I miss it more than I ever thought I would,' he said and his face clouded over. 'Especially the grub.'

'Why did you join up?' George asked him. He was searching for clues about Ned's real age without having to ask him. A direct question might force him to lie, which George did not want him to do.

The youngster creased his brow. His thin face somehow looking older, as if this was a difficult subject. 'A number of things, I guess.' He shrugged and looked away. 'You get two job choices in Cape Breton, either the steel mills or the coal mines and I didn't fancy either. I wanted to learn about wirelesses and televisions, maybe set up my own store someday. Training flights started over my town when the war began and I used to look up and see the aeroplanes. I wanted to be part of it. So I figured that by joining the air force I could get some adventure and learn a skill.'

'And get yourself killed in the process,' Chalky interrupted harshly. One of the crews gathered around the piano and started singing.

I never fly in aircraft 'cos I haven't got the guts,
I sit upon my arse all day and write out lots of bumph,
The Aircrew call me 'Penguin', 'cos I haven't any wings,

I'm one of the Chairborne Airmen, shiny pants and shiny rings.

Ned had clearly thought about Chalky's comment. 'How do you think we'll do, skipper?' he asked, turning back to George.

George took a pull of his beer before answering. 'We're a tight crew,' he replied. 'I think we'll do fine. It won't be a piece of cake but I think we can get the job done and live to bore our kids with war stories.' The only thing that troubled him slightly was that during most flights he had the reassuring presence of Smith next to him. His calm words and dry humour gave constant reassurance. He would miss that.

This answer was not enough for Ned and he continued. 'But what do you think actual flying operations it will be like?'

'That's the question we all ask, Ned,' he began, wondering how to combine honesty with reassurance. 'I think of a bomber stream as being like a herd of caribou and the fighters like wolves. The wolves kill some caribou, but mainly the weak or those that do something stupid. So what I think is that if we're quick and strong and clever, the wolves will look for softer targets.' He knew it was not that simple, but there was some truth in it. Some crews survived multiple tours, while others never came back from their first op. That could not just be luck; there must be something else as well. Ned sipped his beer thoughtfully as across the room other crews joined the chorus.

When the flak went bang, my knees would clang,
My ring would blaze away,
My head would whirl, my tail would curl,
and I'd run the other way

136

He glanced at the rest of his people. Jim Ambiolo was deeply ensconced with his WAAF, talking quietly and doubtless arranging a more private assignation. She was certainly the best looking of the four and George tried unsuccessfully to remember her name. Max was all over another, while she seemed to be half fighting him off and half encouraging him. Dingo chatted happily to his WAAF, gesturing with his hands while both of them laughed over something he was saying. Finally, the studious Dick Scrivener sat transfixed by the final girl, captivated by her every word. They each had a companion and George was pleased, if not a little envious. The thought again gnawed at him that Millie might have met someone else during the past year. Her last letter was warm enough and arrived soon after he wrote telling her he was back but did the irregularity of her other letters mean that writing was an afterthought, a duty rather than a pleasure? The only way to tell was by seeing her again.

'What happens next, skipper?' Chalky asked, bringing him back to the present.

That was a good question. 'Well, once they're satisfied that we're capable of flying the Lanc, which could be any time now, we'll be posted to an operational squadron. No idea which one though, it could be any in 3 Group.' Although he did not say so, this bothered him. There were rumours that some squadrons suffered higher casualty rates than others because their COs demanded reckless aggression. The watchword of those keen types was *'press on regardless'* or POR. If an engine stopped or a system failed, never mind, POR to the target. Turn back and the squadron boss would accuse you of lack of moral fibre, or LMF. In other words, cowardice.

'When we get there, the usual form is that I fly one mission with another crew as 'second-dicky' to get some experience,' George continued, remembering Smith's explanation. 'Our first raid as a team should be against a soft target, mine laying or a quick hop into France. After that we're fully operational and part of the squadron.'

George studied the other crews. Young people without cares for a few hours and taking pleasure in life, the same as people their age did everywhere. Simon Moffet's crew sang by the piano, while he conducted them as if they were a choir. Sam Jones' navigator and a WAAF were racing an obstacle course of chairs and tables with glasses of beer balanced on their heads, while Sam and his crew cheered. The WAAF suddenly lost her glass and deliberately pushed the navigator, spilling his beer over his hair and face. Another crew played cards and others were happy just talking amongst themselves. Lastly, there was his crew and he knew them so well by now. They were all good people, the best as far as he was concerned. As he scanned the room looking at everyone, he suddenly wondered how many would see the war's end and that thought made him shiver.

George dozed comfortably in the darkness of the bus as they drove back to Oakley. Outside rain lashed the blackened streets, giving the road a silvery sheen and he pulled his greatcoat tighter in anticipation of the deluge once they arrived. At the dimly lit gatepost, he noticed the guards had doubled. Even stranger, someone had wrapped chains around the telephone boxes to prevent their use. The bus clattered to a halt and crews shuffled reluctantly into the rain. Even in the dimness, George could see figures running or cycling. There was movement right across the aerodrome; the place was a frenzy of activity.

'Do you reckon this is normal partway through a course?' Chalky asked.

'I don't know,' George replied quietly. 'I never saw anything like it in Canada.'

A dripping wet 'erk' in an oilskin cape, hurried across to the bus. 'CO's orders. Aircrew briefing at zero eight hundred tomorrow,' he called.

'What's up then, chum?' Max asked him.

'No idea Sarg. The CO will tell you I'm sure,' he replied evasively and scurried off to the next bus.

Max turned to the others. 'I don't like the sound of this,' he said suspiciously.

'Maybe the Germans have surrendered?' Ned Anderson asked hopefully.

Max put his arm around Ned's shoulder. 'Yes, and maybe the CO's booked Father Christmas and the Tooth Fairy to do a floor show for us in celebration.'

'Leave the boy alone Max, he doesn't know where you've been,' Dingo warned.

'I could tell him,' Max replied. 'You'd like to know about Uncle Max's battle honours, wouldn't you, little Ned?'

'Come on,' George said leading them away. 'We'll know soon enough.' The following morning they found out why there had been no disembarkation leave.

Chapter 11

RAF Oakley - 10th September 1942

They pushed their way into the crew briefing room and found seats along a table together. Every crew was apprehensive and it showed. The nervousness was contagious and George fidgeted uncomfortably as he waited, listening to snatches of conversation while rumours were swopped across seats.

'I've heard the whole course is below standard and to be scrubbed,' Taff Morgan said.

'Can't see that happening,' Phil Bennet, another pilot replied. 'No, my gunner was told by an 'erk' in admin that we're definitely being posted to the Middle East.'

The air was thick with tobacco smoke and tension. It was like a living thing that fed off rumour and uncertainty, growing stronger with each conversation. George tried hard to appear relaxed and unconcerned but found himself tapping his feet anxiously. The CO arrived ten minutes late, followed by a clutch of staff officers and all the instructors. The crews sprang to attention as he climbed onto the low stage and turned to face the front. The instructors found places at the back, while staff officers took front row seats, each clutching several sheets of paper. It was reminiscent of the day in Perth when *HMS Hood* was lost and George wondered if there was more bad news.

'Please sit gentlemen,' the CO told them. George suddenly noticed the curtains drawn across the blackboards at the rear of the stage, which was unusual.

He nudged Dingo and whispered, 'what do you thinks' behind the curtains?'

Dingo stared for a moment. 'Dunno mate. Nothing good that's for sure.'

The CO stood straight-backed and formal, looking down at them with an expression that dared them to speak. Always a little aloof, especially in the way he dealt with aircrew sergeants, there was previously the promise of humour in his eyes. Now he seemed different as if he had news that he thought best to give briskly.

'When you first arrived here,' the CO began. 'I told you the reason your leave was delayed would become apparent. I will now explain. This year Bomber Command launched a number of large operations against Germany, including the Thousand Bomber Raids. What is less well known is that training squadrons like ours contributed to those missions. Tonight Bomber Command will strike another blow at the Nazi war machine and you will be part of it. Tonight you will join a force of five hundred aircraft taking the fight to the enemy.' He paused and scanned their faces significantly.

The room went silent and George felt a thrill that almost made him shiver. It was not joy exactly but exhilaration, the certainty of combat at last. He glanced sideways at his crew and wondered what they were feeling. Yesterday, operations seemed far into the future, like the distant destination of a train journey. Now the train had arrived unexpectedly and it was time to fight. The spell was broken and everyone spoke until the CO raised his hand for silence.

'You will wonder why training crews have been selected for an operation and the answer is quite simple. The Lancaster and Halifax are our most potent weapons, but they equip only a dozen or so squadrons so far. Stirlings, Wellingtons, Hampdens, and Whitleys have done great service but it has not yet been possible to convert all their crews. You are needed because the Lancaster is needed.'

The CO rocked slightly on the balls of his feet and his tone changed. 'You will also wonder if you are ready for operations. Well, I'm afraid you would ask that no matter how long you've trained. However, your instructors believe you are ready and so take confidence in their opinion. I will also give you some facts that I'm sure will be of interest.' He lifted a sheet of paper. 'The Thousand Bomber raid on Cologne in June comprised of three waves, as will tonight's operation. The losses suffered by succeeding waves were four point eight, four point one and one point nine percent. The last wave was least damaged because as the raid went on German defences became progressively overwhelmed by bombing and smoke.' He paused and looked at them significantly. 'You, gentlemen, will be flying in the third wave. Further, the losses suffered by training crews overall was three point three percent lower than the regular bomber groups. Finally, and no one knows why this is the case, aircraft flown by pupil pilots suffered lower casualties than those flown by instructor pilots.' This drew laughter and whistles from the room. The CO again looked at their faces as if trying to convince each one. Then, like a magician performing a trick, he waved a hand at the curtain to the rear of the stage. It opened to reveal a large map of Europe, with red tapes stretching from various points in England to form a single line over the North Sea. The tapes then went east through Holland and into Germany, ending at Dusseldorf. He picked up a snooker cue to use as a pointer.

'Gentlemen, your target for tonight is Dusseldorf. Takeoff will be at last light, nineteen hundred hours and the bomber stream will assemble at twenty hundred over Southwold.' He tapped the map with the snooker cue. 'The stream will turn southeast and head towards Cologne, Bonn and Frankfurt, which should draw their fighters south.' He tapped the map again. 'At this point, around twenty miles from the Dutch coast, the stream will swing due east towards the Ruhr. You will follow a course between the cities of Rotterdam to the north and Tilburg to the south. Flak batteries are thick as fleas in both cities, so keep between them and do not stray. You are well within GEE transmission range, so there is no excuse for poor navigation.' He waved the cue at the aircrew. 'Are you listening, pilots?'

'Loud and clear, sir,' they shouted back.

'Is that you MacDonnell?'

'Sir!'

'Well, if you tell that navigator of yours there's a brewery in the target area, he might try harder to find it.' That caused some welcome laughter.

'Now, when they detect us over Holland, they will think we are paying the Ruhr a visit. This should again send their fighters to the wrong place. However, once we reach Hertogenbosch, the stream will swing southeast, away from the Ruhr and directly towards Dusseldorf.' He looked at the young faces staring at him and his voice softened. 'Tonight you will join the ranks of those playing their part in the defence of this country. I will remind you of the words spoken by Air Marshal Harris.' He lowered the paper, it was unnecessary. 'The Nazis entered this war under the rather childish delusion that they were going to bomb everyone else, and nobody was going to bomb them. At Rotterdam, London, Warsaw and half a hundred other places, they put their rather naive theory into operation. They sowed the wind, and now they are going to reap the whirlwind.' His voice rose into almost a shout as he finished. 'The Luftwaffe killed over forty thousand British civilians during the Blitz, and so you gentlemen are the whirlwind. You will avenge our dead. Do your duty, remember your training and stay safe. I wish you all good luck and good hunting.'

Cheering and applause thundered around the room. George had to admit that this was just the performance they needed, even young Ned looked fired up. Half the crews seemed ready to grab a bomb and fly to Dusseldorf without an aircraft.

The intelligence officer took the CO's place on the stage and waited for silence. He was a bespectacled man, tall and painfully thin. It was rumoured that he had been a university lecturer before the war and George could well believe it from his appearance. He scanned his notes and looked myopically at his audience.

'Tonight's target is the industrial area of Dusseldorf. There are two chemical works and major factories manufacturing items such as steel tubes, machine tools and magnetic mines. Smaller factories produce enamel, boilers, wire, insulating materials, railway wagons and paper. Success tonight will be a substantial blow to the German war effort.' He picked up the snooker cue and walked to the map.

Dingo leaned towards George. 'The Krauts may turn nasty if we blow up their dunny-paper factory.'

George chuckled. 'Better make sure we carry some spare in case we're shot down.'

Then the IO banged the board with the cue, stilling the whispered conversations and making him seem even more like a schoolteacher. 'German defences around Dusseldorf are heavy, with searchlight and flak gun concentrations, here, here and here.' He tapped red shaded areas to the west of the city. 'Similarly, all cities on the route will be heavily defended.' He pointed to the red tape showing the bombers' course. 'Pathfinders will lead the force and mark the target with green indicators. You will bomb on green unless the master bomber says otherwise. Hopefully the target will be obvious by the time you arrive with the third wave, but nonetheless, listen out for the master bomber as he may ask for a change in target and a change in marker colour.'

He put down his pointer and turned to the crews. 'German air defence is based on their Kammhuber line, a series of radar zones running all the way from Denmark to the middle of France. The zones are layered three deep and each covers an area of about twenty square miles. Every zone has a Würzburg radar to detect aircraft and to control a master searchlight. It also has two dedicated night-fighters also directed by the Würzburg. To minimise the number of fighter intercepts we will swamp their defences. That means all five hundred aircraft passing through each Kammhuber zone in thirty minutes, so timing and good navigation are essential. The bomber stream must be no more than nine miles wide and aircraft height separation will be from seventeen thousand to twenty thousand feet throughout each wave. Timings, course, headings and speeds will be given at a navigator only session immediately after this briefing.'

The German words made him think of Millie and he suddenly wanted to speak to her, to ask about their meanings. Maybe understanding the names would make them less intimidating. Instead, he turned to Dingo.

'No pressure on you then, Dingo,' he whispered.

'Bloody ripper all right, mate,' Dingo replied, as he made hurried notes. 'Just make sure you don't fly us into some other joker. We'll be like canned sardines in that stream.'

The IO handed the stage to the meteorological officer, who lifted a blackboard onto an easel and stood beside it. Chalked on the board was an illustration of weather conditions at different heights along the route and he talked them through the journey. Dingo scribbled furiously but George only wanted to know if he would need to fly on instruments, which was taxing and whether there would be a moon over the continent, which would be dangerous. Thankfully the answer to both was 'no'. Next, the armament officer gave their bomb load as a standard stack of a 'cookie and cans'. This was a single four thousand pound bomb and twelve bomb containers each with two hundred and thirty-six, four-pound incendiaries. After this, the Air Control officer told them about taxiing and landing procedures and that was that, they were ready to go.

Leaving Dingo and the other navigators with the chief navigator, everyone else wandered outside and huddled in groups, talking excitedly and smoking. Even to George, they looked young, more like a group of schoolboys waiting for a football match. He wondered how they managed to appear so calm. After the initial buzz, he was now a bag of nerves.

'Quite a surprise isn't it?' a voice said next to him and he turned to see Smith, his instructor, grinning.

'Have you known for long?'

'Not for sure, not until they locked the gates. That's standard procedure before each raid. This mission's been on the cards for weeks, but word only came down from Group two days ago.' He glanced at the other crews before turning back to George. 'So how do you feel?'

George shuffled uncomfortably. 'I'd be lying if I said I wasn't nervous.'

'Nervous?' Smith fixed him with the same blue eyes that had watched him so often in the cockpit. 'George, you should be scared stiff. Nervous is how you feel before an interview with the CO. Going into the valley of the shadow requires something a bit stronger. I'd say absolutely petrified gets you closer.'

'Is that how you feel?' he asked, surprised. Smith had a DFC, a thirty-operation tour behind him and he knew all there was to know about combat flying. If anyone should be confident, it was him.

'I'd say more on the scared-stiff side of petrified.'

Could he just be saying that to be kind? Then again, only a lunatic would be indifferent to the possibility of death. 'So why are you going? I mean, you've completed a tour, you don't have to go back yet.'

'Ah, now there's a clever question,' Smith said and pushed his disgracefully battered cap back and scratched the top of his head thoughtfully. 'It's a contradiction, isn't it? I suppose I found that only being near to death makes you appreciate life.' He smiled sheepishly. 'When I was flying ops I longed for nothing more than safety. I planned to do so many things once my thirty was over. Then you survive, the fear fades and you lose that zest for life. Everything becomes paler and less vital. So you long to go back on operations and recapture the feeling.' He looked at George questioningly. 'Insane, isn't it?'

George shrugged. 'I'd say more on the barking-mad side of insane.'

Smith laughed and slapped him on the back. 'Well then, just beware, because that's the curse of combat. Now are you ready for war, as the Roman legionaries used to shout?'

'As ready as I could be, thanks to you. Any last minute advice?'

Smith became serious. 'You've got a good kite, a good crew and you're a damn good pilot. Just remember that fear is normal, it keeps you on your toes. Doubt is the killer. Never, doubt yourself or your judgement. If you're in danger, always do something, because even if it's the wrong thing, you'll probably be no worse off. Action is always better than just plain sitting there.'

'I'll remember.' George offered his hand. 'Thanks for everything.'

Smith shook it and said, 'Thank me tomorrow night with a beer or two.' George watched him saunter off with the knot of instructors who would be his crew. They looked solid, confident and capable, and for a moment, he wished he were flying with them.

'What do we do now, skipper?' Dick Scrivener asked.

George turned and saw his crew watching him closely, anxiously. It felt good that they turned to him for leadership, that they needed him to tell them what to do. 'As soon as Dingo gets out we'll take Mother for an air test. Until then, we go over every inch of her, make sure she's on top-line.' It was clear from their faces that like him they needed to be busy. Waiting was the hardest time, and the wait before their first combat might be the hardest of all.

After taking M-Mother for a thirty-minute check flight, Dingo left with the other navigators to prepare their maps while George and the others stood and watched a succession of activities around their aircraft. All afternoon ground staffs fussed over M-Mother, doing all they could to make sure she was ready and would come home again. Fitters performed last-minute maintenance on engines and systems. Riggers swarmed over the aircraft's body checking surfaces, cleaning Perspex and fixing any loose rivets and catches. Wireless specialists returned the secret equipment removed after each flight. Photographic technicians installed the automatic camera to record Mother's bombing. Matador petrol bowsers pumped two and a half thousand gallons of fuel into the tanks. Armourers loaded bombs and armed the machine guns.

The meal was at sixteen hundred and by then the tension was palpable, like an approaching thunderstorm. Crews crowded together along mess tables, taking what comfort they could from each other's company. Many ate normally, seemingly unaffected, while others could only manage a few mouthfuls. A few rushed for the toilets. George forced himself to eat the traditional pre-op meal of chips, bacon and eggs. Rationing made eggs and bacon a luxury, which for some might be their last. He decided that his crew were bearing up well and only young Ned Anderson seemed more subdued than normal. How pitifully young he looked. The boy should have been at home, climbing trees and fishing in rivers, not flying off to war in a bomber. With a feeling of guilt, he realised he should have spent more time with him, talked more, prepared him better. There had not been enough time.

'You OK, Ned?' George smiled as warmly he could.

The young Canadian looked startled. 'Yeah, sure. Everything's good.'

'It's going to be fine, a piece of cake.'

'Really?' His eyes bulged slightly in his pale face.

'Of course it will. Remember, you're part of a handpicked crew. We're the best. Just concentrate on your job because we rely on you.' Ned nodded, but George could not tell if he was any happier. 'Now tell me, what's Group HQ's frequency?'

He came back instantly, 'Three thousand one hundred and ninety kilocycles.'

'Good. How often does Bomber Command HQ broadcast?'

'Twice every hour, at quarter to and quarter past.'

George reached across and ruffled his hair. 'You'll do Ned. Well done.' The boy smiled.

'Course the kid will be fine,' Dingo added encouragingly. 'Never met a Canuck yet that wasn't up for a fight. Just remember that I'm only a few feet in front of you. Come up anytime and say hello, 'cos I'm the one most in need of company.'

'Yeah, keep an eye on Dingo,' Max said. 'He's so full of it, he could flood the aircraft.' He ducked as Dingo threw a chip.

The final briefing was at seventeen hundred, after which they went to the crew room and changed. Temperatures dropped as low as minus forty degrees centigrade at high altitudes and touching the metal airframe with bare skin froze flesh and caused frostbite. George pulled a thick white jumper over his shirt and vest, then the battledress blouse and finally a thick-fleeced Irvin jacket. Below the waist, he wore two pairs of long johns, three pairs of socks, trousers, Irvin leather trousers and fleeced flying boots. Finally, he pulled on pairs of silk and then leather gloves. He left off the gauntlets as these made operating the controls too difficult. Just walking in flying clothing was cumbersome, but they made operating an aircraft gruelling. Being practically immobile in their cramped turrets, the two gunners Max and Jim were especially at risk from cold. The two gunners also wore bulky, electrically heated overalls. Crews were supposed to hand in their locker keys in case they did not come back, but few did, it seemed too much like tempting fate. Next, they queued for parachutes where as usual a cheery WAAF told them to bring back any that did not work. Then another counter for Mae-West life jackets and survival packs. Finally, they each received a thermos of coffee and a bag of sandwiches. Ned Anderson also collected two homing pigeons, housed in small boxes. The birds would carry messages if they ditched in the sea.

George felt for Millie's necklace around his neck and lightly pressed it against his skin. It was like having part of her here with him and he thought of her, wondering what she was doing at that moment. Would she sense the approaching danger and think of him? Would she feel his fear and maybe even the moment if he died?

Outside the sun was setting a blood red colour that he hoped was not ominous. There was little wind and a fine mist obscured the edges of the aerodrome. However, individual Lancasters stood out clearly, strong and purposeful. While they waited for transport, the crews chatted and bantered with each other, raucous with nervous energy. Once again, he thought how waiting was the worst part, particularly before the unknown of first combat. Waiting allowed the imagination to run wild and invent any scenario, see any omen. It would be better once they got to the aircraft and were away. Then again, perhaps he should try to enjoy these last minutes of idleness, the next few hours would be very uncertain. Lost in thoughts, he barely noticed the trucks pull up until Dingo tugged him.

'Where to?' the WAAF driver called.

'How about the Chandos Arms?' Max replied. 'First round's on the skipper.'

'You'll have to wait for that, love, I'm afraid,' she replied. 'The CO's locked the gates.'

Max tutted. 'He really is a wet blanket. I suppose you'd better take us to M-Mother. I'm brassic anyhow.'

'M-Mother it is.' She ground the truck into gear and trundled off towards dispersal.

'Fancy coming with us?' Max continued, winking at Ned. 'Nice and cosy in my little turret, and you get a cracking view.'

'Do you want the polite or the honest answer?'

'Is there a difference?'

'Not really, it's just that the polite one has fewer swear words.'

'I'll take that as a 'no' then.'

'It would be 'no' even if I came with you,' she laughed. It was a short journey and she pulled the truck up beside M-Mother and waited for them to get out. 'Good luck boys, we'll wave you off from the flight line. Be careful.'

Chapter 12

RAF Oakley - 10th September 1942

M-Mother towered over them, black, solid and imposing. There was something about the Lancaster's appearance that was somehow just right. Although for all that, she was vulnerable. Much slower than a fighter and when loaded with fuel and bombs she was an explosion waiting to happen. Their lives depended on whether they saw the enemy in time and, of course, to a dose of luck. They stood in a group and watched the truck drive away; leaving them alone. Their last link with normality gone and M-Mother would now carry them to war and danger. George suddenly realised he was experiencing the same fear that every combatant must feel before battle, a thing that linked soldiers throughout history. The certainty of approaching violence and the uncertainty of survival. Some of the older men in the village where he grew up would have felt the same thirty years before in the trenches. Now he would share in that knowledge if he survived.

Chalky unbuttoned his flies and headed for the tail wheel. 'Come on, you blokes, it's for luck.'

The rest glanced at each other before following. 'An' I thought you engineers were all science.' Max blinked through his cigarette smoke as he sprayed the tyre.

'It is,' Chalky replied. 'We're peeing in the gremlin's eye, blinding him for the journey.'

'Struth, Chalky, anything to make your bloody job easier isn't it.' Dingo finished and did up his trousers.

While the crew clambered aboard, George began ground checks and waited for the sergeant to arrive with the form 700. Even in the dim light, his signature looked wrong, shaky and forced, not something he recognised as wholly his own. Climbing the ladder suddenly felt like a condemned man stepping up to the gallows, but Smith was right, every moment now seemed more vivid, more precious. Fear increased his alertness, made him sharper and he would cling to that positive. It would give him an edge. With finality, he clamped the side door shut, sealing them in the Lancaster until they returned from their seven hundred mile journey and patted the side of the aircraft. *Bring us home safe please, Mother*.

Max was settling into his lonely turret in the tail. Turning forward, George squeezed by Jim Ambiolo's legs in the 'dustbin', the mid-upper gun position, and wished him luck. He slid over the cramped space above the main spar, where just the other side Ned was already setting frequencies on a bank of receivers and transmitters. George gave him the thumbs up and received a pale smile in return. He wanted to reassure the boy, convince him that they would all live through the night. However, they both knew there could be no guarantees; the best he could offer was fellowship.

'Waiting is always the worst part,' George told him. 'We'll all find it easier once we get going.'

Ned nodded, and for a second George thought he was going to say something, but the young Canadian turned back to his dials.

'Come up the front if you get lonely,' George said and patted him on the shoulder. Immediately in front of Ned was the navigator's cubby. Charts and instruments spread across the plotting table while to one side a long strip of map, marked-up and spliced together earlier, coiled like a toilet roll onto a holder, ready to be unwound as the flight progressed. Dingo adjusted the 'Gee' navigation equipment and he looked up at George and nodded, holding out his hand.

'Take care of yourself, bushwhacker.' George said, grasping Dingo's hand and shaking it. The Australian looked his usual competent self, despite any fears he may have felt.

'No worries about me mate,' he said with a sly grin. 'First sign of trouble and I'm out the hatch with my hanky strapped to my back.' He nodded towards his parachute. 'Make sure you follow close behind because I bet I'm the only one that can find Switzerland.'

'I'll remember that.' George smiled and clambered on and into the cockpit next to Chalky. 'Right everyone,' he said over the intercom. 'Let's start ground checks.'

It took thirty minutes before they were ready. George nodded to Chalky to start the engines and he, in turn, indicated the starboard inner to the ground crew. He opened the fuel cocks, pressed the start button and the propeller turned slowly, spluttered, banged and became a blur. With all four Merlin's turning, M-Mother shook and trembled with power. Once George received permission to roll, he signalled to an aircraftman who pulled away the wheel chocks and waved M-Mother forward onto the taxiway.

The Lancasters moved around the perimeter slowly like a procession of black beetles, all heading towards the runway. George joined the queue and crept forward, alternately scanning dials and looking towards the start of the runway where the squadron leader's Lancaster waited at the head of the queue. Suddenly the lead bomber began to move, slowly at first and then quickly gathering speed as the tail came up. Straight away, the next aircraft came to the start line and as the squadron leader lifted into the air and banked to the right, the second was already rolling down the runway and a third moving to the start. This movement rippled down the line and George nudged M-Mother forward gently, careful not to foul the engine plugs. With three aircraft in front, George throttled each engine in turn to full power and watched the revs. Chalky then read out the final checks.

'Elevator trim, two divisions.'

'Check.'

'Propellers set to max rpm.'

'Check.'

'Flaps, twenty degrees down.'

'Check.'

'Superchargers in medium gear.'

'Check.' They finished with just one aircraft in front and with a massive roar, that Lancaster wound up its engines and began rolling. He tried to swallow, but his mouth was too dry, his whole body felt light, insubstantial as if this was happening to someone else. Was it just him that felt afraid? He glanced at Chalky, but Chalky was staring at the controller's caravan, watching for the green light, his face hidden.

'Take off positions everyone,' George said and placed his right hand on the throttles. Then the green light flashed. This was it.

'Green light,' Chalky confirmed and George pushed all the throttles forward, waiting a few seconds for power to build before releasing the brakes. Winding up the engines against the brakes broke the rules, but it was the best way to gain every inch of runway with a heavy load. Another trick Smith had taught him.

'Here we go!' George called and released the brakes. M-Mother jumped forward, straining under the weight like a horse pulling a heavy load. They were laden with fuel and bombs and now he had to get her off the ground.

Over a mile of runway stretched into the distance like a thick pencil line. On either side, flare path lights flickered as speed built. To the right, a group of WAAFs and ground crews waved to them. Further back on the control tower balcony, he could see the CO and his senior staff officers watching.

Despite the load, M-Mother's tail soon came up, but George decided to keep her on the runway until they reached over one hundred and ten miles-per-hour. He took his hand from the throttles and left Chalky to tighten the friction screws. With both hands on the yoke and his eyes set firmly on the runway, he listened to Chalky read the speed.

'Eighty-five... ninety... ninety-five... one hundred...'

They had travelled three-quarters of the runway. Too late to abort if something went wrong. At one hundred and ten miles-per-hour, George pulled back on the column and M-Mother climbed solidly into the air.

'Undercarriage and flaps up please, Chalky,' George asked and felt the speed increase without their combined drag.

Pulling Mother into a climbing right turn, he could see aircraft above them spiralling towards the clouds and their grouping point ten thousand feet over the aerodrome. Now that they were committed, most of what happened next would depend on their ability. Smith was right, they were a good crew and this was a fine aircraft, he must cling to that.

The setting sun shone warm and red as they emerged above the clouds, coating the cockpit in a golden glow. He watched in fascination as Lancaster after Lancaster appeared through the white haze below, rising upwards like birds leaving a misty lake. Grouping in loose vics of three, the training squadron turned northeast towards Southwold and began a gentle climb to fifteen thousand feet. There they would meet the rest of the attacking force, arriving from bases across eastern England, before they all turned southeast and headed for Holland.

'Oxygen on please, Chalky.' George fastened his mask across his face and breathed in puffs of rubbery tasting air. 'Make sure you're getting a supply, everyone. I don't want anyone passing out.'

'We've got company,' Dick Scrivener said. He was in the front, spotting ground features for Dingo. 'Wellingtons at ten o'clock and five thousand feet below.'

George banked the aircraft to get a better view and saw a gaggle of Wimpey's in front and to the left on a parallel heading. Although strongly built and resilient, the twin-engine Wellington was slower than the Lancaster and could not climb as high. Consequently, it was more vulnerable and a more tempting target for night fighters. Perversely, a part of him was grateful for this, although he felt guilty for thinking it. Within fifteen minutes, the sun had set and a half-moon shone its weak light on the cumulus below them, turning it silvery white. Aircraft stood out quite distinctly against the clouds, but there was still some refracted sunlight leaking around the earth's curvature. The sky would darken fully as the sun moved further away. He hoped so; they would be sitting ducks over Holland otherwise.

'Southwold should be coming up.' Dingo said.

'Thanks, Nav. Eyes peeled everyone.' George said. 'This is going to get crowded and I want to know if we're close to other aircraft.'

'Coastline ahead,' Dick said, his voice uncharacteristically excited.

Through broken clouds, George could see the grey English coast and beyond that the dark surface of the Channel sparkling with cresting waves. Directly ahead there was just enough light to make out the bomber stream gathering. It was an impressive sight. A horde of bombers spread across the sky. Wellingtons, Lancasters, Halifax and Stirlings, even a few venerable Hampden's and Whitley's. Dozens and dozens of aircraft converged on Southwold before turning southeast towards Holland. Unbidden, a memory of the Blitz came back, the day he had watched the Luftwaffe swarm head towards London. *Butch Harris is right about one thing*, he told himself, *Germany is reaping the whirlwind.*

'Ned, Dingo. Come up to the front and see this.' Seconds later the two stood behind him and Chalky.

'Jesus,' Dingo said. 'Dusseldorf is in for one hell of a pasting tonight.'

'I thought you should see it while you can. In fifteen minutes it will be fully dark.' George dimmed the instrument lights until he could hardly read the dials. 'You'd better give me the course changes early so I can mark the compass.'

'Will do skipper.' Dingo said and he and Ned went back to their positions. The light faded quickly and cloud colour changed from white to dark grey. There were so many bombers in the sky that collision was now a real danger. Aircraft that had been discernible just a few minutes before disappeared entirely.

'We turn onto our new heading in five minutes, skipper.' Dingo said.

'Thanks, Dingo. Jim, can you see the rest of the squadron?' The upper turret gave a good three-sixty degree view above the aircraft, though very little directly below. There was a moment's silence.

'Negative skipper. I get glimpses of P-Peter to our right occasionally, but apart from that just the odd shape.'

'Nothing from the rear either,' Max added.

The Lancaster suddenly bounced and jarred in another aircraft's slipstream. It must be just a few hundred feet in front, although George could see nothing. He felt the hairs on his neck tingle. There were so many aircraft surrounding them that when they made the next turn, he might fly into one. George took Mother up a hundred feet until they were out of the slipstream, but then a Halifax crossed right in front of them, a looming back shape just a dozen yards away and so close that George could see its tail gunner staring at him.

'My God,' Dick called from the front turret. 'Any closer and we could have shaken hands.'

'Change course to one hundred and twenty degrees, now skipper,' Dingo called.

'Thanks, Nav. Going right and climbing, I'm taking us up and out of this. More revs please Chalky.' The Lancaster could fly higher than other bombers, even a Halifax and he decided to climb and find some space. 'Keep your eyes peeled, everyone.' He pulled back on the column and turned onto the next heading. In front, the horizon's dim outline tilted and dropped down the cockpit glass. They were now flying towards Holland and beyond that to the heart of Germany. M-Mother climbed sluggishly to twenty thousand feet, far less responsive with the weight of fuel and bombs.

'I'm worried about fuel consumption, skipper,' Chalky said. He was looking at the engineer's panel and making calculations on a clipboard. 'I'd like to pull back the revs as soon as possible.'

'Bit early to worry about fuel isn't it?' George asked although he knew Lancaster engineers strived for the golden one point one miles-per-gallon and fretted like misers about reserves.

'It always pays to have something in your back pocket,' Chalky replied primly. 'You never know what's in front.'

'How are we doing for time, nav?'

'Pretty much bang on, skipper. Next turn is in fifteen minutes, new heading fifty-four degrees. Airspeed should be one eighty to avoid creeping up on the blokes in front.'

'OK, bring back the throttle for one hundred and eighty miles-per-hour, Chalky.'

There was little to see outside now, just blackness punctuated by a scattering of stars. Even the weak glow of the moon seemed to have abandoned them. Each second took M-Mother closer to danger and only the thought that they were part of an armada gave him any comfort. The Luftwaffe's radars would be tracking them and bringing night fighters to readiness or already have them prowling the skies. Ground defenders would be fetching ammunition, cranking their gun barrels upwards and waiting to fire thousands of shells at the attackers. George fiddled with the trim wheel. He longed for the next turn, the sooner they made landfall, the sooner it would begin and the sooner it would be over.

'Searchlights coming on to port,' Dick said. He now sounded dispassionate; they all seemed to have calmed down since the mission started. George looked sideways and saw half a dozen beams probing to their left. Then others flicked on either side of these, around twenty altogether.

'Where is that?' George asked no one in particular.

'Must be Rotterdam,' Dick replied. 'I guess the pathfinders are already skirting the city.'

'Next turn in five minutes.' Dingo said.

'How long after that till we cross the coast?'

Dingo was silent for a few seconds and then he said, 'It's difficult to be exact as we may come up one of the estuaries, but after we turn I'd say five to ten minutes to reach Schouwen. Then another twenty minutes to the final turning point at Hertogenbosch.'

'Thanks, Nav. Fighters will be about from now on, gunners. We're relying on you.'

'You're in safe hands with me, skipper,' Max replied. 'Jim's a complete no-hoper, though.'

'You cockney half-pint.' Jim Ambiolo's Norfolk accent was emphasised by the intercom. 'You can hardly see over the gun mounts.'

'Quiet you two or Goering's boys will have the last laugh.'

'Turn now, skipper. New heading of ninety-four degrees.'

George pulled M-Mother to the left and watched the compass rotate. 'We're on course, Nav. Let me know five minutes before the next turn.' He tried to sound calm, but he felt too anxious. This was it; they were now heading straight for the enemy. The Merlins roared, the Lancaster trembled with power and George wondered what the next hours would bring. More than anything, he wondered whether he would be good enough. Despite the CO's words, he did not feel confident. A scan of the dials again and he paused. Was it his eyes or was the port inner hotter now, the needle marginally higher. Chalky noticed it too and tapped the glass. The needle dropped, aligning with the other three.

Their course lay directly towards the string of searchlights. Some beams wandered across the sky, searching for intruders, while others remained vertical, creating a barrier. It was like staring at the bars of a prison cell. There were so many beams, it seemed impossible to slip through undetected. George squinted because he noticed something else in front; bursts of colour that appeared and quickly faded. Then he realised it was flak. A deep layer of orange flashes that left small clouds of black smoke in its wake. Below the flak, dotted lines of coloured tracer arched up, but these faded at around twelve thousand feet, well below the height of the bombers. The Germans were certainly putting on a show, searchlights, heavy calibre flak and medium calibre tracer below that. It was like watching a firework display, mesmerising and deadly. M-Mother inched towards it, the blackness hiding all sense of speed. It felt that they were travelling at little more than a walking pace and involuntarily he began to reach for the throttles, but then stopped. Chalky was right. They might be short of fuel later.

'Someone's coned,' Chalky said.

Away to the right, three searchlights had come together, joining at the top to illuminate a bomber. In the distance, the aircraft was just a white speck, a moth caught in torchlight. Suddenly flak peppered the sky nearby, black smudges with angry orange cores. George gripped the yoke harder. *Move you, idiot. Dive. Get away*, he urged. Then the spec sprouted flames, small at first but growing quickly until it looked like the tip of a struck match. Within seconds, the aircraft was a comet falling through the night sky. George was stunned. Seven lives gone in seconds, *that could be us*, he thought.

'My God!' Dick's voice was shocked, horrified. 'The poor bastards didn't stand a chance.'

'What's happened, skipper?' Dingo asked. He could see nothing outside his curtained area.

'A kite to starboard took a direct hit. It looked like flak exploded the bomb load,' George decided.

'Hell. At least it would have been quick.'

Flak filled the sky around them as they crossed the shoreline. Immediately Mother bucked and wallowed through the broken air as if she was driving along a deeply rutted road. George thought of the burning aircraft and of the thousands of pounds of explosives beneath his feet. It took just one red-hot splinter slicing into the Cookie. There was no defence other than changing height every minute or so and he was not convinced that particularly helped. Many of the flak guns fired in a barrage, their shells exploding randomly and so one piece of sky was no safer than any other. The distance between searchlights grew as they closed and he banked left towards one of the wider gaps, hoping to slip through unnoticed. Then he saw a beam swing towards them. It looked different to the others; silvery blue rather than yellow and with a sinking feeling realised it was the radar-controlled master light. It was startling how quickly it flicked across the sky, like watching a snake's springing attack. Now flying straight would definitely kill them just like the other bomber. He had to evade.

'Hold on everyone!' he shouted and pushed the column and throttles forward. M-Mother leapt downhill, increasing speed as she dropped. The dive was so steep that he became weightless. Across his left shoulder, the beam sliced nearer.

'Two-ten... Two-twenty...' Chalky called out the airspeed.

'Two-forty... Two-sixty...' Was it his imagination or was the blue beam heading astern of them?

'Two-eighty... Three hundred...'

The searchlight's edge grazed M-Mother just for a second and passed on. Its sweep had missed. Now George had to decide whether to continue the dive, in case it swung back, or start climbing and hope the radar targeted someone else. He decided to climb; chasing a fleeing target was more difficult than one coming towards you and aircraft filled the skies. Pulling back on the throttles, he tugged the column and slowly Mother's nose came up. It was hard work; the Lancaster was heavy to manoeuvre at high speed.

A massive blast exploded below and in front, peppering them with shrapnel and pushing Mother's nose higher. Immediately the engines struggled against the steep angle and speed bled away. George instinctively pushed both the column and throttles forward before the Lancaster stalled.

Smoke wafted into the cockpit, filling it with the acrid tang of cordite.

'Everyone OK?' George asked feeling badly shaken. That had been close, too close. The crew checked in and miraculously no one was injured. 'What's the damage?'

'There's a couple of holes in the nose, but nothing serious.' Dick said.

'I think the starboard wing tank is holed,' Chalky said as he clambered up in the cockpit to get a better view. 'There's a stream of vapour. Wait, it's stopping. I guess the self-sealing works.'

'Sounded like a hail storm on a dunny roof back here.' Dingo sounded indignant. 'But nothing came through.'

Had he not pulled up they would have flown straight into the shell. *Don't think about it now, it's a distraction.* He breathed deeply before continuing. 'Well done everyone. We're through the first flak belt. The big danger is from fighters, so eyes peeled gunners. How long is it until we turn nav?'

'Ten minutes skipper. Then right, onto one hundred and fourteen degrees magnetic.'

'Firing to starboard,' Jim shouted. George looked across Chalky in time to see a horizontal stream of tracer rip through the air in the distance.

'Must be a fighter after one of the boys,' Max said. 'Jim, you keep watching that side, I'll scan to port.'

George could see nothing of the two aircraft and there was no more tracer, so maybe the bomber got away. Out in the darkness, two aircraft were playing a deadly game of cat and mouse. He pushed the column down and wallowed back up, hoping this would make them a more difficult target. Simultaneously, he banked steeply to port and then to starboard, giving both gunners a better view below. The thought that a fighter could be creeping up behind them made him shiver. It was like walking down a dark alley with a crazed knifeman on the loose.

'Turn in two minutes, skipper,' Dingo said.

'Thanks, Nav.' George noticed Chalky examining his engineer's panel. 'What's the fuel state, Engineer?'

'We lost a hundred gallons or so before the hole sealed itself. There's a quarter of the reserve left, plenty to get us home as long as we don't go wild.'

'Turn to a new heading of one hundred and fourteen degrees,' Dingo called.

George banked to the right in a slow turn and watched the compass revolve. 'One hundred and fourteen it is, Nav. How long until we reach Dusseldorf?'

'Sixty miles until the start of the bomb run, so with this tail-wind, say about twenty minutes.'

George blanched, it was a long time to sit and wonder if the Luftwaffe was about to blow you out of the sky. Almost as bad as knowing they could easily drift into one of the five hundred bombers surrounding them.

M-Mother seemed to crawl over the black landscape, rocked occasionally as flak shells exploded nearby. No one spoke and apart from the constant background noise of the Merlin engines, the silence became oppressive. Everyone seemed tense, readying for the bomb run. He was tempted to again ask Dingo how much longer but worried that would make him sound windy. Suddenly, a burst of firing ripped through the black sky, half a mile away and five thousand feet lower. This time the victim did not escape. A line of silver dashes created a trickle of flames, which grew rapidly into a tongue of fire on the target. The light from the flames showed the victim to be a Wellington. The aircraft flew straight and level and he guessed the pilot was holding her steady while his crew jumped. Then the fuel tanks ruptured and the entire wing blazed brightly. *Jump. Get out*, George urged. As he watched, the wing snapped back against the aircraft's body and the Wellington rolled onto its side and tumbled like a slowly turning Catherine wheel. The crew talked at once.

'Christ, did you see that?'

'See what?' Dingo asked.

'A kite's bloody wing burned off.'

'Poor bastards.'

'Quiet everyone and keep watching,' George snapped. 'There are more fighters out there.' He dipped the aircraft more vigorously this time and as M-Mother climbed back up he saw a glimmer in the distance.

'Nav and Bomb Aimer. I can see a red glow. I think the first wave has gone in. Dusseldorf's burning.'

Dingo came back immediately. 'Good one. I make it ten minutes until we start the bomb run. Can you see anything below us, Dick?' Dingo asked and George saw the bomb aimer wriggle further forward into the Perspex bubble.

'There's something reflecting in front of us. Could be a river?'

'That'll be the Meuse. We're bang-on then, skipper. Aim for the fires, you don't need me again until we've dropped.'

'You'd better arm the bombs, Dick,' George told him. 'I want to go straight in and out.'

'Wait, skipper, we've got company,' Max interrupted. 'Jim, look behind, about five o'clock and a bit below. Got it?'

Silence and then, 'Got it.'

'What is it, Max?' George asked.

'There's a Messerschmitt 109 climbing up behind us, trying to get on our tail.'

The effect was like having ice water tipped down his back and he jerked into the seat. This was the moment he feared, the moment a night-fighter found them.

'Don't do anything yet skipper. Wait until I say, then drop straight down and corkscrew right.' Max spoke confidently but the worry in his voice was obvious. 'When he comes in, me and Jim'll give him a squirt.'

Should he start the corkscrew now? Did he trust Max? Could he trust him? All their lives depended on the next few moments. Mother's fuel tanks were awash with hundred-octane petrol, and underneath hung a four thousand pound bomb cased in only a thin metal tube. One well-aimed cannon shell could blow them to pieces, and the 109 fired ten each second. George forced himself to think rationally. The 109 was an aircraft, not a demon. Although the pilot flew a nimble fighter, the Lancaster was a great kite and he felt confident that he was a good pilot and had a good crew. He trusted them.

'OK Max,' he decided and pressed Millie's Star of David for luck. 'It's your call. Tell me what's happening.'

'He's still climbing. Just wait a second, skipper.' Max suddenly sounded calm and George pictured him crouched behind his four machine guns, watching the dim shape draw nearer. 'Still got him, Jim?'

'Aye, I'm tracking the bastard.'

'Any second now, skipper.' Max drew out the words as if he was performing a delicate operation. 'Here he comes! Corkscrew right!'

George threw the column forward and yanked the yoke to the right, before pulling back the throttles to slow the bomber and make the Messerschmitt overshoot. Mother dropped sickeningly as if she was tumbling down a cliff. Looking over his shoulder, he saw a hail of cannon shells scream

168

across the left wing and past the cockpit. Instinctively he flinched and leaned away.

'Three hundred... Three-ten...' Chalky called the speeds but George hardly heard him. Although forward momentum reduced, the steep dive angle was causing speed to build. Then, Mother vibrated as both Max and Jim fired. Still looking left, he pulled the throttles back further to begin a slow climbing turn just as the 109 hurtled past yards away trailing smoke. It pitched nose up, rolled over and spun downwards. George stared in shock, frozen until Chalky banged his arm. With a start, he adjusted the throttles and tugged the column with all his strength, it barely moved. Mother did not respond.

'Three sixty... Three seventy...' Chalky droned. The maximum recommended dive speed was three fifteen miles per hour and they were far in excess of that. George pulled the column as hard as he could and swung the elevator trim tab. They were going too fast for the elevators and ailerons to deploy effectively. Despite the sub-zero temperature, sweat slickened his forehead and his arms trembled with effort.

'Lower the undercarriage,' he called to Chalky.

The engineer glanced sideways at him, uncertain. 'You could pull the bloody wings off!'

'We're dead anyway if we don't pull up. Do it!' Chalky pulled the lever, extending the wheels. Immediately Mother bucked and fluttered as if slapped by a red-hot poker, but that and trimming her nose up, loosened the column and using both hands he pulled it back into his chest. *Don't look at the wings*, he told himself. Slowly but surely the Lancaster levelled. It had been a desperate manoeuvre driven by fear, but it worked. They lost five thousand feet and now they had to climb back up again before they reached the target. The attacking force's bombs would fall on them if they stayed low.

'Sod it, you blokes,' Dingo said. 'I've lost all me bloody instruments.'

'It could have been worse,' George muttered shakily. 'Believe me, it could have been a lot worse.'

'Well, you can find your own bloody way home. I'm on strike.'

'I'm going to arm the bombs now skipper.' Dick sounded matter-of-fact, as if the last minutes had not happened.

The red glow in front had now become raging fires spread over a large area of the city. Streets and roads lit up with flames like a fiery crossword puzzle. The Rhine snaked in a meandering black line through the centre of the firestorm, cutting it in half. Dusseldorf burned on one side and Neuss on the other. Bomber after bomber dropped Cookies and incendiaries in an almost constant series of explosions. Shock waves expanded outwards in the fires like raindrops rippling a red pond. It was the most chilling sight he had ever seen. A vision of hell.

'Dingo, stop sulking and work out a course for home after we drop,' George snapped. 'Ned, are you picking up the master bomber yet?' His breathing was rapid, gulping down oxygen as he forced himself to concentrate.

'Yes, skipper. I'll patch you through.' The young Canadian sounded excited, almost as if he was enjoying himself and George shook his head at the change, wondering if war was best suited to the very young. With minutes to go, Mother regained her lost altitude and Dick slid back into the bomb aimer's position. George listened to the master bomber.

'Keep coming, attacking force. You're late, third wave,' the master bomber chided. He would be orbiting somewhere over the city, probably in a fast moving mosquito. 'Ignore the green target indicators and drop on yellow. I repeat drop on yellow.'

'Are you ready, Bomb Aimer?'

'Ready for bombing, skipper.' The words practised so often in training now seemed different, more portentous.

'Over to you, Bomb Aimer.' Now Dick would lead them until the bombs dropped. George was just the driver following directions.

The bomb-run was the most dangerous part of the mission because the bombers had to fly straight and level. There could be no evasive manoeuvres from now on because the electro-mechanical computor, feeding data to the bombsight, only worked if it was relatively stable. They were sitting ducks and only the fear of their own flak kept the fighters away. George gulped down oxygen and scanned the night sky, searching for fighters, although any attack would come from behind, towards Max.

'Open the bomb doors,' Dick instructed.

'Bomb doors open.' George pulled the lever with his left hand and tensed. Now, not even the flimsy skin of the bomb bay doors protected the cookie. Buffeted by a carpet of bursting flak, the Lancaster wallowed and bounced. The defences were far stronger here than over Holland, far more guns and searchlights. Like a wounded beast, Dusseldorf lashed back at its attackers. Again, the aircraft rattled from shrapnel fragments and a strong smell of cordite seeped inside. He gripped the yoke more firmly and prayed they would be over the target soon. In front, each second added fresh fires and explosions to the burning city. Clouds of dense black smoke billowed thousands of feet into the air and the fires were so bright that flames coated the attacking bombers in a dull red glow.

'You're creeping back, third wave,' the master bomber called. 'Drop in the middle of the TIs, not on the edge.'

'Target sighted. I can see yellow target indicators,' Dick announced.

Explosions occurred more frequently as the body of the third wave arrived. Adding to the bewildering visual display of tracer, flak, searchlights, fires and explosions, were the random pops of photoflashes. Each aircraft dropped an exploding flare, set to detonate as their bomb landed. This changed with the aircraft's height but was generally around twenty-five seconds after release. At the same time, the onboard camera automatically took a photograph, capturing the accuracy of the bomber's aiming.

'That's better, third wave,' the master bomber called. 'Right on target. Keep it coming, keep it coming.' To one side George watched a Stirling with its wing streaming fire, pressing on with the attack, seemingly oblivious to its wounds.

'Left, left...' Dick instructed, each 'left' repeated for clarity. 'Steady... Left, left... Steady... Right... Steady...'

George wanted to scream, *just drop the bloody bombs.* A piece of shrapnel zipped across the perspex, leaving a deep groove. Away in front, a Lancaster exploded. Its entire fuselage became a mass of fire before breaking apart and tumbling earthwards like so much flaming confetti. George watched the disaster, fascinated, appalled. *Please drop the bloody bombs*, he pleaded silently.

'Steady... Steady... Steady...'

They were well over the target now and flames lit the aircraft as bright as day. Where were the fighters? The bombers were sitting ducks. George swung his head, craning upwards, searching for movement in the dark sky. *How much longer?* It felt as if the entire aircraft was holding its breath.

He was cold with fear and felt entirely exposed and vulnerable, but at the same time images of the Luftwaffe swarm heading towards London and the bodies he pulled from the wreckage all mixed in his mind. Suddenly he was glad to be there. This was payment for home.

'Steady... Steady... Bombs gone!' Dick uttered the magic words and freed of their weight, M-Mother rose up like an elevator.

'Take that you bastards,' Max shouted and the others cheered.

'Bomb doors closed, now let's get out of here,' George said. He too felt a thrill at the release, exhilaration as the bombs tumbled earthwards. They had flown to Germany and done their job.

'Wait for the photograph, skipper!' Dick called and George relaxed his grip, he had forgotten. His excitement evaporated and he flew straight and level for a further twenty-five seconds, during each one he expected bullets to flay the aircraft or flak to blast it to pieces.

'Photograph taken,' Dick said at last and George pushed the throttles forward and climbed steeply to the right. Chalky could fret about fuel later. Without the weight of her bombs, M-Mother moved like a scolded cat. She was a different creature, faster and more responsive. Now they could go home.

'Course please, nav?'

'Make a ten-mile right turn until we're directly south of the target area. No more than ten miles or we'll run into Cologne's flak belt. Then steer two seven four degrees, skipper.'

'Thanks, Dingo. I'm glad you're not still on strike.'

'Well, we didn't *cark it* on the bomb run and you said 'please', so I thought I'd help a bunch of lost Poms get home to mum.'

'I'm no Pom, you Aussie Dink.' Ned chirped happily.

'Hey, it's young Ned. How you doing Cobber? Still got your feet up listening to Vera Lynn, while the rest of us fight the war?

'Leave the boy alone, Dingo. He's got a sister I want to meet.' Max called.

'You'd be more suited to my old fella's prize ewe. She's half-blind and can't smell.'

Max chuckled. 'That's a good offer, but do you mind me screwing your mother?'

'Pipe down the lot of you!' George called sharply. This was a dangerous time; they were all buoyed up and distracted. A fighter could sneak up and kill them if they lost concentration. 'We're not out of the woods yet. Stay alert.' Without bombs and with much of her fuel used, M-Mother's cruising speed increased by thirty miles-per-hour and she climbed another three thousand feet. It was not a massive improvement, but unless a fighter was already above and in front, it would be a long tail chase and possibly not worth the fuel.

He felt bone weary from the stress of the last hour and pulled his goggles up to rub his eyes. Blinking deeply he glanced over his shoulder at the glow from Dusseldorf, nine miles away to the right. Acres of the city were burning. Bright red patches of flame billowed black smoke high into the air. Although the last of the bombers had now gone, searchlights continued scanning and flak still peppered the sky. In contrast to the horrors over Dusseldorf, the landscape's dim outline below looked serene and peaceful. The silvery surface of the Rhine snaked its way south and he wondered if Millie had ever been there and walked the city's streets or strolled in the countryside. How would she react if she knew they had just destroyed the major part of the city? Maybe it was fear or exhilaration, but he ached for her at that moment. To hold and talk to her, breathe in her scent and nestle his face in her hair. He wanted to tell her about the mission, listen to her thoughts and wait while she made sense of it all.

In no time at all Dick warned, 'Searchlights in front.' Having shut down the bombing system, he was back in the front turret map reading and spotting for Dingo. George replaced his goggles and realised guiltily that he had been drifting, not concentrating. The very crime he had warned the others against committing. Fifty miles away a dozen searchlights swept the sky, hunting for the fleeing bombers. They were passing a river, presumably the Meuse again. It felt like days before when they crossed over it to Dusseldorf.

'We're heading right for searchlights, Dingo. When do I turn?'

'Antwerp's straight ahead and we should turn right onto two nine two degrees in ten minutes.

'Skipper, I think there's another aircraft behind.' Max called. 'Not sure if....' But the rest of his sentence was cut off as George threw the aircraft downhill into a violent corkscrew. As he reached the bottom of the manoeuvre and started to pull back up, he saw a blunt shape pass overhead.

'Junkers 88.' Jim spoke quietly as if the enemy might hear him. George climbed right and left before dropping again. He repeated the corkscrew three times before resuming the standard wallowing motion.

'Any sign of him?' George asked.

'Nothing out the back.' Max called.

'Nothing from up here either.' Jim added in the upper turret.

'Make the turn, skipper.'

'OK, turning right on two nine two degrees. How long until we reach the coast?'

'I make it around...' But Dingo didn't finish. A blur of bright yellow tracer ripped across the right wing, shredding the metal and scattering burning fragments like pieces of tissue paper. Without thought, he threw M-Mother into another dive.

'Starboard inner's on fire,' Chalky called, his voice high pitched with fear. 'I'm shutting her down and turning off the fuel.'

'Remember to feather the prop,' George grunted. He held the column forward and watched Chalky deftly working the engine controls. The starboard inner engine was spewing flames. They were doomed if the fire ruptured the wing tanks. Within seconds, M-Mother dropped a thousand feet.

'Where is the bastard?' George called. 'Anyone see him yet?'

'Nothing,' Max replied, shocked. 'He came out of nowhere.'

'The fire's not dying. Shall I trigger the extinguisher?' Chalky asked. George considered. Once extinguished, they would not be able to restart the engine. However, the Lancaster could still fly on three engines. The bigger worries were that the fire acted as a beacon to the fighter and that unchecked it might ignite the wing tanks.

'Yes. Do it,' George said. Chalky lifted the flap and pressed the button. They both watched the engine, hoping to see the flames subside.

'Skipper, we're heading too close to Antwerp, you need to veer right about fifteen degrees,' Dingo said. The searchlights were just a few miles in front now, so George turned the dive northwards.

'Turning right.' He briefly wondered how Dingo did his job. Shut away in the dark, with constant alarms and evasions outside, and no clear idea what was happening.

'The fire's not going out.' Chalky said urgently. George looked across to the engine; it seemed to be burning just as fiercely. Their altitude was now fifteen thousand feet. There was no point in corkscrewing because the fighter could see the flames. At best, he could only make Mother a difficult target. There was just one option, to increase the dive angle and hope the wind extinguished the fire.

'Hold on tight. I'm taking us steeper.' George pushed the column further forward and immediately the nose dipped at a crazy angle. The faint horizon now rose to the top of the windscreen, while in front was solid blackness. Wings trembled and the howling wind shrieked above the engine noise, flattening the guttering flames against the burning engine.

'Two fifty... Two sixty...' Chalky called out speeds. George wondered how fast he should go. Mother had been difficult to control at over three hundred miles-per-hour when she was heavy with bombs. Without them, maybe he could risk three sixty or three seventy. On the other hand, there were now only three engines to pull them out of the dive.

'Can you see him, gunners?' More pieces of metal skin peeled away from the damaged wing and fluttered away into the slipstream.

'Two eighty... Three hundred... Altitude ten thousand feet.' George glanced at the starboard inner; the flames were smaller, flicking tongues rather than fat blobs. However, unless he extinguished them completely, they would just start again.

'Nothing, I still can't see anything.' Jim's voice sounded confused, scared.

'Look harder. He's out there somewhere following us.'

'Three ten... Three thirty...' George eased back on the throttles. He would pull out at five thousand feet and if the engine still burned, they would have to jump.

'Three forty and eight thousand feet.'

'Three fifty and seven thousand feet.' Chalky became excited. 'It's out, skipper. Thank God. It's out!'

He held the dive for a few more seconds before slowly pulling back on the column. With just three engines, Mother's power had reduced noticeably and she was far less reactive, worse than with a full bomb load. George's heart pounded as he watched the instrument panel. Slowly the dive became shallower until the needle clicked from 'descend' to 'climb'. 'What's our position, Dingo?'

'Bloody dicey, I'd say.' There was a moment's silence. 'North of Antwerp somewhere. Possibly near Zundfort, about forty miles from the coast.'

'There's water in front, some sort of estuary.' Dick chipped in.

'Hopefully, that's the Oosterschelde. You're on course if it is.'

'Skipper, I can see the Junkers. He's about half a mile back and closing.' Jim's voice was squeaky with excitement. George scanned the dials, six thousand feet and speed one hundred and fifty. Mother was dragging slightly to the right because of the feathered starboard inner and wind resistance from the damaged wing, so he increased power to the remaining starboard engine and cut back on the port two. Unless they found some cloud to hide in there was no way to avoid a fight now, and there was nothing close.

'Make sure you track him, gunners. I'm going to repeat what we did to the Messerschmitt. We'll let him get close and drop steeply to the right. You should get in a shot as he overshoots.' That was so easy to say, but when to start the manoeuvre. Their lives hung on the answer to that question. If he were the Junkers pilot he would get as close as possible before firing to ensure a kill. The night fighter had already missed once and so he would want to be certain this time. Also, he'd crept up unseen before, so maybe he'd think he could do it again. There were a lot of 'perhaps' and 'maybes'. Too many.

George levelled Mother off, hoping to convince the Junkers that he had not been spotted and draw him in. 'Call the distances Max. I want him close, around four hundred feet.'

'Christ but the bugger's coming up fast. OK, he's about seven hundred feet away.'

'Chalky, I want full flaps and the wheels down when I say. Got it?'

'Got it.' Chalky moved his hands to the levers.

'Six hundred feet.' George ached with fear. He visualised cannon shells ripping the length of the aircraft, shredding Mother and her crew. They were all going to die if he misjudged the manoeuvre. He clamped one hand on the yoke and the other on the throttle levers. 'Wait for, it,' he cautioned.

'Five hundred feet.' Max's voice was squeaky as if he had difficulty getting out the words. He would die first when the Junkers fired.

'Wait for it. Almost there.'

'Four hundred feet.'

George waited a few seconds to make sure. 'Now!' he yelled and pulled back on the throttles, pushed the column forward and turned the yoke to the right. He saw Chalky pulling the flaps and undercarriage levers.

M-Mother slowed dramatically and dropped right. Seconds later the aircraft shook as Max and Jim fired their machine guns. George swung the yoke the other way, just in time to see the twin-engine Junkers streaking past, yards above.

'I don't think we hit him, skipper,' Jim's voice crackled over the intercom.

After retracting the undercarriage and flaps, George pushed the throttles forward and dropped the nose. The Junkers disappeared into the blackness. Perhaps they had grazed him, but probably not. He turned Mother sharp right.

'I'm taking us low. Without the flames to follow, he'll find it hard to find us again.' He looked down towards the ground. 'Dingo where are we?'

'Christ alone knows. I'm shaking so badly that I can't hold the map steady.'

'We're over an estuary,' Dick offered. 'Not sure if it's the same one that I saw before though?'

'Never mind, water's good,' Dingo said. 'Keep to the middle of it until we reach the sea, then steer north-west. I'll try for a star shot as soon as I can hold the sextant.'

'Searchlights and flak ahead.' Dick called, but this time there were only two lights, one either side on the headlands. George pushed Mother even lower, hoping to slip by unnoticed while the flak gunners focused on high altitudes. A few strings of light tracer arced towards them, firing at their engine noise, but it was inaccurate and disappeared behind.

'How are we doing for fuel?' George asked Chalky.

'Better than I'd hoped. We should have enough to get us home as long as Dingo doesn't take the scenic route.'

'Mate, the only thing I want to see tonight is Oakley's runway and my pit.'

Thirty miles out from Holland, it felt safe to assume that the Junkers had lost them so he climbed slowly up to nine thousand feet. Chalky and Dick did the rounds, handing out the coffee and corned beef sandwiches. George was ravenous and even the bitter coffee tasted good. They had been in combat and survived, and a feeling of deep relief that was almost euphoria swept over him.

M-Mother crossed the English coastline near Felixstowe and he flew the last leg fearful that the tyres might be shredded or the brakes damaged, things that gave no indication until the wheels touched the runway. Ned contacted Oakley to tell them they were flying a damaged aircraft and the controller gave them landing priority. George said a silent prayer and flew straight in. M-Mother got them down on a perfect three-point landing and that was it, they were safe. The fire tender followed them as far as dispersal and waited until the engines shut down. Lifting his goggles, he rubbed his eyes and massaged his face where the oxygen mask had chafed. He wanted nothing more than to see the crew bus trundling around the perimeter track to take them to debriefing, followed by a breakfast of bacon and eggs and eight hours of solid sleep.

After switching off the aircraft systems, they crowded outside. The stillness of the early morning was disorientating following the hours of vibration and roaring engines. The aerodrome felt like an alien world and he staggered slightly, not quite able to believe they were back. He waved the crew over to see the damaged starboard inner engine. The cowling had gone and the Merlin itself was burnt and blackened. Behind it, the wing looked as though a giant can opener had peeled it away. The red painted inner fuel tank was fully exposed and with a start, he realised that they would have died if the cannon shells had gone just a foot lower.

Memories of the Stirling bomber with flames spewing from its wing over Dusseldorf came to him. *That was almost us,* he thought.

The ground crew appeared, all as excited as puppies and asking about the flight. They turned naturally to Max, who they knew enjoyed spinning a tale. Max pressed a hand into the small of his back to relieve the discomfort of being in the rear turret for so long. Then he described the bomber coned in the searchlights and destroyed, their own escape from the flak, the fight with the Messerschmitt and the bombing run itself. He began well, but when the story reached Dusseldorf, his smile faded and the words slowed. His face creased into a deep frown and the words finally dried on his lips. He stood in the middle of the ground crew and looked at George, lost.

'We almost died half a dozen times tonight.' The shock of that realisation etched itself on his face. 'How the fuck can we get through thirty ops?'

The others turned to George, even the ground crew watched him. He shuffled deeper into his jacket, unsure what to say, he had been thinking the same thing. 'I don't know,' he replied at last. 'One mission at a time, I suppose. That's how we do it.' He felt so tired that he could not think clearly and his brain struggled for something clever to say. Swamped with relief at being safe and from the shock at the dangers, he felt as though he was drunk. The truth was that he agreed with Max. They could not live through twenty-nine more operations like tonight's. The odds were just too great. Again, he rubbed at the creases in his face and thought. Yet, they had survived. They fought off two attacks and bombed the target. He had made mistakes and that would change. The others had too; they should have spotted the Junkers earlier. However, somehow they got through and got back.

182

'We get better and we get luckier. We'll make our own luck,' he said at last.

Max glanced at the others before speaking. 'Luck? We had more than our share of luck tonight. We had all the flaming luck there was, and then some.' He took a pull of his cigarette. 'The way I see it we're all dead men.' The ground crew looked at each other and wandered off towards M-Mother.

Dick Scrivener raised his hand tentatively as if he were still in a classroom. 'Look, for what it's worth, I'd just like to say something.' The others turned to him and he paused, gathering his thoughts before speaking. 'Probability doesn't remember what happened in the past; you start afresh with each roll of the dice. If nothing changes, then our chances stay exactly the same. However, we survived and we can improve the odds, mathematically at least. The skipper is right; our chances alter as we do and not in themselves. I don't know how we do it, or what we do, but tonight each of us learned something. As long as we remember those things and build on them, then statistically our chances get better.' Dick finished with a shrug and George was so grateful he could have hugged him.

'What did he just say?' Max asked.

Jim put an arm around Max's shoulder. 'Reading between the lines, you should take up Dingo's offer of the sheep while you can.'

Max thought about it and smiled. 'Fair enough. How is your mum these days, Dingo?'

Dingo moved towards the gunner just as a truck rattled up. They clambered onboard wrestling and laughing, and George could almost taste the bacon and eggs waiting in the mess.

Chapter 13

RAF Oakley - 11th September 1942

After changing, handing back parachutes and returning survival packs, George and his crew went to the main hall for de-briefing. Three teams, each consisting of a sergeant and two WAAFs interviewed crews while the intelligence officer wandered from table to table behind them, eavesdropping and delving further whenever he heard something of interest. They waited their turn behind the crew of P-Peter.

'How was it?' George asked Tim MacFarlane, P-Peter's pilot. He was a dour Scot whose complete lack of humour George always found unsettling.

'Piece of cake,' MacFarlane shrugged. 'Found the target, dropped the bombs and came home. End of story.'

'Any problems with fighters?' Even before he asked the question, George knew what the answer would be.

'Fighters?' MacFarlane shook his head. 'Hardly saw another aircraft except over Southwold and the target. Why don't tell me you did?'

MacFarlane's patronising manner irritated George. It was as if he were commiserating with a particularly dim pupil over a simple maths problem. 'We tangled with a 109 and an 88. My gunners saw them off though,' George added in defence.

'Good for you Watford,' MacFarlane said without enthusiasm. 'Although, I dare say they would have been better avoided in the first place of course. Were you not weaving and changing height?' MacFarlane glanced pointedly at his crew and raised his eyebrows.

'Yes, I was weaving.' George said calmly while gritting his teeth. MacFarlane made him sound like an amateur, which of course he was, but then again so was MacFarlane.

'Well, better luck next time. I suppose you were just unlucky.' The Scot made the word sound like a code for incompetent.

'Unlucky?' Dingo interrupted. 'Mate, if we hadn't been such a good crew, we could have been a damn sight more unlucky. Just like the poor bastards in the burning aircraft we saw.'

'Burning aircraft?' MacFarlane scoffed. 'Are you sure they were not just 'Scarecrows'?'

'Scarecrows? What are they?' George asked.

'I thought everyone knew?' MacFarlane pursed his lips. 'The opposition send up pyrotechnics that explode into the size and shape of a burning aircraft. They hope it will scare some of the 'windier' crews.'

George felt his anger rising. 'Did you see any?'

'Oh aye, we saw some alright.'

'Did they frighten you?'

MacFarline's expression changed. 'No, they most certainly did not. I have a steady crew, Watford. We know what we are about.' With that, he led his people towards a table just vacated by another crew.

'MacFarlane!' George called and the Scot turned. 'When it's our turn, listen in if you like. You'll hear how to tackle something scarier than a firework.' MacFarlane looked as though he wanted to come back and punch George, but his people dragged him on. When it was their turn, George related their flight, backed up by notes from Dingo and Ned. The IO listened over the shoulder of his sergeant. He queried George about the fighter's tactics, the radar-controlled searchlight and the locations of the flak batteries. George then mentioned that he had seen several bombers shot down.

'Forget those, Watford,' The IO advised as he scribbled in a small notebook. 'They were almost certainly Scarecrows.'

George shook his head. 'Sorry sir, but I saw planes blow up, not fireworks.'

The IO looked down his glasses at George and spoke irritably. 'Just consider, man. There would be no point to Scarecrows if they were not realistic, would there? The mind plays tricks in battle, psychological warfare works that way. Have you never heard of the Mons Angels?' He smiled patronisingly, an expression that reminded George of MacFarlane. 'Anyhow, losses were light by all account and the raid was a great success, you all did very well. Now, have a good breakfast and a long sleep. That's the ticket.'

George nodded and stood up; there was no point in arguing. Could those burning aircraft have been fireworks, clever deceptions? The more he thought about it, the less certain he became. Maybe the ones over Dusseldorf, but surely not the others. He pictured the Wellington with its burning wing folded back, toppling through the night sky. That was no firework.

'That drongo's so full of shit his shoes squelch when he walks.' Dingo muttered once they were outside.

Dick Scrivener walked alongside them. 'Agreed. What I saw was no pyrotechnic. In any case, a device that expands to the size of a bomber would be too large for a shell. Only a rocket could deliver it and that would leave a trail like a comet.'

'So why does the twit insist they're Scarecrows?' Dingo accepted one of Dick's cigarettes and they stopped to light them. The others came back and waited for Dick to answer. George was pleased to see how the slight, bookish bomb aimer had quickly established himself as the brains of the team, the one to consult with difficult problems.

Dick took a quick puff and considered. George always thought he looked ill at ease smoking as if it was something he felt he should do, rather than enjoyed. 'Well, maybe he's right and Scarecrows are hard to distinguish from real aircraft. Alternatively, they may know that Scarecrows don't exist, but encourage belief to hide how many aircraft we're losing.'

'But they give our losses on the BBC, don't they?' Max pointed out. 'Or are you saying they're lying as well?'

Dick creased his brow. 'I don't know, but there's a saying that truth is the first casualty of war.'

'Truth had better join the queue,' Chalky said grimly. 'There's a fair few in front in this one.'

'Can we talk over breakfast?' Max asked. 'I've been looking forward to my bacon and eggs since we left Dusseldorf.'

'You go ahead, I'll catch up,' George said, turning away. 'Something I want to check on first.' The others watched him walk off.

'Where you going, mate?' Dingo called.

He looked back. 'To the control room, I just realised the IO didn't say if we'd lost any Oakley crews tonight.'

'Yeah, I guess he didn't at that. Hold on, we'll come too.' Dingo started after George and beckoned to the others. 'Come on.'

Max followed reluctantly. 'OK, but if that twat MacFarlane and his mob snaffle all the grub, I'll swing for him.'

The control room was a squat building, built partway into the ground for protection. The crew waved their ID cards at an armed guard in the vestibule and pushed open a thick metal door. Beyond was a harshly lit windowless room, saturated with the smells of stale air and old cigarette smoke.

Along the centre, a double row of communication consoles bristled with switches and dials, all but two empty now that the operation was over. On a rostrum above the consoles, the control officer chewed his pencil and stared blankly at a piece of paper. From up there he could see both the console operators and the large status boards lining the wall. He looked up as they entered and nodded at George before returning to his task.

George scanned the status boards, huge blackboards painted with a white grid that gave details of each of the squadron's bombers. His eyes flicked across the columns listing the aircraft's name, pilot, bomb load, takeoff time and the latest time it could still be airborne until he came to the final column, which was entitled 'remarks'. Written here was either 'Returned' or 'Diverted' if the aircraft had landed elsewhere. The letters 'FTR', or Failed-To-Return, were shown if the aircraft was lost. Most aircraft were marked as 'Returned'. F-Freddy had diverted to the emergency runway at Woodbridge and for some reason, K-King was down at Coningsby, probably because of low fuel. However, O-Orange piloted by Taff Morgan was FTR. George pictured Morgan, a stocky and good-natured Welshman, fanatically keen on rugby. He remembered seeing him and his crew tossing a rugby ball between them as they waited by their Lancaster. Now they were missing, most likely dead.

'Sorry, Watford.' The control officer had crossed the room without George noticing. 'I know you got on well. He'll be missed by all of us.'

George was confused; he knew Morgan but not that well. 'Thanks, sir, but I wasn't that friendly with Morgan. I think he was close to Phil Bennet.'

'I didn't mean Morgan. I thought you'd read the whole list.'

George quickly looked back at the board, and scanned down, wondering what he had missed. Near the bottom, U-Uncle was also marked FTR. Its pilot was Smith, his instructor. For a second he gaped in disbelief. Steve Smith had survived thirty operations, he was the man who had all the answers, the man who did everything right.

'He can't be missing, there must be some mistake?'

The control officer shook his head. 'No mistake, I'm sorry to say. Someone reported seeing his aircraft go down over Dusseldorf. I understand they were hit by flak.'

George looked desperately at the controller, remembering the Lancaster exploding in front of them, wondering if that had been him. Even if by some miracle Smith or his crew had survived, the target area was a death trap. There were also reports of German civilians hanging downed flyers or throwing them into the fires. The officer patted George on the back in consolation and returned to his desk.

Dingo ushered him towards the door. 'Sorry mate, Smithy was a good sort.'

He nodded; they would write Dingo's epitaph on many graves before the fighting was over. '*Died for his country, he was a good sort.*'

A cacophony of shouted conversations and nervous laughter swept over them as they entered the mess hall. It was crowded with crews, boisterous and noisy. Young men who had survived their first action and could not stop talking about it. George tried to join in, but anything he said felt hollow and false. The best he could manage was to laugh half-heartedly at banter. Whatever he wanted to say was lost in thoughts of Smith, that patient and clever man who had nursed him through a dozen or more flights. He had convinced himself that skill, training and experience could safeguard them, and now that seemed naive.

MacFarlane had not even seen a fighter, so did that mean he was more skilful or was he just lucky? He had to believe that skill was dominant since it would always be there, whereas fickle luck would come and go. How would Macfarlane react when he faced a pair of night fighters? The words of Dick Scrivener, the mathematician, came back to him. *'Chance alters as we do, not in itself,'* and he hoped that Dick was right. However, Smith had skill and experience by the bucket load and he was dead. George shook his head in exasperation. Whatever the factors were that helped them survive; he now knew that the future was uncertain and tenuous. Their first operation had extinguished the lives of fourteen people from the training squadron, and there was the rest of the tour to come. Twenty-nine more times to play Russian roulette with flak and fighters.

Later, they lay in the darkened Nissen hut with their stomachs full of bacon and eggs, and their minds overflowing with memories of the raid. George listened to the others grunting and shuffling as they waited for sleep. Max started to snore first. The small Londoner had a gift for ditching worry like dirty bath water and he wished he could do the same. Once the fear and excitement had subsided and the images became less vivid, he thought about the future and Millie, indulging in his favourite fantasy. One-day he would take over the farm and he tried to imagine living there with her and working the land together. If she still wanted him, he just had to survive and so much could be his. There was something about her spirit and foreignness that would make life in a small Somerset village seem narrow and unadventurous without her by his side. Slowly he drifted into a troubled sleep, uneasy with thoughts of Millie and the night's raid.

They slept late and only woke when one of the other crews barged into their hut with the mail. It was cold and the tin walls ran with condensation. Jim Ambiolo's bed was nearest the door. He cursed, grabbed the letters and dumped them on Max to distribute, while he hurriedly lit the stove. George had two letters, one from his parents and the other from Millie. He snuggled back under the sheets and saving his parent's letter to last opened Millie's.

'Dear George,

Thank you for your last letter, which I greatly enjoyed. It is wonderful now that you are back in England. I missed you greatly while you were away and although I relished your letters, they often made the distance between us seem greater. As always, I apologise that my correspondence was often few and far between. My job is very demanding and it was impossible to write more often at the time hopefully it will be easier now.

I hope that your training is going well. Life continues much as before for me, with work taking up most of my time. The thing you will notice most is that the shortages have grown worse, with more and more items now rationed. Fortunately, we find other ways to make do and the whole country seems to have become increasingly inventive. However, I am certain that the thing people want more than any other is the return of peace. Although, ours are small sacrifices when compared to those fighting or the poor souls bombed in cities.

I expect you are anxious to visit your home and see your loved ones, and my work will only permit a short time off, but if you are able, perhaps you could stop over in London on your way. I should very much like to see you again. If this appeals, please tell me when you will get leave....'

She went on to describe a show that she had seen and filled two further pages with everyday gossip, but the wonderful thing was that she wanted to see him. Basking in warm anticipation, he lay back on the bed and reread the letter. Later, the sentence about *poor souls bombed in cities* began to bother him. Did she mean just British cities or German ones as well? Recently, he had noticed some newspapers expressing doubts about the bombing. Even Butch Harris's Chaplin was against it. Although last night's target was the industrial centre of Dusseldorf, a salvo of bombs took twenty seconds to release and with bombers flying at around two hundred miles-per-hour, even the most accurate bombing spilt into other areas. It bothered him, although not because he felt overly sorry for civilians, the war would stop tomorrow if civilians stopped making bullets and tanks. However, concern for the targets diluted the bravery of bomber crews and he knew first-hand the courage it took to fly to Germany and back. He lay on the pillow and stared at the curved tin ceiling. They had twenty-nine more ops to fly and he felt windy after the first. How would he feel after ten with another twenty to go? Or after twenty-five, if he survived that long? One thing was for certain, it was now near pointless thinking too much about the future because the likelihood was that none of them would live past the year's end. They had weeks of training left before leave and then a very uncertain and violent future waited.

Chapter 14

London - 22nd October 1942

Although the train from Bicester was crowded, George found a seat by the window and tried to ignore the other passengers as they squeezed in beside him. He wiped condensation from the glass and stared at the passing countryside, feeling nervous at the thought of seeing Millie again. A year was a long time and things would have changed. Or rather, there had been so much time for things to change. Soon he would find out, one way or the other. On the luggage rack opposite, his canvas kitbag took up too much space, causing some of the other passengers to sit with bags and cases on their knees. He wondered if he should move it but decided that would be just too difficult. At Risborough, he gave up his seat to a mother and her child and went to stand in the corridor.

Signs of the war became more apparent as the train approached London. At first, it was just the odd damaged building, but he soon saw whole streets destroyed. The house walls just battered shells like row after row of rotten teeth. The destruction seemed worse now than it did back in the Blitz. He wondered if Dusseldorf was like this, or would it be worse? Part of him felt glad that he had repaid the enemy, but another part of him recoiled at the waste. For a fraction of the cost of this war, they could feed and clothe the whole country for years. George shook his head and steadied himself as the train rattled into Marylebone Station.

As soon as they stopped, there was a rush to escape and George was swept along with the crowd. Outside the station the sun now shone and finding a space on the pavement, he took off his greatcoat, hitched up his kitbag and gasmask case and set off along the busy streets. His first sight of

London in two years was both depressing and inspiring. Every building appeared to have its windows either boarded over or taped up, but surprisingly the many bomb-damaged shops were still open for business, although often with sandbag walls built across broken frontages. Teams of labourers cleared rouble, helped by mechanical diggers where the damage was extensive. It seemed that someone in charge had things organised.

It was early afternoon and he had arranged to meet Millie at a café in Bayswater later that day. He knew London reasonably well and decided to walk the few miles to use up time, as well as to gather his thoughts.

Turning a corner, he came across large crowds lining both sides of the road, all looking excitedly back towards Saint Pauls Cathedral. Curious, he craned his head to where they were looking. In the distance, marching columns approached and a band played.

'What's happening?' he asked the person next to him.

The man looked at George in surprise. He was middle-aged and wore a city suit of pinstripes and bowler hat. He puffed at his pipe before pointing the stem towards the sound. 'Why it's the Yanks. They're parading their first troops through the city.'

George watched the band stride past, followed by several columns of marching soldiers. The men themselves looked confident, fit and well fed. The final column wore dark jackets and white trousers, smart enough to be guardsmen. The crowd waved small paper American flags and George joined in the cheering. American aircraft already operated from British bases, but it was particularly reassuring to have their soldiers here as well.

Once the parade passed he continued his journey, humming a tune that the band had played and feeling far more assured than at the start of the day. Just past Paddington Station, the damage to Bishop's Bridge Road was extensive and most buildings were either hollow shells or rubble. There were few people but crossing the road, he suddenly felt certain someone was following him. He stopped quickly, turned and came face to face with her.

'Millie?' he stammered. With hair bunched behind her neck and wearing a brown topcoat over a smart grey jacket and skirt, she looked stunning. He immediately felt the same longing for her, the same tension.

She stood grinning. 'Bother, I thought being disguised as Churchill would fool you.'

'Churchill?' George said in confusion, before realising that she was joking. 'You need a cigar, Churchill always has a cigar.'

'Hello, George. It's good to see you again.'

'And you too,' he replied feeling his senses race and his thoughts becoming leaden. 'How are you?' She looked the same as he remembered, but if anything those dark brown eyes were even livelier and more piercing. She stared as if daring him to do something.

'It's been a year since we last met and all you can do is to ask me how I am.' She put her hands on her hips in the pretence of irritation. 'Well, I'm in good health thank you for asking. Now kiss me.'

George dropped his kitbag and greatcoat on the pavement and took her in his arms. He had thought of this moment for so long that he had to remind himself it was real. However, the feel of her body, the smell of her perfume and the taste the smoothness of her lips were so much more intoxicating than he could have imagined.

'There, that wasn't so bad was it?' she asked, pulling away.

'I could get used to it.'

'And who said you will have the chance?' she laughed.

'How...' he began, but she interrupted him.

'How did I come to be following you? I guessed you would come this way and I've been waiting.'

'You have, why?'

'You ask so many questions George and none of the important ones.' She stepped past him and beckoned. 'Come on, let's dump your bag at my place and then we can eat and drink at a restaurant around the corner. You can ask all the questions you like once we're comfortable.'

'I thought we were meeting at a café?' He trudged along beside her, feeling clumsy and light-headed with pleasure, uncertain what to say and wishing he had planned some clever words.

'There isn't a cafe, but there is a restaurant.'

As they walked, Millie talked about London and the bombing. Close by was the hotel where she lived, taken over for the duration by the department that employed her. It was a Georgian building, fronted with mock pillars and decorated with ornate mouldings. A sign at the door stated, 'MINISTRY OF WATER SUPPLY'. Inside, a guard wearing a civilian suit staffed the reception desk and George noticed a revolver sized bulge under his jacket. The guard waved Millie through with hardly a glance but gave George a hard stare.

'It's OK Charlie, he's with me,' Millie told him. The guard nodded but continued to watch as they headed for the stairs.

'Friendly type,' George commented.

'Believe me, they're not chosen for conversation.'

It was a small but imposing building whose grandeur had faded in line with its new role. Beneath ornate and dusty cornices, black scuff marks streaked the greying walls, while they walked on threadbare carpets and cracked floor tiles.

197

Around the foyer, white squares showed at regular intervals where paintings once hung. Millie led him up a wide staircase to the third floor and down a short corridor whose floor sloped slightly to the left. Deeper inside the building the air smelt stagnant and musty. She unlocked a door halfway along and they entered a compact room just big enough for a bed, wardrobe, chest of drawers and a small desk. However, it was luxurious compared to the Nissen hut that he shared with his crew. Best of all was the view of a park. Dumping his bag and coat, he crossed to the window. It was darkening rapidly, but people still wandered through the grounds. It could easily be a pre-war evening if the majority had not been in uniform. Beyond the park, rows of tall buildings were visible, some damaged but many not. Above it all floated two barrage balloons, ever-present reminders of the war.

Beside the window, a photograph set in a thick silver frame sat on the chest of drawers. The frame was ornate, decorated with silver flowers and leaves interlaced with swirling stems. It looked expensive and out of place. There was also something foreign about the heaviness of the design and he decided that Millie must have brought it from her home in Munich. The photograph itself was of a middle-aged couple sitting on a small settee, with three children behind them. The tallest, and in the centre, was Millie.

'My family,' she said simply, lifting the frame and staring at the photograph. She passed it to him and he tilted it into the fading light. Millie's father was difficult to see clearly, he wore spectacles and sported a thick beard, but Millie's eyes seemed similar to his. Her mother was slight and erect, sitting very primly with both hands clasped on her lap. Her brother and sister were much younger and shorter and both had mischievous half-grins. Millie looked youthful in the photograph, a girl still rather than a woman, but she was full of seriousness and stared directly into the camera.

'You have your father's eyes.' He passed back the photograph. 'Have you had any news of them?'

She replaced the frame and lightly traced the top edge with her finger. 'I make enquires whenever I can of course and my contacts do all that is possible, but no, nothing.'

He suddenly noticed how close she was, the sweetness of her perfume and how the bed was just behind them. She looked at him and he felt dizzy with temptation, but the bed was a step too far. Her eyes searched his but then the moment passed and she turned and crossed to the door.

'Come on, we'd better go or Charlie downstairs will wonder what we're up to.' Again, that teasing smile and those deep, dark eyes.

'Sure you don't mind if I leave my kitbag here?'

'That's why I invited you up to my room, isn't it? I think I can allow it without too much risk to my good name.'

Outside it was now dark and people hurried home along blacked-out streets. Millie looped her arm through his and he tucked her into his side for protection as on-coming pedestrians suddenly appeared in front of them. Millie delved into her handbag and produced a torch, its lens painted blue because of the blackout. It was next to useless but at least it warned of their presence.

'When does your train go? I mean, how long can you stay?' she asked him.

'The last train leaves Paddington at eleven, I should be fine if I catch it,' he replied, even though he knew it would mean sleeping on a station bench in Bath until the first train to his village. 'There's a small station a few miles from where I live. It's not a difficult journey.' Was it his imagination, or did he feel her grip on his arm loosen?

'Then you will be home with your loved ones,' she said quietly. 'That will be nice for you after so long away.'

'Sorry Millie, I can understand how hard it is for you to be apart from your home and family.'

She was silent for a few seconds. 'It's not just the separation; it's more that I don't know where they are or even if they're still alive. Those are the hard things.'

They walked down some steps to a cellar restaurant. Just inside the door, through heavy blackout curtains, was a large area of tables and booths. The light was dazzling after the blackness outside and the air was so thick with a fug of tobacco, alcohol and cooking that he found it hard to breathe. It was noisy too and full of servicemen from a variety of countries. Most looked as though they had been there all afternoon and from the bottles littering the tables they seemed more interested in drinking than eating. A plump waiter with a cloth tucked into his belt bustled across and showed them to a booth where they sat on opposite sides of a small table. The seat creaked dangerously under his weight and the table wobbled when he touched it, threatening to topple a dusty pot of fabric flowers. However, it was intimate, discrete and he hoped, inexpensive.

'So why did you follow me?' He asked once they had settled.

She smiled and picked up the menu card. 'I wanted to see if you were as I remembered before we met again. If you had become fat and bald I would have left you searching for the café.'

'And am I the same?'

'Yes, very much the same,' she said with a grin. 'Still tall and stiff, typically English.'

'Not all Englishmen are tall.'

'Then, maybe their stiffness makes them seem so. At least you haven't gotten fat or lost your hair.'

There was little choice on the menu so they ordered the set dinner and a bottle of wine, which to his relief, and thanks to rationing laws, cost only a few shillings. Although he received flying pay, his wages were no more than his father paid him on the farm, less if you counted his small share from market days. Fortunately, the intensity of flying in Canada gave few opportunities to spend, so he had scraped together some savings. The waiter returned with a bottle and as George poured, he watched her over his glass. This was someone he had known for just a few hours, maybe a day in total. Yet she consumed his thoughts and inhabited his dreams. The yearlong absence in Canada only seemed to have intensified his feelings. But did she feel the same about him?

'I've missed you,' he began, edging his way into a discussion about them.

'I'm just glad you haven't forgotten me,' she replied. 'Didn't you find a nice Canadian girl?'

'Just one. She became very special.'

'Really...' Millie's voice trailed off.

'Yes, she used to sit outside the fence with her bear cubs and growl until I threw them food.'

Millie laughed. 'I thought you were serious for a moment.'

'I was, but it would never have worked, she looked too much like my dad.'

'That's a horrible thing to say. Poor bear, looking like a Watford. I'm sure she was very pretty.' He poured more wine and finished the bottle. A hovering waiter quickly brought another.

Their soup arrived and he stared doubtfully at it, feigning interest until the waiter left. It consisted of small lumps of non-descript vegetables floating in a tomato broth. Still, he had not eaten since breakfast and found it tasted better than it looked. In fact, it tasted pretty good.

'When you came to Scotland you said that we could be more than friends. You said you would be my girlfriend.'

She stared at him for an instant and he could not read her expression. Reticence? Pleasure? It could have been either. 'I would still like to be your girlfriend,' she said carefully. 'But we must take things slowly. I cannot rush into a relationship.'

'We've been apart for a year, it's hardly rushing things. Any slower and we'll need walking sticks when we go out.'

She smiled. 'Yes, but it's not just time. I need to get to know you.'

'You're not certain that you like me enough?' he asked, desperate to know now that he had found the courage to ask.

'No,' she said. 'It's not that. I like you a lot, too much probably.'

'Then what? I don't understand.' She started to speak and then changed her mind. 'I love you, Millie,' he said filling the silence.

'Love?' she said the word slowly. 'That word is so easy to say and so difficult to prove.'

'Then give me the chance to prove it. I have two week's leave. I could stay in London and we could see each other every day. I can prove it if you let me.' Her eyes met his and seemed to search him. Almost every day for a year, he had thought about those lovely clever eyes. It was so frustrating.

'Believe me, George. I would like to spend more time with you, but it cannot happen,' she said finally. 'There are things going on in my life, in my work that means I have little free time. I had to call in a number of favours to see you today.'

'Do you have someone else?' he asked, trying hard but failing to mask his disappointment.

'No, there is no one else,' she said quietly. 'Sometimes I almost wish there could be, but you have claimed that place. I just cannot be hurried.'

'Your letters were so few that I began to feel sure you had met someone else,' he said.

'I wanted to write more, it's just that it was... impossible.'

'This job of yours, whatever it is,' he said in resignation.

'I know it sounds lame, but that's entirely the reason. One day I will explain and I hope you will understand, but not now. Tell me about Canada,' she said and smiled at him. 'Let's not be gloomy.'

Reluctantly he let the subject drop and spoke of the past year. With Millie, he felt able to speak of the real joys without embarrassment. Of Canada's crystal skies and the thousands of stars so bright that he felt able to touch them. High altitude night flights when Calgary's lights shone for over a hundred miles. Clouds that tumbled like foam over the Rockies and the endless flat prairie stretching so far into the distance that it hurt his eyes just to follow it.

'What adventures you've had,' she said sincerely. 'It sounds wonderful. I'd love to see Canada.'

'Maybe we can go there after the war?'

'I'd like that,' she replied guardedly.

He quickly changed the subject. 'I'm sorry you haven't traced your family. Is there no news at all?'

She shrugged. 'Nothing specifically about my family. All I know for sure is that the Gestapo arrested my parents and that before the war my brother and sister were in southern France. I've heard odd snippets, reports that Jewish children from the Kindertransport have been hidden in the mountains.'

'You think your brother and sister are one of them?'

She took another sip of wine and shrugged. 'I have to believe they are safe. If some children have been sheltered by French families then why not my brother and sister? It's possible. Someone has to win in a lucky dip.'

He nodded and tried to look optimistic, but he felt she was clutching at straws. 'I hope you get good news.' The waiter cleared their soup bowls and brought the next course. George went to refill their glasses but found the bottle was again empty, so he waved it at the waiter for another.

Millie smiled. 'I'm hopeful that they are all safe. It's one of the reasons I have to be at work. Things are happening in France right now and there might be news. As we Germans say, '*Tu nur das Rechte in deinen Sachen; Das andre wird sich von selber machen.'* '

'What does that mean?' George asked. Millie's accent was now so English that it surprised him to remember she was German. Then the waiter brought another bottle, just as a group of Polish soldiers by a piano on the other side of the room began singing. It was a sad, plaintive song and after every chorus, a different person sang a verse. They listened silently until George asked, 'do you know what they're singing about?'

Millie smiled. 'Yes, it's a song of regret.'

'What do they regret?'

'They wish they had gone to a country where the lazy natives bothered to learn more than one language.'

George laughed. 'You think you're so bloody clever, don't you?'

'Yes, actually I do. They only take the best brains at the Ludwig Maximilian University and they took me.'

'Well if you're so clever, what are you doing in a dank restaurant with a low life sergeant?'

She looked at him, her eyes dark and searching. 'Because you have something more valuable than intelligence, you have decency.'

He stared at her for a second. *Decency*? Dear God what a joke. Here he was with a girl he loved, a girl he obsessed over and putting on a show of restraint and gentlemanliness when all the while he wanted to make love to her. Before he could speak, a large hand landed on his shoulder. He turned and saw the red face of a drunken Polish officer grinning at him.

'You like our song?' he asked loudly in deeply accented English.

George sensed something good-natured in the expression and smiled back. 'Yes, it was very good,' he replied.

The Pole nodded, satisfied. 'You are flyer? A Pilot?' he continued.

George nodded. 'Yes I'm a pilot,' he answered and wondered how he could get rid of the soldier politely.

'You fly Spitfires. Kill many *boche*?'

'I fly Lancasters,' George corrected.

The soldier looked puzzled. 'Lancasters?' he repeated, sounding the syllables as if he were chewing them. Then he shrugged. 'Never mind. One day they let you fly Spitfires, I know for certain. Now you come sing for us,' and he pulled George's arm.

'What?' George recoiled. 'I can't sing.'

'You like our song, now you sing for us,' the Pole insisted logically.

'Go on, George. It's only fair,' Millie laughed. He glanced at her in desperation but she shoved him forward. 'Show them what an Englishman can do.'

Reluctantly he allowed himself to be steered to the piano, where he mentioned a tune to the pianist. The Pole announced him and the room clapped and banged their glasses on the tables. George took a small bow and waited for the music to begin.

He had sung the song so many times before, but never alone. Each line required a different action and he began with his hands clasped on his heart.

'A young aviator lay dying
At the end of a fine winter's day
When to the surprise of his comrades,
These brave parting words he did say:
Take the manifold out of my larynx,
Take the butterfly valve from my brain,
Remove from my liver the crankshaft
And assemble the engine again.'

The explosion smashed open the door and tore down the blackout curtains. Belatedly, a siren began to wail. 'Air raid!' someone shouted and in a daze, he ran to Millie's side.

'There's a shelter nearby, hurry!' she said urgently. George followed, grabbing something from their table as he passed.

Customers rushed to the door and he forced a space in the press for Millie to slip through. Along the road to the left, a building was on fire. Heat gusted from it like the back-draft of a Merlin engine, scattering showers of burning embers. Millie led him to the right and then at the junction, down some steps and into a tube station. Weary Londoners were already settling for the night, spreading blankets and pillows on platforms. Trying to snatch what sleep they could. Millie tugged him to a space by the wall and they snuggled next to each other on the hard floor. He pulled the wine bottle from his greatcoat pocket and two tumblers. Millie smiled when she saw this.

'There's hope for you after all, George. You're not as dim as you try to make out.'

'And not as decent as you try to make out either,' he replied.

'I very much hope not, decency can be so tedious at times.'

He poured them each a glass of wine and they sipped it gratefully. 'This takes me back to when we first met,' he said.

'You didn't bring any booze with you that time, though,' she reminded him.

'In those days I was just an Erk with dreams of flying. I hadn't even tasted proper wine, only the stuff that my folks make.'

'And now you're a pilot.'

'Now I'm a pilot.'

Millie snuggled closer to him and tipped the glass to her lips. 'You know, this tastes better the more you drink.'

'They say practice makes perfect.' He tried to focus on the advertisements across the underground tracks opposite but gave up. 'I have to say, I'm feeling pretty plastered.'

'Me too,' she replied dreamily. 'But, nicely plastered.'

They must have fallen asleep because he remembered nothing until the 'all clear' sounded and he felt her stir. She stretched and asked, 'What will you do now?'

'Now?' George tried to think, his thoughts muddled from sleep and wine. 'I've been posted to an operational squadron. I guess I'll just try to do my best and hope to survive.'

'No, idiot, I mean tonight. You've missed your train.'

He sat up with a start and glanced at his watch, it was almost midnight. 'Damn. I'll sleep in the station until the first one in the morning.'

She snuggled next to him and said sleepily, 'I can find you a bed for the night and it won't cost a penny.'

He looked into her eyes and felt a stab of excitement. 'That sounds good. I guess even air raids have a silver lining.'

'It's better than you think,' she added.

'How can that be?'

'Because I've just realised that we left without paying for the meal.'

George laughed and held her close.

The harsh swish of curtains and sharp morning light woke him with a start. He blinked groggily, uncertain for a moment where he was. Then a warm glow of happiness as memories of the delicious intimacy of their lovemaking filled him. However, these quickly faded when he saw her expression.

'You must get dressed,' Millie said briskly. 'I have to get you out of here before the others are up.' She was already clothed in her uniform.

'Is everything OK?' he asked doubtfully, confused by her coolness. He reached for her but she turned away and gathered his scattered clothing. 'What's wrong?'

'There's no time now,' she replied evasively and tossed the bundle onto the bed. 'We must hurry.'

She smuggled him out through a fire escape door at the back of the building. Before they reached the main road, he grabbed her arm and turned her to him. 'What is the matter?' he asked, determined to have an answer.

Millie looked away before speaking. 'Last night should not have happened,' she said quietly.

'But you were happy,' he told her, uncertain what to say to make things right.

'It was the wine and the bombing. I didn't want it to happen like that.'

'Well I'm glad it did,' he said defiantly, not wanting to dismiss a memory so pleasant. 'I love you.'

'I told you before that I wanted things to move slowly between us. I'm not ready for... for *this*,' she said spitting out the word.

'So what now?' he asked, as lost and bewildered as a child whose Christmas present is taken away. She did not look at him and he could tell that she wanted to go, to be away from him. He felt desperate.

'I need time to think. I can't decide now.' she said and gently removed his hand from her arm. 'I'll write once I've thought things through.' She kissed him lightly, turned and left, disappearing into the morning crowds. For a long time, he simply stood looking in the direction that she had taken, hoping she might turn back. As the seconds turned to minutes, he felt certain he had lost the only person he had ever loved and almost shivering with grief, he tramped the streets to Paddington Station feeling utterly miserable.

Chapter 15

Somerset - 9th October 1942

The Somerset and Dorset stopping train rattled between Bath and each small station until it finally arrived at the halt near Torcombe. It was mid-morning and the train nearly empty so George enjoyed a compartment to himself, a luxury he rarely knew these days. The countryside passed slowly by the window, occasionally obscured by wafting grey smoke from the engine. It was so familiar that he felt a deep and visceral joy at seeing it again after so long. The rolling Somerset hills and gentle valleys gave him a sense of belonging that he would never feel elsewhere. He admired the vast prairies of Canada and awed at the Rocky Mountains, but this would always be the landscape of home. The train shuddered to a stop and he grabbed his kitbag and stumbled onto the platform. Everything was as he remembered, but as the train pulled away, he worried that he had become a stranger. It had been over a year since he was last home and with only occasional visits in the twelve months before that. Two years had changed him from a farmer's son into someone else.

Millie had changed him too. She loosened the connections with his past and made him realise that there was a whole world where he could be more, or at least, different. Before the war, flying was new, glamorous and available only to the rich. It held a mystery that few would ever experience. She saw him not as a farmer's boy but a pilot and knew nothing of the baggage that life in a remote village carried with it. Thinking of her brought memories of last night. The thrill of them undressing each other and falling into bed. Her softness and scent, and the way she curled her body into his so wantonly. It was perfect. He loved her very much, but would she want him now? Would he ever see her again? All he knew was that he loved her and wanted to be with her, but last night may have destroyed any chance of that. In the restaurant, she said that she wanted their relationship to build slowly. Why had he not listened? Too much wine on an empty stomach was just an excuse and one that he might have to pay for.

Torcombe was over a mile from its tiny station and their farm was two miles further on from the village. In front, the road led up a hill to the school and church, and then down the other side to the village. George hitched his bag onto his shoulder and climbed head down, lost in reflection, striding at a brisk pace as he thought things through. The trouble was that although he loved Millie, he did not really understand her. At heart, he was an English country boy while Millie was German and from a large city. They even had different religions. She was cosmopolitan, educated and their lives and experiences were very different. She wanted to move their relationship slowly so that trust could grow, then after a couple of bottles of cheap wine, they spent the night together. Once again, he felt like kicking himself. How could she trust him now? He should have acted honourably, not drank too much and taken her to bed. What a fool he was.

The village school suddenly appeared on the right and he stood by its low boundary wall, listening to the sounds of children reciting verse inside. The drone of their voices rose and fell in a rhythm of indiscernible words and he smiled at the memory of doing much the same, and with exactly the same teacher. Further up the road, a few yards on from the vicarage, stood the church. It had Norman origins but was not grand enough to boast a steeple and he always thought it looked incomplete with just a stunted bell tower. On impulse, he pushed open the wicket gate and went inside. He believed in God, although apart from RAF's parades his church attendance had been poor these past few years. However, he had several things to thank Him for, one or two requests to make and a large number of apologies to offer.

The muted atmosphere inside the church was more than just spiritual. The building contained serenity and stillness found nowhere else and a peacefulness that affected him deeply. As a child, he once went inside alone and summoned the courage to shout. His sharp voice echoed off the walls with a harshness that felt like sacrilege. He never tried it again. Now his footsteps echoed on the flagstone floor as he walked to a front pew. From here, he could gaze up at the stained glass windows behind the Altar and, as he had done so often as a child, enjoy colours so vivid that they seemed unreal. Bowing his head, he prayed silently. Afterwards, he noticed the verse from Mathew engraved on the wall. *'For what is a man profited, if he shall gain the whole world, and lose his own soul?'* Until that moment, he had never fully appreciated the wisdom of those words and he hoped it was not the reply to his prayer. Suddenly, the contradiction helped him reach a decision. From now on, he would be a person of two parts. When he was a pilot, fighting the war and risking his life, he would be one person, but at home, he would be another, his old self. He would keep the two halves separate so that there was no risk of cross-contamination. Then, once the war was over, he would abandon his wartime self and forget that person as if he never existed. He would wrap him in brown paper and string and bury him deep in a hole at the bottom of his memory, never to emerge.

Beyond the church, the road led down into the valley and he caught his first glimpse of Torcombe, with its thirty houses and a pub lining the single road. His eyes immediately focused on the hill behind, which was the edge of their farm. Now he walked faster, the heavy kit bag feeling light on his shoulder. His old life had seemed so distant minutes before, but now he knew it was still there, just waiting to slip on like a pair of old and comfortable shoes. His mother would be happy to see him, but he wondered how his father would react. His last leave had not been a happy one.

At the start of the track leading to the farm, he stopped and rested a hand on the five-bar gate. In front, he could see his home. The farmhouse was large, solid and unperturbed by wind and rain or the passing decades. Its outbuildings were old, thick-walled, sturdy and so mellowed by age and usage that they seemed part of the countryside. It was a good place, solid and comfortable. Built of light coloured Cotswold stone, it had a roof of thick brown tiles above six windows. Once the war was over, he could settle here and maybe with Millie. That thought pleased him and he hoped it would please her, if she ever spoke to him again of course.

George pushed open the gate and walked up the track to the door. The front garden was barer, with fewer vegetables than when he had tended it, but everything else looked much the same. As he came closer, the bittersweet smell of cows and manure gave way to the rich scents of cooking. During the past year, he had thought about this reunion so often and just for an instant, he savoured the anticipation. Pressing the latch, he stepped into the hallway and put his kitbag on the slab-stone floor. Further into the house, he could hear his mother working in the kitchen, the sound exactly as he remembered. He filled his senses with home and looked around the kitchen door to see her familiar figure.

'Hello, Mum,' he said gently, not wanting to startle her.

She shrieked and spun around, her eyes wide with disbelief. 'George,' she yelled and threw herself at him. 'Oh George, it's you.'

He lifted her from the ground and spun her around, laughing with joy until she cried for him to stop. 'Put me down you great ape or you'll break my back!' He hoped her tears were from happiness and not pain.

'I can't believe you're back at last,' she said, collapsing against him and sobbing. 'Oh George, I was beginning to think I'd never see you again.' She quickly composed herself and pushed him away. Holding him at arm's length, she looked him up and down, taking in every inch of his uniform and all it meant. In turn, George felt a twinge of sadness to see how much his mother had aged. He remembered her as strong, erect and youthful. Now she seemed smaller, thinner and older. She dabbed her eyes with her pinny and pulled him towards the door. 'Come on, your father's in the milking parlour, let's surprise him.'

'Will he be pleased to see me?' he asked, remembering their parting before he went to Canada.

She smiled. 'You know what he's like, son,' she said kindly. 'Your father is a worrier, always has been. But he's missed you and it's changed him, made him realise that we mustn't stand in your way anymore.'

'I'm my own person, mum. I can't change that.'

'I know. It's just that we were both so worried when the war started. Then you got a job on the ground and we thought you would be safe. But being injured in the Blitz and then volunteering for aircrew panicked us, it really did. Dad didn't mean what he said and I know he regrets it now.'

The trouble was that although he understood how his parents felt, they had not seen the Blitz or the bodies. They had not watched hundreds of Luftwaffe bombers destroying London.

'Come on then, let's go and surprise him.'

The back garden was much as the front, tended, but not as carefully as before. Potatoes, carrots and onions grew in coarse rows. His parents had clearly done their best in the time available and they were far luckier than most, but it was sad to see how the war had even diminished their garden.

'Jack!' his mother called towards the cowshed. 'Come out for a moment, please.' Her voice was brisk, giving nothing away. Cows meandered in the yard outside the building bellowing impatiently for the hay and cow cake waiting in the stalls. The door opened and his father shuffled out, hunched over from the effort. His mother's appearance was a surprise, but his father looked much worse. He was drawn, spare and seemed to have shrivelled. He wore a heavy overcoat that was too big for him and looked like a caricature of an old man. Jack Watford muttered something under his breath and looked up. Immediately, his eyes widened in pleasure when he saw his son.

'George!' he croaked and stepped forward.

There was no sign of the disappointment and anger that had been so close to the surface in the past and George rushed to embrace him. 'Hello Dad,' he beamed. 'It's good to see you again.'

'We've missed you,' his father replied simply and George felt him tremble as he held him. 'The farm hand can finish off. Let's go and have some tea, I want to hear what you've been doing.' His father turned back to the milking parlour and shouted. 'Chester, I'm going indoors. Finish off will you?' An acknowledgement sounded from inside the building.

Then his father stumbled slightly and George grabbed him. 'Are you OK?' he asked. 'You don't look well.'

'Of course he's not well,' his mother interrupted crossly. 'He's been running a fever for days now, but he still won't rest.' George knew his mother only become angry when she was worried.

'You shouldn't be working if you're ill, dad,' George told him.

'Outside day and night when he should be in bed,' she scolded her husband

They helped his father into the house and sat him on the sofa. The fire was ready for the evening and it needed only a match to the twists of newspaper beneath the kindling for the flames to take hold. 'There, the room should be warmer soon,' George said.

His father smiled at him. 'Thanks, son,' he wheezed. 'I don't feel so good if I'm honest.'

'You don't look too good, either. Mind you, you were no oil painting to start with,' George replied, grinning at him. He reached out and touched his father's forehead; it felt hot and clammy, feverish. He checked his pulse; it pounded like a steam hammer. The old man coughed loudly and held a rag to his mouth.

'He's worse today,' his mother said quietly. 'It started as a cold a few weeks ago. I thought he was getting over it and he would have too if he'd spent a couple of days in bed. But no, he just has to keep working.'

'I'll get all the rest there is when I'm dead,' his father wheezed.

'No you won't,' she told him sharply. 'I'm going to put your ashes in an egg timer and make you work in the kitchen for a change.'

The old man's laugh turned into a cough and this time when he removed the rag, beads of sweat glistened his brow. His face was white and his cheeks were blotched red.

216

'I think we'd better get the doctor,' George said. It shocked him to see his father so ill. He had always seemed strong and indestructible, but now he looked frail, beaten.

The old man looked confused. 'A doctor? We don't need to waste money on a doctor.' His father put a hand to his brow and felt the dampness there. 'I'm fine. Just let me lay down for a bit.'

'No you're not fine you old fool. You're a long way from being fine,' his mother snapped, looking worried. 'Thank goodness George is home to make you see sense. I'll phone the surgery.' She hurried into the hallway, while George went to the kitchen and searched for a dishcloth to wet in the sink. When he returned his father was slumped back and his right arm dangled loosely on the floor. He looked dead.

'Dad!' George yelled, leaping to his side and shaking him.

The old man's eyes opened. 'Hello George,' he said weakly. 'What's happening?'

'You old fraud, I thought you were dead.'

'Dead? Dear Lord, I hope not. You shouldn't have a headache like this in heaven.'

'Who says you'll go to heaven,' George said, gently placing the cold wet cloth on his father's head. 'It could be the other place.'

'It probably is if you're here. They don't allow the 'Brylcreem Boys' anywhere respectable.' He coughed and adjusted the dripping dishcloth. 'Thanks, that feels better.' He held George's arm and looked at him. 'I'm sorry we parted on bad terms, son. I was wrong to stand in your way, I can see that now.'

George gave a smile of understanding. 'That's water under the bridge, dad,' he said. 'In any case, I'd like to come back to the farm once this is over.'

'Honestly?' his father asked.

'Truly,' George confirmed.

The old man nodded and looked away to hide his misting eyes. 'Now tell me all about flying and Canada.'

'I'll tell you later. It's best that you try to sleep now,' he said and watched his father close his eyes.

Just then, his mother burst through the door. 'The doctor's coming right away,' she said. 'How is he?'

'He needs peace and quiet, let's leave him be until the doctor gets here.' He turned back to his father. 'Try to rest. I'll be in the kitchen with mum.'

Leaving the doors open in case his father called, he ushered his mother away. The kitchen was stiflingly hot from the range, just as he remembered it. Surprisingly, there were eight or nine large pies on the table. Some were cooling and others already wrapped in muslin; it was like a production line.

'Why all the pies, mum?' he asked curiously.

'Oh, that's just my sideline these days.'

'Sideline? What do you mean?'

'Are you hungry?' she asked and George felt sure she was avoiding answering. 'How about bacon and eggs? I picked mushrooms in the field yesterday.'

'Yes, please,' he replied. 'As long as I'm not taking them from you and dad.'

'We've got plenty. Now put the kettle on the stove and we'll have that cup of tea.'

'So who are the pies for?' he asked again.

She looked at him irritably. 'They're for Mr Dryden. He pays us for them.' Mr Dryden was an old friend of George's father. He owned a business in Bath and had many connections, someone who did *favours* for his network of friends. For years, they exchanged vegetables and meat with him for anything that came his way. Clothing, building materials, carpets and furniture, items otherwise too expensive in the cash-strapped times after the Depression. It was an arrangement that suited many people.

George filled the kettle and put it on the stove's hot plate, saying nothing but still confused by her reticence. Selling pies hardly seemed a crime. If it were then most of the Woman's Institute would be behind bars. He raised an eyebrow for her to continue. She frowned and eventually said,

'Don't be cross with us, George. It's not been easy. We needed fuel for the farm machines and even though we get an allowance from the government, it's not enough. Mr Dryden gets fuel from the American aerodrome just the other side of Bath. He trades it for my pies.' She reached into the pantry, lifted out a large side of pork and deftly sliced off four thick rashers. That much meat would have been a rare treat even before the war and these days, it would be a month's ration for a whole family. Then there was the meat used to make the pies. Something odd was going on.

'I don't know what we would have done without him, I really don't.' She put a lump of lard in the frying pan and pushed past George to the range. 'I gave him a pie on one visit and the next time he came he said that if I could make half a dozen, he could trade them with an American for petrol.'

'You make pies so Mr Dryden can get stolen petrol to keep dad in work?'

She looked at him sheepishly and he tried not to smile. 'Well yes, I did at first. Then he offered to pay me for any extra I could make. The pies you get from the butchers these days are just vegetables and gristle. People want proper meat in their pie and they'll pay well for them. So now, he comes every week and I give him six for petrol and the rest for money. I told your father you wouldn't like it, you've always been such an upright child.'

George was not sure what surprised him most, the insight into his character or discovering his mother ran the local black-market pie concession.

'How many pies do you make?'

She fluttered her hands as if the question was an irritating fly. 'Oh, I don't know. It just depends on how much meat I have.'

'How many?' George insisted.

'You know how I like to cook,' she said in self-defence. 'I suppose it's all got a bit out of hand, really. I make twenty to thirty every week.' She looked at him appealingly.

No wonder she's tired, George thought. He frowned until he could no longer keep a straight face. 'I think it's wonderful,' he told her, laughing. 'How can you manage it? I mean, I thought all livestock had to be registered and was government controlled?'

Now his mother really became uneasy. She swept a hand through her hair and glanced at the window, agitated in a way he had not seen before. 'It was an accident. When meat rationing began the government sent inspectors to every farm to list their animals. One day they came here unexpectedly and Chester was alone. He showed them around, but because he hadn't been here long he didn't know about the Gloucestershire Old Spots in the woods. They're fenced in and we've always left them pretty much to themselves, which is how they like it. So Chester didn't know and the inspectors missed them. We didn't realise the mistake until much later.'

'Can't you just tell the inspectors you've made a mistake?' George asked, not understanding why it was such a problem.

His mother shrugged. 'We were going to, but then the papers had a story about a farmer being sent to prison for hiding animals. He claimed it was a mistake too, but they still jailed him. Dad is afraid they'll do the same to him.'

'Then why not just kill the pigs and get rid of the evidence?'

'We could, but you know how many there are. Dozens and dozens. It seems such a waste of livestock, especially now we're at war. Dad loves his pigs. He's bred them for years and got a prize Sounder. We thought we might get away with it if we reduced the Sounder down to just a handful of animals.'

'So you've been slaughtering them and making pies?'

'Not just pies,' she said quietly. 'Chester takes some meat and Mr Dryden sells the rest. But Old Spots have several litters a year, and although we've tried to separate the boars from the sows, they still find ways to mate.'

George smiled, that sounded a bit like the RAF. 'Then I guess I'll just have to put up with having a mother who's a criminal.'

She shrugged. 'I know it's wrong but we've never had savings before and now I've been able to put a bit back for our old age.'

There was a knock on the door and the doctor arrived. Dr Grey was short, plump and bald, with just a white semicircle of hair above his ears. Although now in his sixties, he possessed an energy and vitality that belied his age. George could only describe it as a sort of bustling enthusiasm.

'Mrs Watford,' the doctor called and poked his head around the kitchen door. 'I hear someone's ill?' Then he looked at George. 'My goodness, why it's young George. I hardly recognise you in uniform.' Dr Grey reached out and shook George's hand. 'A pilot too! I always thought you'd do well for yourself,' and he looked more closely at the double winged insignia on George's jacket. 'You must tell me all about it, but I ought to look at the patient first. What's happened?'

Dr Grey listened as they described the symptoms and went to examine Watford senior, closing the door behind him. George's mother stared after him, biting her lip with worry.

'I hope he'll be alright,' she said anxiously. 'This would happen just as we've got you home again.' She shook the frying pan, watching the lard slide from side to side as it melted. The smell made George's stomach rumble. 'Anyway, I want to hear what you've been up to,' she added more brightly and gave him a smile.

George talked as he watched her work. He tried to describe his joy at being a pilot, the freedom, the view from the clouds. How he had sweated over exams and struggled through tests. He spoke about some of the people he had met, Dickinson, Marshall and of course his crew. He told her about the wide prairies of Canada, the towering Rocky Mountains, the shops in Calgary and his visit to Niagara Falls. He did not mention the raid on Dusseldorf or even Millie. Maybe that would come later when he was ready. Dr Grey emerged just as his mother was plating the bacon and eggs.

'How is he, doctor?' George asked.

'He has a high temperature, a bad cough, and his lungs sound like a leaky set of bellows. I'm afraid it's pneumonia,' Dr Grey said. 'He's going to be very ill for a while and that's always dangerous in someone his age.'

'What can we do?' George asked.

'Unfortunately, there's nothing I can prescribe. We have to let the fever run its course. Make him comfortable and give him plenty of fluids to drink. Keep him cool. So no fires and not too many blankets either. Leave the window open if he can bear it. He must stay in bed for at least a fortnight. Keep a careful eye on him and let me know if he worsens. He'll have a bad cough so mix a bowl of hot water and mustard and try getting him to breathe the steam. That might free up his airways.' Dr Grey eyed the bacon and eggs hungrily as he spoke. 'Keep cold water and a flannel by the bed for his headache. I'll come back in a few days to check on him again.' He glanced at the two and returned his gaze to the food. 'My, that smells good; you're a lucky boy George.'

George glanced at his mother who nodded imperceptibly. 'Please have it, doctor. I'm not hungry.'

A smile formed on the doctor's lips and he took half a step forward. 'No, I couldn't rob you of your meal,' he said reluctantly.

George pulled the chair out from the table and offered it to him. 'Please do, Dr Grey. I've lost my appetite seeing dad so ill.'

'Well, if you're sure. I've been out since dawn and I doubt I'll see home again anytime soon.' He sat down and tore into the food, at intervals dabbing fried bread into the egg yolk. 'Marvellous,' he said between mouthfuls. 'Now tell me about your adventures George, I want to hear all about it.'

George told his story once again, trying hard not to watch his breakfast disappear and hoping the doctor would not hear his growling stomach. After Dr Grey left, taking with him one of the pies, George helped his father up the stairs to bed and into his pyjamas. The old man was tired and George waited until he was asleep before creeping downstairs again. His mother cooked more bacon and eggs and he was ravenous. After wiping the plate clean with a chunk of bread, he stretched out his legs and enjoyed the drowsy feeling of a full stomach and a warm room. Tonight he would put the tin bath in front of the fire and scrub himself clean. He was home.

Chapter 16

RAF Blackbrook - 23 November 1942

It was growing dark by the time George arrived at the small local station about fifteen miles from Lincoln. There was no transport to ferry him to RAF Blackbrook, so after getting directions, he set off along three miles of unlit roads. Although he felt depressed that his leave was over, somehow knowing it was ending and that an uncertain future awaited added zest to the time. It seemed that George's presence spurred his father's recovery so that by the time he left, the old man was able to sit in the parlour and even walk short distances around the garden. However, the doctor ordered him to wait at least another two weeks before going back to the farm, an instruction Jack Watford accepted with better grace than they expected.

The sound of Merlin engines snapped him back to the present. One after another, distant engines coughed and growled until their roar filled the air. He walked faster. A squadron was readying for takeoff. The aerodrome's perimeter fence began just past a copse of trees and in the dim light, he could see the distant grey outlines of curved hangars and square buildings. Vehicles gathered beside the control tower, flight vans, an ambulance, fire tenders and a few staff cars. Closer, just a few yards from the wire fence, sat the black shapes of Lancasters. The noise intensified, pummelling the air and as he watched the closest Lancaster, its port-outer began to turn. Blue-grey flames belched and the airscrews blurred. It moved slowly from dispersal, guided by an aircraftman walking backwards and waving his hands above his head. As soon as the bomber swung onto the taxiway, the aircraftman sprinted to the side and gave the pilot a 'thumbs up'. George grabbed his cap as the slipstream washed over him. Other Lancasters lumbered onto the taxiway, their rudders flapping and brakes squealing as they processed towards the runway and the red light on the controller's caravan. Tomorrow he would be part of their number and that thought thrilled him. He was where he belonged. Almost as soon as the first bomber reached the runway, a green light flashed and the aircraft wound its engines up to full power. It moved slowly at first but quickly gathered speed. Flare lights flickered as the Lancaster thundered between them, faster and faster until the black shape lifted into the air and was lost from sight. As soon as the first was airborne, the next began down the runway and a ripple of movement transmitted itself through the queue. George watched until six aircraft launched and with a quick glance at the noise-filled sky, he walked on.

The sergeant's mess was superior to Oakley's, older, better built and more comfortable. Best of all was that aircrew had their own mess. George pushed open the double entrance doors and went inside. The corridor smelt of polish and the tiled floors shone starkly. Paintings of aircraft and aerial combats hung above deep brown half-panelled hallway walls. With the squadron on an operation, the place was deserted and he found Dingo and Chalky playing snooker in a side room with Ned watching them intently.

'Hello chaps,' George said, surprised at just how good it felt to see them again.

'Skipper!' Dingo beamed and they all shook hands.

'Good leave?' George asked. Dingo and Ned had spent the two weeks searching villages for distant relations, while Chalky went home to Newcastle and his family.

'Ripper,' Dingo said. 'We crawled through half a dozen villages and eventually found a relative of Ned's. She put us up for a week and sent us off with ten bob. Can't say fairer than that.'

'Did you trace any of your own relations?' George asked Dingo curiously.

'Nah. Too many generations down-under for anyone to remember us.' Dingo slammed a white ball into a tangle of reds and watched the balls rebound across the table. The white ball rolled straight into the corner pocket and Dingo raised an eyebrow at Chalky, daring him to comment. 'I found a few graveyards with ancestors in them though,' he said as an afterthought.

'You should have dug them up and said hello,' Max's voice said behind them. 'Might have found yourself a girlfriend who didn't yell as much as usual.'

George turned around and saw Max, Dick and Jim grinning at them. They had gone to London together to see the sights. 'How was London?' George asked.

'Full of spivs and criminals,' Dick said, 'and those were just a few of Max's family.'

'That's not fair,' Max protested. 'Aunty Mable's never been inside and she took care of you alright, didn't she?'

'She certainly did,' Jim said ruefully. 'Played Gin Rummy every night and cleaned us out. I've never been so well taken care of.'

They talked about their leave until a gangly steward returned to his desk. After consulting a sheet of paper, he allocated them to Nissen hut number twenty, their new home. Grabbing their kitbags, they wandered across the darkened aerodrome until they found three rows of the familiar curved roofs. It had started to rain and a steady cold drizzle made them look forward to having their own place and a warming fire.

'I hope they've given us fresh sheets and towels,' Jim said as they found their hut.

'And some coal,' Chalky added.

George went in first and switched on the light. He blinked in surprise. Clothes lay on unmade beds. Photographs and books sat on small bedside lockers. The room was scattered with personal belongings.

'They've given us the wrong hut,' George said. 'Someone's in this one.'

'Bloody Hell,' Max swore. 'Back through the rain again.'

Ned wandered over to one of the beds. 'Hey, look at this,' he cried happily. 'This guy's a 'Caper' too.' Emblazoned on a cotton banner above the bed was 'Cape Breton'. 'I'll have someone from home in the squadron.' He beamed at the others.

'Not another mad Canadian,' Max said patting Ned on the shoulder. 'An' I thought this was a respectable squadron.'

'Not if they...' Dingo began.

'Yeah I know,' Max interrupted him. 'Not if they let me in.' He turned to Dingo. 'That was so predictable. You really are going to have to work on your one-liners.'

'Look, this bloke's got a set of silver hairbrushes,' Jim said, picking one up. 'He's obviously out the top drawer.'

'He's obviously a ponce,' Max said. 'Mind you, they'd fetch a bob or two,' he continued, examining one.

George lifted a photograph and stared at a smiling girl in the picture. Not pretty, but she had a kind face and a cheeky smile that made her attractive. 'Come on,' he said, putting back the photograph. 'We shouldn't be nosing through their stuff.' They tramped back through the rain to the admin office.

'You've given us the wrong hut,' George told the aircraftman.

227

'Wrong hut?' the steward repeated woodenly. 'I don't think so. Wait a moment, I'll check.' He ran his finger down a piece of paper. 'No, I'm right. You're booked into hut twenty. What's the problem?'

'The problem is that hut twenty is already occupied,' George explained patiently. 'There's kit all over the place.'

The aircraftman thought for a few seconds, before a glimmer of understanding dawned. 'Hasn't it been cleaned out?' he asked and shook his head. 'I'll chase them up now,' he said and reached for the telephone.

'What are you talking about, chum?' Max asked. 'Have you moved them?'

'No. Not moved them,' the aircraftman laughed as he waited for someone to answer. 'They didn't come back last night. We lost three crews. The Adjustment Board should have gone in today and packed away their stuff. Too busy I expect,' he said and shook his head again. George felt an icy shiver of understanding. The kit and clothes belonged to seven dead men. They had lived together in hut twenty and now they were gone, just memories and mementoes to be boxed up and taken away. He glanced at the others and saw them staring open-mouthed back at him.

It was midnight before they returned to the hut. The Adjustment Board staff cleared away the belongings and left a pile of clean sheets and a towel at the foot of each bed. If anything, the ease of packing away seven lives was more disconcerting than finding their kit still there. Sensing his crew's grim mood George placed one of his mother's pies on the table and removed its muslin cover. He cut it into seven slices as the others watched hungrily.

'Oh well done, skipper,' Max chuckled, helping himself to a chunk. 'Now this is what I call a proper pie.'

Chalky examined the profile of his slice. 'This is almost solid meat,' he said and sniffed it appreciatively. 'There must be a month's ration in here.'

They looked at George for an explanation, which he did not give. 'My mum loves me,' he said and hoped that would defer further questions.

Max bit into his hunk and a dreamy expression crossed his face. 'She must. I reckon she's given her right arm for you.'

'An' maybe a leg as well,' Dingo said through a mouthful of pie.

The thunder of returning aircraft woke them at two in the morning. George lay in bed, listening to the sound of Lancasters on final approach. Three aircraft lost the night before, twenty-one men killed. He closed his eyes and tried to sleep, but the numbers whirled in his mind. The desire to begin operations fought against the fear of what was waiting across the channel. For a few hours, he dozed fitfully before giving up. Weak autumn sunshine gradually filtered through the thin curtains making further sleep impossible, so after checking his watch he grabbed a towel and went to find the shower block. Outside the hut, the day was crisp and the aerodrome already busy as he took his first daylight look at the base. Built pre-war, its buildings were bigger and more substantial than those at Oakley were. Large square redbrick messes and admin blocks sat in well-tended lawns, while further away were four hangars. The original occupant of the aerodrome was a Fairy Battle squadron. Its crew of three meant the accommodation block was undersized for Lancaster's crew of seven and the reason they were once more in a Nissen hut.

The difference in tempo with Oakley was also surprising. Aircraftmen and WAAFs moved purposefully and their expressions were more serious than on the training squadron. After a breakfast of porridge, they reported to the adjutant's office. George knocked on the door and waited until a voice told them to enter.

'Well?' asked an elderly squadron leader from behind a desk piled high with papers. Ribbons from the Great War and the wings on his uniform marked him as an old RFC flyer. He was lean and had steel grey hair, but his most noticeable feature was a luxuriant white moustache that flourished under an aquiline nose. He looked at George quizzically.

'Sergeant Watford and crew, reporting for duty, sir.' George saluted as behind him the others shuffled into the small room.

The squadron leader stroked his moustache and scanned each of them before turning back to George. 'Are you replacements?' He asked and held up his hands in exasperation at the papers littering his desk. 'No one's told me a damn thing about replacements. Cox!' he bellowed. A mouse like corporal squeezed into the room and sidled around George and the others until he arrived at the adjutant's desk. 'Why wasn't I told about replacements?' the adjutant demanded.

'You were sir,' Cox replied patiently and sifted through the chaos until he fished out a form. 'Paperwork's waiting your attention, sir. Has been since last week,' he added self-righteously.

The squadron leader glared at the corporal. 'Well next time bring it to my attention, man.' The corporal looked about to protest but the adjutant cut him off. 'That's all Cox, dismissed.' He looked at the form and said, 'say's here you were to arrive last night?'

'We did, sir,' George replied.

'Never mind excuses, sergeant.' He put down the paper. 'The CO insists on punctuality. It's best to remember that if you don't want to run afoul of him.' Suddenly his frown turned into a smile. 'Anyway, better late than never I suppose. Welcome to 323 Squadron.' He stood up and shook hands with each of them. 'I'm Squadron Leader Russell Templeton, the adjutant, although most people call me *'Uncle'*. No idea why, I suspect most of 'em don't know who their own father's are, let alone more distant relatives.' He guffawed like a choking donkey and George politely joined in, certain that if this man was not actually mad, he was knocking on the door. Suddenly a figure wearing an Irvin jacket pushed his way into the room and came straight up to the adjutant. He was holding a pair of flying boots.

'There's no more flying boots, Uncle,' he said angrily. 'I've just been to the stores and they gave me these!' He held the boots far in front of him in disgust.

The adjutant straightened. 'But those are flying boots, Will,' he protested bewilderedly, completely forgetting George and the others.

'No, Uncle,' the newcomer said waving the boots in front of the adjutant's face. 'These are a bloody travesty. Look at them!'

The adjutant took the footwear and quickly examined them from several angles. 'They're definitely flying boots. Recognise 'em anywhere.'

'God give me strength,' the newcomer replied. He snatched the boots back and handed them to George. 'What's wrong with these?' he asked.

George gave them a quick look and handed them back. Superficially, they looked like normal flying boots. Suede exterior, rubber-soled and thickly fleeced. 'No ankle straps,' he said.

The newcomer turned back to the adjutant, 'Exactly, no ankle straps. Bailout wearing these bloody things, Uncle and as soon as your parachute opens the jolt will shake them off. You end up in enemy territory with only a pair of socks on your feet. Can't get far in socks, Uncle.' He said and thrust the boots at the adjutant before turning to George. 'And who are you?'

Although George could see no badges of rank, he guessed this was the squadron boss, the wing commander. Just shorter than George, he looked to be in his thirties and had a sharp face and long nose. His eyes were clear blue and he exuded authority like expensive cologne. 'Sergeant Watford, sir, and this is my crew.' George said and saluted.

The newcomer touched his cap and held out his hand, which George shook. 'I'm Wing Commander William Stafford, the squadron commander.' George stood back and introduced the others. The CO's clipped tones were almost the music hall caricature of an officer.

'Come along with me,' the CO said. 'Uncle needs time to find some decent boots before we're on ops again.'

'But, Will!' the adjutant protested.

'You heard me, Uncle,' the CO called back from the corridor. 'Before the next op.' George and the others followed him to his office, where he perched on the edge of his desk and turned to face them. 'Uncle's a good man, but like the rest of us, he's more suited to flying a kite than a desk. So, welcome to RAF Blackbrook and 323 Squadron,' he said and began patting his pockets. 'I hope you'll be happy here.' He scowled, stood up and searched his desk until he found a pipe, which he stuck in the corner of his mouth. Then he gave them a more thorough stare and frowned again. George could tell he thought them an odd collection. Dingo and he were tall, Chalky, Dick and Jim were roughly average height, while Max was short and Ned was only a little taller but very skinny. They were not a group to enhance a parade ground.

'Stand easy,' the Wingco said. 'Now, 323 Squadron has three Flights A, B and C.' Stafford took the pipe from his mouth and began filling it from a leather pouch. 'You'll be in 'B Flight' under Squadron Leader Toby Mallard. Toby's a good type and you'll need to see him next.' George nodded and glanced at the others. They were standing loosely to attention and trying hard not to make eye contact with each other. It was important to make a good first impression but the temptation to grin was overwhelming.

'This afternoon I want you to take your kite up and get familiar with the area. Do plenty of circuits and bumps, plus a complete air test. OK?' George nodded. 'Good. I'm afraid that as a 'sprog-crew' you get the oldest aircraft, but they're all airworthy so that shouldn't be too much of a problem.' He looked at George. 'We've been pretty busy recently so we probably won't be on squadron ops for a few days, but when we do, you'll fly as 'second-dicky' with Toby. Just so you can see what an operation is all about.' The CO paused to tap the tobacco down into the pipe bowl and George decided to speak.

'We've been on an operation, sir,' he said. 'Our training squadron took part in the raid on Dusseldorf a few weeks back.' He hoped the CO would not think he was trying a line shoot.

The CO looked up and raised his eyebrows at them. 'Is that so,' he said slowly. 'Well, no need for a second-dicky trip then. How was it?'

George shrugged; he was not sure what to say, or rather, how to say it. If he made the raid sound difficult, the CO might think he was windy. Alternatively, if he made it sound easy he could seem arrogant. 'We bombed the target OK, but lost the starboard inner in a scrap with a Junkers on the way home.'

The CO struck a match and puffed a cloud of smoke into the room. 'Did you indeed,' he said, clearly interested. 'Tell me more.' George briefly outlined the battles with the Messerschmitt and the Junkers and talked through the bomb run, ensuring that he praised each of his crew. The CO puffed and listened attentively as if this was the most interesting thing he had heard all day. As George finished, he stood up and beamed at them. 'Well done, well done indeed,' he said. 'I encourage an aggressive spirit in my crews and I'll be expecting good things from you.' It worried George that there was an almost piratical gleam in his eyes. 'Remember to check in the flight office for battle orders at ten each morning. You'll be kept pretty busy here.'

Someone told them that B flight's commander was in a hangar checking an aircraft. They found him talking to a Flight Lieutenant who George assumed was the engineering officer. Behind the two, ground crew swarmed over a Lancaster. Fitters riveted repair patches while others worked on two stripped engines. The harsh noises of sawing, hammering and banging echoed through the building. All the while, the aircraft waited patiently.

The pair turned towards him and George saluted smartly. 'Sergeant Watford reporting, sir,' George said. 'We're a replacement crew. The CO says we're in your flight.'

The squadron leader glanced at George and then at the others. He looked weary and bad-tempered, dark patches stained the skin under hooded eyes. His lip curled into a brief smile that could equally be mistaken for a grimace and he touched his hat in a minimal salute. 'Squadron Leader Toby Mallard,' he said quietly. The small acknowledgement seemed more from necessity than friendliness. 'Another sprog-crew, you're the third in three weeks,' he said bleakly. George said nothing and stared just above Mallard's head, which was the usual way of reacting when you felt an officer was playing silly buggers, a sort of passive resistance. If he had hoped for a warm welcome from his flight leader then he was disappointed and that bewildered him. Why would Mallard not welcome replacements? From the corners of his eyes, he glanced at the others and saw that they too stared impassively. 'What did the CO say was to happen to you?' Mallard continued with little obvious enthusiasm.

'We've had one operational trip with the HCU training squadron, sir, so the CO thinks there's no need for a second-dicky flight. He told us to report to you and then take a kite up this afternoon for familiarisation.'

Mallard suddenly looked happier, as if he was relieved. 'No second-dicky trip,' he repeated. 'Well, that's good news.' He handed a clipboard to the engineering officer, crossed to George and shook his hand. 'Welcome to B Flight. Good to have you on board.' Then, like the CO, he shook hands with each of the crew. 'Come and see me later after your flight, if you have any problems,' he added before turning and hurrying off, clearly wanting to be away.

'Well, that was all pretty strange,' Dingo said, scratching his head as they watched him go. 'They haven't exactly rolled out the band for us, have they?'

Jim shook his head, mystified. 'That bloke can't decide whether he loves us or hates us.'

'I suppose they do want us here?' Max added. 'I mean I'm happy to go back on leave if it's not convenient right now.'

George noticed that the engineering officer had joined them and he turned to face him. He grinned at George. 'Don't mind Toby,' he said. 'You'll be just the same in a few weeks.'

'What do you mean, sir?' George asked, more than a little confused.

'Flight Lieutenant David Martin,' he introduced himself, 'Only I don't fly and everyone calls me 'Pincher'.' Pincher was short and plump, with a round, good-natured face. He waved at the aircraft. 'This is Toby's Lancaster. He was hit by flak on the last raid and staggered home on two engines. We counted fifty-eight holes in the wings and fuselage. He just made it to the aerodrome before he ran out of sky. That was his twentieth op and this is his third aircraft. The other two were complete write-offs.'

George began to understand. 'I guess he's under a lot of stress.'

'Just a bit,' Pincher agreed. 'This line of work makes people twitchy. Not that they'd admit it of course, but every crew feels the strain and that makes them behave oddly.'

'In what way?' George was curious.

'In every way. Some don't sleep, some can't stay awake. Some become excitable and some depressed. You name it and someone has cornered the market in strange behaviour. Thing is though, as far as I can tell none of them realises.'

'Is that why he wasn't very friendly,' Chalky asked. 'As Max said, it feels like he doesn't want us here.'

Pincher smiled and beckoned them towards an urn. They took turns filling chipped enamel mugs with warm sweet tea. 'Oh, he wants you here all right. Toby needs a full flight of aircraft.' Pincher swirled his mug and watched the oily surface spin. 'It's just that sprog-crews are unlucky and no one likes to get too close.'

Dick Scrivener laughed, but then realised that the engineer was serious. 'Unlucky? Why do they think that?'

Pincher looked as though he was debating whether to continue. 'Because sprog-crews tend not to last,' he said eventually. 'The official statistics are that new crews have a one in three chance of surviving their first five missions.

After five trips, the odds change to evens. Unfortunately, even after twenty trips, it never gets to odds-on.'

'I'm not sure I needed to hear that,' Max said.

'Yeah, thanks mate, you sure know how to cheer a bloke up,' Dingo added.

'It's probably best that you know,' Pincher said calmly. 'It explains why the old sweats will treat you differently.' He glanced at his fitters anxiously before continuing. 'The old crews may seem a bit offish, but sprogs are always coming and going. They won't make much effort to get to know you until you've got five missions under your belt. Did you notice that Toby was relieved not to have you as second-dicky?' He looked at George who nodded. 'Well, that's because every crew thinks that dicky flights are particularly unlucky. It's quite common for them not to come back and that makes people superstitious.' Pincer drained his mug and placed it by the urn. George and the others did the same and Pincer led them to the entrance of the hangar.

It was now grey and drab outside; the earlier clear sky had abandoned them. Four thousand feet above, a thick cover of dark featureless nimbostratus hung in the sky, completely blocking the sun and bringing a light but persistent rain. George felt these were the ugliest clouds of all and the most depressing.

'You'll be flying N-Nuts,' the engineer said, pointing to Lancaster waiting at a nearby dispersal. 'She's old and battered, but a good kite. The two inner engines are new and the outers are rebuilds. Apart from being a bitch to trim, she's structurally sound and as good as any of the others.'

'You sound like an Irish horse trader,' Max said. 'Shall we go and rub her fetlocks and count her teeth?'

'You can pull on the wings and kick the tyres, for all I care,' Pincher told him carelessly. 'She's your kite now whether you like it or not.'

George buttoned up his greatcoat ready for a walk in the rain. 'Anything else we should know?' he asked wearily.

Pincher kicked a rusty bolt towards the edge of the hangar. 'Just take things slowly with the squadron. They're good people, some of the best, but flying bombers is a dicey business and niceties tend to disappear when crews are under this much stress. They'll come round when you show that you'll be around.' There was a loud clang and a curse from inside the hangar. He turned on his heel and went back in. 'Just give things time and try to stay alive,' Pincher called over his shoulder. The rain began falling harder.

'I'm not sure that I'm going to be happy here,' Max said quietly.

'Mate,' Dingo replied, glancing at George. 'From what he just told us, I think happiness is the least of our worries.'

Max shrugged. 'I know, but a man should be happy in his work and I've gone right off this war.'

'Sorry to hear that,' George said. 'Would you like me to order you a new one?'

'Could you?' Max replied. 'Something in civilian colours this time, I've had it with RAF blue.'

After lunch, they drew flying clothes and parachutes from the stores and went to N-Nuts. The rain had stopped but puddles lay deep on the concrete dispersal. The Lancaster towered grimly above them, dripping rainwater from the wings and fuselage. A fitter stencilled a bomb on the aircraft's nose after each bombing mission and N-Nuts was a veteran with twenty-four such markings. A dozen or more repair patches gave her the look of a grizzled prizefighter, but George gazed lovingly at her. She might be old and worn, but faded or not she was still a beauty and she was his. Although he had already been in combat, his war would really begin in this machine and the fact that she was battered and survived, only added to her allure. After speaking to the ground crew and getting their assessment of her condition, he checked N-Nuts's exterior with particular care. Nothing he could see gave cause for concern, but of course, there was always the possibility of some battle damage lurking unseen beneath the skin. They boarded in the usual order with George last and he stowed the ladder and clamped the side door shut. The interior stunk of kerosene, a liquid that ground crews used for cleaning, so George slid back the cockpit window and gulped down some fresh air. Despite everything, he felt excitement building like a head of steam. N-Nuts was about to transition from a pile of metal and fuel into a flying machine, a killer, the queen of the skies. Soon the fuselage would shake, the engines roar and there would be enough power to send them over twenty thousand feet above the earth.

An hour later, N-Nuts lifted smoothly from the ground and they climbed to just below the cloud base that hovered morosely at four thousand feet. Wispy vapour wafted like smoke, obscuring the ground for seconds at a time as he flew in wide circles around the aerodrome. Although they flew at night operationally, it might be light when they returned and in any case, reflective features such as rivers were still discernible in the dark. They practised circuits and bumps until George felt comfortable with the aircraft and aerodrome. Pulling back on the stick, N-Nuts went up through the clag of clouds in a steep climb, emerging into bright sunlight at fifteen thousand feet. This was one of the joys of flying for those lucky enough to experience it. A wet miserable day on the ground would still provide brilliant sunshine above the clouds.

This bomber was old, but she was still a Lancaster and a joy to fly. Her one vice was, as Pincher Martin had warned, that she was difficult to trim. She began to wander up or down as soon George levelled the nose. This was not a problem on short flights, but it would make a six or eight-hour operation taxing. He suspected that the fuselage had bent at some point, which was worrying because there might be other, unknown damage. However, he was happy with N-Nuts and an hour's air test was just the thing to blow the cobwebs away.

After a late dinner of corned beef, potatoes and cabbage in the sergeant's mess, they went across the corridor to the bar. Remembering the warning from Pincher Martin, George pushed open the double doors and paused apprehensively, unsure of their reception. The white-walled room was full of aircrew and a gramophone blasted out a scratchy dance tune. No one looked at them, even to acknowledge their presence. Immediately he felt a tension in the atmosphere as if charged with electricity. The crews stood in groups, talking, nursing beers and smoking, but the way they held themselves looked stiff, almost uncomfortable. His next impression was of their clothing. Only a very few wore 'blues'. Most sported a mixture of flying and ground clothes. Generally, this meant white roll neck sweaters, battle dress and suede flying boots. A few even wore items of civilian clothing. George felt very much an intruder in a private club, one with an admission fee they had yet to pay. They threaded through knots of aircrew as he led the way to the bar and ordered a round of beers. Even Max seemed subdued as they waited. Taking their drinks a little way from the others, they stood in a circle, taking comfort from their own company. Unexpectedly, a figure detached itself from one of the groups and joined them.

'Hello, you look like new boys,' he said with a grin. 'Peter Davies. I'm new myself,' he added brightly. He was a pilot, short and lean with ginger hair and a face full of freckles.

'George Watford,' George said. They shook hands and he introduced his crew. 'How long have you been here?'

'About three weeks,' Davies replied. 'Have you met the CO yet?'

'First thing this morning. What's he like?' He felt it safest to hear Davies' opinion before offering his own.

'Oh, he's good, a very keen type. He looks after his boys and does more than his share of ops. But he expects a lot too. Just make sure you reach the target. He doesn't have any sympathy with early returns from mechanical problems.'

George nodded, he had guessed that much. 'Press on regardless,' he said.

'Very much so,' Davies replied and shrugged as if this were just another of life's inconveniences. 'A few weeks back one of the pilots complained of mag drop just before an op. This was the third time it happened. The CO jumped in his car and drove to the aircraft, kicked the pilot out and flew the kite on the raid in only his jacket. No parachute or anything.' Davies laughed and shook his head. 'The pilot was off the squadron the next day. You've probably met Uncle?' Davies then asked and George nodded. 'He flew S.E.5s in the last lot. Complete lunatic of course. Terrorises the admin staff, but he keeps them on their toes and so overall, he's effective. Just watch out because he tries to hitch lifts on operations. Tug Wilson found him stowed away on his kite and threatened to kick him out without a parachute unless he got off.'

'I'm glad someone enjoys ops,' Max said. 'Shame that it's only a madman.'

'How many ops have you done?' Dick asked Davies.

'Four,' Davies replied and his expression darkened. 'Two nights ago we went to Kiel and that was a real bastard. Three squadron kites went for a Burton.'

'What happened?' George asked.

Davies drank some beer as he remembered. 'No one knows for sure. It was a low-level approach and then a climb to four thousand for the run in. Someone saw two kites go down together and the CO thinks they probably collided in the darkness. No one knows what happened to number three. Low-level ops are a dicey business.'

'That's a tough break, no wonder they look a bit down in the mouth.' Chalky said, nodding at the crews.

Davies glanced around, puzzled. 'Oh, I see what you mean. No, this is normal. Problem is that many of the crews are split between the officers and sergeants messes. It's better when everyone gets together at the pub. In any case, two of the missing Lancasters had sprog-crews and the old sweats don't count us as much of a loss. You'll learn that after a while. The third crew was on their twelfth op and popular so they are missed.'

'Rookie lives don't matter?' Dingo said indignantly, glaring at the crews. 'I bet they bloody well mattered to the boys who didn't come back, and to their families.'

Davies eyed Dingo wearily. 'I didn't say they don't matter. It's just that no one here knew them well, so they aren't missed.' He stepped closer, to ensure they could hear over the noise. 'Going on ops is like nothing else. Everyone's scared, and anyone who says differently is a liar. Everyone in this room just wants to survive their thirty, so we all believe we're something special, that we have something that makes us better than the rest. Something that ensures we'll survive when the others don't. Sprog-crews are easy to discount because we're at the bottom of the heap as far as experience goes.'

'It still doesn't seem right,' Dingo persisted. 'We're all in it together.'

'That's the reality of bomber ops, I'm afraid,' Davies said. 'It's not callousness, it's just that we sprogs stand least chance of surviving and so why be friends with us until we've shown we'll last. I bet you'll be the same before long. You go on missions and you're glad that Wellingtons and Stirlings are in the stream because they're easier targets. You'll see kites blasted to pieces and you'll tell yourself that they got the chop because they just weren't good enough, not as good as you anyway.' Davies nodded over his shoulder at the aircrews. 'Some of these boys are on second tours, yet they still crawl into their tin coffins and go back. We all do what we need to do.'

George sipped his beer and felt Davies was probably right. He had convinced himself that he and his crew were exceptional, out of the ordinary, just as every other crew undoubtedly did. All crews had that unique something, right until the moment bullets shredded the aircraft or flak exploded the fuel tanks. Special crews littered Europe, each as dead as the next. In his mind, flying ops was a weighing scale. On one side, you had knowledge, skill and equipment, but on the other, you had misfortune, the target and the enemy. You could not alter the negatives, but he still believed they could improve the positives.

'Where did you go last night?' George asked. 'I saw the squadron taking off as I arrived.'

'Spoofing.' Davies smiled at what he knew would be a new term to them. 'Sometimes before a raid goes in a squadron will be asked to cross into Europe and divert attention. It puts their fighters in the wrong place so they're low on fuel when the stream arrives. It's not particularly dangerous unless the Luftwaffe sends their fighters after you instead of waiting where they think you're heading. The shame is that spoofing doesn't count towards your thirty.' He held up a hand to one of his crew. 'Anyway, better be going, I don't want my boys to think I've abandoned them. We should be getting more replacements soon and then we sprogs can gang up on the old boys.' Davies winked and went back to his crew.

'Yeah and by then he'll have done his fifth and be one of them,' Dingo said.

'I've had enough of this place,' George said and quickly drank the last of his beer. 'How about we go on our first squadron raid right now?'

'What do you mean?' Chalky asked.

'Follow me,' he said mysteriously, 'and find out.'

They searched for the two vacant Nissen huts and took the dead crew's coal. The metal stove in their hut soon glowed a dull red and with a blazing fire, the place seemed almost cosy. Max had somehow acquired a kettle and tea leaves, and so they each lay back on their beds with a mug of black tea. It reminded George of being with his father in his workshop.

'So what do you think, Skipper?' Max called out. 'Not the most welcoming start was it?'

George considered for a moment. 'I guess we just have to get through five ops and hope the big boys let us join in their games.'

'You blokes know what I think?' Dingo asked and told them anyway. 'I think those drongos are windy. We've done an op and sure it was bad, but we got through it.'

'Yeah sure,' Max said and threw a magazine at the navigator. 'Just another twenty-nine to go. I don't know why anyone's worried, I really don't.'

Chapter 17

RAF Blackbrook - 25 November 1942

Their names were on the 'battle order' in the flight office the next morning, along with Peter Davies and the CO. Just three crews would be flying. Two sprogs and the boss. First briefing was at ten thirty and George felt the same blend of fear and excitement that he had before their first op. The others looked at him, waiting for him to speak, to give his opinion.

'Looks like the day job has started,' he said simply and grinned, trying to make light of it.

'Just the three of us, though.' Chalky scratched his chin. 'It can't be a big job.' Other crews pushed past and then immediately departed when they saw their names were not on the list.

'It's probably a milk run, an easy job to start with,' George said hopefully and led them outside.

The CO was already in the briefing room when they arrived, along with his crew of the squadron's specialist heads, the Navigation, Bombing, Gunnery, Engineering and WOp leaders. Normally these seniors prepared missions and did not fly, but it seemed the CO liked to keep them on their toes. Peter Davies and his crew arrived shortly afterwards and he gave George a friendly nod. The room could accommodate the entire squadron of one hundred and twenty-six and it seemed practically empty with just twenty-one.

The CO stood at the front, arms clasped behind his back. Behind him, the curtains were tightly drawn. 'Good morning gentlemen,' he said brightly. 'Tonight we're doing some gardening and here's where we plant the vegetables.' He waved his hand theatrically and the curtains opened to reveal a large map of Europe with a red tape heading northeast out into the North Sea and then directly east towards Denmark. George sat forward with interest. He knew that *gardening* and *vegetables* were the code names for mine laying and the mines themselves. Even the sea-lanes they mined had plant names. However, that was about all he knew.

'For those of you who didn't pay attention to geography lessons at school, Denmark consists of a mainland and more islands than a dog has fleas. The other side of mainland Denmark are two large islands of Funen and Zealand. Between them is a strait of water known as The Great Belt. This strait is a major route from the Baltic into the Kattegat and Atlantic. Our objective is to mine it between here and here.' The CO tapped the map with a long pointer. 'We will sow nine mines, three from each aircraft. Now gardening is a precise business. In order to drop the mines successfully, we must release at an altitude of fifteen hundred feet and fly no faster than one hundred and eighty miles-per-hour. Any quicker and the parachutes could be torn off the mines. Also, we must drop the mines at four-second intervals to give a good spread.' He turned to face the crews, fixing them with a hawkish gaze. 'Once you have sown the last mine, it's important to continue in a straight line for at least another three minutes so as not to give away where they are. In effect, this will mean flying right across the strait to Zealand and near to its anti-aircraft batteries. Watch out for these.'

Turning back to the map, he lifted the pointer. 'I'll go in first and drop a Target Indicator around here.' He tapped a piece of land on the western side of the strait. 'I'll then circle back and come in again behind you. We start our runs from the TI, each of us crossing it at different angles to give a good spread of mines in the water. Exact angles and timings will be given by the navigation and bomb aiming leaders.' The CO placed his pointer against the wall and came closer to the crews. 'This is a rapid ingress and egress operation, do not hang about. Precision is key so get your timings, angles, speeds and heights right and this will be a piece of cake.' He picked up the pointer again and went back to the map. 'To avoid enemy radar we will approach Denmark at five hundred feet and then go down to one hundred feet for the last hour. I know that this sounds dicey but it will be twilight, so all you have to do is follow my lead and watch your instruments. We will arrive just after it gets dark...'

George sat forward and looked harder at the map. Flying that low at night was dangerous. An hour of holding the Lancaster a few feet off the water when one lapse of concentration, one surge of wind or one mechanical failure would cartwheel them across the surface. In his mind, he could see a dim horizon above smooth black water dappled with foam flecks, all of which would gradually blend into one as the light faded. The squadron lost three crews flying low level just a few days before. He glanced at Davies and saw him scratching his chin thoughtfully, no doubt remembering that raid. It would be a relief just to get to the target safely, whatever the reception waiting for them.

Much of the remaining briefing passed over his head; he was already feeling the controls and scanning the dials as N-Nuts skimmed towards Denmark. He registered that there would be a weak moon and scattered clouds, but the times and courses he left to Dingo, who scribbled furiously on a pad of paper. However, the intelligence officer grabbed his attention when he mentioned that their mission was part of thirty-five aircraft who would be mining the Biscay ports and the Frisian Islands. George wondered why only 323 Squadron was going much further, almost into the Baltic itself. Still, it was an easier op than Dusseldorf and flying low level meant that they should be undetected by radar. Then, once they crossed the Danish coast, they would be gone before the anti-aircraft gunners knew they were there. That was the theory anyway. In reality, the coastal batteries would raise the alarm, and then every gun on both sides of the Kattegat would be waiting for them. Flying straight and level for several minutes after they dropped the mines might not be healthy. No wonder Davies looked uneasy.

George nudged Dingo. 'Piece of cake,' he whispered sarcastically.

'Don't give me the bloody horrors, skipper,' Dingo replied, not looking up as he copied down timings. 'This is supposed to be a milk run. Just keep the kite out the drink and away from the others and we'll be fine. The CO says so and he's a gentleman.' He crossed out a figure and rewrote it. 'What can possibly go wrong?'

George chuckled, but then forced a serious expression as the CO looked at him. 'Something you wish to add, Watford?'

'Just keen to get going, sir,' George replied putting on an earnest expression. The CO studied him for a second.

'Good show, Watford,' he said brightly. 'I'm sure we all feel that way.'

The CO was in high spirits as the crew bus jerked around the peri-track. Pipe clamped between his teeth, he stood with his back against the front and joked with the crews. George had to admit that he had charisma. There was an indomitable spirit about him that made you feel things would turn out well, that this was all just a bit of a lark. However, he also suspected that the man might be too plucky for his own good, or rather for George's own good. The bus stopped at N-Nuts and they struggled out, clumsy in flying gear, parachutes and survival kits.

As the bus pulled away, the CO called out above the grinding engine. 'Remember, stay close!'

'Will do, sir,' George called back. 'But not too bloody close,' he added quietly.

As always, the most unsettling thing was the unknown, the bogeyman waiting in the dark. The noise of the bus faded and George turned to look at his crew, giving them what he hoped was a confident grin. Fear was infectious and he hoped that confidence was too. Whatever he felt inside must not show through on the surface. After a thorough ground check, they stood around the rear tyre and peed. His hands shook slightly as he refastened his trousers. Would experience reduce that fear or would it build over the coming weeks until he had to force himself into the aircraft? He waited for the others to board and followed them inside, patting the aircraft for luck. However, they had stopped just beyond Jim's mid-upper gun position.

'We've got a problem, skipper,' Dingo called back to him. George pushed past to the wing spar and saw the cause of the delay.

'Hello, Watford,' the adjutant said brightly. 'I thought I might join your little jaunt. You don't mind of course.'

George eyed him warily, remembering Davies' warning. 'Does the CO know you're here, uncle?' he asked.

The adjutant's face twitched. 'I'm sure he won't object.'

'So this is unauthorised,' George said and shook his head. 'Sorry, Uncle. I can't do it.' He indicated for the others to squeeze by to their positions and waited as the adjutant clambered dejectedly back over the spar.

'Look, George, I won't get in the way and you're only carrying a light load.' His moustache drooped and he gave a pitiful look. 'For God's sake give this old warhorse a whiff of gunpowder. Being stuck behind a desk all day is driving me bloody well insane.'

George almost laughed at Uncle's hangdog expression. He liked the old boy and was inclined to say yes, but he did not want to fall foul of the squadron boss on his first operation. 'If the CO authorises it you can come anytime, but he'd throw the book at me if I took a passenger.'

The adjutant looked around anxiously. 'No one has to know and I can be a useful friend to have. You scratch my back and so on. For Goodness sake, George, I'm desperate.'

That thought suddenly seemed attractive. Having the adjutant owe him a favour could be useful. He pretended to ponder. 'I don't know, Uncle. It's a big thing to ask.'

'I won't get in the way, old fellow,' Uncle urged, sensing a weakening of George's resolve. 'I'll make it up to you for sure.'

'I really should boot you off you know,' George said and scratched his chin thoughtfully, going through the pretence. In reality, he was considering just what Uncle could do for him. 'I'm risking a lot. You'll be up to your ears in debt to me if I agree.'

'And beyond,' Uncle said readily.

'Well OK, I suppose you can come, but no advice on flying and no distracting the crew.'

'Quiet as the grave,' Uncle crossed himself quickly. 'You're a good man George, I won't forget it.'

'Don't worry, Uncle,' he assured him. 'I won't let you. Now find somewhere to wait while we prep the aircraft.' The adjutant smiled like a child on Christmas morning and scrambled back over the spar.

An hour later, just as the sun was setting, the CO edged A-Able away from dispersal and began the slow crawl around the taxiway. Davies followed in Y-Yoke and then George in N-Nuts. The three Lancasters paused at the start of the runway, waiting in a line for clearance. George settled back into his seat and held the yoke lightly with his fingertips. The time before takeoff was the worst part. In a few moments, he would be too busy flying the plane to think much about the future. But now he remembered Dusseldorf and the aircraft bucking from flak, the wing shredded by cannon fire and he shivered. However, his biggest worry was not the enemy but flying low in the twilight, especially with N-Nuts tendency to wander. A green light flashed from the controller's caravan, A-Able wound up its merlins and started forward. Slowly at first, but then faster until she was just a small shape at the end of the runway clawing skywards and turning to the left. Y-Yoke soon followed. George and Chalky finished the Vital Actions just as the green lamp flashed again and it was their turn. He pressed the intercom.

'Pilot to crew, here we go,' he said and pushed the throttles forward, thumbing the port outer just a fraction more as they spurred forwards. In the distance, Davies' Lancaster climbed away from the field, while in front of her A-Able neared the low cloud base. The three mines weighed one and a half thousand pounds each, a fraction of the Lancaster's maximum load of fourteen thousand pounds. N-Nuts felt light and came off the runway easily. He turned left and followed Y-Yoke into a climbing turn. She was now about a mile away and rising steadily. With a small clump, the wheels came up and the flaps retracted. Two thousand feet overhead A-Able disappeared into the clouds.

'Stay on sixty degrees magnetic, skipper,' Dingo said. 'It's twenty-seven miles until the coast at Saltfleet.' Misty white wisps flicked past the cockpit and N-Nuts rose into the cloud base.

'When do we go low?' George asked.

'Two hundred miles, just before the turning point,' Dingo replied. 'In about an hour's time.'

'Increase revs for two twenty miles-per-hour, Chalky, please. We need to catch up with the others.'

They broke through the clouds at seven thousand feet and continued the climb to ten thousand. Although the sun was still bright at this height, it was swiftly lowering behind some of the higher reaching cumuli, haloing their drab grey shapes with edges of brilliant silver. It was quite stunning. The two Lancasters were directly in front. The plan was to stay high for the first half the journey so German radar operators would think they were heading to Norway. Halfway there, they would drop down and turn right towards Denmark. Thereafter, it would be low level all the way to the target. Although flying low was exhilarating, it was disturbing that N-Nuts would not stay in trim. Flying an unstable aircraft just above sea level was not for the faint-hearted. In addition, the knowledge that two planes had collided just a few days before added little to his happiness.

'Where's Uncle?' George asked.

'Back here, old boy. Keeping Ned company.'

'Not distracting him?'

'Perish the thought. Though I think I might come forward and watch the fun when you go down low.'

'Fun?' Max said. 'Struth Uncle, you've got a strange idea of how to have fun.'

'Best part of flying. On the western front, we used to say '*fast and low is the way to go*."

'Yeah, but they were probably talking about girls, Uncle. I reckon you got yourself confused.'

The Lancasters formed an untidy 'vic' of three and bounced through the choppy North Sea air. Close formation flying was not a skill much used by Bomber Command, a safe separation was far more important during night flying. However, it was not demanding and George relaxed, controlling the aircraft with just the tips of his fingers and small presses on the rudder. Once he was satisfied that they were in a reasonable formation, he tweaked the rev controls to synchronize the four engines. Having every Merlin turning at exactly the same frequency made for a quieter and smoother ride and was far easier to achieve in daylight using shadows cast by the props as a guide. He looked across at the engine temperature gauges on the panel next to Chalky and patted his arm. The port outer was running hot.

Chalky tapped the dial and the needle dropped a little. 'Probably nothing serious, but I'll ease back on it and bring up the port inner just in case,' he said.

'Just when I'd synchronised them,' George muttered. The sun sank lower behind the clouds and their silver halos changed to dark red. Visibility reduced noticeably and he wondered whether they had left it too late for a twilight approach.

'How long till the turn, nav?'

'About ten minutes, skipper. I was just about to warn you.'

George sat up straighter and became more alert. Any second the CO would begin his descent to five hundred feet and bank right, and then it would be hands-on flying every mile of the way. With N-Nuts on the left of the three, he would have to increase power to stay in formation as they turned. The light faded quickly now and the other two Lancasters became little more than dark shapes. When they became even less distinct there would be a strong temptation to close up, but that could bring them too close for safety and it was possibly the reason why two aircraft collided during the last mission. He used two screws around the cockpit glass as visual keys, lining one with the rear of A-Able and one with the front. If he lost sight completely he would drop back, fly on his own and hope to spot the 'pink pansy' target indicator burning on the ground later.

A-Able waggled her wings and descended in a shallow dive. George followed into the clouds and broke through at two thousand feet where it was much darker. At five hundred feet, they banked right and thundered over the sea towards Denmark. The sensation of speed was striking at five hundred feet and it would be greater still when they dropped to one hundred. Below, slate grey water capped with white lines of spindrift rose and fell in an uneven swell. The three aircraft wobbled like merry-go-round horses. Gripping the yoke more firmly with his left hand, he dimmed the instrument lights until they were only just visible. To his right, the CO's Lancaster was now a black shape against a dark background. On the other side of A-Able, Davis' aircraft had disappeared entirely. The sea's surface flicked past and he found the random patterns it created mesmerising. It was far too tempting to take his eyes off the instrument panel and look at the undulating surface. Each time he did N-Nuts lost height. The only safe thing to do was concentrate on the blind flying instruments, the big six. The numbers became a mantra, height five hundred feet, heading eighty-three degrees, indicated airspeed two hundred and twenty miles-per-hour, flat artificial horizon and zero climb or descend.

'Any sign of Y-Yoke, gunners?' George asked.

'Not from back here,' Max replied.

'I think I see him,' Jim said from the mid-upper gun. 'He's pulled up towards the boss; I think he's directly on his other side.'

'Sniffing around the leader,' Dingo said. 'Maybe you should do the same, skipper?'

George smiled, 'I doubt the CO wants us too close on a night like this.' Suddenly a hand patted his shoulder, startling him so much that he dipped the aircraft.

'Take my advice and keep well back.' Uncle's voice said. 'Young Will doesn't like his pilots to fly dangerously unless they're killing Germans.'

'Uncle, you scared the hell out of me. Don't do that.'

'Sorry old chap. Just trying to be helpful,' Uncle replied tartly.

'Well if you want to be helpful, go round with the coffee. We've got a few minutes before we go down to one hundred and I could do with a boost.'

The plan was to approach the coast of Denmark between the German island of Sylt, with its Luftwaffe aerodrome, and the Danish island of Rømø, with its cluster of gun and flak emplacements. The three would fly at low level across the narrow Danish mainland to the east coast, just north of the city of Aabenraa and then on to the island of Funen. Beyond Funen was the Great Belt strait. Codenamed asparagus, this stretch of water between Funen and Zealand islands was their destination.

Here N-Nuts and Y-Yoke would circle in opposite directions while A-Able dropped a target indicator. Using the TI as a navigation point, the aircraft would cross it on different headings like a three prong fork with its left and right tangs bent outwards. N-Nuts would go right, Davies in Y-Yoke was in the centre and the boss in A-Able, having circled back, would come in behind them and be on their left.

A rainsquall suddenly smeared water across the windscreen, obscuring it in a dozen thin streams. However, it was now so dark that looking outside was almost pointless anyway. The horizon blended into the sea and A-Able became more a looming presence than a defined shape. Only the white crests of the biggest waves were visible, although the sensation of speed remained and if anything became more pronounced. Uncle handed him a mug half filled with coffee and he sipped it gratefully. There was a companionship about flying a bomber and being part of a crew. Combined with the roaring Merlins and a needle hovering at five hundred feet, he began to feel an exhilaration that was almost recklessness. Diming the instruments again, he settled back into the intimacy of the dusky cockpit and concentrated on the dials. They must be halfway through the second leg of the journey by now and a quick glance overhead showed the cloud ceiling dissolving into towers of cumulus, between which a few stars shone. The light was also improving and he could suddenly see A-Able quite clearly and even the dim outline of Y-Yoke on its far side.

'Pilot to nav, there's a break in the clouds. Do you need a star shot?'

'Sorry pilot, I'm playing whist with Uncle.'

'Uncle, I'll bloody well throw you out the hatch if you're distracting the crew.'

'But I'm stood right behind you, old boy.' A hand tapped his shoulder again in confirmation. 'Never trust what an Australian tells you about cards.'

Glancing back, he saw Dingo crammed in beside Uncle and pointing his sextant upwards at the glass cockpit roof.

'You clowns will get us all killed one day,' George cursed before draining his coffee and handing the mug back to Uncle. 'Why don't you use the astrodome like normal navigators?'

'Cos' I'm not a normal navigator and Ned gets violent when I stand on him.'

'So would you guys if you had Dingo's backside pressed in your face,' Ned said firmly. 'What with his wind problem and all.'

'It's not me.' Dingo said slowly as he adjusted the sextant. 'I'm the innocent victim of a ventriloquist.' Chalky smiled in the gloom and shook his head.

'We'll be going to one hundred feet soon. One last equipment check everyone please,' George told them.

'I've got a good star shot, skipper. Give me a minute to plot it and I'll tell you exactly where we are.'

'OK Dingo, but hurry. I make it five minutes until we go low.'

'Skipper, A-Able's losing height right now,' Dick said. The bomb aimer's position in the nose gave the best view forward.

'He's keen,' Chalky added.

'No,' George decided. 'He's just taking advantage of the extra light from the cloud break. I'm following him down. Dingo, tell me as soon as you know where we are and the time to the coast. Adjust throttles for one hundred and eighty miles-per-hour please, Chalky.'

George pushed the column forward gently and watched the altitude unwind. Outside the waves grew larger and more distinct as the needle fell. His previous calm evaporated as N-Nuts sunk towards the sea. This was edge of the seat flying, thrilling but dangerous. One hundred feet was nothing. It was the change in height caused by nudging the stick, or from a strong gust of wind. In any case, some of the waves looked as high as small hillocks, so combine any two and you were dead. There was no margin for error, no negative numbers in flying.

'The wash from A-Able's props is whipping up the sea,' Dick said in amazement. Four white phosphorescent trails streamed in the water below the dim outline of the CO's aircraft.

'We're doing the same,' Max said. 'If we go any lower I'm putting in for submarine pay.'

George returned his gaze to the dials, even more determined to focus on height. 'This is too low, Uncle. I thought the first op was supposed to be a breeze?'

'Yes, but it isn't your first op, is it?'

'Don't split hairs, you know what I mean.' The aircraft gave a bump and for an instant, he thought they had touched the water.

'I got a good fix, skipper,' Dingo said. 'I make us about eighty miles west of the island of Sylt. We're a bit south of the course so we should cross the top of the island. Say twenty-five minutes to get there and another five minutes to reach the mainland afterwards.'

'Any hills on the route?'

'Nah, where we're going Denmark is as flat as last week's beer. Only things to worry about are church steeples and power lines.'

'Reminds me of a time on the western front...' a jovial voice began.

'Uncle!' George warned him.

'As the grave old boy,' Uncle replied. 'As the very grave.'

His concentration was absolute, just fine adjustments to the column as he fixated on the instruments. It was so tempting to glance outside at the sea, but apart from a regular peek at A-Able, his attention stayed inside the cockpit and the bank of six blind flying dials.

'I can see breakers,' Dick said after what seemed a short time. 'It looks like land.'

'That'll be Sylt,' Dingo added. 'It depends where we are, but the CO may veer left to make sure we avoid the aerodrome.'

258

George allowed N-Nuts to rise a little. The instruction was to fly at two hundred feet across the land. Ahead a ragged line of white flickered as waves broke on the shoreline. A-Able became more distinct as she banked left in front of them and he adjusted position to stay in formation. Then they soared over a broad sandy beach with a lighthouse to one side and a cluster of houses to the other. It took less than ten seconds to cross Sylt and drop back to one hundred feet over the sea again. Mainland Denmark lay directly ahead.

'Five minutes to the Danish shoreline.' Dingo said. 'I reckon we should be a point or two to starboard.'

'Is that a problem?'

'Could be. Demark is flat but there are a couple of low hills on the other coast just to the left of Aabenraa. On this track, the other two should go over the town but we might clip the hills.' Dingo continued. 'It gets worse after the mainland, Funen Island has hills over three hundred feet high.'

'Crossing the coastline now,' Dick called. They were over Denmark and so far, no one had fired a shot at them.

'Gunners, keep your eyes peeled,' George said. 'We're in bandit country and the fighters back in Sylt may be coming after us.' The Germans must know about them now, although they would not know where they were heading. All he knew of Demark was that its Vikings had once raided England. Well, they were the raiders now. Below, a scattering of buildings flicked past, their white walls reflecting in the weak moonlight and part of his mind registered how attractive they looked. Seconds later, they rushed across a town and he was startled to see A-Able fly alongside a church, its spire higher from the ground than the aircraft. He jerked up a dozen feet, fearing that where there was a town there would also be power lines with cables strung out like trip wires.

'Tell me if we get near the hills, Dingo. I'll pull up to three hundred feet.'

'I can't be that accurate, skipper. We might miss them altogether. Just keep your eyes peeled.'

'OK, but do your best.'

'Searchlights coming on over to the right,' Dick said.

'That'll be Flensburg,' Dingo replied, 'just over the border in Germany. We won't go anywhere near there. Skipper, pull up if you see some small lakes. There's a scattering of them just in front of the hills.'

'We've just gone over them,' Dick said urgently.

'Pull up!' Dingo shouted.

The blackness in front suddenly looked more solid than the rest. George yanked back the column and saw trees flash by below, their tips rushing up at them. He pulled harder. The dark shapes were a carpet quickly rising around them. The Lancaster jarred and pieces of wood sprayed against the cockpit as the propellers lacerated the treetops. To the left, he saw foliage brush against the wing and felt the aircraft tug to port. Just as he was certain the trees would pull them down, they were gone and N-Nuts was clear. He held the column back until his panic subsided and they were a thousand feet up. They had only grazed the edge of the hill but if not for Dingo's warning, they would have flown straight into it. The darkness below looked sinister, full things that could kill but he had to go back into it.

'Christ, that was close,' someone said eventually.

'Too close,' George agreed. 'Well done, Dingo. Check for damage everyone.'

'My trousers are damaged,' Max replied. 'I hope the laundry doesn't charge extra for accidents,' he sounded shaken.

'We've just crossed the other coast,' Dick said. 'A-Able and Y-Yoke are to starboard.'

George glanced across the water to the right and edged N-Nuts down to one hundred feet. Now he no longer concentrated solely on the blind flying instruments, his scan took in the dim outline ahead as well. Not that there was much to see, they were hopping in and out of cloud shadow and where there was no moonlight the water became inky black.

'Ten minutes until we reach Funen island,' Dingo said. 'Pull up to four hundred feet in five minutes. Hold on eighty-three magnetic.'

'Thanks nav, will do.' George glanced at his clock. 'How long until we circle?'

'Around twenty-five minutes, right after we clear Funen.' A break in the clouds showed the sea in the strait to be flat calm and motionless, shining smooth and glassy. He felt tired now, weary. Hours of concentrating on cockpit dials were telling. The added difficulty of keeping N-Nuts in trim made his arms ache and the noise from the unsynchronised port outer engine gave him a dull pain at the back of his head.

'Bring her up, skipper,' Dingo said and looking up he saw the dim outline of Funen, the next island approaching. A gentle pull on the stick took them to four hundred feet just as the coastline rushed below. In front, the ground rose with them. The island consisted of fields as far as he could see. Oblong after oblong, dark and regular with only an occasional wood to alter the view. Nowhere as attractive as the rolling countryside of his Somerset home, or the prairies of Canada.

'Circle left as soon we clear the other side of the island,' Dingo said. 'Passing you over to the bomb aimer.'

Dick would direct them from now on and he spoke carefully as if he sensed that George was tired. 'At the coast, we climb left to two thousand feet and Y-Yoke will turn right to fifteen hundred to give us separation. While we both circle, the CO will drop a TI, so only do a small circle or we'll overshoot. Once you see the indicator, cross it at eighty-six degrees, speed one sixty and come down to fifteen hundred feet.'

'Got it. What angle will Y-Yoke cross at?'

'Fifty-four degrees and the CO will cross at Twenty-one degrees. We go right, Y-Yoke will be in the middle and the boss will be on the left'

'I need you ready to start the run as soon as we circle,' George told the bomb aimer. 'Gunners, shout out when you see the target indicator.'

'Roger, coastline coming up.' Dick said.

George pulled N-Nuts into a rate one climbing circle, levelling off at two thousand feet. 'Anyone see the TI yet?' he asked after a minute. The CO should have reached the aiming point by now.

'There's something away to port,' Jim said from the mid-upper gun position. George looked left. A small bright light flickered on the ground. It looked too dim to be the TI, but suddenly it flared, pink and bright.

'Are you ready, Bomb Aimer?'

'Ready for bombing, skipper.'

'Over to you, Bomb Aimer.' George said.

'Open the bomb doors,' Dick instructed.

George reached for the lever with his left hand. 'Bomb doors open,' he said.

'Come onto eighty-six degrees magnetic, speed one sixty.'

George doglegged to line up and watched the fiery marker disappear under the Lancaster's nose. 'Crossing TI now,' Dick said. 'Come down to fifteen hundred.'

He pressed the column forward and N-Nuts dropped quickly. The Great Belt was only ten miles wide at this point and the mines had to be dropped at five-second intervals, ensuring they got at least one in the central channel. After the last mine had gone they were to fly straight for three minutes, and that would take them over the next island.

'Searchlights coming on ahead and left,' Chalky said, 'and tracer too.'

A quick check of the dials before looking up. In front and slightly to port, two beams shone across the water and bright lines of tracer flickered into the strait. They would be firing at Davies in Y-Yoke who was crossing right in front of their position.

'First mine gone,' Dick said. 'Five seconds to the next. Steady on this course.' The searchlights turned a large stretch of water into a barrier as bright as day. Suddenly a Lancaster flew into the beams. Then about a mile astern of Y-Yoke and further into the strait a second appeared, the CO in A-Able.

'Second mine gone,' Dick repeated. 'Five seconds to the next. Steady on this course.' Both lights converged on Y-Yoke and lines of tracer ripped towards it. The distance looked so short that there seemed little chance of missing and this low Davies could do little to evade.

'Last mine gone,' Dick said. 'Close bomb doors and stay on this course.'

'Negative,' George decided. 'Y-Yoke's in trouble, we're going to rake that flak emplacement. Bomb-aimer, man the front gun and quickly. Gunners, fire to port when I say. Make sure you get the searchlights.' Part of him knew this was reckless, but after destroying Y-Yoke the guns would go after A-Able. George might slip away in the darkness, but the searchlights had the other two trapped. Besides, he hated anti-aircraft guns; it would be good to give them a taste of their own medicine.

'Max revs, Chalky,' he snapped and from the corner of his eye, he saw the engineer push the levers forward.

In the darkness, the emplacement looked evil, a spitting nest of hate, ablaze with muzzle flashes and searchlight beams. He grinned viciously, certain that this was the right thing to do. The Lancaster might be under-gunned compared with a cannon-armed fighter, but its eight machine guns could still lay down a hail of bullets at close range.

George dropped the nose in a rapid dive to five hundred feet and the emplacement closed rapidly. It felt like they were flying into it rather than above. Dull red lights from the enemy's muzzle flashes flickered across the cockpit glass and he edged Mother a fraction to the right and dipped the left wing to give his gunners a clear shot. With luck, the noise from the anti-aircraft guns would mask their approach until they were up close. *Almost there ... Almost...* A short line of tracer lifted towards them and zipped above the aircraft ... *Almost there ...* His mouth was so dry that his tongue felt glued in place. N-Nuts hurtled towards the emplacement.

'Wait... Wait... Fire!' he shouted.

The airframe shuddered as the front and upper twin opened up. Seconds later Max joined in with his four machine guns as they came to bear. Eight bursts of fire raked the emplacement like water spraying from hosepipes, hundreds of rounds flaying the ground. The searchlights blinked off, the anti-aircraft guns stopped firing and they had passed.

'Got the bastards,' Max called.

'I got them,' Jim replied. 'You probably missed.'

'Even you couldn't miss at that range. I could have chucked the bullets out and hit them.'

'Well done, gunners, and you too Dick.' George said. 'Now belt up and keep a lookout.' His arms shook from adrenalin as if he had just run a race. Pulling himself together, he levelled the wings and climbed to two thousand feet. A hand patted his shoulder, but this time he expected it.

'Good show, skipper,' Uncle said excitedly.

'A pleasure, Uncle. Now...'

'Yes I know,' Uncle interrupted, 'silent as the grave.'

'Thanks. Course for home, please nav?' He struggled to talk normally. Thoughts whirred through his head as he replayed the attack like a continuously spooling cinema film. The hurtling approach, the tracer fire from the emplacement, the vibration as their own guns opened up and the lines of bullets flying earthwards. Most of all he replayed his decision to attack, trying to analyse his thoughts and instincts while they were fresh, wondering if they were right and more importantly, whether he could rely on them. Still, they had done it.

'Come around onto three-twenty degrees for about forty miles, say fifteen minutes.' Dingo said and George snapped out of his introspection. 'We need to get into the middle of the strait before heading home, it's safer there,' Dingo added.

'Thanks, Nav. Revs for two ten miles-per-hour, please Chalky. What's our fuel state?'

'No concerns. We've used just under half the load and there's the reserve as well. The port outer is still running hot, but nothing to worry us yet.'

'Ned, are you picking up any chatter from fighters.'

'Nothing, skipper. I think we've caught them out.'

'Don't believe it, they're out there somewhere. If we're lucky, down by the Frisian Islands chasing the other part of the raid,' he added as an afterthought.

The action had driven away much of his weariness and replaced it with exhilaration. It was the feeling of having taken a risk and won, or at least survived. However, he knew it was adrenalin fuelled and once that boost had gone he would feel wearier than ever. They had created carnage back at the anti-aircraft site and it was easy to believe the survivors would call in revenge from their fighters. However, each passing second took them further into the safe and enveloping darkness. They were speeding away from the enemy like bank robbers making off with the loot and that thought added to the thrill. He settled back comfortably into his seat and concentrated once more on the dials. Rather than the crawling sensation at twenty thousand feet, dim shapes whipped past on the ground giving the impression of speed. They were hurtling home. Minutes later, he saw a white line of breakers in the distance.

'Nav, I think we're coming up to another island.'

'Good one, that'll be Samsø. Turn onto two sixty degrees, skipper. We need to cross mainland Denmark and hit the west coast between Blaavandshuk and Fanoe. There're two big gun sites worth avoiding there.'

'Blaavandshuk?' Max said. 'The bloke who named Denmark must have had a cold. That sounds more like a sneeze than a place.'

At a thousand feet and airspeed of two hundred and ten miles-per-hour, N-Nuts crossed onto the mainland just above the town of Fredericia and headed west towards the other coast some sixty miles distant. The Germans obligingly shone searchlights from the gun sites Dingo had mentioned, so he steered an easy course between them. It took twenty minutes to reach the shoreline and apart from odd bursts of tracer that came nowhere near, it was uneventful. Below a white line of breaking waves suddenly signalled the end of enemy-occupied Europe and start of the cold North Sea. N-Nuts banked left in a gentle southwest turn towards England. Twenty miles out from the coast, George decided that any fighters would have a prohibitive tail chase so he pulled back on the column and took N-Nuts up to seven thousand feet. They were going home and it was time for Uncle to dispense more coffee and hand around the sandwiches.

Chapter 18

RAF Blackbrook - 26 November 1942

A truck waited at dispersal to take them to debriefing. After handing back the aircraft to the ground crew and describing the port outer engine overheating problem, they clambered aboard. Uncle slipped out the back and scuttled away before reaching the crew buildings, leaving the others to return his parachute and survival kit. They were the first home and went straight to the intelligence officer's table where the padre offered them mugs of hot chocolate, heavily spliced with rum. At the end of their report, the door banged open and the wing commander stormed in.

'Watford!' he bellowed. 'That was the damndest stunt I've ever seen.' George stood up quickly and turned. The CO still wore his parachute and Mae West and his face looked contorted with anger. 'I should have you bloody well court-martialled.'

Surprise and weariness numbed George's reactions. Staring straight ahead, his face impassive, he waited for the wing commander to continue. Stafford stalked across the room and thrust his chiselled face close to George, glaring menacingly. Then quite suddenly, he broke into a smile. 'On the other hand, it was the best piece of combat flying I've seen in a long time.' He laughed and patted George on the shoulder. 'Bloody first rate. Good show, Watford. Damn good show.'

George slumped in relief and forced a thin smile, uncertain what to say. 'Thank you, sir. It seemed the right thing to do.'

'It was exactly the right thing to do. When in doubt, always attack.' He patted George again and reached across the desk for the rum bottle. 'Let's not be miserly. These boys deserve a proper drink.' The padre smiled weakly and watched

Stafford pour more of his precious rum into their mugs. 'Cheers.'

'Cheers,' they all repeated and took a pull of the fiery liquid. Max drained his mug and reached for the bottle, but the padre snatched it away and smiled apologetically.

'Do you know if Peter Davies made it?' George asked. 'I think his aircraft was hit a few times.'

Stafford reached into his Irving jacket and produced a pipe. 'No one hurt, but apparently, his right wing was shredded and both starboard engines failed over the North Sea. He's put down on the emergency field at Woodbridge.' He swirled the rum in his mug and gave George a sideways glance. 'I dare say the two of us would have got the chop if you hadn't switched off those lights.' George nodded mechanically, unsure what else to say. This was probably as emotional as the CO got, he seemed strictly the stiff upper lip type. 'Now get your boys off to breakfast,' Stafford smiled benignly. 'Just wait till I tell Uncle. This is right up his street. You haven't seen him I suppose?' He stared questioningly at George.

'Not for a little while, sir.' George replied evasively, wondering if the CO knew that Uncle had flown with them. Stafford scrutinised him briefly before beckoning his own crew forward for debriefing.

Outside the building, Dingo stopped and lit a cigarette. He looked back at the door and shook his head with a wistful expression on his face. 'Bloody funny lot,' he said blowing a stream of smoke. 'I mean last night the jokers didn't want to know us and this morning we're the dog's bollocks.'

George put his arm around Dingo's shoulder and steered him towards the mess. 'Just shows what can happen if you do something heroic I suppose.'

'Yeah,' Max joined in. 'But, heroes usually get their nuts shot off. Let's not do anything like that again, skipper. The rest of us just want a quiet life.'

'I don't know, I thought it was exciting,' Jim Ambiolo said carelessly as he combed back his thick blond hair.

Max turned on him. 'Well that's partly because everyone in Norfolk is inbred and stupid, and partly because some woman or her husband will kill you soon anyway.'

Jim put away his comb and set his hat at a jaunty angle. 'Jealousy is such an ugly thing, Maxwell. It's no wonder you have so little luck with the ladies.'

Before Max could reply, Dingo suddenly stopped and pointed a finger at his face. 'And don't start on about me and flaming sheep either.'

George led them laughing into the mess, pleased that no one worried about this raid the way that they had after Dusseldorf. Two missions over, twenty-eight to go and that figure still seemed as impossible as ever. Twenty-eight more raids. What would the next be like and the one after that? How could anyone survive thirty? But at the moment none of the others seemed concerned. Then he realised that was perhaps because he had borne the brunt tonight. This raid had been a pilot's mission, where flying and especially low-level flying was the most demanding part. He had flown the aircraft and even set them up to strafe the anti-aircraft guns. Apart from Dingo navigating, the rest had little to do. Although as he thought back over the night, aside from almost crashing into a tree-covered hill, like Jim he had enjoyed it and that thought worried him.

As he lay in bed later, he again wondered why he had attacked the gun emplacement. He replayed the moment of the decision and tried to understand whether it had been foolishness or clever. Had there been some instantaneous mental calculation that showed the risk was acceptable or had it been instinct and bravado. The first would be reassuring, but the second could be suicidal. And why had he enjoyed it? A memory of the savage joy came back, a clear recollection of the second he knew they could attack and kill the enemy. The knowledge that he was in the right place and at the right time, just like a boxer seeing an opening and landing a blow. It was the same feeling he experienced bombing Dusseldorf. But where did that aggression come from? Generally, he was placid and easygoing, but combat had either found a hidden anger or grown it.

No battle order hung in the flight office that morning, so no operation that night. Somewhere in his underground bunker at High Wycombe, Butch Harris decided to give the jobs to other squadrons, or maybe he was just saving up for a big raid. The crews wondered off to find their trade leaders in case they had training planned. Pilots had no senior specialist so George borrowed a bicycle and pedalled to dispersal where the ground crew swarmed over N-Nuts. In charge of the fitters was Sergeant Alec Simpson and he clambered down from a gantry under the port outer as George cycled up. Simpson was tall, gangling and carried a careworn expression as if every one of the Lancaster's million potential problems would be his fault. Each aircraft's support staff was vital to the aircrew's survival and fortunately, they took a proprietary interest in their aircraft and its crew. It was important for morale to keep them briefed and it was important to tell their sergeant first.

They walked away from the aircraft and George waited while Simpson stuck a cigarette in his mouth and cupped oil-stained hands around a flaring match. 'I hear you did well last night,' Simpson said at last, exhaling a stream of smoke.

'Yes, I think we did OK,' he replied feeling quite smug with himself. His first mission with the squadron and he not only impressed the boss but he made the adjutant indebted to him. A happy state of affairs all considered and he hoped things would not go downhill from here. He leant against a wooden crate and described the raid.

'So, you pasted one of their gun sites,' Simpson smiled. 'Not sure how we should paint that on the kite?'

'Just the usual, it still only counts as one mission,' George decided and glanced at the port-outer engine. 'What's the verdict on the overheating?'

Simpson scratched his head. 'Not sure yet,' he said guardedly. 'The engine gills open automatically to let more air in when it gets hot. We think that for some reason the gills on the port-outer didn't fully open so the engine overheated, but we can't find out why. I've told the boys to change the thermocouples, so fingers crossed that's solved the problem. We'll ground test it later.'

George nodded uncertainly. He liked problems to have definite causes and solutions, anything else could become a major problem in the air. 'How are the airscrews?' The memory of the blades lopping off treetops came back to him.

Simpson raised his eyebrows. 'You could get a job as a lumberjack back in Canada; there were bits of tree all over the place.' He laughed until he coughed and spat on the floor. 'Anyway, two blades were beyond repair so we've replaced them. You'd lost four inches off one and the other was fractured. The rest we'll fix this afternoon.'

'Thanks, Alec and thank the lads for me,' George said, deciding to come back later and watch the ground test. The problem was that mechanical things acted differently in the air. Stresses on an airframe flying at twenty thousand feet were not the same as when sitting on the ground. Things bent in differing ways and just a fraction of an inch could exasperate a problem enough to cause a failure.

The day was dreary, cold, damp and overcast. A monotonous grey cloud covered the sky. It did not rain, but the paths had a wet sheen and windows fogged with moisture. High above the clouds, the sun would be shining as bright as summer, but the maintenance work meant there was no chance of taking N-Nuts for an air test to see it. The Nissen hut was empty when he got back and so he sat at the table and wrote to Millie on a regulation pad of flimsy.

'Dearest Millie,

It was wonderful to spend time with you in London and I hope that you now think the same. I had hoped to hear from you before but I understand how you feel. I miss you greatly and long for my next leave so we can perhaps meet again. I hope you will want that as much as I do.

I have arrived at RAF Blackbrook and it was nice to see the crew again. They all had a good leave and are in fine spirits. The accommodation is much the same as I described at Oakley, although the mess is better. We share a tin Nissen hut that lets out heat faster than the stove makes it, but with a good fire and us all inside, it becomes quite cosy.

The other crews are wary of new boys and so we will have to wait before they accept us as one of them. We are told it takes fives missions before they will even talk to you! It doesn't affect us too much since with seven of us we are never lonely.

We went on our first mission yesterday and I think we did well. The boss was pleased with us anyway. There was little danger and we all came back safely...'

Telling himself to keep the letter's tone light and airy, it was surprisingly easy to fill two pages with tales of life, the crew and even concerns over his father. He desperately wanted to see her again. If he had to live without her, then he knew he would never be free of her. The prospect of years of yearning and never having, depressed him. Then the door burst open and Dingo entered, disturbing his reverie. He stalked across the room and tossed his greatcoat onto to the bed.

'That was the first time I've ever enjoyed a talk from a nav leader,' he said cheerfully. 'He thinks we're the dog's testicles after last night. Kept smiling at me. Gave me the willies after a while.'

George nodded and said nothing. Dingo fished for a cigarette and lit it with his Zippo before sitting on the opposite side of the table. 'What is it, mate?' he asked. 'You look as happy as an orphan on Mother's Day.'

Common sense told him that personal matters were best left personal, but he had no answers and he was growing desperate. 'What's your view on women?' he asked in a roundabout way.

Dingo shrugged. 'Well, pretty favourable on the whole. Why do you ask?'

'I've got a bit of a problem,' George said cagily, 'strictly, between the two of us of course.'

'Don't tell me you've put a bun in some Sheila's oven,' Dingo laughed. 'Bloody horrors George, it's always the quiet ones.'

'It's not that, at least I hope not,' he added as an afterthought.

'Well, what is it then? You haven't caught the pox have you?'

'Look, just shut up and listen,' George snapped. 'This is serious.'

'OK mate, no need to get yourself all cut up.'

'Get your coat and let's go for a stroll. The others could be back any moment and I don't want Max overhearing.'

They left the Nissen hut and walked towards the hangars. While Dingo smoked and waited, George huddled into his greatcoat and wondered how to begin. Ground staff passed and the occasional officer, who they saluted in a perfunctory manner. It was quieter on the perimeter track, with just a few trucks and cyclists hurrying by.

'I pulled a girl out of a building in London during the Blitz,' George began. 'It was in the middle of an air raid and we both ended up in hospital. I guess I sort of fell for her. Mad really, I'd only known her for a few minutes.' He looked at Dingo and smiled sheepishly, but the Australian did not laugh. 'She's a lovely girl, wonderful. But... she kind of disappeared.' George shrugged miserably. Talking about it was not helping that much. 'Well anyway, just before I went to Canada she turned up out of the blue.' They walked on in silence as he wondered how to continue. Apart from the distant noises of fitters working on Lancasters, the only sounds were their shoes crunching the gravel. 'We wrote to each other and this last leave we met up and I... I... spent the night with her.'

'Hey, you sly dog. That's great news...' Dingo laughed and patted George on the back, but then he noticed George was not smiling. 'It is isn't it...? It means you... you know...?'

'I like her a lot, Dingo. The problem is that in the morning, she regretted it and now I'm worried she won't want to know me anymore. I feel bad about what happened as she probably thinks I just used her.'

Dingo sucked his teeth. 'Bloody horrors, skipper. You've been a real galah and no mistake.'

'I know, I know. I just never meant it to happen that way.' George said miserably. 'There should have been romance and dancing. Not a couple of bottles of cheap wine and fumble in the dark.'

'But you didn't stop it happening, did you.'

George felt he should defend himself, blame it all on bad luck and fate, but Dingo was right. 'Look Dingo, I may have been a chump, but telling me what I already know doesn't help.'

'Would your mother like her?' Dingo asked suddenly.

'What? I don't know. Why do you ask?'

'Because I read about it once. Men always want to marry girls who are like their mum, but at the same time, they're attracted to girls that aren't. How did they explain it?' he pondered. 'It's a choice between conforming and rebellion. You feel comfortable with girls who remind you of your mother. So when you fall in love with one who's not like her, it causes emotional conflict. Does that make sense?'

'It makes no sense at all.' George thought about it. 'You're saying I'm like the Greek bloke who was in love with his mother, whatever his name was.'

'No, I'm not saying you're in love with your mum. That's disgusting. What I'm saying is that men go for women who are like their mothers and worry if they're not.'

'Even if that's true, and I don't agree it is, what's it got to do with me?'

Dingo took a final pull of his cigarette and with a quick glance to make sure no one was watching, flicked it towards the fence. 'Dunno, like I said I'm no expert. But to me the answer's obvious.'

George looked at him. 'Not to me, it isn't.'

Dingo wrapped his arm around George's shoulders and said. 'Mate, the chances are that we'll all be dead in the next few weeks. So instead of worrying about having too much of a good thing, just enjoy it while you can.'

George laughed. 'And there you have an Australian's philosophy to life in a nutshell.'

Someone placed the wireless in the middle of the sergeant's mess bar that evening and they all waited while it warmed up. The mess was crowded with aircrews, around a hundred individuals standing in groups of seven, except where some crewmembers had commissions and lived in the officers' mess, then just four or five stood together. As before, the dress was a curious blend of flying and ground clothes, with white pullovers under uniform jackets being the most popular. George and the others dressed similarly, so at least they now looked the part. However, from the corner of his eyes, he noticed several glances in their direction and not a few stares. Clearly, word of their attack on the gun position had spread and he felt the reaction was a small triumph, although it was hard to tell whether the looks were friendly or just driven by curiosity. All the same, it made him hold his head a little higher and laugh a little louder at one of Max's jokes. However, one particular pilot stood slightly apart from his crew and gave George a direct, hard stare. At first, he wondered if the pilot knew him from somewhere but when he met his eyes there was no sign of recognition or greeting, just a blank cold gaze. Very odd.

Churchill was due to speak to the nation and no one wanted to miss it. 'Shut up you lot, he's on,' someone near the front shouted. Conversation stilled and the growly, unmistakable voice of the Prime Minister filled the room.

'*Two Sundays ago all the bells rang to celebrate the victory of our Desert Army at Alamein...*' Several crews cheered at this, lifting their glasses to toast what was the first significant victory. Churchill was off to a good start.

'No mood of boastfulness, of vainglory, over-confidence must cloud our minds, but I think we have a right, which history will endorse, to feel that we had the honour to play a part in saving the freedom and the future of the world...' This was typical Churchill. Pugnacious, certain, his tone and words leaving no doubt that they were doing the right thing, the honourable thing. Churchill went on to describe the war's progress, saving special praise for their American allies. Then he came to Bomber Command.

'Already the centres of war industry in Northern Italy are being subjected to harder treatment than any of our cities experienced in the winter of 1940... the whole of the south of Italy, all the naval bases, and all the munitions establishments and other military objectives wherever situated will be brought under prolonged scientific and shattering air attack.' That made them look up. Italy was a long flight, but it was nice to know where they would be going. Hopefully, the enemy was not listening and expecting them. Later Churchill spoke of the war ending in Europe.

'... If events should take such a course we should at once bring all our forces to the other side of the world to the aid of the United States, to the aid of China and above all to the aid of our kith and kin in Australia and New Zealand in their valiant struggle against the aggressions of Japan...'

'Hey, you blokes,' Dingo shouted. 'How about that! We could all be off down-under.' A scattering of his fellow countrymen cheered and the broadcast ended. Churchill's voice and rhetoric left hope and optimism in its wake like a stirring piece of music. The room buzzed with conversation as a gramophone replaced the wireless on the bar.

278

'What do you think of that, Dick?' Chalky asked. As ever, they deferred to the bookish bomb aimer for the considered view.

'I think he's good, very good,' Scrivener replied. Although he seemed less roused than the others did. 'It was clever how he implied we'll win the war, even though we've yet to set foot across the channel. He even warned that we'll have to fight the Japanese after we've beaten the Germans.'

George had been thinking about Australia and savouring the possibility of going there. He studied Dick for a second. 'You didn't like what he said?' he asked, curiously.

'It's not that so much. Churchill is a brilliant orator, probably one of the best there's ever been, and that's the trouble. He is too convincing, he leaves little room for doubt or question. How could you possibly argue against such eloquence and have an alternative view considered?'

'Alternative?' Max interrupted. 'What alternatives are there? You may not have noticed, chum, but we're in the middle of a bleeding war. What choice do we have other than to fight?'

'Maybe no choice about fighting, it's too late for that. But perhaps some choice in how we fight.'

'Come on then genius tell us how General Scrivener would beat the Germans?' Max chided.

They all watched, waiting for his reply. Dick shrugged self-consciously and glanced at his feet before speaking. 'I don't know... Well, for instance, is bombing really the best use of resources? Until recently, we've been lucky to drop a bomb within five miles of the target, more like fifty miles. Yet the navy is desperate for frigates and destroyers to protect the convoys. The army didn't even have any tanks in the Far East and Singapore surrendered.'

'Yeah, but all the guns in Singapore were pointing out to sea. They couldn't train them landwards,' Jim said. 'Stupid pongoes,' he added.

'Not so. That's a myth. They could turn shoreward, but they didn't have high-explosive shells, just armour piercing and they're no use against land targets. They might have held out if they'd had the right ammunition. That's all I mean. Is Churchill such a dominant force that no one can argue with him?'

'Is that what you think?' George asked. 'That Churchill is getting it wrong?'

'No, I don't think he's getting it wrong at all, but no one's right all the time. With our backs against the wall, Churchill is just what the country needs. But all I'm saying is that it does no harm to question his decisions and I hope people are doing just that.'

'Well, I'm glad you've explained things,' Max said, rubbing his face. 'Personally, I'm none the wiser, but now I'm worried that something that might not be happening isn't happening, whatever it is.'

'You don't strike me as the worrying type,' George said, amused by the pained expression on Max's face.

'Well, I don't hold with it as a rule. But thanks to our bomb aiming boffin here, I think I might have to take it up.' He snatched the cigarette from Dick's hand and took a puff. 'Though, I always believed too much thinking is bad for you.'

Dick dipped his fingers into Max's beer and touched the end of the cigarette, dowsing it. 'So is thievery, you cockney chiseller.' Perhaps it was the effect of Churchill's broadcast, but the mess was far livelier and noisier tonight and that energy was infectious.

'What do you think about the bombing, George?' Chalky asked and they all looked at him.

George did not like philosophising about the war, mainly because he still had to fully crystallise his thoughts. There were too many contradictions and gaps in his views. However, the hatred of seeing the waves of German bombers killing and destroying London was still there, as was the thirst for revenge it created. Someone had to speak for the victims in all this, the ones who could no longer seek justice for themselves. Those whose lives were torn apart and could never be repaired. But confusingly, now there was Millie, a German who he loved. How many other Millie's were there? Decent Germans caught up in a madness they wanted no part of. He could not give a wise answer and he doubted that there was one, so he decided to fall back on gut feelings and the things Millie said about Nazis. How the Germans had begun the bombing campaign and that Bomber Command was the only one who could take the fight directly back to them. But, before he could speak a gangly bomb aimer in Australian uniform joined their group. 'The name's Tim Patterson. I see you got an Aussie in your crew,' he said with a grin.

Dingo reached across and shook his hand. 'Dingo Johnson. Where you from, mate?' he asked.

'Good to meet you, Dingo. I'm a *Gum Sucker* from the Bays. How 'bout you?'

'I'm a *Top-Ender* myself,' Dingo replied proudly.

'Come and meet the boys, the skipper's a Kiwi.'

'Stack me,' Max said in amazement as they followed. 'When they talk it's like listening to Gone with the Wind in Australian.*'

At least this was progress. One action seemed to have won them partial acceptance. Or maybe it was the fellowship of Australians or just the fact that Churchill's speech buoyed everyone up and made them friendlier. Not that it mattered; the main thing was that they were no longer outsiders in a private club. However, as he followed behind Patterson he noticed the other pilot still staring at him. It was now a venomous look, hard and contemptuous. That glare summed up all the mean-spiritedness that he hated. He had seen it so often in people who treated others badly for no better reason than they wanted to.

'Bloke over there's giving you the evil eye, mate,' Dingo said nodding in the pilot's direction.

'I noticed. Maybe I should go and introduce myself?'

'Nah. I'll do the talking if it's needed.'

He looked back at Dingo curiously. 'Thanks, Dingo, but I can fight my own battles,' he said indignantly.

Dingo raised an eyebrow. 'Don't get riled, skipper. I know you can. But, I can navigate with a cracked rib and a black eye, can you fly a kite?'

George shrugged. 'Maybe not,' he had to agree.

'Well then stay out of trouble for all our sakes,' Dingo said and turned to Patterson. 'Who's the drongo over there?'

Patterson glanced across the room. 'He's Tug Wilson, mate,' he said quietly. 'Bad piece of work, well worth avoiding if you can.'

'What's his problem?' George asked.

'He's on his second tour and a bit flak-happy if you ask me. Kangaroos loose in the top paddock. He wants a commission but the CO knocked him back because he gets as mad as a cut snake about stupid things. He won't be happy because you've got in well with the boss. Just ignore the silly bugger, that's what we all do.'

George shrugged and introduced himself to Patterson's pilot, Harry Tate. The New Zealander was blond haired, fresh-faced and looked incredibly young. But as they talked, a tremor flickered disconcertingly above his right eye, which George pretended not to notice. Tate was friendly enough but strenuously avoided any talk of operational flying, despite some pointed questions. It was not clear whether this was superstition or if he thought it bad form to talk shop in the mess. Instead, they spoke of training. Tate had learned to fly in Rhodesia and although he loved the country, the skies were mostly clear and the weather generally fine, which left him badly prepared for the storms and dense clouds over Europe. Despite glares from Tug Wilson, George enjoyed his evening and the first real taste of life in an operational squadron. However, Tate's tremor bothered him. More so as he looked at the other crews and saw signs of stress etched their faces as well. Maybe that was why Tate avoided the subject, knowing how bad the operations were would not help. The scratchy gramophone music stopped and a singsong began around the piano. George and the others wandered across the room to where the crews gathered.

This is my story, this is my song
I've been in this air force too flaming long
So God bless the Rodney, Revenge and Renown
But we can't say the Hood 'cause the blighter's gone down!

From the corner of his eye, he noticed Uncle at the bar with Flight Lieutenant McEwen, the Supply Officer, talking animatedly to the mess steward. This was unusual because officers only came to the sergeant's mess by invitation. Sergeants needed a place to relax away from the glaze of officers, so this must be an official visit. Uncle's face grew redder as they spoke and although his words were lost in the singing, the conversation was clearly becoming heated. At one point Uncle slammed his hand on the bar and the steward held his arms up in a gesture of futility, while the Supply Officer just looked sheepishly at his feet. Max had seen the confrontation too and as soon as the two officers left, he made a beeline for the steward. Ten minutes later, he was back.

'What was it about?' George asked him.

'Uncle's in big trouble,' Max grinned. 'Apparently, they've run out of bacon and there's none in the main stores either. The CO is livid and refuses to send the boys on operations without a decent meal. He completely lost his rag and told Uncle that either he sorts it out or he's posted to the Middle East.'

George thought for a moment and then smiled. 'You can get anything for the right price,' he said happily.

Uncle had his head buried in his hands and looked about as miserable as anyone George remembered seeing. A glass of whiskey sat untouched in front of him on the desk. 'Cheer up Uncle,' he said brightly. 'It might never happen.' Uncle scarcely registered his arrival.

'Already has, I'm afraid.'

George sat on a chair in front of the desk and was amused to see a flicker of annoyance cross Uncle's face. 'Look, old boy, nice of you to drop by but I'm really not in the best of moods for company right now. So if you could come back some other time it would be appreciated.'

'Of course,' he said and stood up. 'I just heard you were in the market for bacon. But I won't disturb you.' He laughed inwardly. It was fun to play knowing he had all the cards needed to win the hand.

Uncle did a double blink and reached to stop George leaving so fast that his hand knocked the whisky glass, splashing liquid onto the desk. 'Wait, wait. You mean you can get bacon?'

'Possibly,' George turned. 'It depends on the price.'

The look on Uncles face was that of a condemned man receiving a last-minute reprieve from the gallows. 'Name it. What do you want?' he spluttered.

Sitting down again, he looked directly into Uncles red eyes. 'I want the going rate for pig meat, whatever that is,' he said simply, starting with his lesser demand.

'You've got it.'

'Plus a Lancaster.'

Uncle remained silent for a few seconds before a thin smile of incredulity spread across his face. 'Be serious, George. I can't give you a bomber. They'd notice one was missing for a start.'

'Don't be an ass, Uncle. I want the next new Lancaster that comes onto the base. N-Nuts is falling apart. Its airframe's bent and the engines are knackered. It's dangerous to fly let alone take on a raid. I want a brand new one,' he said, and that was his bottom line. It had come to him in the mess. Taking Uncle as a passenger on the raid was not enough of a favour to get him a new aircraft, but he hoped this was.

'Be reasonable. I can't give you a new one,' Uncle tried to explain patiently. 'They always go to the most experienced crews.'

George kept a poker face. 'Yes and I'll get another worn out cast-off. Well, not this time. I want the next new one or you end up in a tent in the desert dreaming of an English winter.'

Uncle's mouth opened and closed a few times like a fish chewing food. Finally, he spoke quietly. 'OK, OK, it's a deal. But the bacon has to be on site tomorrow morning.'

'Not possible, Uncle. I need a driver and a truck to go to Somerset and back.'

'Somerset? But that will take a day and we could be on ops tomorrow night.'

Now it was George's turn to frown. He wanted a new aircraft very badly. Flying a wreck like N-Nuts lowered their chances of survival and he wanted every advantage he could get. 'Well, at least you'll have some in the pipeline?'

'That's not enough to satisfy young William, I'm afraid. He told me to get the bacon by tomorrow *ack emma* or get forth.' Uncle tapped his fingers on the desk thoughtfully. Suddenly he brightened. 'I presume you're getting it from a farm?'

'Yes, but I can't tell you which one.' George did not want Uncle thinking he could go directly to his father. Not that it would work, but he might try to obtain the meat himself if he realised the pigs were illegal.

'It doesn't matter. Farms have fields. You could fly one of the station's *hacks* down to darkest Somerset first thing tomorrow morning. We've got a Lysander, you can land in a field and be back before mid-day.' As well as fighting aircraft, every squadron kept a number of odds and sods aircraft known as 'hacks'. Usually, these were planes retired from front-line service and acquired by squadrons for transport and communications.

'I flew the Lysander in Canada,' George said slowly, remembering them with little enthusiasm. The aircraft had some unusual characteristics.

'Good. Then there's nothing to worry about, old boy. You can get the goods and be back before lunch. I'll have Pincher Martin and his boys to fit a fuel tank ready for first light.'

'It was more the landing and takeoff from a field that bothers me.' You needed to use the Lysander's trim wheel to get the nose up and down for short landings and takeoffs; the stick alone would not do it. He remembered that the trim wheel was stiff and awkward, taking about twenty seconds to wind from one end to the other. Then there was landing in an unprepared field to consider. The wheel could hit a rock, roll into a rabbit hole or become stuck in mud.

'You're a good pilot, you can do it.' Uncle urged. He sounded desperate.

There was not much to consider. The dangers of flying a Lysander onto a field were minimal when compared to taking N-Nuts on a mission. 'I need to use your phone to make arrangements at the other end.'

'Good man. Be my guest,' Uncle offered, gesturing at the instrument.

'In private, Uncle.' George wanted to speak to his parents about matters other than meat. 'But before you go, how much bacon do you need?'

Chapter 19

RAF Blackbrook - 28 November 1942

The gentle shaking of his shoulder woke him. He opened his eyes and saw the dim outline of an Erk standing above the bed. 'It's oh five hundred, Sergeant,' the figure said quietly. George mumbled his thanks and swung his legs out of bed. The hut was dark and cold, but he felt a thrill at the prospect of flying to Somerset to see his parents and home. He wondered what their reaction would be to him landing an aircraft in their paddock. After stretching, he nudged Dingo with his foot and they dressed quietly before heading for the shower block and the Met Office. Pale morning light had only just lit the horizon when they stepped off the truck next to the aircraft. The stores' officer was already there and he gave George an envelope containing payment before quickly disappearing. The day was chilly and damp, but with little wind. The met officer predicted it would be sunny later, but temperatures would only just rise into double figures.

With a powerful Bristol Mercury engine in front and gull-wings sited above the fuselage, the Lysander had a strong, chunky appearance. Big glass windows surrounded the cockpit giving excellent visibility, especially below.

'Bit different to a Lanc,' Dingo said eyeing the aircraft suspiciously.

George nodded towards the wings. 'The wing slats and flaps are particularly interesting.'

'In what way are they *interesting*?'

'Or concerning,' George replied thoughtfully. 'Depends on your point of view really.'

'Come on then, Skipper. Give me the good news.'

'They deploy automatically when the aircraft is slow and at an angle to create a large wing area. Then, as speed increases or the kite levels off, they retract giving less support but allowing higher speeds.'

'And the problem with that is?'

'It means takeoffs and landings have to be on all three wheels to keep the aircraft at an angle, otherwise the slats and flaps retract just when you need them the most. If you're level and need flaps you have to wind the trim wheel very quickly to set the aircraft at an angle and that's a bit disconcerting to pilots used to setting flaps themselves.'

'You know, sometimes I wish I joined the navy.'

'We'll be fine.' George told him. 'At least I hope we will.' He added and patted the Australian on the back.

'Bloody horrors,' Dingo muttered and shook his head.

After ground checks, George climbed the wheel housing, dropped into the cockpit seat and plugged in his intercom cable. Dingo clambered up a ladder and slid into the observer's space behind, where he faced backwards.

'You ready, Dingo?' George asked although he was not completely sure that he was. He had become used to the Lancaster's cockpit and having Chalky by his side to take care of the details.

'Yeah, if you're sure you can fly this crate,' was the cautious reply. 'You are sure aren't you?'

'Course I am. I flew one in Canada.' He started priming the carburettor bowl with rapid pumps of the primer handle.

'And you still remember how to do it?'

George thought for a second. 'I remember everything I was taught,' he replied, switching the primer to the cylinders.

'I know I'll regret asking this, but they did teach you everything I suppose?'

'I've got to be honest with you, Dingo. One day a training plane went missing and they sent every available aircraft to search for it. There was only a Lysander left and so I took that. Never actually had any instruction, but I've read the pilot's notes. So I've flown one and I'm still here to tell the tale.' He switched on the main ignition switches and the starting magneto. Finally, he pressed the starter button and the heavy prop turned slowly. After three rotations, the engine coughed, fired and started with a roar. *Well, that part worked anyway*. While the engine warmed, he adjusted his seat height. A great thing about the Lysander was that the pilot was high up and had excellent visibility, he could even see forward above the engine while sitting on the ground.

'Is it too late to swap with Max?' Dingo asked.

'Much too late I'm afraid,' George laughed and slid the glass canopy closed. 'We're off.' He gunned the engine, which clattered like a heavy machine gun and they moved onto the taxiway.

'Bloody horrors, Skipper,' Dingo swore. 'I've just remembered that I don't like flying backwards.'

Climbing to eight thousand feet and at a steady speed of one hundred and twenty miles-per-hour, they headed on a course of two hundred degrees directly towards Bath. A honeycomb of white cirrocumulus hung high above, while all around floated fat round blobs of stratocumulus. The clouds took an orange tint as the sun crept further over the horizon and soon heat from the engine made the cockpit so hot that George opened the side windows to enjoy some fresh air. In that instant, he felt intensely happy. Flying without threat from the enemy and heading towards the people he loved.

'Well I'm looking forward to talking to your folks about this Sheila of yours, mate,' Dingo said after a while. 'We can start planning the wedding. What was her name again ... Molly isn't it?'

George smiled to himself. 'That depends on how much you want me to concentrate when we go on ops. Emotional pressures can make you do the daftest things.' He pushed the stick forwards and shoved up the throttles. The Mercury engine gave a huge backfire and pulled the Lysander into a steep dive. The book said the Lysander could do three hundred miles-per-hour downhill and he was curious about that.

'OK, OK skipper,' Dingo shouted as the aircraft suddenly plunged. 'I won't mention the wedding. My oath I won't.'

They reached two eighty with no wing flutter and so he guessed the book was right. Pulling smoothly back on the stick and throttles, they soared back to eight thousand. *Maybe life as a fighter driver wouldn't be so bad,* he thought to himself. There was certainly a thrill to stunting an aircraft.

'Make sure that you remember that, bushwhacker,' George said. 'Or I'll fly us home inverted.'

'Tell you what, skipper. I will as long as you don't make jokes about sheep, us going to a farm and all.'

'It's a deal. Now I can see a city in front. I guess that's Bath?'

'Unless they've moved Bristol ten miles east.'

'Or your navigation's out.'

'Mate, it's more likely that they've moved Bristol. Give me a compass and a good star and I'll...'

'Find the Pope's private bordello,' George finished the sentence for him. With complete certainty that he would recognise the landscape, he dropped the nose and banked left. He remembered once standing on the barn wall and watching spellbound as an aircraft crawled across the sky, trying hard to picture the pilot's view. Soon he would land this aircraft next to that barn. However, at that moment the

291

countryside seemed so different from above that he did not recognise it. Then the symmetry clicked in and he identified the straight line of a train track, the curving river where he had fished, the undulating roads he had cycled and the fields where he had played.

In the distance was the valley next his farm and he felt a sudden longing for home, stronger than ever before. The farmstead was to the right so he dipped the wing and began a slow descent. He recognised the farmhouse straight away, on the crest of a hill next to a cluster of outbuildings and a milking parlour. Finally, like an old friend he saw the barn in the paddock. Throttling right back, he took the aircraft into a low, slow orbit around the farmhouse. The Lysander's stall speed was less than sixty miles-per-hour and the orbit seemed ridiculously slow.

'Reception committee,' Dingo said. Below to the left, three figures emerged from the farmhouse and waved at them. He recognised his mother and father at once and guessed that the other person was the farmhand, Chester.

Wanting to land as smoothly as possible in front of an audience, he decided the best course was to establish a workable glide angle and then try not to change it or the power setting until touchdown. Any adjustment upwards would cause the flaps to alter and then he would have to swing the trim wheel and bring the aircraft's nose up to deploy the flaps again. Waving back to the three he gunned the engine and climbed away to two thousand feet. There he stood the Lysander on its wingtip, purely for show and lined up with the barn before dropping the speed to eighty miles-per-hour. Setting mixture to rich, pitch to fine and cowl flaps open, he was ready and the paddock raced towards them. His father assured him that there were no holes or ditches hidden in the grass and he hoped he was right. A quick sideslip to line up and he sped over the hedge. After the briefest of flares, all three wheels touched the grass at the same time with no more than a small bump. He breathed a sigh of relief and taxied towards the farmhouse and the group.

'George! George!' he heard his mother call once the propeller clattered to a stop and he slid back the canopy. She ran to the aircraft excitedly. 'My goodness, this is wonderful,' she gasped and walked along the Lysander, touching it lightly as though it was a cow she did not want to startle. He watched her intently; amused by the way the aircraft animated her. It was so genuine. Her hair fluttered in the breeze and her face was pink from the chilly air and excitement.

'I can't believe you flew this. I mean, I know you're a pilot but seeing the aircraft in the air and knowing it's you flying it...' She held her arms wide and looked at him, lost for words.

At that moment, he knew he would never again have to worry about his parents approving of him being a pilot. No longer would he just tell them about flying and hope it meant something. They had seen it and now they knew. 'Would you like to come for a flight, Mum?' he asked on impulse.

'Would I like to?' she asked slowly and stared at him questioningly, debating. Then she looked at the aircraft and back at her son. 'Yes... I'd love to... I want to. You are being serious aren't you?'

'Of course. We can't be up long, but there's time for a quick circuit. Just let me say hello to the others first.' He turned to Dingo. 'Dingo, come and meet my mother.'

Dingo extended a hand and she took it, smiling at the Australian. 'Good to meet you, Mrs Watford,' Dingo said.

'Why you're an Australian,' she said and stared at Dingo as if he was from another planet.

'And a farmer's boy too. Course it's all a little different where I come from.

'Australian,' his mother repeated, dazed enough by the aircraft but now she had met someone from the other side of the world.

'We're just normal folks, Mrs W,' Dingo laughed. 'Just like here.'

His father and Chester stood a little way back, staring suspiciously at the Lysander as if it might decide to start up and fly off by itself. George shook hands with his father, who was so transfixed that he scarcely acknowledged his son.

'An aeroplane in my paddock,' he muttered in wonder, shaking his head. 'Well, I never did.'

'Thanks for providing meat for the squadron, Dad.' George said and offered him an envelope. 'This is a promissory note for payment from the stores' officer. You should be able to cash it at a bank, but any problems and just let me know.'

'That's OK lad,' His father said absently and moved his head slightly to the left so that he could still see the aircraft. 'Well, well. An aeroplane in my paddock,' he repeated in awe.

George smiled, put the envelope in his father's hand and moved on to Chester who was equally enthralled. 'Good to see you again, Chester,' he said patting the big man on the shoulder.

Chester flicked his eyes at George and nodded. 'You too, George,' he said slowly. 'You really are a pilot, then. You really do fly?'

George smiled. 'Yes, I fly. I'd take you up too but I don't think there's time.'

Chester shook his head. 'Thanks, but you wouldn't get me up in one of those for all the tea in China.' He shrugged his shoulders sadly. 'Anyway, I've got to round up the pigs for you.'

George was about to turn away when he suddenly stopped. 'What do you mean, round them up?'

'Well they won't put themselves on your aeroplane, will they?' he said as if George was being dim and looked again at the Lysander. 'Mind you, I don't suppose they'll be any happier about flying than I am. They don't even like it in the back of a truck.'

'You've got live pigs for me?' George asked incredulously.

'Chose them myself,' Chester said proudly. 'Six of the best. Pick of the herd straight from the woods this morning.'

'Chester you lunatic, I can't carry live pigs,' George exploded. Just when things seemed to be going well. 'The back of the aircraft is made of canvas and wood. They'd be through the sides in a flash.'

'You could try singing,' Chester offered. 'Sometimes that quietens them. The big old boar is especially partial to a bit of Gracie Fields.'

His mind whirled with thoughts of whether they could tie them securely or even quickly slaughter the animals. Would the station cooks even know how to deal with live pigs? Then he noticed the others laughing and he cursed himself. 'You're joking, aren't you?'

'Luckily we'd already slaughtered a batch,' his mother told him, her eyes alive with amusement. 'Come on. If you're still willing to take me flying, Dingo can go for breakfast up at the farm. Could you manage bacon and eggs?' she asked turning to Dingo.

'Sure can, Mrs W. The mess wasn't open when we left.'

'I'll send him back with a sandwich for the driver,' his father added. 'Are you really going up in that thing?' he asked his wife incredulously.

'Yes I am,' she said defiantly. 'I've wanted to fly ever since George told me about Canada. So don't you dare try and stop me.'

His father took a step backwards. 'Wouldn't dream of it. Just as long as you don't expect me to go up there as well.'

Dingo gave her his headset and fleeced jacket and George helped her into the observer's seat. As soon as she was strapped her in and knew how to work the intercom they were ready to go. 'I'll leave the canopy open so you can see better,' he said, grinning at her expression. 'Let me know if you feel sick or not enjoying yourself and we'll come straight back. OK?'

She nodded, looking apprehensive but determined.

'I'm proud of you, Mum,' he told her and climbed away into the cockpit and started the engine. Once the temperature gauge showed one hundred degrees and the oil pressure had stabilised at eighty, they were set.

'Are you ready?' he asked.

There was a delay and then an excited voice said, 'Let's just go, George, before I change my mind.'

He pushed the throttle forward gently, determined to be as smooth as possible not to scare her and they bumped off along the grass. The end of the paddock fell steeply into the valley and through the windmilling propeller, sunlight reflected brightly from bare beeches and elms on the other side. To the right was the old barn and he smiled at memories of standing on it and pretending to fly when life was so very different. After just sixty yards speed built to ninety miles-per-hour. He pulled back the stick and they were airborne.

'You're flying, Mum,' he called happily. 'How does it feel?'

Eventually, she said, 'I'll let you know when I've opened my eyes.'

He chuckled and climbed straight to two thousand feet. 'Please open your eyes. It's quite safe and we don't have long.' He waited, tensing in case she screamed.

'It's unbelievable,' she said at last, 'and so beautiful.'

He was relieved that she enjoyed flying. No, delighted was a better word. It was such a big part of his life and not being able to share it with his parents left a gap between them. 'Where would you like to go?' he asked. 'We've got about twenty minutes.'

'Over the village,' she said. 'I'd like to see it from the air.'

George nudged the Lysander around and they did a circuit of the farmhouse again. His father, Dingo and Chester were still there watching motionlessly as he took the aircraft even lower and slower than before. Then he headed to Torcombe and dropped into the valley at just over rooftop height. After a wide circuit to allow his mother time to see it, he came back for another pass. An instructor once said that the Lysander was difficult to stall and he tested that to the limit. This time he motored slowly down the valley at rooftop height and with the nose pointing upwards to give maximum flaps. Then there was no more time and so with a sigh, he wobbled his wings at the few staring villagers and climbed away, looping back towards the farm.

Chester had wrapped six carcasses inside hessian sacks and he hefted them into the back of the Lysander where Dingo tied them securely. George hugged his mother and as she pulled away, he saw her face was wet with tears.

'It's been wonderful to see you again,' she said. 'but it's so cruel that it's for such a short time,'

'We're given leave every six weeks,' he replied. 'It'll soon come around.'

She looked at the ground, biting her lip. 'When do you go to war?' she asked quickly.

'I don't know. Not for a while, I expect,' he replied as lightly as he could.

'Don't lie to me George,' she said firmly.

'Sorry,' he apologised. 'Tonight probably. It's why they wanted the meat this morning. We have a pre-op meal of bacon and eggs as a treat.' He shrugged. 'Also someone said that the gates had been locked last night. They do that just before a mission.'

She nodded as if it confirmed her suspicions. 'Where will you be going?'

'No idea. If we are on ops then there'll be a briefing this afternoon and that's when they tell us. It's why we have to get back now.'

His mother walked in a small circle before coming back to him. She tried to smile but failed. 'I'm not going to be some weepy woman, I'm stronger than that,' she said, defiantly.

'I know you are, mum,' he told her.

'But I'm scared, George. Two boys in the next village have been killed fighting in the army.'

'I'm a good pilot, I'll get through.' He looked at Dingo. 'And Dingo's a great navigator; he'll get us safely home.'

She gave a small laugh and cuffed her eyes. 'Are you a great navigator, Dingo?' She called to him.

Dingo turned and walked across. 'Great? Did he say I was only great?' He puffed himself up. 'Mrs W, I'm better than great, why I'm outstanding. Give me a compass and a couple of stars and I'll find you the Popes private...'

'Bathroom,' George interrupted quickly.

Dingo grinned sheepishly and looked at George. 'Skipper, we need to be going.'

'Yes. Sorry Mum, but Dingo's right.'

'Go quickly then,' she told him. 'Phone me tomorrow once you get back from tonight.'

'I don't know for sure that we'll be on ops.'

'Then call me anyway.' He climbed into the cockpit and turned to see his mother and father waving while Chester just stared. Behind them stood the farmhouse, solid and respectable, its windows watching curiously. For a moment, it brought such longing that his hands froze midway through priming the engine. It was another picture to lodge in the album of his memory and he had to force his gaze away and continued pumping. He had never been materialistic, never wanted money or objects for the sake of it. However, the remote possibility of marrying Millie and living here, then one day becoming its owner, sent a thrill through him. He knew now that he belonged in this place and he desperately wanted to survive and return. Moreover, his parents reminded him of another, deeper duty. There were two sides to his life now and his wartime self was as out of place as the Lysander in the paddock. Both he and the aircraft belonged to another world, one where different rules applied. However, war was finite and one way or another it would end. If he survived, he would return. Then he pictured aircraft burning in the night sky and knew it could so easily be him. But if not for the war he would never have met Millie. Sometimes you had to buy admission to a better life and sometimes that price was just too high.

Uncle and McEwen, the supply officer, eagerly awaited their return. They jogged over to the aircraft even before the propeller stopped turning. McEwen undid the side panels and pulled back one of the hessian sacks to inspect the carcass. He nodded at Uncle and waved to a nearby truck.

Uncle turned to George. 'Well done old boy, you've brought home the bacon,' he said, beaming.

'And saved yours, Uncle. You won't forget our deal.'

'Not a bit of it. In fact, they're delivering a new Lancaster later this week. Funnily enough, when young William heard where you were going, he seemed happy that you should have it. So it's in the bag.'

George nodded gratefully, but then he noticed the activity around the squadron's Lancasters. 'Are we on ops tonight?'

'Afraid so,' Uncle said looking at his watch. 'In fact, the briefing's just about to start.' He turned to McEwen. 'Mac, drop us off at the briefing room pronto, there's a good fellow. The boss knows you're back and he'll wait a few minutes, but best not to push it too far.'

'What's the target?' George asked, feeling a tightening of his stomach.

'No idea, but they're filling maximum fuel, so it's not close.'

George could hear a low babble of conversation from the briefing room before he reached the door. Inside, the first thing he saw was Wing Commander Stafford on the stage, perched on the edge of a desk, his sharp eyes staring straight at him.

'The prodigal son returns,' he announced, although was not easy to tell whether his tone was friendly or accusing. 'Mission successful?'

'Yes, sir.'

'Good, then I shall start the briefing.'

As if they were in a classroom, each crew sat at a small table with maps and notebooks spread in front, ready to copy down information. George spotted the rest of his crew and shuffled over to them, taking the place in the centre of the table with his key people, the bomb aimer and navigator on either side, just as every crew did. A curtain hung across the rear of the stage and behind that awaited their fate. The usual lightness caused by fear grew in his innards, the unreality of forced calmness before a mission. Stillness before the thunderstorm.

'Gentlemen, your target for tonight,' Stafford said with relish and waved for the curtain to be pulled back. *Please not Berlin or the Ruhr*, George said to himself. *Not until we get a new kite.* The instant the curtain was removed his brain scrabbled to identify the target. Coloured tapes stretched from a dozen places in Britain straight down to the south coast, then across to the middle of France before a left turn into Italy. 'Turin' was marked at the end of the tapes and he breathed a deep sigh of relief. It was a long flight but the opposition would be far lighter than over Germany. Immediately his thoughts spun to the long hours nursing N-Nuts as she stubbornly crabbed her way to Italy and back again. Hopefully back again.

'Turin,' Stafford continued. 'It's a long flight, around seven hundred and seventy miles to the target and we'll be airborne for about nine hours. The good news is that flak will be light over the target, plus our route takes us well south of the Kammhuber Line of radar-controlled defences. However, German Bernhard radars on the French coast will undoubtedly detect us before we leave England, so still expect fighters. There will be no feints or doglegs; we will take the fastest and most direct route across France. However, five training squadrons are flying diversionary sorties further north and nineteen aircraft are minelaying off the Biscay ports. This will pull the Luftwaffe left and right. The bomber stream will assemble over Littlehampton and cross into France between Le Havre and Rouen,' he said and tapped the map with his pointer. 'Then it's three hundred miles south to Clermont-Ferrand, where we turn left and head directly across the Alps to Turin. I don't need to tell you that taking a laden bomber over high mountains in winter lacks charm. Therefore, I want a thorough air test of every aircraft this afternoon. I will not accept early returns for preventable reasons. Do I make myself clear?' The crews' mumbled agreement and Stafford continued. 'Timings are crucial if the diversions are to be effective and these will be given at the navigators-only briefing afterwards. We have every reason for optimism. One week ago on the twentieth, there was an identical raid on Turin by two hundred and thirty-two aircraft. Just three were lost.' That sounded encouraging, except to the three crews of course. Young men, who would never grow old, never see their families again. 'Take off is at is at twenty hundred and the meal is at seventeen thirty. Don't be late for either. Gentlemen, I wish you good luck and success. I pass you on to the intelligence officer.'

The IO stood up and took the Wing Commander's pointer. He was rotund, with the red face of a drinker and the worried expression of someone driven to drink. 'Operation Torch began a few weeks ago on the eighth of November,' he began. 'British and American forces of the First Army landed at three points along the Algerian and Moroccan coastline, countries administered by France.' He tapped the bottom of the map. 'The Germans fear this is a precursor to an invasion of Europe through the zone libre, the last part of France still controlled by the Vichy government. Consequently, Axis forces have now occupied the zone and disbanded the remaining French army. Yesterday the French fleet in Toulon scuttled itself to avoid capture. French troops stationed in North Africa have yet to decide whose side they are on and appear to be having a go at both us and the Germans.' This brought a chorus of hoots from the crews.

'German and Italian forces are even now rushing into Algeria and Morocco. Therefore, tonight two hundred and thirty aircraft will bomb the industrial centre of Turin. This will disrupt the Italian war effort and reduce the morale of their soldiers. There is also evidence that bombing has caused increased public discontent with Mussolini and may even lead to his overthrow. Our mission will contribute significantly to the war effort.' The IO then spoke of Turin's industries, its Royal Arsenal and of the flak concentrations along the route.

'Marking will be by Pathfinders dropping green incendiaries, so bomb on green unless they change the target and the colour. Make sure you listen to the Master Bomber for updates. As an aside, 106 Squadron under Guy Gibson is dropping the first of the new eight thousand pound bombs on Italy tonight, so look out for larger than usual explosions.' Everyone had heard of Gibson, he and Lenard Cheshire were the bright stars of Bomber Command, the ones who always got through and got back. Next, the Met Officer warned of cloud and winds on route and then icing when they reached the Alps. Ice would weigh them down and lower the height at which they could fly and too much could destabilise the aircraft and bring it down. George wondered which would be the more dangerous tonight, fighters or N-Nuts in bad weather. Maybe God was on the other side after all.

As they changed before the raid, the atmosphere in the crew room became a mixture of anxiety combined with relief that the target could have been much worse. That an identical raid had lost just three aircraft the previous week helped, yet guaranteed nothing. After Churchill's speech, maybe the enemy would put in more effort this time just to spite him. George finished dressing and pressed Millie's Star of David against his chest. All around the room, others carefully

303

checked their own talismans. In his crew, Dingo wore the stuffed foot of some Australian animal on a silver chain. Max had a lucky doubled headed coin that he rubbed obsessively, Chalky tied one of his wife's stockings around his neck, Ned had a maple leaf charm pinned to the inside of his jacket, Dick held a small bear made by his sister and Jim Ambiolo carried three pairs of knickers.

'Time to fly,' George said and led them to collect parachutes and survival packs.

'Bring them back if they don't work,' the WAAF said for the hundredth time.

'Not heard that one before,' Max replied wearily. 'How about saying something different?'

'Like what, love,' she asked indulgently.

Max pretended to consider. 'I don't know. Maybe... bring it back unopened and I'll spend the night with you.'

She laughed. 'There's over a hundred of you, what sort of girl do you take me for?'

'We all have to do a bit more in wartime,' Max persisted. 'You know, make the odd sacrifice.'

'Well, mine is to stand by a freezing cold runaway and wave you all off. Now hurry along or you'll miss the bus.'

Outside they huddled together in the shelter of the building, waiting for the trucks to arrive. The temperature had dropped several degrees and freezing droplets of mist coated their clothes with a damp sheen. Everyone tried to protect their parachutes by holding them under their jackets to prevent moisture sticking the folded silk shrouds together. The day had begun fresh and bright, now it had grown cold, damp and dangerous.

Come on, he silently urged the trucks. They should have been waiting outside, ready to take them to their aircraft. *Don't look for omens, just wait, always bloody wait*. He glanced at the others and saw pinched cold faces struggling to force calm. Hurriedly puffing on cigarettes, their eyes were too wide and their speech was too quick. Of his crew, only Max looked truly relaxed. He would have expected the volatile Londoner to grouse about the delay but instead, he was telling a joke. George tried listening but his mind was too full of the flight, of what would happen and what could happen. Hours of crawling through dark enemy skies, constantly wondering if a fighter was about to kill you. *Come on, come on, come on.* Then he realised that it was always going to be this moment, the time just before. The rest was only an interval, a way of passing the hours until this moment arrived again, the time just before.

'Halleluiah,' someone called. 'Here comes the cavalry.' A fleet of trucks rumbled up and they clambered aboard, slumping onto the hard wooden bench seats inside.

The others smoked a final cigarette while George ground checked N-Nuts. She looked formidable and he felt some of the old confidence return. He touched her skin and dragged his hand across the riveted panels the way some men stroke their dog. She was battered and a bugger in the air, but he felt she was on their side. She would do her best.

'Come on, skipper.' Chalky called. 'The back wheel needs wetting.'

Chapter 20

RAF Blackbrook - 28 November 1942

N-Nuts waited impatiently at the start of the runway, her engines uneven and stuttering at low power. George flicked his gaze between the instruments and the controller's caravan, forcing himself to breathe evenly. Now it was so close to takeoff he just wanted to be gone, to feel the aircraft cutting through the air, to know that with each passing second they were nearer to the target and closer to coming home again. His left hand rested on the column and his right on the throttles. *Any second now*. Then the green light flashed, stinging him alert and he pushed the levers to the stops, feeling power build as the Merlins wound up. As the noise reached a crescendo, he released the brakes and N-Nuts leapt forward. She was very heavy, maximum fuel and maximum bomb load. From the corner of his eye, he saw a crowd of WAAFs waving beside the runway and that felt good. From now on there would be nothing but fighters and flak until they returned, but the WAAFs hopes would go with them and that meant a lot. The aircraft thundered along the runway, speed increasing with every foot but he could feel the heaviness in her responses. Slower to gather speed, more effort to push the stick forward and raise the tail, and much longer on the runway. They reached one hundred and ten miles-per-hour just as the bomber roared and rattled to within sight of the runway's end. It was mesmerising to see the darker black of the tree line hurtle towards them. With a final bounce, N-Nuts slid heavily into the air and climbed slowly away. Turning to Chalky, he saw him grin in the dim light from the cockpit dials and nod his head.

'Wheels and flaps please, Chalky,' he said, pulling N-Nuts into a tight climbing turn. It was now dark but the clouds were just white enough to see other squadron bombers silhouetted above, circling upwards like flies against a ceiling. N-Nuts wallowed after them, crabbing a little and dismissing any attempts to stay in trim. He felt better now that they were airborne, but God, he had been jumpy just before the trucks came, when everything had seemed an omen or a warning.

'We're grouping at ten thousand feet before heading one eight zero, skipper,' Dingo said. 'The bomber stream will gather over Littlehampton at twenty one hundred, distance about a hundred and sixty miles.'

'Thanks, Dingo,' George replied and set the compass 'bug' to the next course. 'Revs for one seventy miles-per-hour, please Chalky.'

They were to fly in a loose 'V' shaped gaggle with the other five aircraft of B Flight, headed by Squadron Leader Toby Mallard in D-Dog. A gaggle really meant staying close enough to see the others but without getting too close. Americans flying daylight raids relied on tight box formations for self-defence, whereas flying at night the British simply needed the maximum aircraft to transit simultaneously while keeping a safe separation. D-Dog was three aircraft in front and just entering the clouds. Mallard had not lost his coolness in the few times they had spoken since their first meeting and it still felt more like politeness than friendliness. Maybe that would change if they had five operations under their belt and it looked as though they would stay the course, but maybe not. Perhaps Mallard was another Tug Wilson, someone who had formed an immediate dislike of him.

Above the clouds, he slid N-Nuts two aircraft away from Mallard and fifty feet lower as they began the climb towards twenty thousand feet. There was just enough light to see nearby aircraft, but high above in the night sky, the stars were invisible behind a curtain thin layer of cirrostratus. The stream of bombers headed for Turin in two waves, each one staggered into three different height layers. Their squadron, 323, flew at twenty thousand feet in the third layer of the first wave. Somewhere below and in front were squadrons of Halifax, Stirlings and Wellingtons. A similar wave was forming just behind, while miles out in front of the bomber stream, two squadrons of pathfinders should already be heading for Turin to mark the target before the main force arrived. Most aircraft came from bases in Lincolnshire and so the sky was already crowded and that was both comforting and concerning.

'Keep a good lookout gunners; it's going to be pretty busy.'

'It's as dark as a mother-in-law's heart back here,' Max came back. 'I can see a couple of C-Flight aircraft behind but sod all else.'

'Same up here, skipper,' Jim added. 'I'm pretty sure that there's nothing above us though.'

'How about some music, skipper?' Max asked.

George thought about it. 'Sure, why not. Just until we reach the coast. Ned, can you pick up the BBC?' Although strictly against the rules, many crews listened to music for part of the journey and he trusted his crew not to be distracted by it.

'No problem, skipper.' A few seconds later big band music wafted through their headsets.

By the time they reached Littlehampton, N-Nuts had lived up to her name by having to be coaxed constantly onto a level flight path. The thought of another eight hours spent fighting her was dismal.

'Turning point coming up,' Dingo said. 'Change course to one fifty degrees magnetic. Now.'

George glanced at the clock, twenty-one hundred exactly. Bang on time and he turned the yoke gently to port until the compass aligned with the marker. They were heading directly for the enemy coast between Le Havre and Rouen. He pressed a hand against Millie's Star of David for luck and hoped the diversionary raids had drawn the fighters away. Had he been home only this morning? That seemed far more unreal than the fact he was now flying to Italy to bomb Turin.

'Searchlights coming on ahead, port and starboard,' Dick said. 'Must be Rouen and Le Havre.'

'Thanks, Bomb Aimer. What can you see gunners?'

'Still the square root of sweet FA, back here,' Max said. 'I catch slight of some of C Flight occasionally, but apart from that, we could be on our own.

'Jim?'

'Same, skipper. Just blackness.'

'Five minutes till we cross the French coast,' Dingo interrupted. 'No course change for three hundred miles. Navigator going silent to use the Elsan.'

'That's great,' Max said. 'Now we won't know if we've been hit by flak or it's Dingo using the thunder bucket.'

'Careful as you go, Dingo,' George warned. 'I'm going to start weaving soon. Remember to plug in your headset.'

'It was flying facing backwards this morning. It always upsets my stomach.'

'Flak ahead,' Dick continued reporting. 'Crossing enemy coast now.'

'Starting to weave, everyone. Eyes peeled for fighters.' He dipped the nose and N-Nuts dropped easily.

'I've got a problem,' Dingo said after a while.

'I can smell it,' Jim replied. 'Have you been eating dead rats again?'

'I'm stuck to the seat.'

'Stop buggering about, Dingo,' George snapped. 'Now's not the time.'

'Seriously. My backside's frozen to the flaming seat, I can't get off.'

George shook his head. 'Off you go Chalky and be quick, I need you up here.'

'Why me?' Even half hidden by his oxygen mask Chalky looked desperate.

'Because you're the bloody engineer and his arse is a mechanical problem,' George snapped. 'Take a thermos and pour coffee around his backside, see if that thaws it. Now go.' Flak exploded nearby and N-Nuts lurched, dropping two hundred feet before George could pull her up again.

'A kite's coned, below to starboard,' Dick said. 'Looks like a Wimpey.'

George tilted the aircraft to the right and saw three beams converge onto a single point, illuminating a twin-engine Wellington. The aircraft tilted almost onto its wingtip and dived, just as flak burst around it.

'That boy knows his stuff,' George said. 'I just hope he can pull out.' Two of the three beams broke away, but the third stayed on the Wellington, following it down. Then that beam gave up and returned to the sky. There was no explosion so with luck the Wimpey managed to pull up. George could guess the relief felt by the pilot. More explosions rattled outside, making N-Nuts wallow and crab. The urge to increase revs and go faster through the flak belt was palpable, but they had to fly at the speed of the slowest if the stream was to stay together. Chalky returned and slumped into his seat, wiping his gloved hands on a piece of rag. The engineer stared bleakly ahead and George decided not to ask. Some things where better left unknown.

Soon the flak was behind and the sky seemed empty despite over two hundred aircraft surrounding them. He wondered how the Wellington pilot would be feeling now. No doubt relief from having evaded the searchlights but scared half to death from ferocity of his dive, and all the while putting on a show of calm for his crew. George could see little outside and other than the dull glow of the instruments and the roar of the Merlins; there was nothing to show they were moving. It was a hateful feeling, the sensation that they were stationary targets just waiting for a fighter to pounce. The thought that tracer could shred the aircraft without warning made him snuggle deeper into his armoured seat. They flew a straight course, every second travelling further from the safety of home and further into danger while knowing that they would have to crawl the hundreds of miles back again. Still, they had not seen a fighter attack yet so it looked as though the distraction sorties had worked.

By far the busiest member of the crew was Dingo and he worked like a demon. Now they were outside of GEE coverage he recalculated their position every five minutes and gave minor course adjustments to compensate for side winds. Not every navigator would be as skilful or diligent, and even those that were had to make assumptions when using a system reliant on map, compass and clock. This meant that the bomber stream, which started out nicely grouped over Littlehampton, was now gradually spreading itself across miles of sky.

'Where we are, navigator?' George asked, after using up some time synchronising the engines.

'Gimme a moment, skipper,' Dingo replied. 'I'm just calculating the winds... Right, I reckon we're fifteen minutes from Clermont-Ferrand, maybe near the town of Bourges. The master navigator wants us to go ten miles past Clermont-Ferrand before we turn to make sure that we don't fly over Lyon.' The place names meant little to George, but he always liked to hear the certainty in Dingo's voice as he said them. It was reassuring, like listening to the BBC shipping forecast before the war.

'When do we reach the Alps?'

'We get to the tall stuff forty minutes after the turn. Some of the ranges are over eleven thousand feet high, so if you have to dive, try to stay above that.'

A tinge of worry made him sit up straighter. Memories of flying over the Rockies in Canada. The sudden wind shear across jagged peaks and the danger of flying into clouds. He checked the engines oil temperature dials on the engineer's panel and saw that the port-outer needle was elevated. Not by much, but it was higher than the others were. 'Have you seen that, Chalky?' he said pointing.

'Yeah, it's only just gone up. They were supposed to have fixed it as well. Maybe we should pull back the revs a little on that engine and see if it cools?'

Could they still cross the Alps if they lost an engine? The book said one hundred and forty miles-per-hour and ten thousand feet was the limit on three, and Dingo had just mentioned peaks of eleven thousand. 'Give it a try, but only as long as we can maintain one hundred and seventy miles-per-hour. I don't want to start drifting back into the second wave.' Chalky reached for the rev and throttle levers, adjusting them so the port-outer did less and the others a little more, while George adjusted the rudder trim to keep N-Nuts flying straight.

'Pilot to crew, the port outer is running hot, just like over Denmark. We may have to abort if we lose the engine. Dingo, can we get to the target flying at ten thousand feet?'

'Yeah, I guess so, but we may have to make a detour around some of the higher mountains to get there. Let me check.'

'What can you see, gunners?'

Jim replied. 'Sky's clearing and I can see some of the squadron left and right of us. No sign of tracer so I guess the Luftwaffe's ignoring us.'

'Same back here. In the last few minutes a dozen or more kites have appeared,' Max added. The high cirrostratus had gone and a host of stars shone steely cold through the cockpit roof. However, a glance at the wings showed a silvery layer of ice forming. Thin now but that would get worse above the mountains.

'Make the turn, Skipper. New heading of one-oh-five degrees magnetic.' They were now heading directly for the Alps and Turin. Chalky reduced the revs and throttle on the port-outer but the temperature gauge was still high, higher than before if anything.

'What do you think?' George asked him.

Chalky was silent for a while. 'It's high but it's not going through the ceiling. Hopefully, we'll be OK on this setting,' he said eventually, but he did not sound confident.

Way out in front, moonlight reflected off Alpine snow creating a thick line of white. Below this, pinpricks of lights appeared where mountain villages ignored the blackout. The closer they came to the snow the brighter the ambient light became and now he could see other bombers flitting over the whiteness. However, Icing also increased in the frigid air above the peaks and soon a layer some inches thick coated the wings and fuselage. N-Nuts began to sink.

'I think I might need that engine, Chalky,' George said pulling back on the stick. 'We've got a couple of tons of ice on the wings. What do you think?'

'At the moment it's doing some work, but if we lose it altogether we get nothing. Your call, but I'd say emergencies only.'

A glance at the instruments showed their speed had fallen to one hundred and fifty miles-per-hour and the rate-of-climb indicator gave a decent of almost a hundred feet per minute. Altitude was down to eighteen thousand feet. They were slowing down and going down. 'Dingo, we've got problems. The weight of ice is pulling us down. We'll be lighter on the way home once we've dropped the bombs, but can we cross the Alps losing height at this rate?'

Before Dingo could answer, Dick's voice cut through on the intercom. 'It's not a linear problem. The aircraft's shape changes as we ice, which has different effects on the aerodynamics. Also, icing creates a bigger surface area for more ice to stick to, so we will ice faster. You can't assume things will continue as they are.'

George sucked his teeth in annoyance. 'That's probably true, but it doesn't help. Look, we have a choice of turning back and this op not counting towards our thirty or taking the risk and continuing. From the way the snow line in front is climbing, I think we have to decide now. My view is that we should continue, but I want it to be a group decision.'

Chalky spoke first. 'If we turn back we have a mystery problem to explain and ten to one they won't be able to find it. I don't want to be labelled LMF by the boss. I'm for going on.'

'I'll take the mountains on this raid rather than the Luftwaffe on another,' Max said. 'I say go on.' One by one, they all agreed. Their height was now seventeen thousand feet and falling.

Dingo spoke last of all. 'On this course, there's nothing much above ten thousand feet. The first range is in a couple of minutes and that goes up to eight thousand. After that, it's a roller coaster of mountains for seventy miles. We should clear the last range, but we'll be low.'

'We're going on then,' George said grimly. 'Press On Regardless.'

'POR,' a chorus of voices repeated in his earphones.

Once they reached the Alps, the air temperature dropped lower than he had ever known before. The cockpit heater was on but it felt almost ineffective. Only Ned would be warm with the fuselage heater right by his feet, the rest of them would gradually freeze. Intense cold made you sleepy, dulled reactions and brought lethargy. Despite the layers of clothing, George could feel cold creep into his body and he sat up straighter, fighting off drowsiness. The Lancaster continued to sink as rime continued to build. Occasionally, ice on the propellers shook free and smashed against the cockpit like rifle shots and sheets of ice, torn from the wings slammed into the rear of the aircraft with a bang that jarred throughout the fuselage. Sharp snow clad peaks slid by below and in between them narrow valleys dipped away into blackness. The part of his brain not occupied with flying and ice wondered at the mountains and pinpricks of village lights. Before the war, a day trip to Weston-Super-Mare was the summit of his travel possibilities. Only the richest would see the Alps or go to Italy. Now he was there and he vowed that one day he would come back when the madness was over. Other places too, France and even maybe Australia to visit Dingo. Then he remembered the conversation with Steve Smith, his instructor at Oakley. What did Smith call it, the curse of combat? How fear made life feel sharper and more urgent, but once the danger was past, apathy closed in like a miasma, dulling and robbing. Their altitude dropped to thirteen thousand feet just as the snow disappeared and the mountains fell towards the plains of Italy.

'Searchlights coming on forty miles ahead,' Dick called. 'That's Turin.'

'Ned, have you got the Master bomber yet?' George asked.

'Negative, skipper. He's not broadcasting,' Ned replied, the worry clear in his voice.

'Have you checked your set?' Chalky asked.

'It's working OK. I can pick up other frequencies, but there's nothing from the Master Bomber. He's just not transmitting.'

'Where the hell are they?' The pathfinders should have marked the target by now. 'Can you see any fires, Bomb Aimer?' George asked. This was wrong; there should be green markers burning in the city. They were twenty minutes from the target; the first part of the wave would be much closer. The aircraft juddered as ice worked loose from the wings in the warmer air and span free. Their altitude was now only twelve thousand feet, which was not a healthy place to be when every other aircraft in the stream was higher. N-Nuts would be under a rain of bombs. He told Chalky to bring up the damaged engine's rev and throttle levers and pulled back the column. Of the two evils, this felt the lesser.

'There's nothing. No TI's burning. We'll have to circle and wait,' Dick said.

'Negative, not at this height and not with a damaged engine. We're going straight in and drop. You'll have to do your best.'

'Wait, I can see an aircraft low over the city. I think it's a Stirling,' Dick said. 'They must be looking for the target. My God that takes balls; he's getting a lot of anti-aircraft fire.'

George craned forward to watch. Illuminated by searchlights and anti-aircraft muzzle flashes, a dark shape flew at two thousand feet above Turin. Suddenly a string of explosions erupted on the ground as the Stirling released its bombs. One became a tall orange column. They had hit something significant.

'Drop where he did,' George said. 'He must have found an aiming point.' They were almost at the city and he hoped Dick had enough time to arm the bombs. 'Are you ready, Bomb Aimer?'

'Almost... That's it... Ready for bombing, Skipper.'

'Over to you, Bomb Aimer.' George was now just the driver.

'Open bomb doors,' Dick said.

'Bomb doors open,' George pulled the lever.

'Left, left...Steady... Steady... Left, left...'

Dick spoke slowly, carefully and George tweaked the yoke, nudging the aircraft onto each new heading.

'Steady... Steady... Bombs gone!'

Freed from the bombs, N-Nuts leapt upwards. This time felt different to Dusseldorf. There was no sense of savage joy as he pictured the cookie and incendiaries tumbling into the city. Instead, grimness replaced euphoria, a cold satisfaction at having done the job. No one else spoke so maybe everyone felt the same.

'Wait for the photoflash,' Dick said. Below the searchlights stopped sweeping and the anti-aircraft guns became silent. Presumably, the crews had dived for shelter and left the city defenceless. Without pathfinders to mark the target, the main force bomb aimers now took their best shots. Bombs rained down and explosions erupted over a wide area of the city. Something big and black fell just in front of N-Nuts' nose, missing them by feet. Too fast to see clearly, but it must have been a bomb. He held the aircraft steady, waiting for the photograph and glancing nervously upwards. Just above, a dark shape slowly overhauled them. The urge to turn away was overpowering.

'Photograph taken,' Dick said before adding. 'I think we were almost hit by a cookie.' George said nothing, but banked to the right and increased speed.

'Skipper!' Chalky shouted a warning and he turned to see the engineer pointing at the port-outer oil temperature gauge, which was high against the stops.

'Shut it down, now. Emergency feathering drill,' he shouted and pulled that engine's throttle and rev levers back. Chalky immediately reached to turn off the fuel cock. If the engine seized with the propeller spinning, the momentum and wind pressure on the blades could rip the engine off the wing and that would almost certainly bring them down. With trembling fingers, he pressed the feathering button for a few seconds, just long enough to make sure it stayed in. Feathering turned the blade edges into the airflow, creating minimal drag. Quickly the blurred propeller solidified into windmilling blades and then stopped. George gulped down some oxygen and tried to steady himself. *Where were they?* Explosions ripped across the ground about ten miles in front and to the right, so they must have circled and be somewhere southeast of Turin. Altitude fourteen thousand and speed one seventy, but both were decreasing now they only had three engines. They were in trouble. The Alps were between them and home and some of the mountains were higher than N-Nuts would soon be able to fly. He quickly thought through the choices of which none looked attractive.

'Pilot to crew. We've just lost the port-outer, so we can't stay higher than ten thousand feet. Dingo, what are the options for getting home?'

Dingo had clearly given this some thought and spoke immediately. 'There're only three choices, apart from landing in Spain and being interned. We could loop around the Alps by flying west along the border between France and Spain, before heading north. That's a long flight and we'll need plenty of fuel. We could fly to North Africa, Tunisia's the best bet, find an airfield and wait for repairs. Problem is we might land somewhere still controlled by the other side and I'm not sure how they'll treat a bomber crew. Lastly, we could chance it back through the Alps, along the ravines and valleys. But one wrong turn and we'll be a nasty mark in the snow.'

'Scrub going the long way home,' Chalky said. 'The wing pump packed in just as we started bombing. I can't transfer any more fuel from the wing tanks.'

'An' I don't fancy North Africa,' Max said. 'If we pick the wrong airfield it's either a bullet in the head from the Germans or some Frenchman doing unnatural things to my body.'

'You should be so lucky,' Jim said. 'Even a Frenchman would turn his nose up at you.'

'Ned,' George interrupted. 'Can you contact anyone in North Africa?'

'Negative, skipper, I don't have the codes. Maybe Gibraltar or Malta, but I can't see them broadcasting the latest situation in Tunisia because of security, even if they know it.'

'Can't we land in Malta?' Chalky asked.

'It's a fighter runway, probably too short for us.' George drummed his fingers on the yoke they had to decide now. 'Dingo, can you get us through the Alps?'

'In theory, yes. But that's betting our lives on the map's accuracy and that there's no cloud. You want to make that bet?'

319

'What choice do we have?'

'Buckley's choice. At least we won't ice up at this height. Budge up Dick, I'm coming up to the front turret to get a good view. I'll need you working with me.'

Moments later Chalky stood up so Dingo could squeeze past him and down into the bomb aimers position. Dingo clutched a map and nodded grimly at George as he disappeared. Soon his voice came through the intercom.

'Keep turning clockwise, about five mile's radius from where we bombed.' George looked right, towards the fires. Although dozens more had started, he could still see the large orange conflagration begun by the Stirling. 'Tell me when the orange fire is due east of us, Skipper. You'll need to bring the speed down as low as you can, there may be some sharp turns ahead and we'll need to take them slowly. Look out for small lakes coming up below, Dick.'

'Flaps fifteen degrees and revs two thousand six hundred please, Chalky,' George said. Quickly he loosened his harness and cranked the seat higher, giving himself the best forward view. A few turns of the trim wheel brought the nose down slightly and he was ready. Had it been solely his decision he would have headed for North Africa. Mainly, he supposed, because he wanted to see it and because he was so cold. The chance to sit in the heat and see the continent where elephants and camels lived was persuasive. On the other hand, flying into a combat zone was just plain stupid. Strange, now that they had made the decision, a part of him felt excited at the prospect of negotiating the Alps and pitting his skills. The compass clicked quickly. 'Due east now,' George said.

'A lake's reflecting below,' Dick added.

'Turn two seven five degrees,' Dingo snapped. 'We're going into the first valley. It's fairly straight for fifteen miles and then curves left and right for another fifteen. At the end is a sharp left into the next valley. I'll count you down when we get there.'

He banked N-Nuts hard left, watching the compass intently. A glance outside showed snowy peaks a little lower than they flew and about five miles distant on both sides. However, directly in front, a high mountain line stood at the valley's end, clear and hard as iron in the moonlight. *Please, God, keep us free from clouds or this will be a short flight*, he thought. Speed was now one hundred and thirty, about the limit for slow flying a Lancaster and their altitude fell to five thousand feet. Far ahead, he could see that the valley curved just before reaching the mountain. At the moment there was still room to turn around, but the peaks rose ominously further on and the valley narrowed. Soon there would be no possibility of going back. Although he had faith in Dingo, he had never relied on anyone this much before. Being a pilot had always placed him in control, given him the final decision, but now that had changed. There was nothing he could do alone to escape the mountains. Even if he managed to crawl over the top of one peak, a higher one would almost certainly be waiting on the other side.

The mountains became mesmerising. Shards of brilliant white, streaked in vertical black shadows and patches of deep grey where crags were exposed. After twenty minutes, they reached the end of the first valley and he began to feel more comfortable about flying with unyielding rock on either side. Tiredness, however, was a problem. It had been a demanding twenty-four hours and he craved a mug of the bittersweet coffee waiting in the thermos.

'The lights in front are the town of Oulx,' Dingo said. 'Turn left over it and onto two hundred degrees for three minutes.'.

Pinpricks of light shone from the valley floor and as he banked N-Nuts onto a new heading, he was grateful for their lack of air raid discipline. 'Count me down, Dingo. I need to keep my eyes out of the cockpit.' All around the peaks were much taller now, almost twice their height, but thanks to the snow there was plenty of reflected moonlight. As long as he could stay above the snow line, he felt he could fly accurately.

'Get ready to turn right. New course two four five degrees... steady... steady... Turn right now.' Dingo's voice was calm and measured. George banked N-Nuts sharply and they entered a valley whose narrow sides towered thousands of feet above. There was definitely no turning back from here. All he could do was keep in the middle of the valley and hope Dingo got it right. A few hours ago, he had assured his mother that Dingo would always guide them home. Well, now was the test. The valley wound crookedly between mountains, never straight for more than a few miles. The twists and turns were mostly gentle, but three miles ahead, a towering peak blocked their way entirely and a new valley seemed to curve sharply right. He sat forward against the seat straps and pulled up his goggles.

'Dingo, do we turn right ahead?' he asked quickly.

'Ah, negative, Skipper. The map says it's another bend to the left.'

'I can't see a left bend, are you sure?'

There was a pause, seconds from a decision. 'I don't know. It does look like a right, but the map says left.' Dingo said slowly, his indecision obvious. 'Jesus, I don't know... Follow the map I guess, go to port.' The mountain loomed above them and George had to decide. At the last moment, he banked the aircraft left, certain it was wrong. Immediately a snowy range appeared in front, just higher than they flew.

'Emergency climb!' he shouted at Chalky and in one swift movement, he jammed the throttle and rev levers fully forward and pulled back hard on the column, while Chalky grabbed the flaps levers.

N-Nuts climbed slowly, lumbering upwards, all three engines screaming under full power. The nose came up steeply and with nothing to see forward except the turret, he glanced at the instruments. Three thousand revs, maximum sixteen pounds of boost and airspeed creeping up past one forty. *Come on Nuts, come on.* To both sides the mountain rose sharply, sliding closer, jagged fingers of black rock poking through the snow, reaching out. He tensed his body waiting for the impact. *Come on Nuts, come on.* Suddenly the noise of the engines muffled and a blizzard of snow whipped up by the blades surrounded the cockpit. It lasted seconds and then disappeared like a puff of steam from a kettle. No one spoke.

'We missed it,' Dick said at last. 'We bloody well missed it!' The others started to shout their relief down the intercom, but George stopped them.

'Quiet you lot! Where are we Dingo?' He was shaking and his heart pounded wildly, but they were only halfway through the Alps and he forced himself to focus. For seconds there was no reply and George could visualize the horror of being at the front and watching helplessly as they hurtled towards the snowy ridgeline.

'Uh... We're now in France,' Dingo replied eventually, his voice quieter than usual, less assured. 'The lights ahead are a place called Briançon.' Was it shock or had his uncertainty unsettled him? 'Make a slow right turn over the city and come onto three twenty degrees. After that, it's seventy miles of winding through a valley until we reach Grenoble. No more sharp turns just bends. Once we pass Grenoble we're out of the Alps.'

'Revs and throttles for one thirty again, please Chalky. Set flaps to fifteen degrees.' George forced himself to sound calm as he let N-Nuts drift slowly back to five thousand feet, and concentrate on the snaking route ahead. Thankfully, the mountains looked smaller here, just occasionally rising above six thousand feet.

'The map definitely says that pass is only four thousand feet,' Dingo said shakily after a while. 'We should have cleared it easily.'

'We did clear it,' Max said. 'There can't be any snow left. I've got most of it back here in the turret. I'm not sure whether to laugh, cry or build a snowman.'

This was not the time for inquests. Confidence was an elusive quantity and they all needed Dingo to have it. 'Maybe there's been an avalanche or heavy snowfall. Who knows?' George said. 'I would have turned right back there and killed the lot of us. So forget it. You did well.'

'Well I'm not convinced,' Max joined in. 'I think we should turn around and do it again, just to make sure it wasn't a fluke.'

'Maybe we should lighten the aircraft by dumping an idiot rear gunner,' Dingo snarled.

Max was unabashed. 'Hey, while we're here, how about popping down to Rome and seeing if Dingo really can find the Popes private knocking shop,' he continued. 'We could sit out the war in a house of ill-repute. Or as it says in the song...' and he began singing down the intercom.

'I don't want to join the Air Force
I don't want to go to war.
I'd rather hang around, Piccadilly Underground

Living off the earnings of a high-class lady.'

The others joined in and George let them get on with it. Better that they worked off the scare this way rather than fretting about it. The valley widened and the mountains were shrinking. Hopefully, there would be no more surprises.

They were the last to land and waited at the end of the queue for the intelligence debrief. Tiredness swamped all of them, but none more so than George who staggered slightly whenever they shuffled forward. The padre bought steaming mugs of hot chocolate laced with rum that they sipped gratefully. However, Dingo nursed his silently while standing a little apart from the others.

'You OK, chum?' Max asked him.

'Yeah, just bonzer mate,' he replied unenthusiastically and turned away. George put his hand on Max's shoulder and steered him gently back. He would talk to Dingo later and sort it out.

'So what happened to you?' a voice boomed out, startling him. George jumped slightly and spilt some of his drink, burning his fingers. Wing Commander Stafford had come up unseen and was standing by George's side.

'An engine failed on the way, sir.' he replied simply. 'We lost it completely over the target and had to limp back.'

'Through the Alps?' Stafford raised an eyebrow.

'It wasn't so bad,' George said, trying to downplay it. 'I've got a great navigator.'

Stafford eyed George speculatively. 'Some would have turned back at the start,' he said at last.

'We still had three good engines,' George shrugged. 'It seemed a wasted trip not to carry on.'

'Good man, that's the attitude. Press on regardless.' Stafford nodded and walked off. Suddenly he stopped and turned back. 'Uncle tells me you want a new Lancaster?'

'It would be appreciated, sir,' George replied, embarrassed that his deal with Uncle was exposed in front of the other crews and he wondered whether Stafford had chosen to announce it this way so everyone would know he had asked for a new aircraft rather than being offered it.

Stafford stared for a few seconds, 'I think we can manage that. Good show.' He turned and was gone.

Jim Ambiolo patted George on the shoulder. 'Good show, Skipper,' he said mimicking Stafford. 'Jolly good show.'

'Sod off,' George smiled at him, although he did feel quite pleased with himself.

Suddenly a harsh voice snarled nearby. 'You've stolen my new kite, you thieving piece of shit.' Even as he turned, George knew it would be Tug Wilson. He came barrelling up with his face twisted in anger and his fists clenched. George eyed Wilson casually as if he was of little concern, but shifted the grip on his mug just in case he had to use it as a weapon.

'Your new plane?' George queried. 'I didn't know you could buy them?'

'One tour and ten ops, that's what I've paid. It should be mine, not some rookie who won't last two weeks,' he snarled in George's face. 'I got the right to that Lanc' through flying operations, not kissing the bosses arse.'

'Even his backside would object to being kissed by you,' George smiled. 'Don't be such a bad loser, Tug. I'm sure you've had a lot of practice.' In truth, he felt a tinge of guilt at jumping the queue for a new aircraft, but Tug's current one would be in much better condition than N-Nuts and he was not going to risk his life just out of politeness. In any case, this was a direct challenge and he would lose face backing down. Tug stepped back a pace, looking to throw a punch and George readied to duck sideways and throw the scalding chocolate in his face.

'Sergeant Wilson!' another voice called. 'We're waiting for you.' The intelligence officer looked at them suspiciously.

Wilson glanced back at George. 'You'll be dead soon and I'll piss on your grave, Watford.'

George smiled. 'Well I won't care then, and I sure as hell don't care now.' He watched Tug and his crew head towards a table and turned back to his own people, wondering how they felt. Max was the first to speak.

'Don't worry about it, Skipper,' he said breezily. 'All's fair in love and war, and this is definitely war.'

'N-Nuts is a wreck,' Chalky said next. 'You did the right thing. Screw Tug. I took a look at all the authorisation books the other day and his crate isn't that old.'

'Even if we get cold-shouldered by the old sweats,' Jim said thoughtfully. 'It's better than flying in a death-trap. Well done, skipper.'

The crew seemed happy, despite the possibility of the other crews siding with Tug. Eventually, it was their turn to tell the IO about their flight, including the bravery of the Stirling crew over Turin. There were no losses from their squadron that night, although overall the raid lost three aircraft, two Stirlings and a Wellington. The same number as the previous raid on Turin.

Afterwards, as they headed for the mess and breakfast, George pulled Dingo to one side. 'What is it?' he asked. 'What's the problem?' Chalky looked back and saw them talking, so he ushered the rest into the mess hall. Dingo watched them go and when they were out of sight, he shrugged. 'I gave myself a bit of a fright, that's all.'

'Well, I'm scared from the moment I know we're on ops,' George told him. 'Everyone is.'

'It's not that sort of fear,' Dingo replied and kicked at something on the pavement.

'What sort is it then?'

'It's hard to explain.'

'Try me.'

It was six in the morning and the sky was lightening. Dawn would break soon and George had been awake for twenty-five hours. In that time he had flown to Somerset and then to Italy and back. He was exhausted and finding it hard to think of anything but sleep, but he knew this was important.

Dingo struggled to find the words. 'I dunno, I guess it's being raised in the outback. I've always known where to go, never had doubts before. It's not just a skill back there, it's a way of life and I've always had it. But just for a moment back in that ravine, I wasn't sure. It was as if I'd suddenly become deaf or blind. Something that always worked fine before just failed.'

Then George understood. 'And you're worried it will happen again on one of the raids?'

'Yeah, well I got to thinking about me mate, the one who carked it on the way back from Germany. Maybe that's what happened to him or his nav? Maybe one of them just froze up at the wrong time.'

What could he say? His brain was so numb from tiredness that any wisdom just escaped him. 'Welcome to the club, you're fallible just like the rest of us. But I guess now you know it can happen, you can be ready for it.'

'Yeah, sure,' Dingo said. 'Thanks, Skipper.'

'That doesn't help?'

'About as much as I did with your love life.'

'Not at all, then.'

'That's the number I was thinking of.'

George patted him on the back. 'Come on; let's go and spit on Tug Wilson's breakfast.'

Dingo smiled. 'Now that would cheer me up.'

Chapter 21

RAF Blackbrook - 30 November 1942

Millie's letter waited for him in the mess like an unexploded bomb. Written on blue paper so delicate that it was almost transparent and lightly scented with perfume, it was as seductive as its author.

Dear George,

Thank you for your letter. I am pleased that you had an enjoyable leave. I have thought long and hard about us and I now regret my words. I would very much like to see you again. I am travelling to Scotland next week and I have decided to break my journey in Cambridge in the hope that we can be together. I shall arrive at the Old Ferry Boat in Holywell on Thursday evening and stay until Saturday morning. If you are free, I have booked a room under the names of Mr and Mrs Watford.

With love,

Millie

He was ecstatic. She wanted to see him again and the fact she was pretending to be his wife made him laugh with delight. Maybe she had excused what happened in London, blamed it on a combination of drink and bombing. The thought of her was pervasive and overpowering. It felt like a fire burning inside. As the day went on, he persuaded himself that this time he would make his intentions clear, tell her that he wanted a future with her. He would stare into those dark eyes and be completely open before booze and lust befuddled him. This time he would do things properly and show he was more than just a country yokel. However, even as he planned the scene and formed the words, he wondered if he could do it well enough. If he had the skill to persuade her to spend the rest of her life with him.

That afternoon he visited Uncle to wrangle a forty-eight-hour pass and it seemed that fate was conspiring to help. A note in the flight office said that the squadron was off ops for four days to allow training and essential maintenance. It felt like the lull before the storm, that Butch Harris was drawing breath before launching hundreds of aircraft in another flurry of blows.

'I need a pass Uncle,' George told the adjutant. He decided it was best to be direct. Demand rather than request. Once he had a new Lancaster they would be quits, but until then he would keep the pressure on by reminding Uncle of his debts.

Uncle crinkled his eyes in annoyance, an expression that George noted. Although operational squadrons were less formal, certain proprieties such as the occasional '*sir*' and salutes were still expected.

'And I need more bacon,' Uncle replied tartly, putting down his pen and leaning back in his chair.

'I'm sure we can come to an arrangement,' George said. 'But first, the pass.'

The thick moustache quivered slightly. 'Just a pass or do you want another bloody Lancaster?'

'Just the pass, Uncle. But now you mention it, when do I get the new kite?'

Uncle muttered under his breath and shuffled the papers on his desk, which as usual was a thing of organised chaos. He found a sheet and scanned it. 'All it says here is that we're getting delivery this week.'

'In time for the next op?'

He glanced at his desk calendar. 'Should be, course you can never be sure.'

'Well make certain you are, Uncle. I won't bring home the bacon without one.' George stood and went towards the door. 'I need the pass from Thursday evening until Saturday morning. An old friend is coming to visit,' he called over his shoulder.

Millie sat at a corner table near the fire reading a newspaper, the glass of red wine in front of her untouched. Her RAF uniform fitted so well that it looked tailored and he paused in the doorway to catch his breath, drinking in her shape, her face and eyes. In his mind, he could already hear her voice and breathe her scent. For a while, she was his. The next forty-eight hours would shape his life, however short that might be. She looked up, saw him staring and smiled. He crossed the room and they embraced.

'It's lovely to see you again,' she said. 'I thought you might not come.'

'I wanted to see you very much,' he replied earnestly.

'So I should hope,' she laughed and led him back to her table. 'I meant I thought you might not be able to get away.'

'I was lucky. The adjutant owes me a few favours.'

'Really? What have you done? Found him a girl?'

'No,' he smiled. 'Nothing so interesting. I got him some bacon. Pretty mundane stuff really, but he was grateful.'

She looked confused. 'Why did he want bacon? Don't they feed him enough?'

'It's for the squadron. We get bacon and eggs before each mission and again when we come back. Sometimes the stores run out so I flew to my parent's farm in Somerset and fetched some. He owes me a favour.' He suddenly wanted to describe the farm, make it sound so attractive that she would want to live there, married to him. *Take it slowly* he told himself. 'How was your journey?' he asked instead.

'Still stuck with a stiff Englishman,' she told him.

'What?'

'George, I've come all this way to see you,' she laughed. 'You could tell me I look beautiful. Instead, you ask about travel.'

He grinned sheepishly; she had said something similar when they met in London. 'Sorry. You look ravishing... beautiful and I love you,' he told her.

Her expression hardened for a second as if she felt a stab of pain, but then she smiled. 'And I love you as well,' she said and that made him soar. She loved him. That was it. There was a future together after all.

'It feels that every time we meet, I've been certain I'd never see you again,' he said slowly. 'Let's not do that anymore. It's bad for my nerves.'

Millie smiled and looked away. 'I'm sorry. Sometimes... sometimes, I just want to hide away. I suppose it's because I find it so hard to trust, even in my own judgement.'

'You can trust me, Millie. That I promise.'

The dark brown eyes flicked at him and she nodded. 'Yes, I believe I can.'

'Would you like to eat?'

'Are you hungry?'

'Only for you. Why don't you show me our room, Mrs Watford?' *So much for taking things slowly*, he chided himself.

Later, when it was dark, he stood by the window staring at the sky. A fading drone told him that somewhere a squadron was going on ops and he pictured the aircraft, struggling off the runway and circling upwards into the clouds, emerging minutes later into the clear air on the other side. That moment above the high cumulus when the vapour thinned and the cockpit slid into hard cold black sky always took his breath away. Halfway between earth and heaven, under a ceiling of sharp white crystals and alone with God. She came to his side, naked apart from the loop of his old identity tags around her neck and placed her hand on his shoulder.

'What are you thinking?' she asked.

He shrugged. 'About how this war takes so much and gives so much.'

'How do you mean?'

He nodded towards the window. 'That's the sound of a squadron going to war and some of them probably won't come back. Lives are about to be lost, snuffed out, but here with you, I couldn't be happier.' He sensed her looking at him in the darkness. 'It's such a contradiction.'

'You do love me don't you, George?'

'From the first time I saw you in the hospital,' he said and squeezed her body against his chest. She tensed, began to speak and stopped. 'What is it?' he asked and suddenly felt moisture from her tears on his skin.

Millie gently pushed away and her dim outline climbed back into bed. 'We need to talk,' she said, although her voice did not sound enthusiastic. A chill of apprehension swamped him, a certainty that she was about to say something to destroy his happiness. Minutes ago, just before the engine noise disturbed him, she nestled in his arm and he imagined them married and sleeping together every night. It had been a good fantasy and he tried to commit the moment to some indelible part of his memory so he could return to this room again and again. He climbed onto the bed and sat against the wall, apprehensive, waiting for her to begin.

'I need to tell you things,' she said simply. 'So many things that I don't know where to begin.' He put his arm around her thinking it would help, but she pushed it away. 'No George,' she said quietly. 'This is difficult enough; please don't make it harder for me.' He moved to the edge of the bed and watched her silently, his previous happiness fading with the noise of the aircraft.

'Go ahead,' he said simply, wondering what was coming.

'I'm sorry, but this needs to be said while I have the courage,' she brushed her hands through her hair and rubbed her palms against her eyes. 'I know you've wondered what I do and believe me I've wanted to tell you. Now is the time for honesty. I work for the Special Operations Executive, the SOE. They do many things but one is to send agents to organise resistance groups in occupied countries. That's what I've been doing and it was the reason I didn't write much while you were in Canada. I was in France.'

'You've been to France?' he sat forward and looked at her. She made it sound ordinary, like a trip to London. He remembered the searchlights and flak waiting on the French coast, a massive organisation trying to kill anyone who came close.

'Three times in total. Wireless operators have a life expectancy of around six weeks once they start transmitting, so I had to move constantly.' Words tumbled out as she began talking. There had always been something deep about her job, something hidden, but he thought she was doing secret work in Britain, not slipping into Europe. Maybe he should have realised. There were clues, after all, the remote base at Arisaig and the armed civilian guard at her accommodation.

He suddenly realised something. 'That was the thing worrying you when we first met, wasn't it? That was the problem you mentioned?'

'Yes. I volunteered to go but I was terrified. Because of what I knew about the SOE I thought they might imprison me if I changed my mind.'

'But you went.'

'I did. The training in Arisaig is very good, it made the risks seem ...acceptable. The Nazis are less suspicious of women so I was able to travel, but you can never relax. You never know who to trust. While I was there, I searched for my brother and sister, and although I found nothing, I made useful contacts. Then, just a few weeks ago I heard they had been found safe and well.'

'That's great news,' he said but she did not reply. 'Isn't it?'

'It's wonderful, but now the Nazis have occupied Vichy France and their troops are searching for Jews. If they find them, they will send the family sheltering them to a Konzentrationslager and they will not risk it any longer. So I've had to move them.'

'Can you get them out? I mean you've been to France and back. How did you do it?'

'The SOE uses aircraft based in RAF Tempsford.'

That puzzled him. 'I've never heard of Tempsford,' he said racking his memory.

'You wouldn't have. It's a secret base, not many miles from here,' she said and then paused. 'The SOE cannot get them, or will not. No agents are scheduled for insertion into that part of France for several weeks and they will not risk an aircraft and pilot just to collect a couple of children.'

'So what's wrong with waiting a few weeks?' he asked. 'I know you're keen to see them, but it's not long.'

She slapped her hands on the eiderdown. 'Because they don't have a few weeks,' she cried, suddenly angry with disappointment. 'There are two separate parts to the Resistance. One fights a guerrilla war through sabotage and assassination, while the other is a pipeline for smuggling airmen back to Britain. The pipeline passes people quickly, no more than a week in each place. I managed to get my brother and sister into the pipeline, but children are not so easy to move.' She waved her hands in frustration. 'For security, each section of the pipeline is isolated from the others like links in a chain. Escapees go to a location and wait until the next link feels it safe to approach them. But children cannot just be given directions and sent off alone. They are stuck at a farm between Poitiers and Tours and every day they stay there puts them and the Resistance in danger. I worry they will be forced to take them far away and abandon them.'

'They wouldn't just dump children?' That seemed too harsh.

'Wouldn't they?' she came back. 'What would you do? The Nazis search regularly and shoot Resistance members. Never doubt the courage of the Resistance, but they have families and only survive through being careful.'

Although he could understand her fears, part of him wondered if impatience was making her irrational. 'Look, I understand, but even if they are taken by the Germans, it won't be forever. Now the Yanks have arrived, we'll invade Europe soon. At most, they'll be imprisoned for a couple of years. It won't be fun but it won't kill them.' She stared at him with a haunted expression. He was confused and concerned. 'Why are you looking at me like that?' he asked.

'Because there are rumours from Poland and Germany, bad rumours,' she said quietly as if talking about something too dark and evil to mention. 'Everyday trains take thousands and thousands to concentration camps.'

'And we'll free them when we invade,' he said. He did not want to argue but challenging her views might make her see sense.

She shook her head. 'You don't understand. The camps couldn't possibly hold all the people going there. Something is happening to them.'

'I don't follow,' he said. 'What does that mean?'

337

'They are being killed, exterminated. The Nazis are murdering Jews as soon they arrive in the camps.'

'But that's impossible,' he spluttered. 'They wouldn't do that. Germans are hard, ruthless at times, but they're honourable.'

She laughed almost hysterically. 'Honourable? Which planet do you live on? There is a world of difference between the *Wehrmacht* and the *Schutzstaffel*. Maybe the ordinary serviceman in the *Wehrmacht* has some decency, but not the *SS*.' She put her head in her hands for a moment. 'Allied governments believe that Nazis are killing Jews. A senior person in the SOE has been told that your Foreign Secretary, Anthony Eden will announce it in Parliament this week.'

'I can't believe it,' he said shaking his head. 'The troops would refuse, surely?'

'You don't know them,' she snapped and wrapped a blanket around her shoulders as if it was armour. 'The soldiers in the *Schutzstaffel* are either thugs or brainwashed.' When she again spoke, her voice was quiet and unsteady. 'You once asked me if there was someone special back home and I said I would tell you one day.' He nodded slowly, watching her. 'Well, there was someone. Kurd and I were friends from childhood. His family lived nearby and we even went to the same university. Then he joined the *SS* and everything changed. He became surly and fascinated by Nazi doctrine. It was as if he was under their spell. I was stupid, just a girl. I thought we were like Kay and Gerda in the Snow Queen. Kay changed because a poisoned shard entered his eye, but Gerda's love saved him. One day after classes, I determined to persuade him to leave the *SS*. I found him in a lecture room with four others.' She shuddered and tears streamed down her face. He reached to comfort her but she pushed his hand away.

'No, let me finish. I want you to know what they're like. I need you to understand.' She steeled herself and continued. 'I asked him to leave the SS and come with me, but they just laughed. Then he told them I was Jewish and the laughter stopped. They surrounded me, touching me and lifting my skirt. I tried to push them away, but the *Unterscharführer* in charge slapped me hard across the face and pushed me to the floor. ...They raped me one after the other, even Kurd. I screamed and fought but no one came. ...No one came.' She repeated, quaking at the memory. 'When it was over they kicked me to the door shouting 'Jüdische Hündin', Jewish bitch... My father called the police, but the Schupo would do nothing, they didn't even want to know. He was so angry that he went to the SS offices to demand justice and they beat him. It was then he decided we must leave Germany.' She seemed exhausted by the memory and slumped forward. 'I know my parents are probably dead, but I can't let my brother and sister fall into their hands, I just can't.'

'I'm so sorry,' he whispered and now she let him hold her. They clung to each other in the dim room until her tears stopped and the shaking subsided. The thought of her rape was terrible, almost more than he could bear and it made him cold with anger. It would be one more thing to remember when he flew. Another reason added to the list. 'I understand. I wish there was something I could do to help.'

'There is, George,' she said and pushed herself away so she could look into his eyes. 'There is something you can do.'

'What?' he asked doubtfully, knowing a lowly Sergeant had less than zero influence.

'You can fly me to France and collect them.' She said in a tone that made it perfectly obvious he should have thought of it himself. 'George, we can go straight away. I only need telephone London to have a transmission sent to France.'

Stunned, he sat back on the bed and looked at her. A half smile of incredulity formed on his face. 'I... I... can't.' he stammered. 'You can't land a Lancaster in a field...'

'I know that,' she replied as if he were being wilfully dim. 'We'll borrow an SOE aircraft from RAF Tempsford. I can get us onto the base and we'll take one, you can fly it.'

'Steal an aircraft?' he said incredulously. He wanted to help, but this was crazy, a half-baked scheme and doomed to failure. Even if they got airborne, RAF fighters would shoot them down before they reached the coast. Besides, stealing a military aircraft was a crime almost certainly punishable by death. Thoughts and options swirled giddily through his mind. The sensible thing would be to explain the difficulties, the impossibility of success and refuse point blank. However, he knew with absolute certainty that he must help. Not just because her story angered him but also because he loved her. 'We can't steal an aircraft,' he said eventually. 'But there is another way. No guarantees it will work though.'

She sat up eagerly and watched him. 'Tell me,' she said leaning closer.

'Do you have connections, I mean people that will help?'

She nodded. 'The two girls you saw in London. We are like sisters. They will help.'

He was thinking wildly, dismissing options and planning others. Finally, he said. 'I can get an aircraft but it doesn't have the range. We'll need to refuel somewhere on the south coast.'

'The SOE uses RAF Tangmere,' she told him. 'I flew directly to France in a Lockheed Hudson, but I think the smaller aircraft are fuelled there.'

'Can you arrange for Tangmere to fill us up? I don't know... Maybe have someone send a signal authorising it?'

'I think so,' she said thoughtfully, brushing back her hair.

'Then we go tomorrow night,' he said and glanced at the window. 'The moon is in its last quarter and fading fast. I can't land in a field in total darkness, so we must go tomorrow night or there won't be enough light for well over a week. By then I'll be back on ops.' He held her shoulders to make sure she understood. 'Although there's a chance, so many things can go wrong. It still might be better to wait for your organisation.'

She shook her head. 'It can't wait. They are good people in France, but they've taken too many risks already,' she said and kissed him. 'I know this may get us in trouble and I love you for it.'

Trouble was a huge understatement. *Dead* would be more accurate. 'Come to the aerodrome at fourteen hundred tomorrow and have someone ready to collect the three of you from Tangmere the following morning,' he added, though he felt far from confident they would be there.

She laughed happily at the prospect. 'Thank you. I always knew you were decent but I was so worried that you wouldn't help. I'll get busy first thing in the morning.' she gave her eyes a final wipe. 'Now come back to bed.'

Chapter 22

RAF Blackbrook - 4th December 1942

Uncle hunched over his desk reassembling a fountain pen. Ink stains covered his fingers and a bright blue smear ran across his brow where he had wiped a hand across it. 'You're back early,' he said flicking an eye in George's direction. 'Didn't she turn up?'

'She?' George replied innocently.

'Don't tell me you wanted forty-eight hours with a male friend?' Uncle chuckled, but then frowned. 'Good God, you weren't with a man, were you?'

'No Uncle. Things just didn't work out that's all, so I'm back.'

'Sorry to hear that. *Cherchez la femme* and that sort of thing.'

George dropped into a chair and smiled winningly, he needed Uncle on his side. 'So I thought I would go get some more bacon for you. I'd like to fly down to Somerset this afternoon, spend the night with my folks and come back first thing tomorrow.'

Uncle looked at him sceptically. 'This isn't a private taxi service, you know. Go now and be back tonight.'

George swallowed. This could be scuppered before it began. 'Come on, Uncle,' he retorted. 'My father's ill, the doctor's not sure how much longer he's got. It's just for one night.'

Uncle tapped the fountain pen on his desk as he considered. Parts came away and scattered across the floor. 'Sorry to hear that,' he said, staring in surprise at the remnants of his pen. 'But what if it rains overnight? The wheels could sink into the field.'

'I'll taxi onto the farmyard, its solid concrete and large enough,' he said and waited while Uncle considered.

'I don't know. It's a big thing to ask. It's my neck on the chopping block if anything goes wrong you know.'

Uncle needed a shove. 'Look, Uncle, do you want the bacon or not? I'm not asking for a Lancaster this time, just a night with my folks. It's really not a lot.'

The fountain pen and the mountain of paperwork pulled Uncle's attention and George sensed he was now just a distraction. 'I'll make arrangements. Just make sure you're back early tomorrow and that the kite is in one piece,'

'Thanks, Uncle. Mind if I use the phone?'

Uncle scowled. 'Not at all,' he said, kneeling to retrieve the pen fragments. 'You know where the phone box is.'

After speaking to his parents, he found Dingo and they walked the perimeter track together as he repeated much of what Millie had said. He wanted the Australian to understand in case things went wrong, but he also needed his help. Dingo's eyes narrowed as he listened.

'Bloody horrors, George,' he said at length. 'Do you really think the bastards are butchering Jews?'

'I believe her,' he said simply. 'I don't think she would make up something so extreme. In any case, she says that Eden is going to make a statement in parliament and so we'll know for sure then.'

'But she didn't show you any proof?'

'No, but I don't suppose she could in any case.'

'Tell me about her again. How you met and so on?'

Dingo was silent as George talked. Eventually, the Australian stopped and turned to him. 'Look, mate, you won't like what I'm going to say, but I'll say it anyway. How do you know she hasn't just set you up all along? I've never heard of

343

this organisation, what did you call it, the SOE? I don't want to rain on your parade, but for all we know she could be a Nazi agent,' he said and shrugged. 'How do you know she isn't just after a free ride home?'

There was no proof and Dingo could, of course, be right. All the time he fretted that he was using Millie, maybe it was the other way round. He felt sure she had told the truth, but suddenly it worried him because he was not a great believer in coincidences.

'You may be right,' he said slowly. 'But I don't think so.' He turned to Dingo. 'I want you to trust my judgement because I need your help.'

Dingo blew a long stream of smoke and nodded. 'OK, mate. I'll go along with it, but just think about what I've said before it's too late, OK?' George nodded, but it was already too late. He would follow his instincts. So far, they had been good ones. 'What do you need?' Dingo asked reluctantly.

Right on time her green Austin snaked its way around the perimeter track and pulled up beside the hangar. Immediately they took her inside to an empty storeroom. Dingo stood back and watched, only offering the briefest of handshakes when George introduced them.

'Nervous?' he asked her.

'Terrified,' she replied but happily. 'Although I can't wait to be off.'

'Dingo has marked a route to the coordinates you gave me that should avoid guns and airfields.' He pointed at a flight suit. 'You'll need to wear this over your clothes. It belongs to Ned, one of the crew who's about your size. We'll wait by the plane while you get changed.'

Outside Dingo lit a cigarette and smoked silently. 'Have you thought about what I said?' he asked after a few puffs. 'Cos, I still don't like the smell of it.'

'I've thought, but I'm going,' George said firmly. 'Look, she's arranged fuel at Tangmere. She couldn't do that if she wasn't legitimate.'

Dingo took another puff and looked at something in the distance. 'Do you think you're the only person she could fool? Maybe she's hoodwinked a whole string of people.'

He felt a flash of annoyance but Dingo was his friend, his best friend, and he was not going to lose that. 'If I'm back tomorrow morning then I'll be right,' he said. 'If I'm not then you will be. Can we leave it at that; it's my skin I'm risking.'

Dingo turned on him. 'No it's not just your flaming skin, mate. If we lose our pilot then who replaces you? Some drongo not fit to wheel a pushbike? You want to know why I wanted you as my pilot?'

George nodded, 'Shoot Dingo, let's hear it all.'

'When you gave up the floor-space on that train, I knew you would be someone who would put their crew first. You'd hold the kite straight and level while the rest of us jumped. Yeah, a selfish reason maybe, but we started this together and we were going to see our thirty through together. Now you're risking it for everyone.'

'He will come back, Dingo. I'll make sure he does.' They turned and saw Millie standing just behind, watching them carefully as she hitched a bag over her shoulder.

'Well just make sure he does,' Dingo spat. 'Because if he doesn't and I survive this war, I'll come looking for you and find the reason why. My bloody oath I will.' With that, he threw down his cigarette and stormed off. George watched him go before turning back to Millie. Maybe Dingo was right and maybe not, but the die was cast now and he would see it through one way or the other. Sometimes the best thing was not the right thing and sometimes you just had to roll the dice.

'He likes you a lot,' Millie said.

'He's a good man and we're a tight crew,' he replied, zipping up his fleeced jacket. 'He thinks I'm doing the wrong thing.'

Her eyes flicked back to him. Did he see concern? Guilt? 'And what do you think?' she asked.

George smiled. 'I think we need to put some blankets in the back of the aircraft. Your brother and sister are going to be cold and uncomfortable.' Millie kissed him.

RAF Tangmere was a hundred miles away and dusk was falling by the time they arrived. Just a few miles further on nestled Bognor Regis and beyond that, the sea glittered in the fading light. Two years before Tangmere had been in the front line of the air battles, its pilots often flying three or more interceptions a day. A flight of Spitfires lifted off on an evening patrol and once they had gone, George flew straight in and landed without contacting the ground controller, hoping that clandestine flights kept wireless silence. Parked to the side of a hangar was a petrol bowser, so he taxied nearby and switched off the engine. The stillness after the noise and vibration was forbidding. While the blades were turning, he had options, a measure of control. Now his power had gone. They needed more fuel to get to *Poitiers* and back and this was the moment where it could all go wrong. Sliding back the hood, he climbed down from the aircraft and waited for someone to come. It was growing dark quickly now and a chill wind whipped in spurts across the aerodrome adding to the feeling of unwelcome. *Come on someone*, he urged. When the moon came up it would be a waning crescent, twenty-six days old and as dim as a Toc H lamp, but the weather forecast was for clear skies and as long as the clouds stayed away it should be enough. He would not want to try landing on a field in pitch darkness. *Come on someone, finger out.*

A car pulled away from the control tower and trundled slowly around the perimeter. He watched it anxiously, anticipating what would happen when it arrived. It parked a few yards away and an officer walked across. His thin, sharp features and dark eyes glared hostilely.

'And who the hell are you?' he asked after returning George's salute.

'Special ops flight, sir.' George replied simply. He had decided that minimal answers would be best. Actual SOE pilots would doubtless use phrases and code words that he did not know.

'This isn't an SOE aircraft,' the officer barked, nodding at the Lysander. 'They're painted black for a start.'

George stood stiffly and did not make eye contact. 'Sir, I regret that I'm not at liberty to discuss this flight or the aircraft. Authorisation to refuel should have been forwarded.'

The officer moved closer and scrutinised George carefully. He did not wear aircrew wings and his breath was rancid. George disliked him immediately. 'We had a signal from SOE, but our authorisation comes from RAF Tempsford and they know nothing about you.'

This was beginning to unravel and George felt a tinge of panic. 'This is not a Tempsford aircraft, sir.'

'I can see that. So as I said before, who the hell are you?'

'Sir, I regret that I'm not at liberty to discuss this flight or the aircraft. We need fuel. Unless you intend to scrub our mission, of course.' He looked at the officer pointedly, making sure he realised who would be responsible.

The officer seemed about to flare, but instead, he swallowed and snorted. 'You sound like a stuck bloody gramophone. This is damned irregular,' he said eventually, his Adams Apple bobbing wildly. 'I shall write to SOE about it.'

'Very good, Sir,' George replied and ended the conversation with a salute. The officer glared for a moment and stormed off to find the bowser crew, while George pretended to ground check the aircraft, feeling certain his nervousness would betray him if they had to speak again. Half an hour later it was finished, the Lysander had a maximum fuel load and they were heading for France.

'You did it, George!' Millie said her voice high pitched with relief.

'For a moment I thought he'd call the guards.' George replied almost laughing with relief. 'We were lucky he worried more about his career than proper procedures.' Reaching for the map that Dingo had prepared, he unfolded it across his knee. The carefully drawn pencilled route had timings and bearings clearly marked and ground features circled five miles on either side of the line in case the wind blew them off course. With a full fuel load, the Lysander had a range of seven hundred miles and as their destination was two hundred and fifty miles away, it left plenty of juice to get them home again. If everything went well he would drop Millie and her siblings off at Tangmere, wait until dawn and then fly straight to his farm to collect the meat. That was if everything went well. The next and biggest challenge was finding the right field in France. Worrying whether Tangmere would refuel them had been his focus, but with so little moonlight, the real problem was navigation. In hindsight, he should have left Millie behind and brought Dingo, but it was too late for that now.

Choppy wave tops flickered as darkness fell on the channel and they crossed at one hundred feet to stay below British and German radar coverage. Their route approached France just west of Caen and a searchlight flicked on as they neared, attracted by their engine noise. A few token lines of tracer quickly followed but thankfully, nothing came near. With a small course adjustment, he headed south on a track that would take them down a line between Le Mans and Angers. Fortunately, the land was flat and he could safely stay at three hundred feet. This was low enough to spot ground features but high enough to avoid most spires and pylons. A week before the moon would have been almost full and the ground clearly visible, but now the weak moon gave precious little away. He sat back and followed the compass, hoping the side wind was minimal. After thirty minutes and eighty miles, they should have crossed the train line running between Paris and Rennes, only it was not there. Given that the line bisected this part of the country, he had to assume he had missed it. Maybe it was hiding in a deep cutting or even a tunnel as he crossed it, but it added to his uncertainty. Unless the wind was blowing directly in front or behind, it must be pushing them off course and the further they flew the greater that error would be. Without a landmark soon, they could easily end up twenty or thirty miles from where the Resistance waited.

'What will you do with your brother and sister when you get them back?' he asked, wanting to hear the sound of a voice and missing the reassuring banter of his crew.

She hesitated. 'They'll stay with me in Tangmere Cottage for a few days. That's a house the SOE uses. After that, I'll take them up to London and find a boarding school. Somewhere nearby, so I can visit.'

'What will you do then?' he asked, trying not to sound too curious.

'Then I'll go back to work of course,' she replied and offered no more.

Then he saw it, a train line flicked past below. They crossed it at an angle, which was right because the line dipped between Laval and Le Mans. That made them six minutes behind schedule, so the wind must be blowing from in front, from the south. But, southeast or southwest? Anyway, it was something to remember when landing. Dingo had circled a town and a wood shortly after the rail line, about five miles either side of the pencil route. A clutch of buildings appeared to the right, which he assumed was Évron. That meant the wind was blowing from the southeast. He was almost five miles off course and banked left a couple of degrees to compensate. The next landmark would be a forest and then the river Sarthe. If he was back on course they would cross the river where it formed a horseshoe.

'Who will be waiting for us?' he asked, trying to make the comment sound casual. It was easy to be over-imaginative in the dark but the more he thought about the coincidences the less he liked them.

'I haven't met them before,' she replied after some hesitation. 'There are usually around ten people, although some may be keeping watch nearby so you won't see them.' Darker tree shapes slid by below as they flew over the forest. She began to speak again but then stopped.

'What is it?' he asked.

'I think we are playing games with each other,' she said at last. 'Why don't you just say what you are thinking?'

'I don't know what to think,' he said and that was the truth. If Dingo was right and Millie had fooled him, there would be a squad of German soldiers waiting. In truth, he did not doubt

Millie, but he did doubt his own judgement with women. He knew so little about them. As a child, girls were sugar and spice, nicer and more honourable than boys were, but his parents sometimes talked in coded half-whispers about women who were plain bad. One thing might prove her honesty. 'Tell me why you help the British, why you joined the SOE?'

'So you don't trust me. You think Dingo is right,' she said and even across the intercom, he could hear her disappointment. 'Well, it was revenge,'

He wanted to believe her but that was not the truth. 'Really?'

She paused. 'No, not entirely. When the war started I expected to be interned, but the authorities invited me to join the SOE instead. So I jumped at the chance because it was a way of finding my family.'

That was what he had guessed. Finding her family was the real motivation and why not? He would probably do the same. A river sparkled in the moonlight on both sides of the cockpit. They were flying down the horseshoe and bang on course. There was just one more thing he had to know.

'You turning up in Perth just as I passed flight training feels more than coincidental. You could have written, but you waited until I passed. Then as soon as I got back from Canada and fully trained you invited me to London. I don't want to doubt you, but it feels like you kept me hanging on in case you needed a tame pilot one day.'

'You think I've used you!' Her voice in the headset was incredulous. 'Have you understood nothing about me? Do you think rape is like a bad cold, something you get over after a week?' She was silent and he imagined her in the rear seat, angry and hurt as she relived painful memories. He hated himself for asking but he had to know. If landing looked

351

dangerous, he would have to decide whether to take the risk or abort, and he wanted to be sure of her before risking his neck. 'Afterwards... I never wanted a man again,' she continued quietly. 'The very thought of being touched sent me into a panic. But you stayed with me through the bombing and... and I saw something decent. It confused me.' Millie paused and he could sense her struggling to form the words. This was no act it was genuine. When she spoke, the words tumbled out. 'It took a long time to see that just perhaps you were different. There is no mystery, no great scheme. I fell in love and that's why I invited you to London. It's why I slept with you and why it hurts so much to discover you doubt me.'

'I'm sorry, Millie. I really am. After you disappeared I thought I'd lost you and every day since I've been expecting you to vanish again,' he said slowly. 'I guess that having you with me seems too good to be true. Can you understand that and forgive me?'

She was silent for a long time and he waited, desperate for her to say something. 'I love you, George, so yes I can forgive you. But never doubt me again. I've had everything of value stripped from me. I want to be able to depend on you.'

'You can,' he told her. 'Once we get back I want us to spend the rest of our lives together.'

'Is that a proposal?' she asked, suddenly laughing.

With a start, he realised that they must be near the end of the pencil line. 'We're almost there,' he said. 'Yes, it is. I want to marry you. Think about it before you say anything.' Pulling back the stick, he climbed steeply to two thousand feet and circled in a wide orbit. For minutes he had not looked for landmarks, they could be miles out.

'Look for lights below,' he said and banked the aircraft. From up here, the ground was solid black, although just ahead the dim moonlit the silver shape of a large river. *That must be the Loire,* he decided and rotated the map to orientate himself. Flying a mile or so along the river and back, he compared its bends with the map until he felt confident that he knew where they were. Then after using his thumb to measure rough distances, he banked sharply to the left and dropped to a thousand feet before heading towards the village of Sainte-Catherine-de-Fierbois.

After six minutes, he had gone too far and so climbing to two thousand feet again, he retraced the path. This was taking too long. Luftwaffe radar operators would be watching and realise what was happening. They would send either a fighter or troops to the area, maybe both. The Loire appeared below again and he cursed, they were back where they started. Once again, he swung the Lysander around but this time climbed to three thousand feet. He had no idea how brightly the Resistance's lamps would shine. Perhaps they only used bicycle lights.

'I can see something flashing,' Millie cried out. 'About a mile away to the left.'

A pinprick of light twinkled, just discernible in the gloom. A check of the compass and he banked slowly, drifting in a wide orbit, allowing speed and altitude to bleed away. Another light flashed a little apart from the first and as they closed, four more appeared in a static line between the two. They had marked a landing spot. Anxiety was threatening to make him careless, fear of losing sight of the lights. He forced calmness, stifling the urge to just drop down and land. Taking another good fix, he flew a rate one turn of one-mile radius before swinging back into the wind. Because he could not see the field, he worried about landing too hard and either damaging the Lysander or putting it onto its nose, so he tried for a very shallow approach angle, even shallower than when he landed at his parent's farm.

Slowing to eighty miles-per-hour and with the nose well up, he set the mixture to normal, pitch to fine and opened the cowl flaps. That was it. He let the Lysander drift earthwards towards the lamps. In front of him, the big propeller span slowly, hardly cutting enough air to support them and through it, he fixated on the lights. Blackness rose around as if they were sinking into ink and the altimeter slowly unwound. This was the gut-wrenching part. He could see nothing clearly outside the cockpit and prayed there were no tall trees in their path. Before he expected it, the Lysander touched with a thud on all three wheels and bounced along the field. Absolute relief surged as he realised they were down and in one piece. Quickly he pulled back the throttle and slowed towards the last lamp. The Lysander's brakes were soft at the best of times, but he dared not use them in case that pivoted the aircraft onto its nose.

With a burst of power, he span the aircraft around and idled the engine, not risking shutting down in case it would not start again. Outside, shadowy figures ran forwards and he watched worriedly until he saw they were not soldiers. Millie's glass canopy slammed back and he looked back to see her fixing the ladder to the side. Time to get out.

It took a while to adjust to what was happening in the field. Several people scurried around Millie speaking to her in French, their tones urgent. Then she gave a shriek and ran towards two shorter figures, wrapping them in her arms, crying and talking at the same time.

'*Venez vite*!' a man nearby called. '*Amenez-le ici,*' and he waved at something in the distance. Mystified, George shrugged and turned back to the aircraft, where he began unfastening the starboard panel to the rear storage. The sooner they got away the better. Stupidly, he had assumed that Millie's brother and sister would be much the same size as they were in the photograph, but these children were bigger and heavier. The Lysander could carry two adult passengers at a pinch, but three would be too much. It just depended on how much they weighed. As he got the hatch open, the three came up behind him.

'George, this is my Klaus and Agata,' Millie called happily above the stuttering engine.

Their faces were indistinct in the gloom but he could see them smiling. The girl whispered something to Millie and she laughed. 'Agata thinks you are handsome.'

'Tell her that I am in the dark,' George replied and ruffled her hair. 'We need to get them inside now. Explain that it will be uncomfortable but they are not to be afraid.'

A scrum of men shuffled up carrying someone between them. '*Mademoiselle. Nous avons un aviateur malade.*'

'What's happening?' George asked.

'*Il a une fièvre,*' said another.

'They have an injured airman,' Millie interpreted. 'He has a fever and they want us to take him.'

'We can't. Tell them there isn't room.' George said. 'Surely, they can keep him a few weeks until the SOE flight comes.'

Millie spoke to a Frenchman and turned back. 'They say he becomes delirious and shouts. The Germans have many patrols nearby. They cannot keep him in case he starts ranting if one searches the farmhouse.'

'This is nonsense,' George snapped and crossed to the airman. 'He can't be that bad.'

Unable to support himself, the aviator drooped like a sack of potatoes between the shoulders of two burly Frenchmen. A rough bandage circled his head. George reached a hand to the man's brow and felt his temperature. It seemed only a little hotter than normal.

'It's not fever,' he said. 'He's concussed,' and that could be more serious depending on the size of the blow. From the look of the bandages, it had been a sizeable knock. Someone shone a torch illuminating their faces and his heart sank as he recognised Dickinson. For an instant, he wanted to turn away and retreat into the shadows but Dickinson's eyes flicked open and stared straight at him.

'George? George... is that you?' Dickinson said weakly. 'Thank God.'

'James? What are you doing here?'

'... OTU sortie,' Dickinson replied after some thought. '... Covering a raid on Turin. We got bounced off the coast. I drifted ashore... don't know where my crew are. I don't remember much at all. I think I hit my head... Feel pretty woozy.' He sagged against the two Frenchmen again.

'You know him?' Millie asked.

'He's a friend; we went through early training together. I thought he was still in Canada.' George said and remembered the Turin briefing. How training squadrons were to mount diversions that would pull the fighters away from the bomber stream. It was another reason why he should help Dickinson.

She looked at the children and hesitated. 'Then you must take him,' she said.

'There isn't room,' he explained desperately. 'In any case, we'll be too heavy. I'll never get off the ground.'

Her face was close to his and he was puzzled to see her expression become sad. 'The children don't weigh much and you're a good pilot,' she said slowly.

Memories of Perth and their weeks of training flashed through his mind and he knew he must try to take them all. His friendship with Dickinson was too strong to abandon him. 'Tell them to slide him in the hatch,' he decided. 'Your sister can lie in front of him and your brother can sit at your feet. But be quick.' They had been on the ground too long and he had no idea if they could get airborne. Maybe after a longer takeoff run or if he sat on the brakes while they powered up as he did with a laden Lancaster. Most likely, they would end up in a ditch on the far side of the field, but he had to try. The men shoved Dickinson through the hatch and onto the narrow boards lining the tail. Agata squeezed in afterwards and curled into a foetal position above Dickinson's head and while George closed the panel, Klaus climbed the ladder and dropped onto the floor.

The shot sounded with a sharp crack, followed immediately by a volley of others and something whickered above his head. '*Allez vite. Une patrouille est ici,*' One of the Frenchman shouted and dropped to his knee before firing a burst from his Sten gun into the darkness. '*Vite, vite.*'

'It's a German patrol,' Millie cried and pushed George towards the Lysander. He scrambled up the wheel, fell into the cockpit and gunned the engine. Over his shoulder, he saw Millie still on the ground, shouting up at her brother. Her bag flew through the air and catching it, she blew her brother a kiss. The Frenchmen were pulling back from the Lysander, evaporating into the night. Millie turned towards George and shook her head sadly before touching a hand to her heart and holding it briefly towards him. Then she turned and fled after the others.

For seconds George was too stunned and shocked to move. He shouted out her name, but she had gone. He wanted to leap from the aircraft and fetch her back but a bullet slammed into the cowling just in front of the glass and tore a grove through the thin metal. He stared at it before wrenching open the throttle. The Lysander bumped away across the field and lumbered slowly into the air. Looking down over his shoulder, he could see nothing except blackness.

Chapter 23

RAF Tangmere - 5th December 1942

It was still dark when they crossed the channel towards Tangmere. During every mile of the journey, George replayed the agony of Millie's sacrifice and pictured her final expression before she ran into the night. No longer caring about the consequences, he contacted Tangmere's air-control and asked for runway lighting. After a long pause, the voice granted permission. Miraculously, they were only around ten miles off course and he easily spotted the double row of lights flickering in the gloom. At the end of the runway, a car flashed its lights and he followed it around the taxiway to a spot hidden from the view of the control tower by a hangar. As soon as the vehicle stopped, it doors swung open and two women dressed in army uniform rushed towards the aircraft. George shut down the engine and sat back in his seat, exhausted, drained and empty. One of the females started shouting at him, but he could not understand what she was saying. Woodenly he slid back the cockpit canopy and climbed down.

'Where is Millie?' she demanded.

'I don't know,' George replied. 'Gone. We were bounced by a German patrol and she went off with the Resistance.'

The woman's stare was hard, tight-lipped and expressionless. He recognised her at once, the last time they met she had pointed a gun at him. 'Do you have Klaus and Agata?' she then asked.

George turned back to the aircraft and saw the boy's head above the rear seat, watching them. The ladder had blown away so he held out his arms and Klaus slid down the fuselage into them. Then he opened the rear panel and helped

Dickinson and Agata out. Dickinson was only just conscious and shivered so much that it looked like he was having a seizure. Agata was confused and became tearful when she realised that her sister was missing.

'Who is this?' the other woman asked, looking at Dickinson.

'An injured pilot, Millie gave up her place for him. You must take him to the base medical wing.'

The two women glanced at each other. 'No,' one said firmly as she hugged Agata. 'We cannot risk the children being discovered. They might take them from us.'

'He needs to be in a hospital,' George almost bellowed and helped Dickinson into the car. After losing Millie, he was damn sure he would do the right thing by Dickinson. 'Take him to your SOE hospital if you must, but he needs a doctor.'

The closer of the two shook her head. 'There is no SOE hospital. That was just a story Millie invented.'

'What?' he jerked back, confused. 'But she said they transferred her to a private hospital.'

'Fool,' she snapped. 'That was just a story. She left because she was afraid to become involved with you. You know what happened to her in Germany.'

'But... where did she go?' he stammered. 'I don't understand?'

'She hobbled to my lodgings and I looked after her.' She replied and pushed the children into the car alongside Dickinson. 'I'll drop him at the guard post. That's all I can do.' They both climbed into the car and the engine started.

'Wait!' George shouted and banged on the roof. 'Wait... Will you tell me when you find out what's happened to her?'

'She'll tell you herself,' the woman answered briskly and then quite unexpectedly smiled. 'Don't worry I think you'll see her again.'

George shivered as the car disappeared into the darkness. Now all the pieces had fallen into place, he knew all the secrets. He also realised why Millie had brought a bag with her. Resourceful as ever, she was prepared in case things went wrong. Somewhere in France, he hoped she was hidden and safe. As he tried to picture her, a NAAFI van drew up by the hangar entrance and fitters working overnight inside gathered around for a mug of tea and a bun. George joined the back of the queue and took his food away, sipping and chewing gratefully. Nothing had ever tasted so good. Inside, someone began a song.

'We'll meet again,
Don't know where, don't know when,
But I know we'll meet again
Some sunny day.'

A harsh voice shouted, 'My boot will meet the end of your arse if you don't fix that bloody gun sight. Now put a sock in it.'

George looked towards where the sun would soon rise and smiled as he hummed the tune. It seemed to fit his mood exactly. Every time he met Millie, he never expected to see her again and each time she appeared. Somehow, he was certain that this would be no different. He would fly to his parent's home, sleep for a few hours and then return to Blackbrook. Tell them a Home Guard unit had taken a pot shot at him and damaged the cowling, which seemed more believable than the truth. Then he would talk to Dingo and take the crew into town for a few beers. After that, he would just wait. The horizon was lightening and it might be a good day after all.

Printed in Great Britain
by Amazon

46296293R00209